Blooming Renewal

Luna Grey

Published by Luna Grey, 2024.

This is a work of fiction. Similarities to real people, places, or events are entirely coincidental.

BLOOMING RENEWAL

First edition. October 20, 2024.

Copyright © 2024 Luna Grey.

ISBN: 979-8227229434

Written by Luna Grey.

Chapter 1: The Distant Whisper

I watched her, momentarily forgetting my troubles, as she murmured to the plants, her voice a soft melody blending with the rustle of the leaves. There was an inexplicable warmth radiating from her, as if she carried the sun in her very being. I couldn't tear my gaze away, fascinated by the tenderness she exhibited, a stark contrast to the harsh realities I faced. She looked up, her emerald green eyes meeting mine, and in that instant, the weight of my financial burdens seemed to lift, if only for a heartbeat.

"Careful there," I called out, managing a half-hearted smile despite the knot of anxiety tightening in my chest. "Those ones are a little delicate."

She chuckled, a sound like wind chimes in a gentle breeze, and stood, brushing dirt from her knees. "I might have a knack for delicate things," she replied, her tone playful yet earnest. "But I think they just needed a little encouragement. Plants can be as stubborn as people, don't you think?"

I crossed my arms, my own stubbornness bubbling to the surface. "I don't know. Some days, I think they're far worse than the folks around here. At least people can talk back."

Her laughter bubbled up again, and I felt an unfamiliar flutter in my chest. "Maybe that's the secret," she mused, glancing back at the plants. "If they could talk, they might tell you exactly what they need. But, then again, wouldn't that complicate things?"

We fell into an easy rhythm, the conversation flowing like the breeze rustling through the fields. She introduced herself as Lena, an aspiring botanist with a passion for sustainable farming. My heart warmed at the idea that someone could have a vision as vivid as mine, yet I couldn't help but feel a twinge of envy. Here I was, struggling to keep my family's legacy alive, and she seemed to float through life with an effortless grace that made it all look so easy.

"I've read about your farm," she said, a glimmer of admiration in her eyes. "The history, the family ties. It's incredible."

The compliment brought a flush to my cheeks, but it quickly faded under the weight of my reality. "Incredible is one word for it. Sustainable is another. I'm just trying to keep it afloat, honestly. The bills are piling up faster than the weeds."

"Then let's do something about it!" Her enthusiasm was infectious, and for the first time in weeks, I felt a spark of hope igniting within me. "What if I helped? We could brainstorm ideas together, figure out a way to revive the crops and attract more customers."

I hesitated, my instincts screaming to protect what little I had left. "It's a big commitment, Lena. I can't afford to pay anyone right now."

She waved her hand dismissively. "I'm not looking for payment. I want to learn, and I think we could create something special here. Your farm has so much potential; it just needs a little... magic."

Her words hung in the air, and I couldn't help but wonder if she might be right. The farm was my sanctuary, a place where I had grown up watching my parents toil, pouring love and sweat into the land. Yet the reality of its decline loomed large, and my dreams of cultivating organic produce felt more like fantasies with each passing day. Lena's enthusiasm was a balm to my frayed nerves, a reminder that perhaps there was still something worth fighting for.

"Alright," I said, my voice firmer than I felt. "Let's give it a shot. But no promises. If things go south, I won't hold you to it."

"Deal!" She grinned, her smile radiant against the backdrop of the sprawling fields. "I have a few ideas already. How about we start with a community event? We could host workshops on organic gardening, maybe even some cooking demonstrations. People love fresh produce, and they love to learn."

As she spoke, I could see the visions dancing behind her eyes, a kaleidoscope of color and possibility. I felt the tendrils of my own dreams wrap around hers, intertwining like the roots of the very plants we hoped to nurture back to life. Perhaps this unexpected partnership could breathe new life into the farm, a venture where both our passions could flourish.

"What if we also included local artisans?" I suggested, my mind racing ahead. "We could showcase their products too—handcrafted goods, baked items. It could turn into a real festival of sorts."

Lena's eyes sparkled with excitement. "Yes! A celebration of everything local, everything fresh! It'll draw people in, build a sense of community. We could even have a small section for children, maybe plant some seedlings together."

As we brainstormed, the weight of my worries began to lift, replaced by a sense of purpose I hadn't felt in a long time. The distant whispers of my dreams, once muffled by doubt, now echoed with clarity. I could almost hear the laughter of children mingling with the rustling leaves, the scent of fresh produce wafting through the air, beckoning people to join us in this endeavor.

"Lena," I said, my voice softer now, "thank you for believing in this place. It's been hard to find hope in the shadows lately."

"Hope is just like those stubborn plants," she replied, her tone serious yet warm. "It often lies hidden beneath the surface, waiting for the right conditions to thrive."

Her words resonated deep within me, a reminder that even in the bleakest of times, there exists a flicker of light waiting to break free. Together, we would cultivate not just the land, but the very essence of what it meant to belong—to find community in the richness of the earth and each other.

With Lena's enthusiasm igniting a spark within me, we set to work the following week, determined to breathe life into the farm and, by extension, our dreams. The air was crisp with the promise of a new season, the sunlight dappling through the trees, casting playful shadows that danced upon the earth. I could almost hear the land whispering its secrets, urging me to listen, to take heed.

As we meticulously prepared for our community event, I realized that my reservations about letting someone into my world were fading like morning mist. Lena was a whirlwind of ideas and energy, her laughter echoing through the fields as we pruned, planted, and painted signs for the upcoming festival. With each passing day, her presence felt more and more like a vital part of the landscape—a splash of color against the earth tones of the farm.

"What do you think of this?" she asked one afternoon, holding up a bright yellow sign she'd painted in bold letters: "Willow Creek Fresh Fest! Taste the Love!"

I chuckled, the corners of my mouth pulling up in a smile. "It's a bit... enthusiastic, don't you think? What if people just come for the free samples and leave?"

"Let them," she replied with a wink, her eyes sparkling with mischief. "At least they'll leave with a taste of what we offer. Plus, we'll reel them in with our charm, right?"

Her confidence was infectious, and I couldn't help but imagine the festival transforming into something magical, filled with laughter, the scent of baked goods wafting through the air, and the promise of fresh produce from our hard work.

We spent days reaching out to local artisans, farmers, and chefs. The anticipation grew with each response, and soon the modest farm was buzzing with the energy of possibility. I had set my heart on reclaiming what felt lost, and Lena's relentless optimism fueled that fire. She had this uncanny ability to see beauty where others might see failure—a gift I had almost forgotten existed.

As the days passed, the festival drew closer, and with it, an unexpected wave of anxiety washed over me. What if no one came? What if we poured our hearts into this event and it flopped spectacularly? I voiced my concerns to Lena as we sorted through a stack of hand-painted signs.

"Look, I get it," she said, her voice steady, "but you have to remember that every big dream starts small. People love authenticity, and that's exactly what you're offering them—your story, your farm, your food. They'll feel that."

"Or they'll feel pity," I countered, though I couldn't help but smile at her unshakeable spirit.

"Pity is just a misguided form of admiration," she shot back, placing a hand on my shoulder. "Trust me. Just look at you—your passion is the most attractive quality. If they can see how much this means to you, it'll resonate."

I was about to retort when a rustle in the nearby bushes drew our attention. We turned to see a scruffy little dog with floppy ears and an overabundance of enthusiasm bounding toward us. He skidded to a halt, his tail wagging like a flag in the wind.

"Where did you come from, little guy?" I knelt to stroke his fur, the warmth of his body grounding me.

Lena laughed, her amusement lighting up the afternoon. "Looks like he's decided to join our festival preparations. Maybe he'll be our mascot!"

As if on cue, the dog let out a playful bark, as if to confirm his new role. "What should we call him?" I asked, looking into his soulful brown eyes.

"Sunny," Lena suggested, her tone earnest. "Because he's bringing sunshine into our day."

Sunny seemed to agree, darting around us in circles before collapsing at my feet with a contented sigh. It was a ridiculous, sweet moment that filled my heart with a sense of lightness, an unexpected reminder that joy could come from the simplest of things.

In the days leading up to the event, the air buzzed with excitement. We transformed the farm into a haven of vibrant colors, flowers blooming in every corner, and booths sprouting up like wildflowers. I watched as Lena connected with everyone, her charm wrapping around them like a warm blanket. It was her gift, this ability to make others feel valued, and I found myself admiring her more each day.

On the morning of the festival, the sun rose bright and clear, casting a golden glow over the farm. I woke early, the soft light filtering through my window, illuminating the remnants of sleepless nights spent worrying. I moved through the house with a nervous energy, preparing trays of fresh muffins and steaming pots of coffee, hoping they'd provide a warm welcome to our guests.

Lena arrived shortly after, her red hair a fiery halo in the morning light. "Ready for the big day?" she asked, her excitement palpable.

"As ready as I'll ever be," I replied, trying to mask my jitters with a smile.

"Let's make some magic happen!" she proclaimed, grabbing my hand and pulling me outside, where a tapestry of laughter and chatter awaited us.

The festival unfolded with a surprising vibrancy that caught me off guard. People arrived in droves, eager to sample fresh produce and handcrafted goods, their smiles wide as they enjoyed the atmosphere. I felt a sense of pride swelling within me, watching families wander through the rows of booths, their laughter intertwining with the chirping of birds and the gentle rustle of leaves.

Just when I thought the day couldn't get any better, a familiar figure appeared at the edge of the crowd. My heart dropped. It was Marcus, my childhood friend and the one who had moved away years ago in search of bigger dreams. He was as charming as ever, with his easy smile and tousled hair.

"Wow, I hardly recognized you!" he called out, weaving through the throngs of people toward me. "You've turned this place into a wonderland!"

Lena caught my eye, her expression a mix of intrigue and amusement as she observed the interaction. I swallowed hard, suddenly self-conscious about the festival and all it represented.

"Marcus! What a surprise!" I managed to say, my voice a little too bright. "What brings you back to Willow Creek?"

"Just passing through, and I heard about this festival. I couldn't resist seeing what you've been up to." His gaze swept across the festival, then landed back on me. "You've really put your heart into this, haven't you?"

I nodded, my heart racing as he took a step closer, his presence stirring up memories I thought I'd buried long ago. "It's a new chapter for me—one I'm still figuring out."

He grinned, his smile infectious, and I felt the weight of my past collide with the hope of my present. Little did I know that this unexpected reunion would shift everything I thought I knew about the path I was on, intertwining our fates once more amidst the laughter and warmth of the festival.

The festival thrummed with life, the air rich with the mingling scents of fresh basil, ripe tomatoes, and the sweet allure of baked goods. As laughter erupted from the crowd, I felt a warmth seep into my bones, a contrast to the cold uncertainty that had gripped me for so long. I stood there, momentarily entranced by the sight of families weaving through the rows of stalls, children darting between them like butterflies. The bright banners we'd hung danced merrily overhead, and I couldn't help but feel a swell of pride at what we had created.

Lena was a blur of motion, her fiery hair bouncing as she flitted from booth to booth, chatting with vendors and visitors alike. The joy she exuded was contagious, drawing in people like moths to a flame. It was as if she were the very heartbeat of the festival, a force of nature igniting everyone around her.

"Willow Creek Fresh Fest! Taste the Love!" a nearby vendor shouted, drawing laughter and applause. The atmosphere buzzed with an energy I hadn't dared to hope for, and yet, beneath the surface, a flicker of anxiety still danced within me.

Marcus lingered close, his presence both comforting and disarming. "You've really outdone yourself," he said, leaning closer so only I could hear. "It feels... alive here."

"Thanks," I replied, a mix of pride and vulnerability washing over me. "I just wanted to give the farm a fighting chance. It's been tough keeping things going."

He studied me, those familiar green eyes holding an intensity that sent a shiver up my spine. "You've always been good at that—fighting. I admire it."

I blinked, taken aback by his sincerity. "I've had to be. It's either that or watch everything fall apart."

"That's not an option for you, is it?" he asked, his voice low and steady. "You're too strong for that."

Before I could respond, Sunny darted past us, chasing after a fluttering butterfly with wild abandon, dragging my attention back to the festivities. I grinned, watching him tumble through the grass, oblivious to the chaos around him. "At least someone's having a good time," I said, laughter bubbling up.

The day unfolded in waves of joy and laughter, but as the sun dipped low, painting the sky in hues of orange and pink, I felt a shift in the atmosphere. The crowd began to swell, a sea of eager faces flocking toward the stalls, and for a moment, I reveled in the chaos. It was exhilarating, each new face a potential friend, a potential supporter of my dreams.

Then, just as I was beginning to lose myself in the excitement, a sharp voice sliced through the air like a knife. "What is this circus?"

I turned, heart sinking as I recognized the figure striding toward us. It was Leonard, a local businessman known for his shrewdness and his glaring lack of respect for the farming community. His dark suit was a stark contrast to the vibrant surroundings, and I braced myself for the confrontation I knew was coming.

"Leonard," I greeted, my voice steadier than I felt. "What brings you here?"

"Business, as always," he replied, eyes scanning the festival with disdain. "I hardly expected to find you parading around like this. It's hardly dignified for someone in your position."

"Dignified?" I echoed, incredulous. "You think a festival celebrating community and sustainability is undignified?"

"More like a desperate attempt to cling to the past," he sneered, his smile devoid of warmth. "You're wasting your time. No one's interested in your quaint little farm anymore. It's only a matter of time before this place becomes another commercialized nightmare."

A knot formed in my stomach, anger mixing with fear as I met his gaze. "You don't know what you're talking about, Leonard. People care. They want to support local farms, local businesses."

He chuckled, a cold, humorless sound that echoed against the joyous backdrop. "Delusions of grandeur won't save you, sweetheart. You're just prolonging the inevitable."

Lena appeared at my side, her eyes blazing with defiance. "Excuse me, but what do you know about these people? About this farm? This is about more than just profits; it's about community and connection."

He waved her off dismissively. "You think your little vision matters? In a world driven by profit, you're just a distraction. This is a game you can't win."

"Maybe so," I said, feeling a flicker of defiance igniting within me. "But I'll play it anyway. I refuse to let you dictate what this farm means to me or to this community."

"Ah, the brave little dreamer," he said, his tone dripping with mockery. "Just remember, reality has a way of crashing down on idealists like you."

Before I could respond, the sound of a nearby commotion drew our attention. A group of children had gathered around a booth, pointing and shouting in excitement. I moved to investigate, hoping to distract myself from the uncomfortable confrontation.

As I approached, my heart sank. One of the displays had toppled over, spilling jars of honey across the ground. A child stood in the middle of the chaos, his face smeared with honey, a mixture of glee and horror playing across his features.

"Oh no! I'm so sorry!" the vendor cried, rushing to the scene. But as he bent to pick up the jars, a shadow fell across us, and I looked up to find Leonard hovering, a predatory glint in his eyes.

"See? This is what I mean," he said, gesturing dramatically. "Your quaint little festival is just a recipe for disaster."

My heart raced, an unfamiliar fire igniting within me. "We can fix this," I said, determined. "We'll clean it up, and it will be fine. It's not over yet."

But Leonard wasn't finished. "Do you even know what you're doing? If this fails, it'll be the end of your little dream. Your farm, your hopes—they'll be buried along with your pride."

With those words hanging ominously in the air, the wind picked up, sending a chill down my spine. I glanced around, feeling the joyous atmosphere shift as whispers of uncertainty rippled through the crowd. Just as I was about to reply, a loud crack echoed across the field, and all heads turned in alarm.

A massive tree at the edge of the festival cracked and splintered, its trunk quivering as it began to fall toward us. Panic surged through the crowd as people scattered in every direction, and in that split second, I realized how fragile everything I'd built was.

As the tree crashed to the ground, uprooting a portion of our carefully laid festival, I caught sight of Marcus's horrified face just before everything went dark. In the chaos, I reached out for him, but the world spun around me, and I was swallowed by the shadows, uncertainty tightening its grip as the weight of everything I had fought for came crashing down.

Chapter 2: The Unlikely Alliance

Every morning, the sun spilled golden light across the fields, casting long shadows that danced playfully between the rows of crops. It was during those early hours, while the air still carried the sweet perfume of dew-kissed earth, that I found myself looking forward to Sophie's arrival. She glided onto the farm like a gust of wind—unexpected and invigorating, her hair a cascade of auburn waves that seemed to catch the sunlight with every movement. As she approached, her practical boots crunching against the gravel, I felt an electric anticipation tingling beneath my skin.

"Ready for another adventure?" she asked, a teasing smile playing on her lips.

"Adventure?" I scoffed, rolling my eyes with a playful exaggeration. "It's just farming, Sophie. You know, dirt, plants, maybe a few stubborn weeds."

"Ah, but within every weed lies a hidden treasure!" she proclaimed, arms wide, as if she were summoning the very essence of nature itself. "Every plant has a story to tell. All we have to do is listen."

It was hard not to be charmed by her enthusiasm. As we worked side by side, she instructed me on how to prune the apple trees that had long since been neglected. I wielded the shears with a clumsy determination, mimicking her graceful motions, while she imparted her knowledge with a gentle confidence. The way she spoke about the trees—how each branch needed nurturing, how they would flourish under careful attention—reminded me that there was beauty in nurturing not just the land, but also the connections we formed.

With each passing day, the landscape transformed into a tapestry of color and vitality. Sunflowers stood proud, their heads nodding in agreement to Sophie's laughter, while the sweet smell of tomatoes ripening in the sun wrapped around us like a warm embrace. There was an undeniable magic in the air, something that danced between us, an unspoken bond formed over shared toil and giggles that echoed through the crisp morning air.

But for all her warmth, a cloud of mystery hung over Sophie. Occasionally, I would catch her staring into the distance, her gaze clouded with thoughts she wouldn't share. When I asked, she would quickly deflect, her smile dimming just enough for me to notice. It was as if she were a puzzle with a few missing pieces, and each time I tried to lean in, the edges grew sharper, more obscured. I wanted to understand her better; I craved the full story behind those sparkling green eyes.

One afternoon, as we rested beneath the sprawling limbs of an ancient oak tree, I decided to press a little further. The sun filtered through the leaves, creating a mosaic of light and shadow on her face. "You know, I've realized something," I began, trying to keep my tone light. "You're not just a horticulturist. You're like... a plant whisperer."

Her laughter rang out like chimes in a gentle breeze, but there was an edge to it. "If only it were that simple. But, you see, plants are far more forgiving than people."

"Is that why you're avoiding my questions?" I shot back, an eyebrow raised. The moment hung between us, charged with something unsaid.

She tilted her head, her expression a mixture of amusement and hesitation. "I'm not avoiding anything, just prioritizing the immediate. Right now, the plants need me."

I wasn't satisfied with that answer, but before I could respond, she changed the subject with a deftness that caught me off guard. "Did you know that the best time to plant a tree is twenty years ago? The second-best time is now."

"Sounds like a very philosophical way to avoid answering," I said, leaning back against the tree and crossing my arms, a smile tugging at my lips.

"Touché." She laughed, but her eyes still held a hint of that elusive sadness, a flicker of vulnerability that made me want to reach out, to pull her into the light.

As the days turned into weeks, our bond deepened. We planted more than just seeds; we planted trust, laughter, and maybe even a little bit of hope. I began to reveal pieces of my own past, sharing tales of my late parents and the dreams they had for the farm. In turn, Sophie offered tidbits about her life—stories about her travels, her passion for horticulture, but never the details that lay beneath. I caught glimpses of her passion, the way she would light up when discussing her favorite plants or the thrill of helping a garden flourish, yet the core of her remained shrouded in mystery.

One evening, as the sun dipped low on the horizon, splashing the sky with hues of orange and pink, we found ourselves sitting on the porch, watching the world slow down. The cicadas began their nightly symphony, and a cool breeze swept through, carrying with it the scent of impending rain.

"Do you ever feel like you're running from something?" I ventured, my voice barely louder than a whisper, afraid of shattering the moment.

She turned to me, her eyes wide, the surprise evident. "What makes you say that?"

"I just... I see how you are with the plants, how you nurture them, and it feels like you're trying to escape something, something that's still tied to you," I said, my heart racing as I spoke the truth I had sensed all along.

For a heartbeat, the air stilled, and in that quiet, I saw the walls around her start to crack. But then the moment passed, and she chuckled softly, the sound light yet edged with something brittle.

"Maybe we all are running from something. Or maybe we're just trying to find where we belong."

Her words hung heavy in the air, an echo of truths unspoken. I wanted to unravel the layers of her, to peel back the façade she wore like armor, but I sensed that would require patience and trust—two things I was ready to invest in, but she had yet to fully embrace.

As twilight deepened and stars began to pierce the darkening sky, I felt a shiver of something unnameable flit between us. It was more than friendship; it was an alliance forged in the shared sweat of our labor and the weight of our secrets. Each day we worked together, the ties binding us grew stronger, yet the shadows from her past loomed ever larger, whispering of a story waiting to be told.

Perhaps, I thought as I looked out over the fields stretching into the night, there was still hope for both of us—hope that the truth could be nurtured like the plants we tended, coaxed into the light of day where it could flourish, unhidden and free.

The days passed like a breath, a seamless blend of sweat, laughter, and the earthy aroma of fresh soil mingling with wildflowers. I had quickly learned that every plant had a personality—a unique quirk that Sophie seemed to read as easily as I read the weather. The corn stalks swayed in agreement with her animated storytelling, while the daisies bobbed their heads, as if they were part of our clandestine discussions. Sophie spoke with a passion that made even the most mundane tasks feel like an adventure.

"You know," she said one afternoon while we were uprooting weeds that had taken a stubborn hold in the flower garden, "gardening is like a metaphor for life. It requires patience, resilience, and a fair bit of faith. Some seeds take time to germinate, just as some dreams need years to bloom."

I chuckled, swiping at a particularly resilient dandelion. "If my dreams were plants, I'd say they're currently in hibernation."

"Maybe they just need a little more water and sunshine," she quipped, her eyes sparkling mischievously. "Or perhaps some gentle encouragement from a horticulturist."

We shared a laugh, but beneath her playful banter lay an earnestness that disarmed me. It was as if she saw the potential in everything—every withered leaf and every patch of bare earth. But I found myself longing for her to reveal the potential within herself, the parts of her that remained locked away, hidden behind a smile that sometimes felt like a mask.

As we worked, I noticed how she would pause at certain plants, her fingers gently brushing over their leaves as if she were coaxing them to share their secrets. I would often catch her staring into the distance, her thoughts far away, her expression a mixture of serenity and storm. One evening, I attempted to bridge that chasm of silence, but it was like trying to catch smoke in my hands.

"Tell me about the last garden you tended," I asked, wiping the sweat from my brow as the sun began to dip below the horizon, casting long shadows across the land.

Her eyes shifted, a flicker of something dark dancing in their depths. "It was a small garden in a community center," she replied after a beat, her voice steady yet laced with a distant melancholy. "We created a sanctuary for the kids, a place where they could learn about plants, about growth. It was wonderful... until it wasn't."

I leaned in, sensing the story lurking just beneath the surface. "What do you mean?"

"It got vandalized," she said, her tone clipped. "The kids poured their hearts into it, and someone destroyed it overnight. I couldn't save it, no matter how hard I tried. Sometimes, it feels like the world has a way of crushing the beautiful things we create."

Her vulnerability pierced through the atmosphere, filling the space with an unspoken tension. I wanted to reach out, to comfort her, but I hesitated, uncertain of how to breach the walls she had erected around her heart. Instead, I gently nodded, letting the weight of her words linger between us.

The following days found us immersed in the rhythms of the farm, each sunrise unveiling new tasks and opportunities. The initial excitement of our collaboration had solidified into a comfortable routine. I marveled at how easily we fell into sync, our movements choreographed by a shared understanding of each other's strengths and weaknesses.

One particularly sunny afternoon, as we dug a trench for a new irrigation system, I found myself sharing more about my past—how I had inherited the farm from my parents, how their love for the land had been infectious, instilling in me a sense of responsibility I sometimes found suffocating. "I feel like I'm carrying their dreams, but I'm not sure I know how to fulfill them," I admitted, my voice tinged with uncertainty.

Sophie paused, leaning on her shovel, her expression softening. "You're not just carrying their dreams, you're creating your own," she said, a warmth emanating from her that made my chest tighten. "It's okay to carve your own path. Your parents would want you to flourish in your own way."

Her words washed over me, a soothing balm on a long-held wound. I wanted to believe her, to trust that my journey didn't have to mirror theirs. But just as I began to feel the weight of expectation lift, the unmistakable sound of gravel crunching under tires interrupted our moment.

Turning to see a pickup truck rolling up the drive, I felt a twinge of anxiety. I recognized it instantly—Carter, my neighbor, known for his habit of popping in unannounced. As the engine sputtered to a halt, I exchanged a glance with Sophie, her brow furrowing slightly, and I knew she felt it too.

"What do you think he wants?" she whispered, a hint of concern threading through her tone.

"Probably to complain about the noise we've been making," I sighed, rolling my eyes. "Or to remind me that I should be planting more than just sunflowers."

Carter climbed out, a tall figure with a broad frame and an expression that could sour milk. "Hey, Sophie!" he called out, waving with exaggerated cheerfulness. "What are you doing here? Shouldn't you be in the city with the other plant nerds?"

I cringed at his lack of tact, and I could see the irritation flash across Sophie's face, quickly masked by her unwavering smile. "Just helping a friend," she replied, her voice steady.

"A friend?" He looked between us, a skeptical eyebrow raised. "You know this place has been in shambles for years. I wouldn't expect you to waste your time here."

The air thickened with unspoken tension, and I could sense Sophie bristling at his words. "It's called revitalization, Carter," I shot back, crossing my arms defensively. "Maybe you should try it sometime instead of sitting on your porch and judging everyone else."

His grin faltered for a moment, but he quickly recovered. "Sure, just remember that not all weeds can be turned into flowers. Some of them just choke the life out of everything."

With that, he turned to leave, but not before Sophie spoke up, her voice cutting through the tension like a knife. "You know, Carter, maybe you should spend a little more time cultivating kindness instead of tearing down those trying to grow."

I felt a surge of admiration for her. There was a fierceness in her words that I hadn't seen before, a fire that lit up her eyes. As Carter drove away, the heaviness in the air dissipated, replaced by a bubbling laughter that sprang forth from both of us, as if we had just shared a secret rebellion against the world.

"Who knew you had it in you?" I teased, nudging her playfully. "I didn't take you for the confrontational type."

She grinned, the spark returning to her eyes. "Sometimes, you have to stand your ground. Weeds might not realize they're weeds until someone pulls them up."

As we resumed our work, I couldn't help but feel a shift within us. Each day brought new challenges, yet with Sophie by my side, it felt less daunting. The shadows from her past still lingered, but in those moments, I felt as if we were building something together—something resilient, something vibrant, something that could weather the storms. And maybe, just maybe, we were both learning how to grow in ways we hadn't imagined before.

Mornings rolled into afternoons seamlessly, each day a delicate tapestry woven with the threads of our growing camaraderie and shared aspirations. The farm transformed under our diligent hands; rows of vibrant vegetables flourished alongside the budding flowers, creating a patchwork quilt of color and life. I had always thought of the farm as merely a place of labor and obligation, but with Sophie, it began to pulse with potential, as if it, too, had a heartbeat.

One afternoon, while we were knee-deep in the cool, dark earth, I turned to her, splattered with mud and full of determination. "I've been thinking we should plant some more herbs. Basil, thyme, rosemary—the essentials. Imagine a farm-to-table dinner with everything fresh from right here!"

Her eyes lit up, and the thought seemed to ignite something within her. "Herbs are the soul of any kitchen," she said, her voice dripping with enthusiasm. "They're not just flavor; they're magic." She paused, brushing a stray lock of hair behind her ear, and looked at me as if I held the secret to the universe in my hands. "You have to talk to them, you know. Herbs are especially responsive to kindness."

"Talk to them?" I laughed, shaking my head. "What am I going to say? 'Hey, rosemary, how's your day going?'"

"Exactly!" she shot back, laughter bubbling up like champagne. "And if you start singing to them, even better. They thrive on affection. It's like you're cultivating a relationship, not just a garden."

I couldn't help but feel the warmth of her spirit infuse the air around us. Each day, I was learning more about her perspective, her playful take on life. Just as I began to feel a deeper connection forming, however, a fleeting look crossed her face—one of uncertainty, like a shadow crossing the sun. It was a reminder that, despite the laughter and growth, there was still an underlying current of something unsaid between us.

That evening, as twilight wrapped the farm in a blanket of indigo, we settled on the porch, our tired bodies sinking into the old wooden chairs. The cicadas sang their evening serenade, a melody that felt both familiar and soothing. I could see the last rays of the sun clinging to the horizon, painting the sky with streaks of crimson and gold.

"What do you miss most about your old life?" I asked, bracing myself for the shift in the air. I had been wondering if this might be the moment she would let her guard down.

Sophie's smile faltered, her gaze focused on the horizon, where the last light faded into a canvas of stars. "I used to be in a place where I thought I could make a difference," she said slowly, her voice tinged with a weight that felt almost tangible. "But sometimes, the harder you try, the more you realize how little control you actually have."

"Sounds like you learned that the hard way," I said softly, sensing her walls beginning to crack. "What happened?"

She took a deep breath, and for a moment, I thought she might finally share the story I had sensed all along. But then she straightened, shaking off the moment like water droplets from her hair. "Let's just say not every garden survives, no matter how much you nurture it."

The words hung heavy in the air, laden with meaning. I could feel the distance between us stretching, like the darkening sky above. "You're right. Some gardens need a little extra attention, a little resilience to get through the tough times."

"Exactly," she replied, though her tone felt more guarded. "Just like people."

A silence fell between us, thick with unsaid thoughts and buried feelings. I wanted to reach out, to bridge that gap, but something held me back. Maybe it was the fear of what I might uncover, or perhaps it was the realization that we were both grappling with our own demons.

The next few days unfolded with the same rhythm, each sunrise punctuated by our shared laughter, yet I sensed an unshakeable tension hovering just out of reach. Sophie's thoughts remained elusive, slipping through my fingers like the delicate petals of the flowers we tended. I decided I would give her space, trusting that she would come to me when she was ready.

One warm afternoon, as we were mulching the newly planted herbs, I caught sight of Sophie glancing at her phone, her expression shifting to something unreadable. The light in her eyes dimmed momentarily, and a tightness formed around her lips. "Everything okay?" I asked, my voice laced with concern.

"Yeah, just... checking in," she said, too casually, as she tucked the phone away. "Sometimes you have to keep in touch with the world, you know?"

"Right," I replied, my instincts flaring. "What's happening out there that's so important? Are you thinking of leaving?"

Her head snapped up, and the intensity of her gaze held me captive. "Leaving? No! This is where I want to be. I just... I have obligations. Responsibilities."

"Responsibilities?" I pressed, feeling a sense of urgency creeping into my chest. "Sophie, you don't owe anyone anything. You've poured your heart into this place, into us. Don't let the past dictate your future."

She inhaled sharply, the tension in her shoulders betraying her calm facade. "It's not that simple. Sometimes the past finds a way of catching up to you, no matter how far you run."

The weight of her words struck a chord deep within me, reverberating like a distant echo. I could see the pain flickering beneath her surface, a fire tempered by regret. "You can't just let it hold you back," I insisted, desperate for her to see that she had the power to reclaim her life, her choices. "You deserve to thrive, not just survive."

Our eyes locked in a fierce battle of wills, and for a heartbeat, the world around us faded. It was as if we were suspended in time, caught between the urgency of her unspoken truth and my desire to pull her into the light.

But just then, the sharp sound of gravel crunching broke our moment, shattering the intensity like glass. A dark figure emerged from the shadows, standing at the edge of the yard—a man I recognized all too well. Carter.

"What do you want?" I snapped, irritation rising as I watched him approach, a smug grin plastered across his face.

"I thought I'd check in on you two lovebirds," he said, his voice dripping with sarcasm. "Heard some interesting things about your little farm project here. Sounds like someone is getting a little too cozy with the weeds."

Sophie straightened, her demeanor shifting instantly to a more guarded stance, the vulnerability of our earlier conversation evaporating like mist. "We're just fine, Carter," she said coolly. "Thanks for your concern."

He laughed, a sharp, mocking sound. "Concern? Oh, I have plenty of that, especially when I see someone trying to waste their potential in the middle of nowhere. You should be careful, Sophie. Some roots are harder to pull than they seem."

An uneasy tension hung in the air, thick as molasses. I could see Sophie's jaw tighten, her eyes narrowing. "You have no idea what you're talking about," she shot back, but I could sense the flicker of fear hiding beneath her bravado.

Carter took a step closer, a predatory gleam in his eye. "Or maybe I do. I know the kind of weeds that can choke out your dreams, and they're not just in the ground."

My heart raced as I exchanged glances with Sophie. What had he meant? What was lurking in the shadows of her past that was now threatening to break free? The weight of his words loomed large, an ominous cloud hanging over us.

"Stay away from us, Carter," I warned, stepping protectively in front of Sophie, my voice steady despite the adrenaline coursing through me. "You have no business here."

"Right, right. But you know what they say about weeds—sometimes they just won't die." With that, he turned to leave, a smirk lingering on his lips as he sauntered back to his truck.

I could feel the tension crackling between us as he drove away, leaving a silence that echoed louder than words. I turned to Sophie, ready to break the tension, but her face was pale, her eyes wide, a storm brewing beneath her calm exterior.

"What was that all about?" I asked gently, trying to coax her back to the moment we had just shared.

But before she could respond, the distant rumble of thunder rolled across the sky, an ominous prelude to the impending storm. The air felt charged, electric, and I could sense something dark and unresolved thrumming between us, the shadows of the past converging as the sky darkened.

"Let's go inside," I suggested, the unease in my gut twisting tighter. But as we turned to make our way inside, I caught a glimpse of something in the distance—a shadow flitting through the trees, a figure moving silently, watching us.

I paused, my heart racing as the first drops of rain began to fall, mingling with the growing tension. "Did you see that?" I whispered, my breath hitching in my throat.

Sophie looked over her shoulder, her eyes narrowing as she peered into the darkening woods. "See what?"

But I was already moving toward the edge of the porch, a sense of dread pooling in my stomach. "There was someone out there. Someone was watching us."

As the storm began to rage above us, a clap of thunder shook the ground, and I felt the air thrum with foreboding.

Chapter 3: Beneath the Surface

The sun dipped low on the horizon, casting a warm, golden light across the sprawling fields of Willow Creek. The vibrant greens of the lettuce and the rich reds of the heirloom tomatoes contrasted sharply with the fading light, creating a tapestry of color that felt alive with possibility. I stood beside Sophie, the soft earth beneath our feet and the faint scent of ripe fruit hanging in the air. It was a heady mix, invigorating and calming all at once. This was our sanctuary, a place where dreams could sprout like the seedlings we tended, and yet, as I watched her gaze drift toward the distant hills, I felt a chill.

"What are you thinking about?" I asked, my voice barely above a whisper. The evening wind toyed with her hair, framing her face in a halo of golden strands, but it couldn't quite mask the shadows in her eyes.

"Just... memories," she replied, her voice steady, but I could hear the quaver beneath. It was a simple answer, yet it felt weighted, as if she was trying to carry the weight of the world on her shoulders alone. I had come to know her well—the way her laughter filled the air, how she tended to the crops with a passion that was infectious. Yet, beneath that exterior lay an enigma I yearned to solve.

We had spent countless evenings working late under the stars, sharing stories and laughter, but tonight, there was a distance, an unspoken barrier I sensed hovering between us. I leaned closer, intent on bridging that gap, but before I could gather my thoughts, Sophie turned abruptly, her expression shifting. "Let's check on the squash. They should be coming in soon."

I followed her into the field, my heart racing not just from the thrill of the work but from the pulse of something deeper brewing between us. The squash vines sprawled across the ground like a green tapestry, their yellow flowers bursting forth with life. As we knelt to examine the plants, I caught her eye again, hoping to coax more of her thoughts out into the open.

"You know, for someone who's so passionate about growing things, you seem to have a knack for hiding." The words slipped out before I could stop them, a blend of playful ribbing and genuine curiosity.

She shot me a sharp glance, eyebrows arching in surprise, then her lips curled into a wry smile. "Touché. Maybe I just prefer to cultivate my crops rather than my past."

Her words hung in the air, thick with implication. "But what if the past is what helps us grow?" I countered, daring to press further, fueled by the connection we shared, the way the air seemed to crackle with tension and something unnameable.

Sophie sighed, her shoulders dropping as she gathered her thoughts like stray petals in the wind. "It's just easier to focus on the future. Here, I can plant seeds, nurture them, and watch them flourish without the weight of old burdens."

Her voice trembled with vulnerability, and in that moment, I realized I wanted to help her shed those burdens. "But what if we faced them together? I know I'm not a therapist, but I'm a pretty good listener."

She laughed softly, the sound warm and inviting, but her eyes betrayed the flicker of fear that lay beneath. "And what if I told you that the past is a place filled with ghosts? Not everyone has a story that ends happily."

"I've dealt with my own ghosts," I admitted, surprising even myself. "And I learned that burying them only makes them louder."

Her expression softened, the defenses crumbling just a bit. "Okay, let's say I entertain this idea of facing the past. Where do we start?"

"Let's start with today," I suggested, my heart racing as I realized how intimate this moment had become. "Tell me something about yourself that I don't know. Something you wouldn't mind sharing."

Sophie hesitated, her fingers fiddling with the fraying hem of her shirt, and I could almost see the thoughts swirling in her mind. "I once had a life in the city. A job in a high-rise, lots of money, parties..." She paused, her gaze faraway. "But it was all so hollow. I was surrounded by people but felt completely alone. I wanted something real, something that grounded me. So, I came here."

"Just like that? You uprooted everything?"

"It wasn't quite that simple." She chuckled, but it was laced with sadness. "I had to leave behind more than just a job. There were people... promises. And I thought I could escape."

A part of me wanted to delve deeper, to ask about those people and promises, but I held back, sensing her hesitance. "I get it. Sometimes the hardest thing is not just leaving but knowing what we leave behind."

She nodded, her expression softening. "You're right. It's a constant balancing act, isn't it? We nurture the future while trying not to let the past choke us."

"Exactly." I took a deep breath, encouraged by the connection we were forging, and shared a part of my own story. "I left my own past behind when I moved here. I was running away from a suffocating job, a life that felt like a treadmill. But in escaping, I found something unexpected—an urge to connect, to build something worth keeping."

Our laughter faded, replaced by a comfortable silence, the kind that settles between friends who are becoming more. I felt lighter, buoyed by the shared weight of our confessions. Beneath the twilight sky, I saw not just Sophie, the woman with untold stories, but the beautiful spirit fighting to find her place in the world.

Just then, a rustle in the bushes nearby broke the spell. My heart leaped, thinking it might be a critter come to steal our precious crops. But as I turned, my gaze fell upon a shadowy figure watching us from the edge of the field. The air thickened, and I felt a shiver of unease creep down my spine, as if the past was reaching out to touch us both in ways we had yet to understand.

The figure lurking at the edge of the field shifted, an unmistakable tension crackling in the air. My heart raced as I instinctively stepped closer to Sophie, ready to shield her from whatever shadows might emerge. The fading sunlight cast elongated shadows across the ground, mingling with the encroaching night, and for a moment, I thought I could hear the whispers of secrets lost in the wind.

"Did you see that?" I asked, my voice low, the earlier warmth of our conversation evaporating in an instant. Sophie's eyes widened, a mixture of surprise and concern flaring up.

"Yeah, I did," she replied, her voice barely above a whisper, as if saying it louder would summon whatever lurked beyond the vines. "It could just be a deer, you know. Or a raccoon."

I nodded, but the gnawing feeling in my gut told me otherwise. "Or someone... watching us."

She frowned, biting her lip as if weighing her options. "Let's go check it out."

"Are you sure?" I hesitated. The last thing I wanted was to spook her further, to drive the wedge between us deeper.

"Come on," she said, her voice gaining strength. "I won't let a little rustling in the bushes scare me off."

With a surge of determination, we crept toward the source of the movement, the underbrush crackling softly under our feet. My mind raced with possibilities, each more absurd than the last, but the thrill of the unknown propelled us forward. Sophie was ahead, her silhouette strong against the darkening sky, and I found comfort in her bravery.

As we approached the edge of the field, the figure slowly became clear, emerging from the shadows like a wraith. It was a man, tall and lean, with tousled hair and clothes that looked as if they had seen better days. His expression was hard to read, a mixture of caution and curiosity. He looked just as surprised to see us as we were to see him.

"Can I help you?" I called out, my voice steady despite the quickening pulse in my throat.

"Uh, I was just... passing through," he stammered, his gaze darting between us, as if weighing his next words carefully.

Sophie straightened, crossing her arms over her chest, exuding an aura of authority. "What brings you out here? This is private property."

"Just wanted to see the farm," he replied, a sheepish smile creeping onto his face. "I've heard a lot about Willow Creek, and I thought it might be a good time to check it out."

I exchanged a glance with Sophie, her wariness mirrored in my own. "And how did you hear about it?" I probed, wanting to peel back the layers of this unexpected visitor.

He hesitated, the bravado slipping slightly from his demeanor. "I used to work for a food distribution company. Your name came up a few times. Thought I'd come see for myself."

His explanation seemed plausible, yet something still felt off. "Is that right? And what's your name?"

"Jake," he said, relaxing a fraction as if he felt the tension dissipate.

"Jake," Sophie repeated, her tone lightening just a notch. "So, you're a foodie?"

"More like a food enthusiast," he replied, a grin breaking through. "I enjoy visiting local farms. There's something magical about fresh produce, don't you think?"

"Magical?" I chuckled, unable to resist the playful banter. "That's one way to describe weeding for hours on end."

He laughed, and for a moment, the tension melted away, replaced by the warmth of shared humor. But as the laughter faded, I couldn't shake the feeling that Jake wasn't just a curious visitor.

"I suppose I could show you around if you're interested," Sophie suggested, glancing at me with a mix of uncertainty and intrigue.

"Sure, I'd love that," Jake replied, his eyes sparkling with interest.

As we walked deeper into the heart of Willow Creek, Sophie took the lead, her confidence blooming like the flowers in our fields. "Here's where we grow the heirloom tomatoes. They're the best in the county, if I do say so myself."

I could see Jake's interest intensifying, his attention focused on her with a mix of admiration and intrigue. "Impressive," he said, leaning closer to inspect the plump red fruits dangling from the vines. "You've really created something beautiful here."

"It's a labor of love," Sophie responded, her voice softening, the pride evident in her tone. "Every day is a new challenge, but it's worth it."

As we continued the tour, Jake peppered us with questions, and I found myself relaxing into the rhythm of the conversation. The way Sophie lit up while sharing her knowledge was captivating, and I could see Jake hanging onto her every word. It was thrilling, but I couldn't help but notice the flicker of something deeper in his gaze, a spark of curiosity that felt like it was reaching for Sophie's hidden truths.

"So, what's the hardest part about running a farm?" he asked, pulling her further into his orbit.

Sophie hesitated, glancing back at me as if gauging whether to reveal more of herself. "There are a lot of challenges, but I think it's the unpredictability that gets to me. Weather, pests, market fluctuations... sometimes it feels like you're battling against nature itself."

"Sounds a bit like life, doesn't it?" he replied, his smile fading slightly, a shadow passing over his features. "Always throwing curveballs at you when you least expect it."

His words hung in the air, and I could see Sophie's defenses slipping back into place. "That's true," she said, her voice tightening. "But we manage to adapt."

"Adaptation is key," Jake agreed, a hint of something unspoken in his eyes. "You've got to keep evolving to survive."

With those words, I felt the atmosphere shift. The playful banter had transformed into a more serious undertone, and I sensed a shared understanding between them, a connection forged from battles fought and scars earned. I watched them exchange glances, and it stirred a mix of protectiveness and jealousy within me.

"I think it's time for a snack," I said, trying to lighten the mood. "We've got some fresh strawberries in the fridge. They're as sweet as a summer day."

"Count me in!" Jake exclaimed, his enthusiasm returning as we headed toward the farmhouse. The thought of ripe strawberries felt like a sweet distraction, but I couldn't shake the feeling that we were on the brink of something far more complex.

Inside, the scent of berries mingled with the warm air, and I busied myself in the kitchen, slicing strawberries and adding a touch of sugar. I could hear Sophie and Jake chatting behind me, their voices low, but the laughter that trickled through made my heart ache with longing. I was reminded that even in this close-knit space we had built, there were still walls around Sophie's heart that I couldn't breach.

"Here you go," I said, turning with the bowl, a smile plastered on my face. "Fresh strawberries, the pride of Willow Creek."

Sophie took a bowl, her fingers brushing against mine, sending an unexpected jolt through me. Jake accepted his share with a grin, and as the three of us settled at the kitchen table, I felt the threads of tension weave in and out of our interactions, stitching together a complicated tapestry of friendship and something far more tangled.

"So, what's next for Willow Creek?" Jake asked, leaning forward with genuine interest, his eyes brightening with curiosity.

Sophie glanced at me, a hint of mischief in her smile. "We've been toying with the idea of starting a community farmers' market. It could be a great way to bring people together."

"That sounds amazing!" Jake replied, his enthusiasm infectious. "Count me in. I'd love to help out."

I felt a pang of unease as I watched the sparks fly between them, but a small voice in my head reminded me that the more people we had involved, the stronger our community could become. And yet, beneath the surface of laughter and shared dreams, the shadows of our pasts lingered, waiting for the right moment to unfurl and catch us off guard.

The sun dipped below the horizon, painting the sky in hues of orange and lavender, casting a dreamlike quality over Willow Creek. I could almost forget the knot tightening in my stomach as Sophie and Jake continued to bond over the berries, their laughter ringing through the farmhouse like the sweetest of melodies. I watched them share stories, each word laced with the chemistry that crackled like static in the air, and I felt a pang of something bittersweet: the unmistakable urge to protect what we had built, juxtaposed against the fear of what lay beneath the surface.

"Did you ever think about how different things could be?" Jake asked, leaning back in his chair, the empty bowl of strawberries forgotten for the moment. His gaze flitted between Sophie and me, his curiosity palpable. "If you hadn't made the leap to start this farm?"

Sophie's smile faltered for a split second before she masked it with laughter. "Honestly? I try not to think about it. It's too easy to spiral into a what-if situation, and trust me, I've done enough spiraling to last a lifetime."

Jake leaned in, intrigued. "Spiraling can be a good catalyst for change, though. Like those wild tomatoes—pushing through the dirt, fighting to survive."

Sophie arched an eyebrow, clearly caught off guard by his analogy. "Are you trying to say I'm a wild tomato?"

"More like a resilient one," he replied smoothly, and my stomach knotted at the ease of their banter. "And hey, if I'm a tomato, I'd want to grow next to you."

I cleared my throat, attempting to inject some levity back into the room. "Well, if we're all tomatoes, I must be a slightly bruised heirloom—perfectly imperfect and just waiting for the right sauce."

Sophie burst into laughter, the sound brightening the room. "You'd make a fantastic marinara! I can already taste the garlic."

Jake grinned, clearly enjoying the playful exchange. "Count me in for the sauce-making competition. It sounds like the start of a culinary reality show right here at Willow Creek."

As the conversation flowed, I felt the edges of my earlier unease begin to dissolve, if only temporarily. Perhaps this wasn't the rivalry I imagined. Perhaps it was a partnership—if only I could keep my own insecurities at bay.

"So, what's the next step for our farmer's market?" Jake asked, turning his attention back to Sophie, who seemed invigorated by the prospect.

"We need to decide on a date, recruit some vendors, maybe even organize some entertainment," she said, her voice quickening with enthusiasm. "I was thinking we could have local musicians perform. Make it a real community event."

Jake's eyes lit up. "I can help with that. I have a few contacts in the local music scene who'd love to play for fresh produce. It could be a win-win!"

"Sounds like you're already invested," I teased, trying to keep my voice light, but my heart raced with the knowledge that this could turn into something more than just a simple farmers' market. It could deepen the bond between Sophie and Jake, and I wasn't sure I was ready for that.

"Absolutely! I think it could be a great way to get everyone involved," he said, his voice animated, eyes shining. "People crave connection, especially after everything that's happened in the past few years."

Sophie nodded thoughtfully, her gaze drifting away again. "You're right. After everything, it would be nice to bring the community together, to show that we can still thrive."

A flicker of worry crossed her face, and I sensed the shadows creeping back. "And it might help us connect with others too," I added gently. "To show them what we've built here, what we're capable of."

She looked at me, a mix of gratitude and unspoken questions swirling in her gaze. "I'd like that," she said quietly.

As the evening wore on, we continued to discuss ideas for the market, with Jake leading the charge, his energy infectious. I found myself caught in a whirlwind of ideas and possibilities, but beneath the excitement lay the persistent thrum of anxiety. I wanted Sophie to open up to me, to share her secrets, yet there was something about Jake that made me feel like I was standing on the edge of a cliff, teetering on the brink.

When Jake finally stood to leave, the atmosphere shifted once again. He glanced at Sophie, his expression earnest. "I really appreciate you both letting me hang out tonight. I'd love to get more involved in Willow Creek. Maybe we can start planning together?"

"Of course," Sophie replied, her voice bright, and I couldn't help but feel a twinge of something—jealousy, perhaps?

As Jake walked toward the door, he turned back, a playful smile on his lips. "I'll bring my guitar next time. We can have a jam session in the fields. Nothing like music and fresh air."

"Sounds like a plan," I replied, though my heart sank a little. I was all for community spirit, but my inner voice was now screaming at me, warning me of potential storms brewing beneath the placid surface of our lives.

Once Jake left, the house settled into an unsettling silence, a palpable tension thickening the air. I turned to Sophie, finding her staring out the window, her silhouette framed against the dim light. "You okay?" I asked, concern lacing my tone.

"Just thinking," she said softly, her gaze distant. "About everything we talked about, the market, the community. It feels like we're on the brink of something, doesn't it?"

"Yeah, it does," I said, matching her tone. "But what about your past, Sophie? You mentioned it earlier—what if it comes back to haunt you?"

She turned slowly, her expression tightening. "I thought I had left it behind, but sometimes it feels like shadows never really go away."

The words hung in the air, heavy with unspoken fears. I took a step closer, driven by an urge to reassure her. "You're not alone in this. Whatever it is, we'll face it together."

"Sometimes, together isn't enough," she murmured, a hint of pain in her voice.

Just then, the sharp trill of her phone broke the tension, and she reached for it with shaky hands. Her expression shifted dramatically as she read the message, her eyes widening in disbelief. "Oh no. Not now..."

"What is it?" I asked, my heart racing as I sensed a shift in the atmosphere.

Her hands trembled, and she bit her lip, staring at the screen as if it were a snake ready to strike. "It's... it's my old life. They've found me."

The gravity of her words hit me like a cold wave, and the air grew thick with fear and uncertainty. The past, once a ghost lurking just out of reach, had come crashing back into our lives, and I was left standing on the precipice of an unknown storm, wondering just how deep the shadows really ran.

Chapter 4: The First Seed of Doubt

The morning sun poured through the kitchen window, casting a golden hue across the checkered tablecloth where Sophie and I had shared countless breakfasts, both mundane and magical. Today, however, a palpable tension hovered in the air, thick enough to cut with a knife. I busied myself with preparing a fresh pot of coffee, the rich aroma weaving through the house like a familiar friend. Sophie was still asleep, her peaceful face nestled in the cushions of the sofa, an array of bright quilts draped over her. I glanced at her, my heart swelling with love and anxiety in equal measure.

Just yesterday, a sleek black car had pulled up to the edge of my property, interrupting the delicate tranquility we had nurtured since moving here. The representatives from AgriCorp had arrived, two sharp-suited men with smiles that didn't quite reach their eyes. They stepped out with an air of superiority, the kind that screamed corporate takeover and had my gut twisting into knots. I had hesitated as they introduced themselves, their voices smooth and persuasive, promising the world while quietly aiming for my land.

"Your farm has potential," one of them had said, his tone oozing with feigned enthusiasm. "With our resources, you could scale up, reach new markets, and really make a name for yourself. Think of the financial stability!"

As they spoke, I could almost hear the gears turning in their heads, calculating profits and future expansions like a game of chess where I was merely a pawn. I had smiled politely, nodding, but inside, I was screaming. What they called partnership, I saw as a cage, gilded and enticing, but a cage nonetheless. The farm wasn't just a plot of land for me; it was a living, breathing entity filled with memories and dreams. I had carved out this sanctuary for Sophie and me, a place where we could thrive away from the noise of the city, and I wasn't about to let anyone tear it apart.

As I poured the coffee, I couldn't help but let my mind wander back to the moments that had led me to this point. It had been a rocky road, each turn littered with doubt and uncertainty. The initial weeks of moving to this rural paradise had been filled with challenges—fixing leaks, battling weeds, and figuring out how to convince stubborn chickens that I was, in fact, their benevolent ruler. Yet, with each obstacle, we had woven tighter threads of connection, both with the land and with each other.

I felt a shadow cross my thoughts, the image of those suits looming large. The idea of signing away even a fraction of what we had built together twisted like a knife in my chest. A partnership with AgriCorp would mean changing everything about our way of life, shifting our focus from sustainability to profitability. It felt wrong, a betrayal of the very values I had worked so hard to instill.

Sophie stirred on the sofa, her sleepy eyes fluttering open. She smiled at me, that bright, genuine smile that made all my worries fade, if only for a moment. "What are you thinking about?" she asked, her voice still thick with sleep.

"Just... coffee," I replied, keeping the tension from my voice. "How did you sleep?"

"Like a rock. Did you hear the owls last night? They were practically serenading me." She stretched, the quilt slipping off her shoulders, revealing a soft, cotton nightgown that swayed like petals in a gentle breeze.

"Not a peep from me. I must have been exhausted." I poured her a cup, watching as the steam curled upward, a small comfort amidst my swirling thoughts.

As she took the mug, I braced myself for her inevitable question about the men in suits. It was hard to keep secrets from Sophie; her intuition was sharper than any blade, and I admired that about her. But at the same time, I wanted to shield her from the burden of my doubts. "They were just some folks from AgriCorp," I said casually, as if they were nothing more than a couple of friendly neighbors dropping by for a chat.

Sophie raised an eyebrow, suspicion dancing in her eyes. "Just? What did they want?"

"They're interested in partnering with us," I said, my voice betraying a slight tremor. "Promised all kinds of resources and support."

Her expression shifted, a flicker of concern crossing her face. "That doesn't sound like a good idea. What's the catch?"

"They want a stake in the farm. You know how these things go, Sophie. They might offer help now, but it could lead to us losing control of everything we've built."

Sophie set her coffee down with a deliberate clink, the sound reverberating in the silence that followed. "You can't be serious. This is our home. We've fought too hard for this."

"I know. That's why I didn't tell you right away. I didn't want to worry you."

Her eyes softened, but the steel in her gaze remained. "You should have told me sooner. We're in this together, remember?"

I sighed, feeling the weight of my hesitation. It was true; we had weathered storms hand in hand, and yet, here I was, trying to shoulder this burden alone. "I didn't want to drag you into it," I said, rubbing the back of my neck nervously. "I thought maybe if I figured it out on my own—"

"Figuring it out alone doesn't work like that. We're a team, even when it's uncomfortable." She leaned closer, her sincerity wrapping around me like a warm blanket. "What are you really worried about?"

I hesitated, searching for the right words. "What if I say no? What if they retaliate? What if I'm putting us at risk by standing my ground?"

Sophie's hand found mine, squeezing gently. "If they want to intimidate us, they don't know who they're dealing with. We've faced bigger challenges than some corporate bullies. Together, we can handle anything."

I let out a breath I didn't realize I was holding, her faith in me stirring something deep within. Perhaps I had underestimated us. Perhaps we were stronger than I believed.

Outside, the morning chorus of birds began to crescendo, filling the air with an optimism that clashed with the storm brewing inside me. I could feel it in my bones—the seeds of doubt were being planted, and while they were small now, if left unchecked, they could grow into something unmanageable, something that could threaten the fragile peace we had fought so hard to cultivate.

And yet, with Sophie by my side, I felt a flicker of resolve igniting in my chest. Together, we had built this farm, and together we would decide its fate.

The sun climbed higher in the sky, spilling warm light over the rows of crops that danced gently in the breeze, each stalk swaying as if in agreement with my turbulent thoughts. As I stepped outside, the earthy scent of freshly tilled soil filled my lungs, grounding me in the reality of what I had cultivated. This land, with its quirks and imperfections, was not just my livelihood; it was a testament to resilience, a canvas painted with sweat and laughter, with memories of Sophie and me sharing jokes over lunch in the shade of the old oak tree.

Sophie emerged from the house, her hair tousled, a bright smile illuminating her face despite the weight of our recent conversation. She wore a pair of overalls, the kind that had seen better days but were lovingly patched and softened by years of wear. "What's the plan for today?" she asked, her eyes sparkling with enthusiasm as she reached for a worn straw hat that seemed to belong to her as much as the land itself.

"We need to check on the tomatoes and see if those pesky crows have returned," I replied, grabbing my own hat and adjusting it to shield my eyes from the sun. The little red fruits were almost ripe, dangling like jewels from the vine, and I couldn't help but feel a sense of pride whenever I glanced their way. "I'd like to put up some scarecrows, too, if we have time."

She laughed, a sound that seemed to chase away the remnants of my doubts. "Scarecrows? I think we should go for something more inventive. How about a scare-robot? Just imagine the neighbors' faces!"

"Scare-robot?" I raised an eyebrow, smirking. "And what exactly would that entail? A tin can for a head and a broomstick for arms?"

"Hey, don't mock my genius! It could have flashing lights and everything." Sophie twirled in place, her excitement infectious. "Think about it—a little disco party in the fields to scare away the crows. It's foolproof!"

The lighthearted banter allowed me to temporarily shelve the unease that had been simmering beneath the surface since AgriCorp's visit. We walked hand in hand toward the garden, the familiar path lined with wildflowers that swayed gently in the breeze. Each step felt like a small rebellion against the pressures pressing in from the outside world.

As we reached the patch of tomatoes, I noticed Sophie crouching low, her fingers brushing the leaves. "Look!" she exclaimed, pointing. "These are ready! We'll have a feast tonight."

I knelt beside her, our shoulders almost touching. "Just the two of us?" I teased. "I was hoping for a dinner party, maybe even an invitation for those corporate guys."

"Please, I'd rather eat dirt than share a meal with them," she replied, scrunching her nose in mock disgust. "You know what they remind me of? Those fancy jars of preserves that look beautiful but taste like nothing."

Her words rang true, and I chuckled, the tension from earlier easing ever so slightly. "Well, if we're going to stick to our plan of not inviting them for dinner, we'd better get to work."

The next few hours flew by as we harvested the tomatoes, our hands stained red and our laughter echoing through the garden. It was a rhythm I cherished, the kind that forged a bond deeper than any corporate contract. Each plump fruit was a victory, a reminder that success didn't have to come with strings attached. We talked about the upcoming market, our dreams of creating a name for ourselves, and I felt my spirits lifting with each passing moment.

Just as we finished gathering the last of the tomatoes, a rumble of thunder rolled through the sky, dark clouds sweeping in like a curtain falling on our little world. "Well, that escalated quickly," I murmured, glancing up at the ominous clouds.

Sophie groaned, her playful demeanor shifting to a more serious note. "We can't let the weather ruin our day. Let's finish the scarecrow before the storm hits!"

We dashed back to the shed, gathering supplies and working in tandem to assemble a figure that would hopefully frighten off any feathered intruders. As we laughed and crafted, I couldn't help but marvel at how effortlessly we made a team. It was a dance, a choreography of sorts, where our movements complemented one another without the need for a single word.

Just as we were securing the last piece of straw into place, a shrill honk split the air, and I turned to see a car—a familiar, sleek black one—pulling up the drive. My heart sank. AgriCorp.

"Uh-oh," Sophie said, glancing at me, her playful spirit dimming slightly. "What do they want now?"

"I have no idea," I muttered, my stomach churning. "Stay close."

The representatives stepped out of the car, their polished smiles back on display, but now there was something sharper in their gazes, a sense of urgency that put me on edge. "Just checking in," the taller one said, adjusting his tie as if it had suddenly become too tight. "We wanted to see how you were doing and if you'd thought about our offer."

I forced a smile, my grip tightening around the scarecrow's arm. "We're busy at the moment, but thank you for stopping by."

"Busy is good," the other one chimed in, his voice dripping with condescension. "But we're here to help. The offer is still on the table. You're going to need more than just tomatoes to sustain this venture."

Sophie stepped forward, crossing her arms defiantly. "We're doing just fine without your help, thank you very much."

The men exchanged glances, clearly taken aback by her boldness. "With our resources, you could expand your crops, reach new markets, and increase your profits exponentially. Think about it—imagine the possibilities!"

"Imagine the possibilities?" Sophie echoed, her tone playful yet edged with seriousness. "How about we imagine keeping our farm intact, our values intact?"

I could see the tension in the air, a strange electricity that crackled between us and them. It was almost tangible, and I felt a surge of protectiveness for the sanctuary Sophie and I had built together. "Look, we appreciate your concern, but we have everything we need right here," I asserted, stepping forward.

The taller representative's smile faded, replaced with an unsettling glint in his eyes. "You may think that now, but it's a competitive market. Opportunities like this don't come around often."

"Yeah, well, neither do thunderclouds," Sophie shot back, glancing at the sky as if daring them to challenge her. "And we both know they can change things in an instant."

With that, the clouds above seemed to respond, darkening and rumbling ominously as if the universe was backing up her claim. I felt a swell of admiration for her bravery, even as my heart raced with the realization of how precarious our situation had become.

"Consider our offer carefully," the representative finally said, his voice suddenly more serious, almost threatening. "It might not be on the table forever."

As they turned to leave, Sophie and I stood rooted in place, our hearts racing, the weight of their words sinking in like stones in a still pond. The distance between us and the world outside felt more pronounced than ever, a chasm of uncertainty that we would have to navigate together.

The dark clouds overhead thickened, casting an ominous shadow across the farm, as if nature itself had taken offense at AgriCorp's brazen intrusion. Sophie and I stood together, the tension crackling like static in the air, our hearts pounding in sync. The representatives slipped into their sleek car, exchanging furtive glances that hinted at the power plays behind their polished facades. I felt a surge of defiance rise within me as they drove away, but unease churned in my stomach.

"What do you think they'll do next?" Sophie asked, her brows furrowed, genuine concern painting her features.

"I don't know, but they're not the type to take no for an answer," I admitted, glancing back at the path they had taken. "They have resources, connections... we're just two people trying to make a life here."

Sophie snorted lightly, an inflection of humor bubbling through her worry. "We're not 'just two people.' We're two people with a garden that grows better than their spreadsheets."

"True," I conceded, the corner of my mouth twitching upward. "But they're playing a game we didn't even know we were in."

We stood in the cooling breeze, the scent of impending rain mingling with the earthy smell of the farm, and I felt a resolve harden within me. Whatever AgriCorp was plotting, we had to be prepared to protect what was ours. "Let's get the scarecrow finished and figure out our next steps," I suggested, redirecting my focus back to the task at hand.

As we resumed work, we crafted our scarecrow with care, embellishing it with old clothes, a tattered straw hat, and a crooked smile that was meant to charm more than frighten. Sophie added the finishing touch, a bright red bandana around its neck, and stepped back to admire our handiwork. "Now, that's a scarecrow with character," she proclaimed, hands on her hips, pride radiating from her.

I couldn't help but smile, the camaraderie lifting my spirits. "If nothing else, we'll be the best-dressed farm on the block."

With the rain beginning to patter softly against the soil, we decided to retreat indoors, the cozy confines of our little house calling to us like a warm embrace. As I brewed a fresh pot of tea, Sophie settled into her favorite chair, curling up with a blanket, her eyes sparkling with mischief.

"Want to make a plan?" she asked, her tone shifting from playful to serious. "Because if those guys think we're going to roll over and give them what they want, they've got another thing coming."

The kettle whistled, and I poured the steaming water over the tea leaves, allowing the aroma to envelop the room. "Absolutely. I've been thinking... we need to gather information. If we can understand what they're really after, we might be able to strategize."

"Like spies?" She grinned, her eyes lighting up. "I've always wanted to don a trench coat and sunglasses while snooping around corporate offices."

"Perhaps we'll need more than a trench coat. I'm thinking more along the lines of research—scouring the web, checking public records, that sort of thing," I replied, trying to keep a straight face.

She feigned disappointment but then winked. "You're no fun. Fine, I'll save the spy fantasies for my next novel."

"Next novel?" I raised an eyebrow, intrigued. "You're writing a novel?"

"Just a little something on the side," she said, waving her hand dismissively. "A light-hearted tale about a farmer who fights corporate greed while saving the world with homegrown tomatoes."

"Now that's a plot twist I can get behind," I chuckled, imagining her as the heroine of her own story, fiercely defending our little corner of paradise against all odds.

As we sipped our tea, the storm began to pick up outside, rain beating against the roof, the sound a comforting rhythm. "What if we invited some locals over for dinner tomorrow?" Sophie suggested, her enthusiasm bubbling back to the surface. "It would be nice to connect with the community and find out what they know about AgriCorp."

I nodded, liking the idea. "A farm-to-table feast it is. We can showcase our bounty and get to know our neighbors better. They might have insights we can't find online."

The rain continued to fall, the world outside becoming a blurry canvas of colors as the sky darkened. We spent the afternoon cooking and preparing, laughter filling the kitchen as we chopped vegetables and stirred sauces. The air was thick with warmth, and in that cocoon of comfort, I could almost forget the looming threat of AgriCorp.

By the time evening fell, the rain had subsided, leaving behind a fresh, earthy scent that wafted through the air. We set up the dining table outside, fairy lights strung overhead twinkling like stars in the now-clear sky. It was a picture of serenity, and I felt a surge of gratitude wash over me.

As guests began to arrive, I welcomed them with a smile, introducing them to Sophie, who was busy pouring glasses of homemade lemonade. The locals filled the space, their chatter mingling with the clinking of cutlery and the fragrant aromas of the meal we had prepared.

"Did you hear about AgriCorp's plans for expansion?" one neighbor, a jovial man named Tom, asked as he settled down beside me, his eyes alight with the thrill of gossip. "Word is they're trying to buy up as much farmland as they can around here."

I leaned in, my interest piqued. "What do you know?"

"Let's just say they're not exactly loved in these parts," he replied, lowering his voice conspiratorially. "Many farmers have fought them off, but it's a struggle. They promise money and resources, but there's always a catch. Those of us who've been here long enough know to be wary."

Sophie, overhearing our conversation, joined in. "So, you're saying we should keep our guard up?"

"Definitely," Tom nodded emphatically. "Stick together, that's the key. We might be small, but there's strength in numbers."

As the night unfolded, stories were shared, laughter echoed, and a sense of community enveloped us. Each smile exchanged, each anecdote told, fortified my resolve to protect our home. I could see Sophie beaming, her spirit lifted by the connections we were forging.

But as the evening wore on, I couldn't shake the feeling that we were still being watched. The back of my mind echoed with AgriCorp's menacing words, their intent clear: they weren't going to let go of their pursuit easily.

Just as I was about to dismiss the thought, the lights flickered momentarily, casting shadows that danced against the walls. I brushed it off as a mere glitch, but a prickling sensation crawled up my spine.

The laughter died down for a moment, a collective pause as everyone turned to look toward the far end of the property. My heart raced as I caught a glimpse of a figure standing in the darkness, partially obscured by the trees—a silhouette that felt both familiar and foreign.

"Is that someone?" Sophie asked, her voice barely above a whisper.

I squinted, the figure shifting slightly, and just like that, the laughter faded into an unsettling silence, leaving only the sound of the wind rustling through the leaves. "I think..."

Before I could finish, the figure stepped forward, revealing a face I hadn't seen in years, one that was etched with urgency and a hint of desperation. A chill rushed over me, as recognition ignited an overwhelming surge of dread.

"Help me!" the figure called out, and my heart dropped as I realized I was staring at someone I thought I would never see again.

Chapter 5: The Storm Clouds Gather

The wind rustled through the fields, a symphony of whispers that spoke of both promise and peril. I stood at the edge of our small farm, my fingers brushing against the weathered wood of the fence that had seen better days, just like us. The sky was an unsettling shade of slate gray, clouds gathering like dark thoughts in a restless mind. I could feel the weight of the world pressing down on me, a heavy mantle I hadn't signed up for but was bound to wear. My heart raced with the urgency of my circumstances, the burgeoning threats from AgriCorp looming larger than the storm clouds overhead.

Sophie had become a stranger, her laughter now a distant echo that haunted the corners of my consciousness. I often caught her staring into the horizon, her emerald eyes glimmering with secrets that danced just out of reach. Each time I approached, she would retreat, an instinctual step back into her protective shell. It was infuriating and heartbreaking all at once. I wanted to shake her out of her reverie, to pull her back to the present where we stood together against the encroaching darkness. But each time I reached for her, she slipped further away.

"Why are you acting like this?" I demanded one afternoon, my voice cracking under the pressure of frustration. We stood in the field where wildflowers swayed in the gentle breeze, oblivious to the tempest brewing within our lives. Sophie knelt, her hands brushing the petals, and for a moment, I wondered if she was more at home in the soil than in my world.

"It's not what you think," she replied, her voice soft yet edged with something sharp—an unyielding barrier. She refused to meet my gaze, choosing instead to focus on the tiny life forms that thrived under her touch. I felt a surge of anger, mixed with a sense of desperation. If she wouldn't let me in, how could I protect her, how could I fight alongside her?

"Then tell me what I should think, Sophie! You can't keep shutting me out. We're in this together, whether you like it or not." The words tumbled out before I could rein them in, frustration spilling into the open air between us. I could see her shoulders tense, a physical manifestation of her internal struggle.

She finally looked up, and I was met with a storm of emotions in her eyes—fear, sorrow, and something else that sent a shiver down my spine. "You don't understand," she said, her voice barely above a whisper. "It's not just the farm that's at stake. It's everything. My family, our history... this land holds secrets that some would kill to exploit."

The weight of her words settled between us like a stone, and I felt a chill creep through the warmth of the afternoon sun. "Secrets? What secrets?" I pressed, hoping to unravel the threads of her past. I needed to know who she was beneath the layers of pain and mystery.

Her fingers curled around a vibrant blue cornflower, its delicate petals trembling in the wind. "My family has been here for generations," she began, the tremor in her voice betraying the strength of her resolve. "We were caretakers of this land long before it was a commodity. There are things, rituals that connect us to the earth, to the spirits that dwell within it. The same spirits that warn me against AgriCorp and their plans."

"Spirits?" I echoed, unsure whether to dismiss her words as fanciful or embrace the intrigue they ignited within me. I stepped closer, wanting to bridge the distance that felt like a chasm between us. "What do you mean? Are you saying they're actually—"

"Real," she interrupted, her gaze fierce now, the flicker of determination igniting in her eyes. "They are real, and they are angry. The land is sacred to them, and they know when it's being threatened. If AgriCorp gets their hands on this place, they won't just destroy our livelihood; they'll shatter something far more profound."

Her passion was infectious, wrapping around me like the vibrant tendrils of the ivy that climbed the nearby fence posts. I wanted to believe in the beauty of her convictions, to find strength in her connection to this land. Yet the practicalities of our situation clawed at the edges of my thoughts, reminding me of the hard truth that loomed like the storm overhead. "But what can we do? They have resources, power... they won't stop until they take everything."

"They will stop if we show them we're not afraid," she replied, her voice steadying with newfound resolve. "If we stand together, we can fight back. I won't let them take this land. I can't."

A surge of affection washed over me, knitting the fabric of my heart closer to hers. In that moment, she became more than just a partner in a shared struggle; she became the embodiment of everything I had ever admired—resilience, passion, and an unwavering commitment to something greater than ourselves. But with that admiration came the stark realization that her fight was now my fight too, and the weight of that responsibility settled heavily on my shoulders.

"Then let's fight," I declared, a fierce determination rising within me. "I may not have the knowledge you do about the spirits, but I know how to stand my ground. We can rally the community, gather support. They can't silence us all."

Sophie's expression softened, a flicker of hope lighting up the shadows in her eyes. "Together," she agreed, her voice a balm against the anxiety thrumming in my chest. As the first rumble of thunder echoed in the distance, I felt an unexpected thrill—a mixture of fear and exhilaration, as though we were standing on the brink of something monumental. The storm might be closing in, but so was our resolve. Whatever came next, we would face it side by side.

The air crackled with anticipation, thick with the scent of impending rain and something deeper, something that lingered just beneath the surface like a storm waiting to break. As I stood beside

Sophie, the weight of our newfound resolve wrapped around me, grounding me in the moment while lifting the veil of uncertainty. We exchanged determined glances, a silent pact forged in the eye of the storm. The world around us began to shift; the very soil seemed to hum with a vibration I could only barely perceive, a low, resonant echo of the struggles that had come before us.

"Okay, what's our first move?" I asked, trying to sound braver than I felt. Sophie studied me for a moment, her eyes narrowing as if she were peeling back layers of my intentions, searching for the truth beneath. I'd never wanted to be seen so clearly before; it felt raw and unsettling.

"We need to gather our allies," she replied, her voice steady, weaving an intricate web of plans as she spoke. "There are others who care about this land, who've felt the shifts in the winds just like I have. We can't take them for granted."

"Allies, right. Like the guy who runs the general store? He loves a good gossip." I couldn't help but inject a hint of humor into the conversation, hoping to lighten the burden I could feel settling over us. Sophie's lips twitched in a half-smile, her demeanor shifting slightly, and I felt a flutter of warmth at the corners of my heart.

"Gossip can be powerful. If he spreads the word about AgriCorp's plans, it might stir some action." She paused, her brow furrowing in thought. "But we'll need more than just words. We need people willing to stand with us, not just talk."

"Right. So we need to be persuasive." I considered the different ways to rally our small community, thinking of my friends and neighbors—those who had their own struggles but also the fiery spirit to protect what mattered. "What about old Mrs. Hawthorne? She's got more stories than the local library and enough feistiness to rival a tornado."

Sophie chuckled, the sound light and freeing, and I felt the tension ease just a fraction. "Mrs. Hawthorne would definitely bring some flair to our cause. She used to be a part of the community board, remember? If she rallies the retirees, we'll have a solid base."

"Let's not forget she makes a mean pie, too. We might need some sweetening up to get people on our side." I flashed a grin, but beneath the banter, the weight of the task ahead loomed large. As we strolled back toward the farmhouse, the wind picked up, swirling around us like an eager dance partner, hinting at the chaos that could soon unfold.

The farmhouse stood solemnly against the backdrop of the darkening sky, its weathered walls telling stories of resilience and warmth. Inside, the familiar smell of fresh coffee drifted through the air, an inviting embrace that beckoned me forward. I grabbed two mugs and set them down on the old wooden table, the surface scarred with years of shared meals and laughter.

As we sipped the rich brew, the rhythmic patter of raindrops began to tap against the roof, a gentle prelude to the storm brewing outside. "Do you think they'll listen?" I asked, my voice breaking the comfortable silence. "Will they care enough to join us?"

Sophie leaned back in her chair, contemplating. "People can surprise you. They may not realize what's at stake until we shine a light on it. Sometimes it just takes one person to spark a movement." Her conviction ignited something in me, a flicker of hope that burned brighter with every passing moment.

"Then let's be that spark," I declared, the words feeling like a declaration, a commitment to ourselves and to each other. I wanted to be more than a passive observer in our lives; I wanted to be a catalyst for change.

The rain intensified, a drumming rhythm that echoed our mounting urgency. As the storm unfurled its fury outside, we mapped out our plan, a hodgepodge of ideas and strategies. Sophie's passion was infectious, and soon I found myself swept up in her enthusiasm, envisioning gatherings at the community center, pie-baking contests that doubled as rallies, and maybe even an old-fashioned barn dance to unite the townsfolk under a shared cause.

"Now we just need to ensure our enemies don't get wind of it," Sophie said, her voice dipping into a serious tone again. "AgriCorp has eyes everywhere."

I felt a shiver race down my spine at the mention of them, the shadow of their presence looming large in my mind. "So, we need to work in secret, like ninjas of the community. Except without the cool costumes," I joked, trying to lighten the mood again.

She laughed, the sound like a balm against the anxiety creeping back in. "I'd prefer not to dress up like a ninja, but I get your point. Subtlety will be key."

After brainstorming strategies, we decided to set our plan into motion the next day. The morning light would bring fresh hope, and we would face the day together, ready to harness the spirit of our community.

As the storm raged on, thunder rolling in the distance like the drums of war, I found myself contemplating the path ahead. I glanced at Sophie, her profile illuminated by the dim light, and felt a rush of gratitude that she was by my side. She was fierce and steadfast, a force of nature in her own right. I could sense that beneath her calm exterior, a tempest brewed, echoing the chaos that surrounded us.

"Do you ever wonder what life would have been like if we'd never crossed paths?" I asked, my voice quieter now, vulnerable in the intimacy of the moment.

"Every day," she replied, her gaze steady, holding mine. "But I wouldn't trade this for anything. We have the chance to fight for what matters. That makes it all worth it, don't you think?"

Her words hung in the air between us, a declaration of defiance against the encroaching darkness. It wasn't just the land we were fighting for; it was a piece of ourselves, our future, and something beautiful we were building together. With each heartbeat, I felt the weight of my responsibilities shift, transforming into a shared burden, a testament to the bond that was forming between us in the face of adversity.

As the storm broke outside, I knew one thing for certain: no matter how dark the skies grew, together, we would find our light.

The next day dawned with the kind of heavy stillness that often precedes a storm, the air thick with the scent of wet earth and anticipation. I rose early, my mind racing with the plans Sophie and I had woven together like a tapestry of resolve. The day ahead felt like standing on the precipice of something monumental—something that could either soar or crash spectacularly. I could hardly swallow my breakfast, my stomach a tight knot of nerves and excitement.

Sophie was already in the garden when I stepped outside, her fingers deftly weaving through the verdant leaves, tending to the plants as if coaxing them to stand strong against the encroaching threat. She looked up, catching my eye, and for a fleeting moment, the weight of the world lifted as a genuine smile broke across her face. "I'm glad you're up," she said, brushing a stray curl from her forehead. "We have a busy day ahead."

"I'm ready," I declared, the words tumbling out with more bravado than I felt. "Ninja-style ready, even." I struck a mock pose, arms crossed and feet planted as if I were about to take on an army.

Sophie laughed, the sound ringing through the morning air like a bell. "Just remember, stealth is key. We can't afford to let AgriCorp catch wind of our plans."

"Right, stealth and ninja-like skills. Got it." I held my hand to my chin in deep contemplation, pretending to strategize, when really, I was just captivated by the way her eyes sparkled with purpose. It was impossible not to admire her, the passion radiating from her like sunlight breaking through clouds.

With a shared resolve, we set out to gather our allies, beginning with Mrs. Hawthorne. Her house stood at the end of a winding dirt road, a picturesque cottage that looked like it had leaped straight from a storybook. The garden was a riot of color, a testament to Mrs. Hawthorne's talent for coaxing life from the soil. As we approached, the scent of lavender wafted through the air, calming my racing heart.

Mrs. Hawthorne greeted us at the door, her eyes twinkling with mischief as if she already knew why we were there. "Well, if it isn't my favorite troublemakers! Come in, come in! I've just made a fresh batch of cookies. What's the cause for such a serious look?"

"We need your help," I said, the gravity of the situation pressing against my chest. "AgriCorp is planning something big, and we're rallying the community to stand against them."

Her laughter rang out like music, but it quickly faded as she caught the seriousness of our faces. "Oh dear. I had a feeling something was amiss. You know they've been eyeing this land for years. What's your plan?"

Sophie and I exchanged glances, and I began to explain our vision, weaving the threads of our ideas into a compelling narrative. Mrs. Hawthorne listened intently, nodding along, her expression shifting from curiosity to determination.

"I'll help you, of course," she said, her voice firm. "I have lived here long enough to know the value of this land. And I won't let those corporate giants take it away. We can organize a town meeting, gather everyone to discuss our options. But we'll need to do it quickly."

With her support secured, we moved on to other allies—neighbors, farmers, and families who shared our love for the land. Each encounter filled me with renewed energy, the spark of hope igniting brighter with every person we spoke to. Even the most skeptical souls listened intently, their curiosity piqued by our determination.

As the sun dipped lower in the sky, casting a golden hue over the fields, we gathered at the community center, a small building that had hosted countless gatherings, celebrations, and, more recently, quiet resignation. The room buzzed with murmurs as people filed in, their faces a mix of curiosity and concern.

Sophie took center stage, her presence commanding as she began to speak about the threats we faced. "We are not just fighting for our livelihoods; we are fighting for the soul of this community," she urged, her voice rising with conviction. "This land has given us so much, and now it's time we return the favor. We must protect it."

Cheers erupted from the crowd, a wave of enthusiasm crashing over the initial apprehension. My heart swelled with pride watching her. This was the Sophie I had come to admire, a force of nature wielding her passion like a sword. The room filled with voices, a chorus of determination resonating as people began sharing their own stories of the land and its importance to them.

But as the energy in the room reached a fever pitch, the door swung open with a crash, silencing the crowd instantly. There, framed in the doorway, stood a tall figure in a crisp suit, eyes dark and assessing. It was Donovan Hart, the sharp-dressed CEO of AgriCorp, flanked by two imposing security guards. My stomach sank as his presence loomed over us, an unwelcome storm cloud in our midst.

"What's this?" he drawled, a smirk dancing on his lips as he surveyed the gathering. "A little meeting of the minds? How quaint."

"What are you doing here?" Sophie challenged, her voice unwavering, even as the tension in the room thickened. "This is a private meeting."

"Private? Oh, sweetheart, you've got it all wrong. This concerns me too, doesn't it? After all, I'm just trying to do what's best for the community." He stepped forward, arrogance rolling off him like a wave, his eyes glinting with disdain. "And that means moving forward with progress, which you seem to be resisting."

"Progress?" I shot back, unable to contain my anger. "Is that what you call bulldozing our lives for profit? You don't care about this community; you care about your bottom line."

"Such passion," he mocked, amusement dancing in his eyes. "But let's not be hasty. We could work together. I'm sure there's a deal to be made that would benefit everyone."

The crowd stirred, whispers rippling like a stone thrown into still water, uncertainty mingling with anger. I could feel Sophie's tension radiating beside me, a storm ready to unleash its fury.

"You'll find no one here is interested in your deals," she retorted, voice steady but fierce. "This land is not for sale."

"Interesting choice of words, considering it might be mine soon enough." His gaze swept across the room, calculating, assessing the strength of our resolve. "I'd advise you to reconsider your position. You're outmatched."

As he turned to leave, a sudden crash erupted outside, followed by the screech of tires and frantic voices. My heart raced as I rushed to the door, fear curling in my stomach. When I stepped outside, the sight that met my eyes stole my breath.

A group of men, faces obscured by masks, were tearing down the community center's sign, a declaration of war against us, a message we couldn't ignore.

"Get back inside!" I shouted, urgency slicing through the air as chaos erupted behind me. But in that moment, as the reality of our fight hit home, I knew we had crossed a line. The battle was no longer just a matter of words; it was tangible, volatile, and ready to explode.

With Sophie by my side, we faced an uncertain horizon, the storm clouds finally breaking. We had ignited something far bigger than ourselves, but would we have the strength to weather the impending storm?

Chapter 6: Harvesting the Truth

The earth breathed a sigh of relief as the days grew longer and the sun dipped low in the sky, bathing the fields in a golden hue. I stood on the edge of our land, a patchwork quilt of greens and browns, each row a testament to our toil. The sweet scent of freshly turned soil mingled with the crispness of approaching autumn, an intoxicating perfume that filled my lungs and whispered promises of the harvest to come. Sophie worked a few paces ahead, her hands deftly sifting through the soil, ensuring that the seedlings we had nurtured would be ready to flourish in the embrace of the season. She had a way of breathing life into the earth, as if she could coax out the best in every seed, and with every passing day, I admired her more.

Yet, even in this pastoral paradise, shadows lurked on the fringes. My heart thudded uncomfortably against my ribcage, the familiar pang of anxiety striking as I recalled the whispers of AgriCorp—the monolithic farming conglomerate that seemed intent on sowing seeds of destruction wherever they tread. They were the giants in this land, towering over the little guys like us, their deep pockets fueling their relentless ambition. I had watched them suffocate smaller farms one by one, swallowing up the land and leaving behind lifeless patches where dreams had once thrived. But I refused to let them take us down.

"Sophie," I called, my voice wavering slightly as I approached her. She glanced up, her hazel eyes sparkling with that infectious determination that could shatter even the thickest clouds of doubt. "Do you think we can really do this? I mean, beat them at their own game?"

She chuckled, brushing a loose strand of hair behind her ear, the sunlight catching the golden flecks within it. "Of course we can! The soil knows what it's doing. We just need to trust it." Her optimism was like a warm blanket, wrapping around me, soothing the frayed edges of my anxiety. Still, a nagging dread tugged at the back of my mind, a dark storm brewing on the horizon of our hard-won peace.

As the days passed, Sophie and I worked tirelessly, our laughter echoing across the fields, blending harmoniously with the symphony of crickets chirping and leaves rustling. Each evening, we would gather at the wooden table on the porch, a sanctuary where we celebrated our small victories. I would recount the day's events, relaying the mundane and miraculous alike—the sight of our first blossoms, the fleeting encounter with a curious deer, and Sophie's comical attempts to chase away the crows. Each story was like a thread, weaving a tapestry of our shared life, one that sparkled with possibility and, unknowingly, the looming threat.

But as the harvest drew nearer, AgriCorp's presence felt increasingly suffocating. Whispers turned to threats, and I could see the shadows of their hired guns lurking just beyond the edges of our property. It wasn't long before they made their move, sending a chilling message that slithered into my heart like ice. I received a phone call one evening, the voice on the other end smooth as silk, yet laced with a venomous undertone.

"Your friend Sophie, now there's a fascinating story," the voice purred. "You might want to consider how far you're willing to go to protect her."

Panic surged within me, an uncontrollable wave crashing against the fragile dam of my resolve. The truth about Sophie's past, a secret she had carefully guarded, was the one thing I had feared most. I had never pried into her history, never wanted to. Sophie was a woman of resilience and grace, and that was all that mattered. Yet now, the specter of AgriCorp hung over us like an executioner's blade, waiting to fall.

I was torn, caught between two worlds—the love I felt for Sophie and the vision I had for our farm. Protecting her might mean sacrificing everything we had built, the crops that had become our lifeblood, our rebellion against the giants. But how could I let her face the wrath of AgriCorp alone? She deserved a chance at redemption, a chance to prove herself beyond the shadows of her past.

That evening, the sun dipped below the horizon, and with it, my last shred of calm. I found Sophie on the porch, her fingers absently tracing the grain of the weathered wood. "What's bothering you?" she asked, her voice soft yet perceptive, a beacon cutting through my turmoil.

I hesitated, my heart racing as I wrestled with the words that felt lodged in my throat. Finally, I met her gaze, feeling the weight of unspoken truths heavy between us. "They... they know about your past," I confessed, each word dragging me deeper into a well of dread. "They've threatened to expose you if we don't back down."

Her expression shifted, shock giving way to an unyielding fire. "Let them try," she declared, her voice steady despite the tremor in her hands. "I won't be their victim. I've fought too hard for this."

I shook my head, overwhelmed by admiration for her strength. "But what if they succeed? What if they destroy everything?"

Sophie stepped closer, her presence grounding me like the roots of an ancient oak. "Then we fight. Together. I won't let fear dictate my life anymore. I want to face this, even if it means dragging the truth into the light."

Her conviction sparked something deep within me, igniting the smoldering embers of defiance. I couldn't let fear dictate our fate. But what would it take to rise against AgriCorp? In that moment, with the weight of the world hanging between us, I knew we had a choice to make: to either buckle under the pressure or turn the tides, to expose the darkness lurking beneath their polished veneer.

The morning sun broke over the horizon, spilling liquid gold across the fields, and with it came a newfound sense of purpose. I stood at the edge of our farm, the dew-kissed grass cool beneath my bare feet, and watched as Sophie made her way down the rows of crops. She was a force of nature in her own right, her hands gentle yet fierce as she tended to the plants that had begun to sway in the soft breeze. My heart swelled at the sight of her, but a lingering dread gnawed at the edges of my mind. The threat from AgriCorp still loomed large, a shadow cast over our little piece of paradise.

"Hey, farm girl!" I called out, trying to keep my tone light, even though my insides felt like a coiled spring. "How about you give me a hand with the morning chores? I think the chickens are plotting something."

Sophie glanced back at me, a playful grin tugging at her lips. "Plotting? Please, they're probably just debating whether to lay eggs or stage a coup. I hear the rooster's been particularly charismatic lately." She shook her head, her dark curls bouncing as she moved closer, her eyes sparkling with mischief.

I laughed, momentarily forgetting the tension that had been suffocating me. "Charismatic, you say? Maybe I should run for office on that ticket. 'Vote for the Rooster: Strong Leadership, Delicious Breakfast.'"

She threw her head back, laughter ringing out like chimes in the wind. "I'd vote for him. The egg selection has been abysmal lately." The moment felt precious, a fleeting escape from the reality lurking just outside our sanctuary.

Yet, as we trudged through our morning tasks—Sophie wrangling the feathery beasts and I gathering fresh vegetables for market—I couldn't shake the feeling of impending doom. The crops were vibrant, a kaleidoscope of colors bursting forth as if they were in on our secret rebellion, but AgriCorp's threat loomed larger than any storm cloud. I had to protect Sophie, even if that meant exposing the truth that we both dreaded.

Later that afternoon, while we rinsed the vegetables in the cool stream that snaked through the property, the conversation took a more serious turn. I couldn't hold back the thoughts that had been swirling like leaves caught in a whirlwind. "Sophie, what do we really know about AgriCorp's plans? I mean, are they just going to sit back and watch us succeed, or will they pull a fast one when we least expect it?"

She paused, the water splashing against her arms as she considered my question. "They'll definitely try something. They're not just going to roll over because we're planting organic. We're a threat to their empire." Her gaze sharpened, a flicker of determination igniting in her eyes. "But we can't let them intimidate us. We've got the truth on our side. If they want a fight, we'll give them one."

I admired her fierce resolve, but the thought of her past being dragged into the light made my stomach churn. "But what if they expose you? What if the truth is worse than we imagined?"

A shadow crossed her face, but she quickly regained her composure. "You think I haven't thought about that? My past is mine, and I won't let anyone twist it into a weapon against me." She stepped closer, water dripping from her fingers, each drop a testament to her strength. "Besides, I'm not the only one with secrets. Every single person who looks at us with envy has their own skeletons in the closet."

The air crackled with a tension I couldn't ignore. "So, you're saying we should play dirty? Fight fire with fire?"

"Not dirty, just smart," she replied, her eyes locking onto mine, steady and unwavering. "We need to gather intel, find out what they're planning. If we know their next move, we can counter it before they even make a play."

The idea had merit, but it felt like walking a tightrope over a pit of snapping jaws. "And how do we do that? We're not exactly spies."

"Leave that part to me," she said, a sly grin creeping across her lips. "I have a few connections. Old friends from my past who might be able to help. Trust me."

Her confidence was infectious, but a knot of apprehension twisted in my stomach. "Sophie, if this goes sideways—"

"Then it goes sideways," she interrupted, her voice resolute. "But I won't let fear dictate our actions. We need to harness the chaos, flip the narrative. AgriCorp thinks they hold all the cards, but they don't know what we're capable of."

The determination in her voice lit a spark within me, urging me to face the storm head-on. Maybe we could turn the tables, but my heart was still heavy with the knowledge that her past could rear its ugly head at any moment.

As dusk settled in, the fields took on a magical quality, the setting sun casting long shadows that danced around us. We retreated to the porch, where the world outside seemed to fade into the distance. I poured two glasses of iced tea, the clinking of ice a soothing melody against the backdrop of chirping crickets.

"So, tell me about these connections of yours," I prompted, curious yet cautious.

Sophie took a sip, her eyes narrowing as she weighed her words. "There's Leo. He used to work for AgriCorp before he got fed up with their practices. He knows the ins and outs. If anyone can help us, it's him."

"Leo?" I raised an eyebrow. "Sounds like a wild card. Is he trustworthy?"

"Trustworthy enough," she replied, a hint of a smirk playing at the corners of her lips. "Besides, he owes me a favor. I helped him out once when he was in a bit of a pickle. I'd say we're even."

A chuckle escaped me, imagining the circumstances that could put a man like Leo in a pickle. "And what kind of favor are we talking about? The kind that involves a daring escape or just a good old-fashioned loan?"

"Let's just say it involved a few too many margaritas and a very angry goat," she said, her laughter infectious.

We shared a moment of levity, the weight of our fears lifting just a fraction, allowing the warmth of camaraderie to seep in. But as the shadows deepened, I felt the familiar knot of anxiety tightening again. "And if Leo refuses to help?"

"Then we improvise," Sophie declared, her eyes glinting with determination. "We've come too far to back down now."

The resolve in her voice resonated deep within me, but doubt still lingered like a specter in the corner of my mind. Our lives had become a precarious balancing act, each decision a step closer to either salvation or disaster. The stakes were higher than they had ever been, and I couldn't shake the feeling that we were teetering on the edge of a precipice. As the stars began to twinkle overhead, I vowed to stand by Sophie, no matter what the coming days might bring. Together, we would face the storm, ready to fight for our future, even if it meant wrestling with the shadows of the past.

As the moon rose high, casting a silvery glow over the fields, the air hummed with an electric charge, a prelude to the chaos that awaited us. The plan was taking shape, but uncertainty clung to us like morning mist, wrapping around our hearts and whispering doubts that made the brave seem foolish. I could feel the weight of our situation pressing down on me, an invisible cloak of anxiety that turned the delightful sounds of the night—crickets serenading under the stars, the soft rustle of leaves—into a cacophony of warning bells.

Sophie and I had decided to meet Leo the next evening, a figure shrouded in mystery and mischief, whose previous connections to AgriCorp left me questioning his loyalty. As I cleaned up the kitchen after dinner, each clank of the dishes echoing in the silence, I couldn't help but replay the day's conversations in my head. It was a small comfort to see Sophie's optimism, yet the undercurrent of her past felt like a tide ready to pull us under.

"Are you nervous?" Sophie's voice broke through my thoughts as she leaned against the kitchen counter, arms crossed. The way she studied me, her brow slightly furrowed, showed she was perceptive enough to catch the worry I tried to hide.

"Just thinking," I replied, scrubbing a stubborn spot on a pan with more vigor than necessary. "What if Leo doesn't want to help? Or what if he has his own agenda? We might be walking into a trap."

"Trap? You've been watching too many spy movies," she teased, though her playful tone didn't quite mask the glimmer of concern in her eyes. "Besides, what do we have to lose? Our secrets are already out in the open, and we can't let AgriCorp scare us into submission."

"True," I admitted, pushing the damp hair from my face. "But I'd prefer to avoid more skeletons tumbling out of closets than necessary."

"Speaking of skeletons, you think the chickens will finally accept me as their queen after all this hard work?" She gestured toward the coop with a mock seriousness that made me chuckle, easing some of my tension.

"Your majesty, the chickens await your decree," I declared dramatically, raising an imaginary goblet. "And they demand organic feed and plenty of sunshine."

"Ah, I'll take that into consideration for our future reign," she replied, a smile breaking through her facade of worry. Yet beneath that lighthearted banter, I could see the weight of our reality pressing down on her, too.

As the evening wore on, we prepared for our meeting with Leo, each of us retreating into our own thoughts, the shared laughter morphing into quiet contemplation. I couldn't shake the notion that we were stepping into a storm, and I feared what might happen when the winds shifted.

The next day dawned bright and clear, a stark contrast to the turmoil brewing within me. We met Leo at a nondescript diner on the outskirts of town, its worn neon sign buzzing softly in the late morning light. As I stepped inside, the smell of coffee and sizzling bacon wrapped around me, an inviting aroma that masked the tension thick in the air.

Leo was already seated in a booth, leaning back with an air of casual confidence that felt disarming. His tousled hair and easy smile made him seem approachable, yet there was something sharp in his eyes, a glimmer that spoke of hidden depths and unspoken truths.

"Ladies," he said, raising his mug in a casual toast. "I hear you're trying to take on the big dogs. Brave of you, considering the bite they have."

"Brave or foolish, that's the real question," I replied, sliding into the booth opposite him. "But we're here to gather intel, not to entertain your metaphors."

"Fair enough," Leo said, his expression shifting to one of interest. "What's your angle? I've been hearing rumors that AgriCorp is planning something big, but the specifics are a bit hazy."

Sophie leaned forward, her determination shining through the shadow of her past. "We want to know what they're up to and how we can protect ourselves. They've made threats, and I'm not about to let them bury me with my history."

Leo's brows knit together, his demeanor shifting to something more serious. "They're playing a dangerous game. But it seems you already know that." He paused, weighing his words. "What I can share is that AgriCorp's interests have shifted toward acquiring local farms, especially ones that threaten their monopoly on organic produce. You two are on their radar."

I swallowed hard, the implications of his words sinking in like stones in water. "And what do you propose we do?"

He leaned back, a smirk playing at the corners of his mouth. "Let's just say it's time for a little counteroffensive. I've got a few contacts who can help gather information from the inside. If you play your cards right, you might turn their game against them."

Sophie shot me a glance, her excitement palpable. "That sounds promising. What do we need to do?"

"First, you need to gain their trust. Make them think you're on their side," Leo explained. "I can set up a meeting with one of their regional managers. If you play it smart, you might even glean some valuable insight into their operations."

"Or fall into a trap," I murmured, the caution spilling from my lips despite my desire to charge ahead.

"Or find out how to exploit their weaknesses," he shot back, his smile unwavering. "This isn't just about defending your farm; it's about turning the tables on them. They've underestimated you, and that's their first mistake."

The conversation took on a life of its own as we strategized, ideas bouncing back and forth like lively sparrows in spring. The diner's ambience faded into the background, the clatter of dishes and the murmur of other patrons becoming a mere whisper as we huddled together, plotting our rebellion against the corporate giant.

As our plans solidified, the sun dipped low in the sky, casting long shadows that danced like specters against the diner's walls. "We'll need to act quickly," Leo said, glancing at the clock on the wall. "The longer you wait, the more vulnerable you become. You can't let them catch wind of your intentions."

With our course set, I felt a surge of adrenaline, a blend of fear and excitement coursing through me. The storm was coming, and it was time to prepare for the tempest. As we rose to leave, Sophie squeezed my hand, her touch a lifeline anchoring me amid the chaos.

"Just remember," she said, a fierce light igniting in her eyes, "we're not just fighting for our farm. We're fighting for every small farmer who's been crushed by their greed."

With that rallying cry echoing in my heart, we stepped outside, the air charged with possibility. But as we made our way to the truck, the familiar chill of unease washed over me. Something felt off, a prickling sensation crawling along my skin.

That's when I spotted them—figures lurking near the edge of the parking lot, their silhouettes shrouded in shadow. My heart raced as I recognized the men from AgriCorp, the same ones who had been watching us from a distance. They were closing in, their eyes locked on us with predatory intent.

"Sophie," I whispered urgently, urgency flooding my veins. "We need to go. Now."

But as we turned to flee, the figures stepped forward, blocking our path, their expressions twisted into knowing smirks. The air thickened with tension, and I felt the ground shift beneath me, uncertainty spiraling into chaos.

"Running away already?" one of them sneered, his voice dripping with malice. "We just wanted to talk."

A rush of adrenaline surged through me, my mind racing with possibilities. This was it—the moment we had dreaded was here. The storm had broken, and now we had to face it head-on. I took a deep breath, steeling myself for what was to come, knowing that the next few moments could change everything.

Chapter 7: The Betrayal

The sky hung low that evening, a thick quilt of gray clouds suffocating the last traces of sunlight as I paced the rows of withering corn in the field. The air felt charged, bristling with an energy that mirrored my unease. It was a heavy, damp sort of silence, the kind that settles in just before a storm. Sophie had been my anchor in this wild endeavor, a relentless spirit who breathed life into our dreams of independence from AgriCorp's looming shadow. But now, the absence of her laughter echoed louder than the cawing of the crows perched on the fence posts.

I reached into my pocket, fingers brushing against the note she had left. It was crumpled, stained with tears I had shed when I first read it. "I'm sorry, but I can't do this anymore. I have to go." It was a simple message, yet it spoke volumes. The way it had crumpled in my palm felt like a physical representation of my heart. Betrayal coiled around me like a viper, sharp and unrelenting. How could she abandon our fight? Didn't she understand the stakes? The thought clawed at me as I called her name, my voice hoarse and desperate, but the wind merely mocked my cries.

"Where the hell are you, Sophie?" I shouted, my voice trembling with a mix of fury and fear. The emptiness swallowed my words, and I pressed deeper into the field, pushing through the rows of corn as if they might reveal her hiding behind the tall stalks. The sharp scent of earth mingled with the fading aroma of the day's labor, a heady reminder of the work we had poured into these fields. It felt like a betrayal of its own—this land, once a symbol of hope, now seemed to conspire against me.

The sun dipped lower, casting elongated shadows that danced menacingly around me. I stumbled over a fallen ear of corn, the crispness of it cracking beneath my feet, a sound that echoed my internal turmoil. My mind raced, replaying the moments leading up to her disappearance. Had I missed something? A sign? A moment of hesitation that might have hinted at her intentions?

I had always prided myself on being observant, but this time I felt like I had been blindsided, left standing in the dark while she slipped through the cracks. The memories of our late-night strategy sessions flickered in my mind—her unwavering passion, the fire in her eyes when she spoke of a future unshackled from AgriCorp's chains. How could she have walked away from that? The question gnawed at me, a relentless reminder of her absence.

A low growl broke the silence, and I froze, heart pounding. The familiar rumble of the AgriCorp trucks rattled in the distance, creeping along the dirt road that framed our property. My instincts flared, a warning tingling in the back of my mind. I knew they were watching, lurking just beyond the edge of my vision, ready to pounce on any sign of weakness. With Sophie gone, I felt like a ship adrift without a captain. My fear turned to anger as I clenched my fists, my knuckles whitening. I would not cower.

Taking a deep breath, I pivoted on my heel and made my way toward the office, a dilapidated structure that had seen better days. The peeling paint and cracked windows mirrored my sense of loss, but I pushed through the door with a determination that surprised even me. The musty air enveloped me as I crossed the threshold, the faint scent of mildew mingling with the remnants of old paperwork and forgotten dreams.

As I rifled through the files strewn across my desk, the panic morphed into a steely resolve. I needed answers, and I knew where to get them. The corporate representatives were slick, charming, and utterly ruthless, often masquerading as benevolent allies. They would have Sophie, or at least information about her. Confrontation was inevitable, and my heart raced at the thought.

I slammed the last file shut and snatched my jacket off the back of the chair. The night air was brisk, a sharp contrast to the heaviness that clung to my skin. I made my way down the gravel path to where the trucks idled, their headlights cutting through the gloom like predators' eyes. My heart thundered in my chest, a wild drumbeat urging me onward as I approached the glistening metal behemoths.

"Hey!" I called, my voice a mix of bravado and uncertainty. The workers turned, their eyes narrowing as they recognized me. I wasn't a mere nuisance anymore; I was a woman desperate for answers, and desperation has a way of sharpening the edges of one's courage.

"Look who decided to wander out of her little field," one of them sneered, his smirk revealing too many teeth. The others chuckled, their laughter echoing off the trucks, a mocking symphony that set my nerves on edge.

"Where is Sophie?" I demanded, my voice steady despite the fear creeping into my veins. "You know where she is."

His laughter died abruptly, replaced by a glint in his eye that sent chills racing down my spine. "Why would we tell you?" he asked, leaning against the truck as if he owned the night. "You're just a farmer's daughter, playing with forces far beyond your comprehension."

"Try me," I shot back, stepping closer, the ground crunching under my feet, fueling my determination. "She's not just some pawn in your game. You took her, didn't you? What do you want with her?"

Their smirks deepened, an unspoken bond of conspiracy that clung to the air like smoke. "Maybe you should consider what she's really worth," he said, his tone dripping with contempt. "You might be surprised at the lengths people will go for power."

A surge of anger shot through me. "Power?" I echoed incredulously. "You think this is about power? This is about people! Our people!"

"People?" he scoffed, the disdain palpable. "You're out of your league, sweetheart. And I'm afraid your little crusade is about to come to an end."

As he turned away, dismissing me with a wave, I felt the rage bubbling over. I had to do something; standing there, seething in helplessness, would get me nowhere. I had to fight, not just for Sophie, but for everyone trapped under AgriCorp's thumb.

"Wait!" I called out, my voice cutting through the air like a knife. "If you know where she is, I'll make a deal."

He paused, glancing back over his shoulder, curiosity piqued. "A deal? What do you have to offer?"

With a flicker of inspiration, I shot back, "I'll work for you. I'll gather intel on our operation here. Anything you need."

A moment of silence stretched between us, thick and palpable, before he laughed again, a deep, rumbling sound that echoed in the dark. "You think we'd trust you? You're nothing but a thorn in our side."

"Maybe so," I retorted, refusing to back down. "But you need someone on the inside. I can be that person."

His eyes narrowed, weighing my words. It was a gamble, one I didn't know I was willing to take until that moment, but I had to know. I had to save Sophie. The seconds ticked by like hours, the tension thick enough to slice through.

Finally, he stepped closer, lowering his voice to a conspiratorial whisper. "All right, farmer's daughter. Let's see what you can do."

The storm clouds loomed overhead, but I felt a flicker of hope ignite within me. This was just the beginning.

The moment he agreed to my proposal felt like stepping onto a rickety tightrope suspended over a canyon of uncertainty. The air around me buzzed with adrenaline, and I suppressed the urge to shiver as I watched the AgriCorp representative's grin widen. A mix of exhilaration and dread tightened my stomach. I had no plan, just a reckless hope that Sophie was safe somewhere, and if I could play their game long enough to find her, I would do it.

"Great, sweetheart," he said, his voice dripping with condescension. "We'll get you a nice little badge. Maybe a lunchbox, too, if you're good." The mocking tone barely concealed a thread of intrigue in his gaze. I held back the retort bubbling in my throat and simply nodded. The last thing I needed was to make an enemy of him when I was already standing on shaky ground.

The moon had risen high, casting an ethereal glow over the landscape as I made my way back home. Each step felt heavy, weighted with the gravity of my decision. This was not just a game; it was a desperate gamble, one that could end in failure or, worse, put Sophie in danger. I envisioned her in some sterile room, trapped in AgriCorp's grasp, and the thought ignited a fire within me. I had to stay sharp, play their game, and learn what I could while keeping my head above water.

The next day dawned with a peculiar brightness that felt dissonant against the turmoil churning inside me. I donned my work clothes, the familiar fabric grounding me amidst the uncertainty. The fields stretched before me, golden and green, a comforting reminder of home. I grabbed a shovel and started digging, my hands working while my mind raced.

"Is that a new way of planting?" a voice called out, laced with playful sarcasm. I looked up to see Jason, my neighbor and longtime friend, leaning against the fence, arms crossed, an amused grin plastered across his face.

"Very funny, Jason. I'm just trying to keep my mind off things," I replied, wiping sweat from my brow and forcing a smile. He had always had a knack for breaking through my brooding moments, and I appreciated it more than I could say.

"Not exactly the most efficient technique. You should let me handle it; I have all the right tools," he said, walking closer, his light-hearted demeanor brightening the oppressive weight of the situation.

"Right, because you digging around in my fields will solve all my problems," I shot back, an edge of playful banter lacing my words. He chuckled, and for a brief moment, I felt a flicker of normalcy. It was a reminder of life before AgriCorp loomed over us, before the fear of losing everything took root in my heart.

"You're not fooling anyone, you know. You've got that look—the kind that says you're about to plunge into the deep end without a life jacket." Jason's expression softened, his teasing demeanor shifting to genuine concern.

I sighed, leaning on the shovel, the metal cool against my palm. "It's complicated, Jay. Sophie's gone, and I think AgriCorp knows something about it. I need to find her, and I'm not sure how far they're willing to go."

His brow furrowed, and he stepped closer. "AgriCorp? What do you mean? What do they have to do with Sophie?"

"I can't explain everything right now, but I'm going to work for them. I'll find out what they know," I confessed, my voice barely above a whisper. I could see the concern deepen in his eyes, but there was also something else—an understanding of the reckless bravery that comes when you're fighting for someone you love.

"That's dangerous, Liv. You know they'll use you," he warned, his tone serious now, slicing through the levity of our previous exchange.

"I know," I replied, crossing my arms defensively. "But I can't just sit here and do nothing. I won't."

Jason shifted, rubbing the back of his neck as he pondered my determination. "Okay, but you need to be careful. They're sharks, and you're just a little fish. Just... promise me you'll watch your back."

"I promise," I said, but even as I spoke, a knot of uncertainty coiled tighter in my stomach. The way he looked at me—a blend of admiration and worry—only heightened the weight of the choice I had made. With a light touch on my shoulder, he turned and walked back toward his property, leaving me standing in the golden fields that felt more like a battleground every day.

The hours drifted by, my focus shifting between the chores at hand and the impending shadows of AgriCorp creeping into my life. As the sun began to dip below the horizon, I heard the rumble of the trucks again. It was time for my first day on the job, and while my heart raced with anxiety, it also thrummed with a sense of purpose.

The office was a stark contrast to the warmth of the fields, a sterile environment of bright lights and white walls that felt as cold as the corporate suits roaming the halls. I navigated the maze of cubicles, each one filled with employees who looked far too absorbed in their screens to notice me. A few glanced up, their expressions indifferent, as if I were merely an annoyance rather than the newest recruit in their world.

"Ah, the farmer's daughter!" a voice boomed from behind me, making me jump. I turned to find the same representative who had initially laughed at my plight, his smirk all too familiar. "Glad to see you've decided to join the winning team. You'll find it's much more exciting than digging in the dirt."

I forced a smile, trying to mask the irritation bubbling beneath my surface. "Exciting is one way to put it. I prefer to think of it as treacherous."

He laughed, a hollow sound that echoed off the walls. "Good, you're catching on. We thrive on treachery here. Now, let's get you acquainted with the real work."

He led me to a small conference room that smelled faintly of stale coffee and desperation. As he explained my tasks, I realized quickly that my role was nothing more than a glorified informant. They wanted me to gather information on local farmers—who they talked to, what they were planting, any whispers of rebellion against AgriCorp's dominance.

"This will be easy for you," he continued, leaning back in his chair, confidence radiating from him like a noxious gas. "You're one of them. Just a little espionage on the side. How hard could it be?"

I swallowed hard, the knot in my stomach tightening once again. "I'm not a spy. I'm just a farmer trying to survive."

He waved a hand dismissively. "It's all the same, really. Just remember, if you want to find your friend, you'll need to play your part."

The pressure of his words weighed heavily on my shoulders. I nodded, feeling the precariousness of my situation. I had stepped into the lion's den, and now it was up to me to survive.

As the hours dragged on, I absorbed every piece of information, my mind working in overdrive. I scribbled notes on a notepad, trying to piece together how I could maneuver in this corporate labyrinth. In moments of silence, I replayed images of Sophie, her laugh, her passion, and the fire in her eyes. I wouldn't let them extinguish it; I couldn't.

At the end of the day, I felt both exhilarated and drained. My resolve solidified. As I made my way back to the farm, the cool night air filled my lungs, invigorating me. Each step echoed with determination, a reminder that I was not just a pawn in their game. I would outsmart them, piece together their secrets, and reclaim Sophie from their grasp.

As I crossed the threshold into the familiar chaos of my home, I realized that each day would be a battle, but I was ready. I would forge ahead, even as the darkness loomed, armed with the knowledge that love and courage could ignite even the fiercest flame against the shadows.

The days blurred together in a haze of work and worry as I settled into my role at AgriCorp, a tightrope walk through a world that felt increasingly hostile. I kept my head down, gathering information on fellow farmers while crafting a facade of compliance. Each evening,

I returned home, the weight of my dual existence pressing heavily on my chest. But my resolve did not waver; every detail I learned brought me one step closer to finding Sophie.

On a particularly gray afternoon, the office felt more stifling than usual. I was hunched over my desk, trying to decipher a jumble of reports when the door swung open, and a voice cut through the tension. "There you are, farmer's daughter! Looking as lovely as a wilted plant." It was my smirking handler, the same man who had brought me into this twisted game. His insincere grin made my skin crawl.

"Flattery will get you nowhere," I replied, forcing a smile as I straightened in my chair. "What do you want?"

"Oh, just checking in on my star recruit." He leaned against the doorframe, arms crossed, his smugness palpable. "Word has it you've been quite busy snooping around."

"Not snooping," I corrected, my voice steady despite the anxiety gnawing at me. "Just doing my job."

"Right. Your job." He stepped closer, his eyes narrowing as if trying to penetrate the facade I wore like armor. "You know, I'd hate to see you fall into a rabbit hole you can't climb out of. You wouldn't want to end up like your little friend, now would you?"

The reminder of Sophie sent a jolt through my body, a fresh wave of panic rising. "What do you know about her?" I snapped, the words escaping before I could rein in my composure.

"Relax, sweetheart. We don't have her locked in a cage. At least, not yet," he chuckled, enjoying the power he wielded over my emotions. "But you need to focus on the job at hand. Gather what you can from the others; we have our eyes everywhere."

The thinly veiled threat hung in the air, heavy and suffocating. I clenched my fists under the desk, feeling the heat of anger pulse through me. "I'll do what I need to do," I said, my voice unwavering.

"Good girl," he replied with a wink, turning on his heel and striding out, leaving a chill in his wake. I took a deep breath, forcing myself to focus on the task ahead. There was no time for fear; Sophie was depending on me.

As the days unfolded, I wove deeper into the web of corporate dealings, collecting snippets of conversations and documents. I learned about AgriCorp's plans to expand their operations, their hunger for control seeping into every facet of our community. Each piece of intel I gathered felt like a small victory, yet the deeper I delved, the more perilous my situation became.

One evening, I found myself in a small diner on the edge of town, a refuge from the cold corporate world. The fluorescent lights buzzed overhead, illuminating the faces of weary locals who whispered about the changes AgriCorp was forcing upon our community. I hunched over a cup of coffee, pretending to read a newspaper but eavesdropping on the conversations around me.

"You hear what they're planning?" a woman at the next table murmured to her companion. "If they get their way, we won't have any say in our land anymore."

"I can't believe those fat cats think they can just walk all over us," her friend replied, anger simmering beneath the surface. "Someone needs to stand up to them."

My heart raced as I recognized the passion in their voices. Here were the seeds of rebellion, and I was standing on the precipice. I leaned in closer, the scent of stale coffee and fried food grounding me in reality.

"Hey, you two," I interjected, hoping to spark a connection. "What do you think we can do? They're not going to back down easily."

The women turned to me, surprise flickering across their faces. "Who are you?" one asked, suspicion lacing her tone.

"Just someone who's tired of being pushed around," I replied, my resolve strengthening. "I want to fight back. Together, we might stand a chance."

Their expressions shifted from wariness to intrigue, and after a moment's hesitation, the conversation flowed freely. They shared stories of their struggles, the way AgriCorp's practices suffocated their livelihoods, the fear creeping into their homes like a thief in the night.

"You're brave to speak up," the woman said, her gaze steady. "Most people are too afraid to go against them."

"Bravery is relative," I replied, a hint of sarcasm coloring my words. "Sometimes it's just desperation in disguise."

We exchanged numbers, a tentative alliance formed under the dim lights of the diner. As I left, I felt a spark of hope igniting within me. Perhaps I wasn't as alone in this fight as I had feared.

Back at the farm, the familiar sights greeted me like old friends—the rustling corn, the vibrant sunset painting the horizon. But tonight, unease settled over the land like a shroud. As I stood on the porch, gazing out into the fields, the weight of the world felt heavier than ever.

My phone buzzed in my pocket, pulling me from my thoughts. I pulled it out to see a message from Jason. Meet me at the barn. I found something.

A surge of urgency propelled me forward. I raced across the yard, the shadows stretching around me as I approached the barn. Each step echoed with anticipation, my heart thundering in my chest. What had Jason discovered? My mind raced with possibilities, both thrilling and terrifying.

As I reached the barn, I pushed the door open, the creaking wood announcing my arrival. Inside, the scent of hay and aged wood enveloped me. Jason stood in the dim light, his expression grave. "You need to see this," he said, urgency threading through his voice.

"What is it?" I asked, scanning the space.

He stepped aside, revealing a makeshift table covered in papers, photographs, and diagrams. My breath caught in my throat as I recognized the images of Sophie, her smile frozen in time amidst a flurry of documents detailing AgriCorp's sinister operations.

"They're planning something big, Liv. Something that involves her," Jason said, his brow furrowing in concern. "Look at this." He pointed to a map, dotted with red Xs marking locations—farms, including ours.

"No," I whispered, the reality crashing over me like a wave. "They can't do this. We have to stop them."

"We will," he assured me, determination flaring in his eyes. But just as I felt a surge of hope, the sharp sound of tires crunching on gravel reached my ears.

My heart dropped. "They're here."

We shared a look, and without a word, we moved, instinct kicking in. I grabbed the closest stack of papers and shoved them into my bag, the fear igniting my resolve. We had to get out of here, but as we turned to leave, the door swung open, and the menacing silhouette of an AgriCorp representative filled the doorway.

"Going somewhere?" he drawled, his eyes gleaming with the thrill of the hunt.

Before I could react, I felt Jason's hand on my arm, pulling me back, a silent plea for us to stay calm. The room felt small, closing in on us as I clutched the bag tighter, knowing that whatever happened next could change everything.

"Looks like the little farmer's daughter has gotten herself in over her head," the representative sneered, stepping further into the barn, the shadows consuming him.

In that moment, I realized that I wasn't just fighting for Sophie; I was fighting for our entire community. The stakes had never been higher, and the air crackled with tension as I braced myself for whatever was to come. Would I be able to outsmart them and protect everything I loved? The answer loomed, uncertain and heavy as the night pressed in around us, and just as I opened my mouth to speak, a sound echoed from behind him—a low growl that promised danger.

Chapter 8: The Rescue

The soft glow of dawn crept through the trees, casting a delicate light on the forest floor, where shadows danced and whispers of the night lingered like a half-remembered dream. I moved cautiously, each step a careful negotiation with the soft earth beneath my feet, as if the ground might give way beneath me. My heart thrummed in rhythm with the gentle rustling of leaves, a chaotic symphony underscoring my resolve. The scent of damp soil and wild honeysuckle filled the air, rich and intoxicating, blending with the faintest hint of fear that clung to my skin like an unwanted cloak.

When I first stepped into the woods, it felt like walking into an ancient painting, where every tree stood sentinel, its gnarled branches whispering secrets of old. I had scoured this place many times before, and yet today was different—charged with purpose, driven by a desperation that clawed at my insides. Each rustle of a nearby bush sent a shiver through me, not just from apprehension but from the hope that I might finally find her. Sophie had been missing for far too long, and the weight of her absence had become a palpable thing, a stone in my chest that threatened to drag me down into despair.

Then, there she was. The moment my eyes fell upon her, a jolt of electricity surged through me, igniting a fire I thought had been extinguished by weeks of searching. Sophie sat hunched against the base of an ancient oak, her once-vibrant hair now dull and matted, her cheeks sunken and pale. The sight of her like this felt like a punch to the gut, the world around me narrowing to just her. My breath hitched, a rush of emotions swirling within—relief, fury, love—each more potent than the last.

"Sophie!" I called, my voice breaking the delicate silence, reverberating off the trees like a desperate plea. She looked up, her eyes meeting mine, and for a moment, the darkness that enveloped her seemed to lift, revealing a flicker of the vibrant woman I adored.

"Liv?" Her voice was barely a whisper, laced with disbelief and pain, but it was enough to send my heart racing.

I rushed to her side, falling to my knees in the damp earth, clutching her face in my hands as if I could absorb the sadness etched in her features. "You're safe now. I'm here. We're going to get out of here," I promised, my voice fierce and unwavering, as I brushed a thumb over her cheek, trying to coax life back into her.

She shivered, and I could see the tremors that ran through her body, not just from the chill in the air but from the memories of what she had endured. "They... they took me, Liv. AgriCorp's men. They wanted to use my abilities—to control the land, to manipulate everything," she stammered, the words spilling out like a dam that had finally broken.

"Shh, you don't have to talk about it yet. Just focus on me," I murmured, pulling her into an embrace, feeling her thin frame shake against mine. I could feel the weight of the world on her shoulders, and in that moment, it was as if I could absorb it all—her fear, her pain, her exhaustion. Together, we could bear it, just as we had borne everything else.

As I held her, a fire ignited in my chest, an urge to protect her, to fight against whatever evil had dared to snatch her from our lives. I had always known Sophie was special; her connection to the land was profound and inexplicable, a bond that seemed almost otherworldly. But this? To weaponize that connection? It made my blood boil. I pulled back to look into her eyes, the deep wells of sorrow reflecting a steely resolve. "We'll make them pay for this," I said, my voice low and fierce. "They have no idea who they're dealing with."

Sophie offered a faint smile, though it was tinged with sadness. "I'm not sure I can do it again, Liv. I'm so tired."

I brushed my fingers through her hair, wishing I could take away the exhaustion that had settled in her bones. "You're stronger than you know. We'll figure this out together. You're not alone anymore," I promised, every word laced with conviction.

With her hand clasped tightly in mine, we made our way through the dense underbrush, each crack of a twig beneath our feet echoing like a drumbeat of urgency. The world around us was alive with sounds—the chirping of birds, the rustling of leaves—but all I could hear was the thudding of my heart and the soft gasps of Sophie beside me. We were navigating a maze of trees, but I couldn't shake the feeling that we were being watched, as if the shadows themselves were holding their breath, waiting for the right moment to pounce.

"Do you think they're still looking for me?" Sophie asked, her voice barely above a whisper, tinged with fear.

"Probably," I replied, trying to sound more certain than I felt. "But they won't find us. We know these woods better than they do. We'll use that to our advantage."

A flicker of determination ignited in her gaze, and I knew we were both thinking the same thing: We couldn't let AgriCorp win. The air crackled with tension as we forged ahead, each step bringing us closer to freedom, to a future I dared to dream of—a future where Sophie could reclaim her power and we could reclaim our lives.

Then came the sound of crunching leaves behind us. My breath caught in my throat. I turned, heart racing, and instinctively positioned myself in front of Sophie, ready to shield her from whatever threat lay in the shadows.

"Keep moving," I whispered urgently, every muscle in my body coiling with tension as I strained to listen.

But just as the rustling intensified, a familiar voice broke through the tension, calling out with a frantic urgency that felt both like a lifeline and a looming disaster. "Liv! Sophie! Are you out there?"

"Liv! Sophie! Are you out there?" The voice, strained and filled with an urgency that shot adrenaline straight into my veins, snapped me back to the present. I recognized it instantly—Mason, Sophie's brother, a steadfast presence in our lives, whose loyalty was as fierce as his protective instincts.

"Mason!" I called, relief flooding my chest like a spring thaw. "We're here!"

He burst through the foliage, a whirlwind of movement and concern. His disheveled hair and frantic eyes told me he had been searching for us, the hint of wildness around him a stark contrast to the calm that had enveloped Sophie and me just moments before. He skidded to a halt, taking in our disheveled forms, and I could see the tension in his shoulders ease as he focused on Sophie.

"Thank God," he breathed, the relief evident in his voice. "I thought I was losing my mind."

Sophie stood tall beside me, her grip tightening around my hand. "You nearly did, but we're not done yet. They're still out there," she warned, her voice steady but edged with the remnants of fear.

Mason nodded, scanning the area with a soldier's vigilance. "I saw the men as I came through the east side of the woods. They're searching for you. We need to get out of here, now."

The urgency in his tone hit me like a slap, and I exchanged a glance with Sophie, who nodded, determination igniting in her eyes. "Lead the way," I urged Mason, my heart racing again. The stakes had never been higher, and I could feel the looming danger like a storm cloud overhead, heavy and threatening.

As we retraced our steps through the forest, the once-familiar paths felt altered, as if the trees themselves were closing in, their gnarled roots and thick branches conspiring to trap us within their embrace. I focused on the rhythmic crunch of leaves underfoot, a reminder that I was alive and moving, that every step was a victory against despair.

"What happened, Sophie?" Mason asked, his voice tight with concern. "Where have you been?"

"AgriCorp's men," she started, her voice trembling slightly. "They took me when I was gathering herbs for the shop. They wanted to use me, to bend the land to their will. They think they can control everything."

"Bastards," Mason spat, his anger palpable. "This is bigger than we thought."

"Bigger than we imagined," I murmured, recalling the rumors I had heard about AgriCorp's intentions. They were a faceless corporate giant, and their ambitions were notorious. If they could harness Sophie's connection to the land, they could twist it to suit their greedy purposes. It felt like a tightening noose around my heart, and I refused to let that happen.

As we pressed on, the weight of the trees seemed to amplify the urgency of our situation. The underbrush was thick, snaring at our legs like unwanted memories. But with Mason leading us, we navigated the labyrinthine paths, and I felt a flicker of hope reignite within me. The world outside this forest felt distant, but every rustle behind us reminded me that danger was still lurking.

"Mason, do you think they've sent out search parties?" I asked, glancing back over my shoulder.

"Definitely," he replied, his brow furrowing in concentration. "They won't give up easily. They need Sophie. You know how powerful she is."

Sophie squeezed my hand tighter, her eyes reflecting a mixture of fear and determination. "We need to show them just how powerful I can be," she said, her voice gaining strength.

"Exactly," I chimed in, feeling a surge of pride for her. "We're not going to let them win. We're going to turn this around."

A sudden crack echoed through the trees, sharp and loud. My heart dropped. "Did you hear that?"

"Yeah," Mason replied, his eyes narrowing. "It sounded like a branch breaking. We need to keep moving."

We accelerated, but the forest felt alive, whispering warnings as we pushed deeper into its heart. The tension thickened the air, and my senses heightened; I could almost taste the fear on my tongue, a bitter reminder that we were not safe yet.

"Do you think they can track you?" I asked Sophie, my voice barely above a whisper.

"I don't know," she admitted, her brow furrowing. "They might have some way to sense my abilities."

"Then we need a plan," Mason said, his gaze intense. "We can't just run into a trap."

Sophie nodded, her face now resolute. "If we can reach the creek, we might have a chance. The water will mask my scent."

"Then let's move," I urged, my heart pounding as we sprinted through the underbrush, adrenaline coursing through my veins. The sound of our hurried footsteps became a rhythm, a heartbeat of resistance against the impending threat.

The creek was a few yards away, its babbling water a comforting promise amidst the chaos. As we neared it, I could hear the gentle splashing of water against rocks, the cool air carrying a sense of clarity that felt almost surreal. I could almost imagine dipping my toes into the refreshing stream, washing away the fear that clung to me.

But as we reached the edge of the creek, a shadow flickered just beyond the trees, and my stomach dropped. "Mason, look out!" I shouted as a figure lunged from the underbrush, a dark silhouette against the sunlit forest.

He turned just in time to dodge the man's grasp, the sudden burst of movement propelling him sideways. The mercenary stumbled, momentarily disoriented. But I didn't wait to see what would happen next. "Sophie!" I yelled, yanking her toward the water. "Now!"

We plunged into the icy creek, the shock of the cold water jolting me awake, sending shivers through my body. I glanced back at Mason, who was still grappling with the mercenary, his instincts kicking in as he fought to keep the man at bay.

"Go!" he yelled, his voice fierce and commanding. "Get to the other side!"

Sophie's grip on my hand tightened as we swam against the current, the water pulling at us with a force that felt almost alive. My heart pounded, fear surging through me like a tidal wave, but we couldn't stop. We had come too far, endured too much.

Just as we reached the bank, I turned to see Mason wrestle the mercenary to the ground, fists flying. The moment felt suspended in time, as if the world was holding its breath, waiting to see who would emerge victorious. I felt a fierce surge of anger. We weren't just fighting for ourselves; we were fighting for everything we believed in—the land, the future, each other.

"Mason!" I shouted, desperate. "We need you! Come on!"

With one last effort, he tossed the man aside and lunged toward the creek, his determination evident. "I'm coming!" he called back, his voice a mixture of exertion and resolve.

The three of us huddled at the bank, the water splashing around us, both a barrier and a lifeline. "What's the plan now?" Mason gasped, catching his breath.

Sophie looked at both of us, her eyes ablaze with conviction. "We fight back. Together."

With that, we stepped into the water, ready to confront whatever lay ahead, determined to reclaim our lives from the shadows that sought to snatch them away.

The water enveloped us, a cool cocoon that seemed to hush the chaos of the world above. As we caught our breath, I glanced back at the bank, where the mercenary had momentarily fallen to the ground. I could see Mason clenching his fists, ready to spring into action again if needed. The adrenaline surged through me, a wild, electrifying current that fueled both fear and determination.

"Okay, we're all here," I whispered, a thread of urgency woven into my voice. "What's the next move?"

Sophie, shaking droplets from her hair, looked at me with an intensity that sent shivers down my spine. "We need to get to the old barn by the eastern edge of the farm. If we can reach it, we can fortify ourselves and think of a plan to deal with AgriCorp."

"Right, because nothing screams 'safe haven' like a rickety old barn," Mason quipped, forcing a smile to lighten the heavy atmosphere. "But I'm all in. Let's do it."

We shared a determined glance, the kind that says no words are necessary, as we emerged from the creek and shook off the cold water clinging to our skin. The chill invigorated me, sharpening my senses. The familiar scent of damp earth mixed with the wild, floral aroma of the woods surrounded us, a reminder that we were still in the land we loved.

"Stay low," I murmured as we began to move, darting between the trees, the forest becoming our cover and our camouflage. My heart raced as I led the way, feeling the weight of both Sophie's and Mason's presence behind me, their energy buoying my resolve.

Every rustle in the underbrush heightened my awareness; it felt as though the forest itself was alive, holding its breath for what would happen next. I couldn't shake the sense that we were not alone, that the eyes of unseen watchers were tracking our movements.

"What if they've already set up a perimeter?" Sophie asked, her voice tight with concern.

"We can't think that way," I replied, glancing back at her. "We need to act. Remember, we have an advantage—they're looking for you, not us."

Mason nodded, his gaze flicking back toward the direction we had come from. "We'll outsmart them. That's what we do best."

We navigated the underbrush, weaving through trees and low-hanging branches. My mind raced as I calculated each step, urging us forward. The old barn loomed ahead, a dilapidated structure that had seen better days. Its weathered wood and rusting tin roof had once been a place of joy, a hub of summer adventures and laughter. Now it stood as a potential sanctuary, a shelter from the storm gathering outside.

As we approached, I noticed the doors were slightly ajar, creaking ominously in the gentle breeze. "Stay alert," I whispered, pushing the door open just enough to peer inside. The dim interior was cloaked in shadows, the beams of sunlight filtering through the gaps in the walls casting eerie shapes on the floor.

"Looks like a great place for a horror movie," Mason joked, trying to keep the mood light, but his bravado couldn't completely mask the tension in his posture.

"Right? Just us, a barn, and the lurking terrors of AgriCorp," I replied, stepping inside. The air was musty, filled with the scent of old hay and forgotten memories.

"Okay, let's secure the place," Sophie said, her tone shifting to businesslike. She moved to one side, inspecting the windows, while Mason and I took to the other.

"I'll block the back entrance," Mason said, positioning a few barrels to obstruct the doorway. "If they come, at least we'll have a few seconds to prepare."

I focused on the front entrance, glancing out through the cracks in the door. The world outside was eerily quiet, but the stillness felt wrong, like the calm before a storm. "I don't see anyone, but that doesn't mean they're not out there," I muttered.

"Let's hope they're as clueless as we are," Sophie said, sliding down to sit on a nearby hay bale. She looked drained, and I hated seeing her like this. "What's the plan now?"

"We wait," I replied, trying to sound more confident than I felt. "We need to gather our thoughts and assess our resources."

But the unease crept in, whispering that waiting was the worst thing we could do. I turned to Sophie, a fierce sense of protectiveness surging within me. "You're not alone anymore, Soph. We're in this together, remember? Whatever happens, we face it as a team."

She nodded, a small smile breaking through the worry etched on her face. "Together."

Minutes ticked by, and the silence wrapped around us like a thick fog. I could feel the tension building, an electric current humming beneath the surface. Suddenly, a distant sound pierced the stillness—a roar of engines, the unmistakable growl of trucks approaching.

"Do you hear that?" I hissed, my heart racing as I peered out again.

"Yes," Mason said, his expression hardening. "They're coming. We don't have much time."

"Okay, we need to act fast," I said, feeling the urgency creep into my voice. "Sophie, can you draw on the land? Maybe we can create a barrier or—"

"I can try," she interrupted, determination shining through the remnants of her fear. "But it will take concentration."

"Then let's create a distraction," Mason suggested. "Something to divert them while she works."

I glanced at the door, the sounds growing louder. "I can make noise—draw them away from here."

"Not alone," Mason said firmly. "We need to stick together. How about we set up something that can lure them? If they chase after the noise, it buys us time."

Sophie looked thoughtful, her brow furrowed. "The old grain silo to the north. If we can set something to catch their attention—"

"I'll do it," I interrupted, adrenaline surging through me. "Just tell me what to grab."

"Anything loud and flashy," Mason said, urgency seeping into his words. "A couple of old metal sheets should make a racket."

I nodded, steeling myself for the task. "Keep an eye on Sophie. If things go south, get her to safety."

"Liv, don't—"

"No time to argue!" I cut him off, my heart pounding with both fear and a strange sense of exhilaration. I knew I had to do this. The safety of Sophie—and our future—depended on it.

Without waiting for another word, I slipped out of the barn, the cool air hitting my skin like a shockwave. The noise of the engines grew closer, and I dashed toward the silo, dodging the trees and brambles that clawed at me. Every instinct screamed for me to turn back, to seek safety, but I pressed on, determined to create the diversion we needed.

I reached the silo, my hands trembling as I fumbled for the metal sheets that had lain abandoned for years. As I banged them together, the loud clanging echoed through the woods, a cacophony that filled the silence with a promise of chaos. I glanced back, catching a glimpse of movement at the barn; Mason was helping Sophie prepare, readying her for what was to come.

The trucks rolled into view, their headlights cutting through the twilight, illuminating the forest in an eerie glow. Panic clawed at my throat as I waved the metal sheets above my head, shouting into the night. "Over here! Come and get me!"

The trucks came to a screeching halt, headlights sweeping across the trees, and I felt my heart race with a mix of fear and exhilaration. They were here, just as I hoped.

But before I could take another step, I heard the unmistakable sound of a voice I'd never wanted to hear again, a voice that made my blood run cold. "Liv! There you are! You thought you could hide from us?"

The blood drained from my face as I turned slowly, dread curling in my stomach. The mercenaries were here, and their eyes locked onto me like predators spotting their prey. The world around me blurred, and all I could think about was getting back to Sophie and Mason, but there was no way I could let them know I was alone out here.

"Run!" I shouted back toward the barn, but my voice barely broke through the growing chaos. The trucks opened up, and mercenaries poured out, each one armed and menacing.

I stumbled backward, desperate to escape, but I could already hear the sound of footsteps closing in behind me, their shadows looming ever larger as they moved with predatory precision.

And then it hit me—one of them had spotted the barn, where Sophie and Mason waited. My heart plummeted as realization settled in; I had to act, and I had to act fast.

Just as I turned to sprint back toward the barn, a sharp pain lanced through my shoulder, and I staggered. I looked down in shock, my heart racing as I realized the wound was a gunshot. Panic flooded my senses as darkness encroached on my vision, and I fought to stay upright, to run, to get back to the only people who mattered.

But with each step, the world began to spin, and all I could hear was the distant echo of Sophie's voice fading into silence as the shadows closed in around me, threatening to engulf everything I had fought for.

Chapter 9: The Turning Tide

The scent of fresh earth lingered in the air as I walked through the fields of Willow Creek, my boots squelching slightly in the damp soil. It was early morning, the sun peeking over the horizon, painting the sky in hues of orange and pink, a canvas splattered with the promise of a new day. Birds chirped a symphony of greetings, their melodies intermingling with the distant hum of bees busy at work. Every heartbeat echoed the rhythm of the land, a pulsing reminder of why we were here—why I was here. I ran my fingers over the tall stalks of wheat, feeling their strength, their resilience, and it filled me with a sense of purpose that I had never fully embraced until now.

Sophie was already at the community center, her fiery spirit igniting a spark in everyone who gathered. She stood at the makeshift podium, her hands gesturing animatedly as she spoke. I caught snippets of her impassioned speech, her words rolling over the crowd like waves of inspiration, stirring the hearts of farmers and families alike. They were here, not just for the land, but for each other—an unbroken circle of hope and determination. The sky darkened with clouds, but it felt more like a dramatic backdrop to our impending showdown than an omen of bad weather.

As I stepped closer, the crowd erupted in applause. I spotted Sophie's familiar auburn hair shining like a beacon, her eyes sparkling with determination. She was radiant, every ounce of her being consumed by the cause, and it made my heart swell with admiration. I could hardly wait to join her on stage, to add my voice to the cacophony of dissent rising against AgriCorp's predatory practices. My hands trembled slightly with the weight of my commitment, and I inhaled deeply, letting the scent of the land ground me.

"Together, we stand against the tides of greed!" Sophie's voice cut through my thoughts, pulling me back to the moment. She was in her element, and I felt a surge of warmth and courage radiating from her, like the sun breaking through the clouds above. It was infectious, an electrifying current that passed through each of us as we raised our fists in solidarity. "They may think they can drown us in their corporate lies, but we are the roots of this land, and we will not be uprooted!"

I took a step forward, my heart pounding, and raised my voice to join hers. "We know the truth! We know what sustainable farming means for our community, our children, and our future! AgriCorp's promises are nothing but smoke and mirrors, designed to snatch away what we hold dear!" My words fell into the rhythm of the crowd, fueling the momentum. Faces turned towards me, eyes wide and hopeful. I had once been hesitant to step into the spotlight, but now it felt as though my entire being was meant for this moment, to fight not only for our land but for Sophie as well.

The protest gathered momentum, a vibrant tapestry of voices and wills woven together. Banners flapped in the wind, their messages bold and defiant. "Protect Our Farms!" "AgriCorp: No Thanks!" Each slogan felt like a lifeline, connecting us all, binding us together in this fierce endeavor. I glanced around, taking in the faces of neighbors and friends—people who had shared harvests, stories, and laughter with me over the years. Their resolve bolstered my own; I was no longer just a woman fighting for a cause; I was a part of a living, breathing entity, a community determined to preserve its way of life.

But even as our unity grew stronger, a nagging doubt twisted in my stomach like a vine trying to choke the very roots of my resolve. The power of AgriCorp loomed like a shadow, a goliath against our modest band of farmers. I knew their resources were vast, their reach insidious. The thought of facing them sent a shiver down my spine, but it only steeled my determination. I had Sophie by my side, and that was more potent than any corporation's money.

"Listen up!" Sophie called, rallying the crowd. "Our message must be clear. We are not just fighting for our farms; we are fighting for the integrity of our food, the health of our families, and the future of our planet. If they think we'll roll over and let them take our land, they have another thing coming!"

The crowd roared, a chorus of voices uniting in purpose. With each chant, I felt the fear recede, replaced by a fierce sense of duty. I had spent too long feeling trapped between my ambitions and my heart. Now, with every chant echoing through the fields, it became clear that my ambition had found its purpose within the love I felt for this land and for Sophie. It was a revelation that ignited a flame inside me, a resolve that spread like wildfire through the crowd.

Just then, as if to punctuate our determination, the sky opened up, and rain began to fall—a soft drizzle at first, then a steady downpour. The drops soaked us, a baptism of sorts, cleansing the fears of the past and fueling the fire of our rebellion. We laughed and danced in the rain, our spirits soaring as the world around us transformed into a vibrant celebration of defiance. The colors of our banners bled together, the earth embraced us as we joined in a jubilant chorus, our voices melding with the rhythm of the raindrops.

In that moment, the storm felt less like an enemy and more like a partner in our dance—a reminder that sometimes, chaos can bring clarity. I caught Sophie's eye across the throng, her smile illuminating the gray skies, and I knew without a doubt that whatever lay ahead, we would face it together. We were no longer simply a group of farmers; we had become a movement, and I was ready to fight for what we believed in, with every ounce of strength I possessed. The tide was turning, and with it, we would carve our own path through the tempest that awaited us.

The rain continued to drench the earth, each droplet a reminder that our fight was as elemental as the land itself. As I stood there, exhilarated and drenched, I noticed something in the crowd that sent a jolt of uncertainty through my veins. A few figures on the periphery were watching us intently, their expressions unreadable. Clad in dark jackets, they seemed out of place amidst the vibrant colors and lively chatter of our protest. My heart sank slightly; I recognized them from AgriCorp's headquarters—sharp suits and sharper eyes. Their presence felt like a dark cloud amidst our storm.

"Is this a protest or a water park?" Sophie quipped, shaking her hair, droplets flying like confetti around her. "Because I didn't sign up for a splash zone!"

I forced a smile, trying to push the tension aside, but my instincts buzzed like angry bees. "Just keep an eye on the crowd," I murmured back, trying to sound nonchalant. "I think we might have some uninvited guests."

As the rain poured, it became a chaotic symphony of voices—laughter mingling with shouts of protest, the rhythm of our unity undeterred by the ominous figures lurking in the shadows. I noticed how Sophie's eyes sparkled even in the gray, the way her determination lit up the dreary day. It made me realize that no matter what storm we faced, we had each other, and that was worth fighting for.

The crowd began to disperse as the rain fell harder, and I felt a pang of disappointment that the momentum was slipping away. Sophie approached me, her face flushed with enthusiasm. "Did you see the way they responded? We're making waves!" She twirled around, her soaked clothes clinging to her, yet she seemed utterly unbothered. "I think we've officially turned this protest into a performance art piece."

"Just don't expect a standing ovation," I replied, my heart racing. "Unless, of course, those guys from AgriCorp decide to join in. I hear they're not great at taking hints."

We shared a laugh, the tension momentarily lifted, but I couldn't shake the feeling of unease. I spotted one of the men in a dark coat stepping closer, his posture straight, gaze locked onto Sophie. "I'll be right back," I said, my voice tight. "I need to find out what they want."

"Be careful," she warned, her brow furrowing. "I don't trust them."

I navigated through the crowd, each step heavy with anticipation. The rain slowed, turning into a light drizzle, but the atmosphere crackled with unease. When I reached the man, I found my voice, firm yet steady. "What do you want?"

He smirked, his demeanor oozing confidence. "Just observing, really. Your little protest has drawn quite the crowd. You've got people riled up."

"Observing or scouting?" I shot back, crossing my arms defiantly. "If you're here to intimidate us, it's not going to work."

"Intimidation? Please." He waved his hand dismissively. "We're in the business of opportunity. You see, we could help you."

"Help us?" I echoed, skepticism creeping into my voice. "What's your angle?"

He leaned closer, his voice dropping to a conspiratorial whisper. "You're fighting a losing battle, you know. AgriCorp has resources you can't even imagine. But here's the thing: we respect passion. You and your little friend have got that in spades. What if we could channel that energy into something more... profitable?"

I narrowed my eyes. "And what's the price? Everything we've built?"

"Not at all," he said smoothly, a predatory smile forming. "Just a partnership. Think of it—a way to expand your reach, bring your ideals to a larger audience. With our backing, you could be the face of sustainable farming, rather than just another protester in the rain."

My gut twisted. I had always been wary of shortcuts, of shiny promises that seemed too good to be true. "I'm not interested in selling out," I replied firmly. "This is about our community, not profit margins."

He shrugged, an insufferable calmness in his demeanor. "Suit yourself. But just remember, when the tide rises, it's not just the boats that get lifted." With that, he turned, disappearing into the dwindling crowd, leaving me standing there, drenched and unsettled.

I returned to Sophie, my heart heavy. "What did he say?" she asked, concern etched on her features.

"Just trying to lure us into a trap," I replied, anger bubbling beneath the surface. "They think they can buy us off with their slick promises."

She let out a breath, her eyes flashing with determination. "Let them try. We're not going anywhere. This is our land, our fight. We'll find a way to turn their tactics against them."

As the rain lightened, we began to gather the remnants of our protest, folding banners and picking up signs, laughter still lingering among us like a warm embrace. But beneath the laughter, the seed of doubt had taken root. What if they were right? What if we were outmatched?

Sophie's voice cut through my spiraling thoughts. "You know, I always thought the saying 'don't bring a knife to a gunfight' was a little misleading. What if we show up with a water pistol instead?"

I chuckled despite myself. "Water pistols aren't going to save us when they bring out the big guns."

"True," she admitted, her smile faltering slightly. "But what if we were to turn their weapons against them? They're betting on our fear. What if we make it clear that we're not afraid?"

I contemplated her words, the way they swirled in the air like a fragrant breeze. "And how do we do that?"

"By being louder, prouder, and more united than ever," she replied, her conviction palpable. "We take this fight beyond the fields. Social media, town halls, everywhere we can. We'll expose AgriCorp's real intentions. Show the world what's really at stake."

Her words ignited something within me—a flicker of hope amid the uncertainty. I realized that while AgriCorp had the resources, we had the community, the passion, and the drive to protect what was ours. It wasn't about fighting fire with fire; it was about outsmarting the flames entirely.

"I'm with you," I said, my resolve strengthening. "Let's take this fight to them. We'll show them that Willow Creek isn't just a dot on the map; it's a force to be reckoned with."

As we stood together, rain-soaked and invigorated, I felt an electric thrill course through me. We were a team, our dreams entwined like the roots of the crops we nurtured. The road ahead might be rocky, but together, we could weather any storm.

The days that followed our protest were a whirlwind, a flurry of meetings, strategy sessions, and endless cups of coffee that seemed to fuel our newfound momentum. The community rallied around us, each voice contributing to the growing narrative of resistance against AgriCorp's overreach. We filled town halls, bustling with energy, ready to educate our neighbors on the importance of sustainable farming practices and the long-term benefits of preserving our land. The more we spoke, the more we believed in our cause, transforming our fear into a palpable force that rippled through Willow Creek.

Sophie had taken to social media with the zeal of a new evangelist, crafting posts that were both informative and engaging. "You know," she said one afternoon, scrolling through the hashtags we'd created, "if we keep this up, we might just become the poster children for eco-warriors."

"Or the target for AgriCorp's 'eliminate the competition' campaign," I replied, teasing a strand of my hair behind my ear. "I'm still waiting for their hitmen to show up at my door with corporate contracts and a very sharp pencil."

"Don't give them any ideas!" she laughed, but I could see the concern flicker in her eyes. The stakes were high, and I felt the weight of our decision more heavily than I'd ever anticipated.

Despite the tension, we forged ahead, fueled by our unwavering commitment. Sophie and I spent hours brainstorming ideas, plotting our next moves. We established a schedule for community meetings, guest speakers, and events that would keep our message alive. Yet, amid the flurry of activity, I couldn't shake the feeling that we were being watched, the gaze of AgriCorp's representatives lingering like a fog.

One evening, while sorting through flyers in her cozy kitchen, Sophie turned to me, her brow furrowed. "What if we hosted an open forum?" she suggested. "Get everyone together, let them voice their concerns. It could show AgriCorp we're united."

"An open forum?" I raised an eyebrow, intrigued. "You mean a town hall where they can throw tomatoes at us while we spill our guts about sustainable farming?"

"Exactly! The tomatoes are optional, but it would show we're not afraid to engage with our neighbors," she insisted, her eyes sparkling with mischief. "Think about it: a chance for everyone to share their stories, their experiences. We could even invite a few experts to back us up."

"Alright, let's do it," I replied, feeling the fire rekindle within me. "If we can turn that into a rallying point, we might just pull this off."

The plan came together quickly. We set the date, booked the town hall, and reached out to local farmers, activists, and experts in sustainable agriculture. Word spread like wildfire, and the excitement was contagious. Posters adorned every telephone pole in Willow Creek, vibrant colors promising a night of knowledge, unity, and resolve.

As the day of the forum approached, however, I noticed something unsettling. A few townspeople had begun to waver, their enthusiasm tempered by whispers of doubt. "What if AgriCorp is right?" I overheard one neighbor say. "Maybe their methods are the way forward."

Sophie and I tackled these doubts head-on, meeting with anyone who expressed concern. "We're fighting for our land, for our future," Sophie would say, her voice steady and passionate. "It's not about whether AgriCorp's methods are effective; it's about whether they're ethical."

"Can you really put a price on our community?" I would add, hoping to ignite a sense of pride. "Look around you—this is our home, and we have to protect it."

Finally, the night of the open forum arrived, and the atmosphere buzzed with an electric energy that filled the town hall. Sophie and I stood at the front, flanked by experts and eager farmers ready to share their stories. The seats filled quickly, and soon, the room overflowed with neighbors, friends, and families united in purpose.

Sophie opened the discussion, her voice unwavering as she welcomed everyone. "Thank you all for being here tonight. We're not just talking about farming; we're talking about our future." The crowd murmured in agreement, a wave of solidarity washing over us.

One by one, local farmers took the stage, sharing personal anecdotes of their struggles against corporate encroachment and the loss of traditional practices. Each story added another layer of conviction to our cause, weaving a narrative that was hard to ignore. Laughter punctuated the serious tones as we all connected over shared experiences, a sense of kinship blossoming.

But just as the momentum reached its peak, a figure in a crisp white shirt and tailored suit strode in through the door. The room fell silent, a hush rippling through the audience as we recognized him—one of the men from AgriCorp, the very one who had approached me after the protest.

"Good evening, everyone," he said, his voice smooth and charming, an unsettling contrast to the weight in the air. "I hope I'm not interrupting. I merely wanted to remind you that AgriCorp is always open to discussions regarding the future of agriculture in Willow Creek."

Murmurs of disbelief swirled around the room, and I felt a surge of anger rise in my chest. "This is not a negotiation," I shot back, my voice rising above the whispers. "This is about defending our way of life!"

"Isn't it possible to find common ground?" he countered, glancing at the crowd, his smirk unyielding. "After all, we all want what's best for Willow Creek, don't we?"

Sophie stepped forward, her eyes narrowing. "Common ground? You mean, like your plans to monopolize our farmland? Because that sounds like the opposite of common ground to me."

The tension crackled like electricity, and I could see the agitation in the crowd as they processed his words. I felt the need to take control of the situation, to turn the tide back in our favor. "We've seen what your 'common ground' looks like, and it's paved with greed," I asserted, my voice steady. "Willow Creek deserves better."

He feigned a laugh, leaning back as if amused. "Well, isn't this adorable? A community of dreamers fighting against a reality they can't change. Let's face it, sustainable farming is a quaint idea, but it's not sustainable in the real world."

The crowd shifted uncomfortably, and I sensed the doubt creeping back in. This was not just a battle for our land; it was a battle for our beliefs, our very identity. Just as I prepared to respond, the lights flickered ominously, and a low rumble echoed outside.

"What was that?" someone shouted, panic lacing their tone. The tension in the room heightened as we all turned toward the window, peering into the darkness beyond.

Suddenly, a loud crash resonated from outside, and the building shook slightly. "Stay calm!" I shouted, though my own voice felt thin against the rising tide of chaos. "We need to find out what's happening!"

The AgriCorp representative smirked, clearly enjoying the chaos unfolding. "Looks like the real world has come knocking, folks. Perhaps it's time to reconsider your stance."

Just then, the doors swung open, and a group of locals rushed in, their faces pale and frantic. "It's AgriCorp! They're—"

Before the words fully formed, the lights cut out completely, plunging us into darkness. A collective gasp filled the room, the air thick with tension and uncertainty. My heart raced, pounding like a drum, as I felt the weight of our fight pressing down on me, and I realized that we were standing on the precipice of something monumental.

As the shadows danced around us and the voices rose in panic, I grasped Sophie's hand, squeezing tightly. "Whatever happens, we face it together," I whispered, determination igniting within me.

But just then, a loud crash echoed from the back of the room, followed by the unmistakable sound of shattering glass. My stomach dropped, and all at once, the air grew heavy with a sense of impending doom.

And in that moment of uncertainty, the flickering light returned, revealing a chilling sight that would change everything. The AgriCorp representative stood at the door, his expression twisted in delight, and behind him loomed a dark silhouette, a figure cloaked in mystery and menace.

"Welcome to the real fight for Willow Creek," he said, a glimmer of triumph in his eyes.

Chapter 10: The Gathering Storm

The air was thick with anticipation, a warm breeze threading through the trees, rustling the leaves like whispers of old friends. I stood in the heart of Willow Creek, a quaint town nestled between rolling hills and lush fields, where the golden sun cast long shadows on the pavement. Each breath tasted like the promise of change, mixing with the scent of freshly turned earth and blooming wildflowers. The protest had started as a flicker of an idea—a small gathering of like-minded souls who shared a vision of preserving our way of life. Now, it was a wildfire, and I was fortunate to be at the center of it.

Banners waved like the flags of a new kingdom, each hand-painted slogan a testament to our shared resolve. "Save Our Soil!" read one, bright and bold, flanked by images of vegetables bursting with life. Another proclaimed, "Farmers Not Foes," a jab at the faceless corporation that threatened to swallow our land whole. I glanced at Sophie, her vibrant hair a beacon amidst the sea of faces, her eyes alight with determination. She had always been the spark, the one who ignited the passion in us all. Today, she was the flame.

"Remember, folks," she shouted, her voice ringing out over the crowd like a siren's call. "This isn't just about us; it's about our children, their children, and the future of Willow Creek. We won't let them bulldoze our dreams!" A roar of approval surged from the crowd, a powerful wave that washed over me, energizing every fiber of my being. Sophie's words wrapped around us, tight and unyielding, knitting our hopes together.

As I took a step forward, I felt the warmth of hands squeezing my own, my neighbor Judy's reassuring grip grounding me. The years spent sharing stories over backyard fences and picking apples during harvest season had forged a bond that felt indestructible. Her voice chimed in beside me, steady and strong. "We're not just farmers;

we're caretakers of this land. And if they think they can take it from us without a fight, they've got another thing coming."

The clamor of voices surged, igniting the air with fervor. My heart raced, not from fear of the corporate giant looming over us, but from the sheer thrill of unity, of knowing that we were a part of something larger than ourselves. Willow Creek wasn't just a town; it was a tapestry woven from generations of stories, laughter, and love.

I scanned the crowd, taking in the faces of my friends and neighbors—the elderly couple who had planted the first apple orchard decades ago, the young couple expecting their first child, and the spirited teens eager to make their mark. Their passion radiated like sunlight breaking through clouds, lifting my spirits even higher. Each one of us represented a thread in this beautiful fabric, and together we would not be torn apart.

Then, the mood shifted. I noticed a figure standing on the fringe of the crowd, arms crossed, a look of disapproval etched on his sharp features. It was Tom Reynolds, the local businessman whose interests lay more with the corporate developers than with the land. A chill crept through me, an uninvited gust that threatened to extinguish the flames of our resolve. Tom had a way of making his presence felt, often a dark cloud on our sunniest days. Today, however, he had brought his own storm with him.

"Nice show of theatrics, ladies and gentlemen," he called out, his voice dripping with condescension. "But you really think this is going to change anything? These protests are just a waste of time."

His words sliced through the crowd like a knife, eliciting gasps and murmurs of disbelief. Sophie's eyes narrowed, her fiery spirit ignited further. "This isn't just theatrics, Tom. This is our life! This is our land! You don't understand what it means to grow something, to nurture it from the ground up."

He shrugged, dismissing her words with a wave of his hand. "What you don't seem to get is that progress is coming whether you like it or not. You can either get on board or be left behind."

The tension was palpable, the air electric with unspoken words. My heart raced, a wild drum echoing in my ears. This was the moment, the clash of ideals that would define us. I took a step forward, adrenaline surging through my veins, my voice steady despite the turmoil inside. "And what kind of progress is that, Tom? The kind that destroys our heritage, our community? We won't stand by and let you dictate what's best for us."

His expression darkened, and I could see the flicker of surprise in his eyes, as if he had never expected resistance from someone like me. But this wasn't just about me; it was about all of us. It was about the children who played in the dirt, the farmers who rose with the sun, and the future we envisioned together.

The crowd began to rally around me, their voices merging into a chorus of defiance. "No more destruction! Save our farms!" The chant built, rolling over the streets of Willow Creek, drowning out Tom's disdain. I felt the pulse of unity swell within me, a fierce determination that we wouldn't back down.

Tom's eyes darted from face to face, finally settling on Sophie. She stood tall, unyielding, her expression fierce. "You may have the money, Tom, but we have the heart of Willow Creek. And you'll never buy that."

The energy shifted again, a collective inhale as the reality of our power settled in. We were not just a group of dissenters; we were the lifeblood of this town, the guardians of its spirit. We had history and passion on our side, and that was a force to be reckoned with.

As Tom huffed in frustration and turned to leave, the tension began to melt away, replaced by laughter and cheers. I felt a swell of joy rise in my chest, the victory of that moment washing over me. We had stood together, unafraid, and our voices had found their strength. The air buzzed with excitement, and I knew, without a doubt, that this was just the beginning.

The applause swelled around us like a rising tide, each clap and cheer washing over me, infusing me with newfound confidence. We had stood our ground, voices raised and spirits unyielding, and I felt an intoxicating blend of hope and exhilaration ripple through the crowd. Yet, even amid our small victory, a sliver of doubt crept into my mind—could we really fend off the impending threat?

As the sun dipped lower in the sky, casting a golden hue over the gathered faces, I noticed Sophie was already formulating the next steps. Her vibrant spirit radiated a mix of enthusiasm and strategy. "We can't just stop here. We need to take this energy and turn it into something actionable. A town hall meeting—let's really organize!" She was practically buzzing, her ideas spilling out faster than I could keep up.

"Okay, so a town hall meeting," I echoed, attempting to keep pace. "Do you think people will show up?"

"Show up? They'll be lined up around the block!" She grinned, a spark of mischief dancing in her eyes. "We'll make it an event. We can invite local musicians, maybe even a potluck. Everyone loves a good potluck."

I laughed, a bit incredulous. "Sophie, if you keep this up, we'll end up hosting the biggest town gathering since the last harvest festival. Do we even have enough casseroles to feed the whole town?"

"Trust me, we'll have casseroles galore," she declared, her confidence infectious. "And pie! Everyone loves pie."

Just as I was about to dive into the logistics of how we might organize such an affair, a familiar figure broke through the crowd. It was Noah, with his easy smile and tousled hair, the kind of guy who could charm the frost off a pumpkin. He sidled up beside me, a gleam of mischief in his eyes. "Did I miss the memo on the protest? I thought you all were just gathering for a spontaneous block party."

"Pretty close," I said, rolling my eyes playfully. "We're gathering to save our town, but feel free to bring the chips and dip."

"Chips and dip?" He laughed, shaking his head. "I'll see what I can do. But I might need a little more motivation than just chips to join the fray."

"You're lucky I'm here to provide that," Sophie quipped, throwing him a grin. "We could always use someone to help put up posters."

"Is that your secret plan? Get me to do all the hard work while you two sit back and enjoy your potluck?"

"Absolutely," Sophie replied with mock seriousness. "It's called teamwork, Noah. Besides, you love a good fight, don't you?"

He raised an eyebrow, that easy charm still lingering, even as the gravity of our situation crept in. "I suppose I do. But I'd prefer to fight with baked goods than against a corporate giant. Are we really prepared for this?"

"Prepared or not, we have to try," I said, meeting his gaze with conviction. "We can't let them take our land, our way of life. And I'd rather go down swinging than stand by quietly."

Noah nodded, a flicker of respect crossing his face. "I'm in. Count me as the designated poster guy and pie enthusiast. But only if I get dibs on the first slice."

"Deal," I said, my heart swelling with gratitude for my friends, the way they rallied around me, fueling my determination.

As we exchanged ideas and laughter, the sun began its slow descent, casting long shadows that danced across the pavement. With each passing moment, my confidence grew. I felt a warm sense of belonging as the community gathered closer, united in our purpose, ready to fight for the land that had cradled generations of families.

In the days that followed, the energy from the protest propelled us into a whirlwind of activity. The town hall meeting took shape, morphing from a vague idea into a tangible event. We canvassed neighborhoods, placing brightly colored flyers on doorsteps and chatting with residents about our cause. Sophie was relentless, her enthusiasm contagious as she convinced even the most reluctant neighbors to join our mission.

"I can't bake to save my life, but I'll be there," Mrs. Jenkins from down the road declared, her voice steady. "I've seen too many changes in this town, and I won't sit quietly anymore."

"Exactly!" Sophie beamed. "Every voice matters, and we want to hear yours."

As we drummed up excitement, I felt the stirrings of hope grow more robust. Our small town, often dismissed as quaint and sleepy, was awakening. We were transforming from quiet farmers and shopkeepers into a force to be reckoned with.

The night of the town hall meeting arrived, the air crackling with anticipation. I stood at the front, a stack of chairs ready to embrace the growing crowd. The town hall itself, with its wooden beams and rustic charm, felt like a sacred space—a gathering place where stories and dreams had been shared for generations.

Sophie took her place next to me, her fiery hair cascading over her shoulders as she glanced at the filling room. "Look at this! They came!" Her voice was a mixture of awe and pride.

As I scanned the crowd, my heart swelled. Familiar faces filled the seats—families I had grown up with, friends who had shared my struggles and triumphs. There were the Thompsons, who owned the dairy farm at the edge of town, their two kids bouncing with excitement. Old Mr. Henderson, whose weathered hands had tended the soil for decades, sat with a determined gleam in his eye.

Just as I was about to speak, the doors swung open with a clatter, and in strode Tom Reynolds, flanked by two unfamiliar figures in sharp suits. A hush fell over the room, the mood shifting as tension prickled the air. I felt a shiver run down my spine; his presence was like a storm cloud overshadowing our bright evening.

"What's he doing here?" Sophie whispered, her expression turning to one of indignation.

"Not a clue," I muttered, my heart racing. "But I don't like it."

Tom surveyed the room with a smirk, his confidence radiating from him like a shield. "I thought I'd pop in to see what all the fuss was about," he said, his voice smooth, dripping with condescension. "Is this a gathering or a town hall meeting? I can't tell."

Sophie stepped forward, fists clenched at her sides. "We're discussing the future of our land, Tom, something you seem to care little about."

"Oh, I care," he replied, a glint of amusement in his eyes. "I just don't think you're fully grasping the reality of the situation."

My stomach twisted as I faced him, feeling the weight of the room's attention. "This is our home, Tom. And we're not going to let you dictate its fate."

The crowd behind me murmured in agreement, their voices rising like a chorus of defiance, and I realized that this was our moment. The tension was palpable, a charged current of energy that danced between us, each word carrying the weight of our resolve.

The air in the town hall felt electric, charged with unspoken tension as Tom Reynolds held the floor. He leaned against the podium, his posture relaxed but eyes sharp, scanning the room like a hawk eyeing its prey. I could feel the collective heartbeat of the crowd—our anxiety mingled with anger, simmering just beneath the surface. Sophie stood beside me, her fists clenched at her sides, a silent vow that we wouldn't back down.

"What's the matter, folks?" Tom drawled, his tone mocking. "Scared? This isn't a playground; this is business. And believe me, I have the backing to make some significant changes in this town."

"Changes that benefit you and nobody else!" I shot back, my voice rising, cutting through the oppressive silence. "You think we don't see through your façade? You're here to destroy what makes this community special."

A ripple of agreement surged through the audience, and I noticed Mrs. Thompson nodding vigorously, her husband whispering words of encouragement from the other side of the aisle. The warmth of their support bolstered my confidence. "We're not backing down, Tom. We're not going to sit quietly while you destroy our farms and our heritage."

Tom chuckled, the sound hollow and mocking. "Ah, the noble farmers of Willow Creek, defending their 'heritage.' But let's get real. Progress waits for no one, and holding onto the past won't save you from the inevitable."

"Progress shouldn't come at the cost of our land!" Sophie interjected, stepping forward. "We can have both sustainable development and preservation of our farming practices. But you refuse to listen!"

"Listening is futile when your minds are set in the mud, my dear," he retorted, shrugging as though our concerns were nothing more than pesky flies. "What I'm offering is a chance for growth—something you'll never get by clinging to your quaint ideals."

The tension in the room tightened like a noose, and I could feel the pulse of uncertainty thrumming beneath the bravado of our voices. This man had the power to bulldoze our dreams, yet here we stood, defiant in the face of intimidation. I caught Noah's eye across the room; his brow furrowed, a storm brewing within those easygoing features. He raised an eyebrow, urging me to stay the course, to maintain our strength.

"Tom, we're not asking for much," I said, finding my voice despite the quivering nerves. "Just the chance to keep our home. Our community is more than just a plot of land to develop; it's our lives, our stories."

He leaned forward, eyes narrowing, as if weighing my words like stones. "Stories? Well, how charming. But stories don't pay bills, do they? The world is moving forward, and you'll either have to adapt or be left behind."

A murmur of discontent spread through the crowd, like a wave pushing against a dam. This was our moment, the crux of our fight, and it was time to show him we wouldn't yield. "Tom, you may think you're invincible," I said, my voice steady, "but you underestimate the people of this town. We've been here longer than you, and we won't let you erase our existence."

Just then, a voice from the back of the room broke through the growing tension. "What do you think you'll achieve, Tom? You don't know us like you think you do!" It was Mr. Henderson, his voice quaking with age yet fierce as a summer storm. "We've survived droughts, floods, and harsh winters. This community is built on grit, and we'll fight for our land!"

The applause that followed was thunderous, filling the hall with a sound that vibrated through my bones. Encouraged, I caught Sophie's eye, her smile radiant, and suddenly the weight of our struggle felt lighter.

Tom's demeanor shifted, the playful smirk fading as he realized that he had miscalculated. The room was no longer a mere audience; it was a battleground of wills. "You think this is about me?" he snapped, anger flashing in his eyes. "This is about what's best for Willow Creek. I'm doing this for your sake, whether you realize it or not."

"For our sake?" I echoed incredulously. "You're doing this for your own gain! If you cared about Willow Creek, you'd listen to us instead of trying to steamroll over our voices!"

As I spoke, I could feel the heat of the moment radiating from the crowd. There was power here, a collective spirit ready to defend our home. Just then, Sophie stepped forward, her fiery hair glowing in the soft light of the hall, a true warrior ready for battle. "Tom, we're not going anywhere. We're digging our heels in, and you'll have to go through us to change this town."

"Digging your heels in won't stop progress," he retorted, but there was a flicker of uncertainty in his eyes. "You think a few speeches will deter me? I have a proposal lined up that will bring jobs, revenue, and a brighter future for this town."

"Jobs that come at the cost of our heritage?" Noah interjected, stepping to my side. "How many jobs are worth the loss of our farms? What happens when all that's left are memories of what was once ours?"

A heavy silence fell over the crowd as Tom's gaze flicked to Noah, his expression morphing from arrogance to something else—perhaps fear. "You really think you can stop me? I have the resources, the backing, and the law on my side."

"That's where you're wrong," I said, a thrill running through me as I seized the moment. "We have something you can't buy, Tom. We have love for this land, a community that won't crumble under pressure, and a bond that can't be severed. You underestimate us at your own peril."

The murmurs grew, voices swelling around us like a rising tide. Tom straightened, attempting to regain control. "You'll regret this, all of you. This isn't just about land; this is about your futures. If you push me away, you'll find out just how easily I can make things disappear."

I swallowed hard, the implication hanging thick in the air. "What do you mean by that?"

His smirk returned, but it was cold, devoid of warmth. "Let's just say, I've made a few friends in high places. If you want to keep your farms, you'd best start cooperating."

Fear flickered through the crowd, an undercurrent of anxiety that rippled around us. I felt the color drain from my face, but I couldn't show weakness. "You're bluffing," I asserted, trying to project confidence even as uncertainty coiled in my gut.

"Am I?" He leaned back, his posture relaxed but eyes sharp, watching us as if gauging our reaction. "Let's see how this plays out then. I'll give you a week to consider my proposal. If you choose to defy me, don't say I didn't warn you."

With that, he turned on his heel, striding out of the hall, his suit trailing behind him like a shadow. The silence that followed was deafening, a heavy blanket of unease pressing down on us.

Sophie was the first to break the tension. "We need to strategize," she said, determination flooding her voice. "This is far from over."

I nodded, my heart pounding, but a creeping dread settled in my stomach. As we began to discuss our next steps, I couldn't shake the feeling that we were teetering on the edge of a precipice, and the fall could be devastating.

Just then, a loud crash echoed from the back of the hall, the sound reverberating through the air. Heads turned, and we all gasped as the doors burst open once more, revealing a figure cloaked in shadows, their presence electrifying and ominous.

"Tom's not the only one who's interested in Willow Creek," the figure said, stepping forward, a wicked smile playing on their lips. "And I'm here to make sure you all understand just what's at stake."

Chapter 11: Shadows of the Past

The late afternoon sun draped the room in warm hues of gold and amber as Sophie settled onto the worn leather couch, her fingers absently tracing the patterns embossed on the cushion. She was a juxtaposition of strength and vulnerability, and in that moment, the weight of her past seemed to fill the air between us. I watched her, heart racing, as she took a deep breath, the kind that seemed to summon courage from the very depths of her being. "You know," she began, her voice soft yet steady, "growing up in Oregon wasn't just about the trees and rivers. It was about understanding the whispers of the earth."

Her eyes shimmered with a light that hinted at both nostalgia and sorrow. I could picture the lush forests, thick with towering evergreens, their scent a blend of pine and earth that clung to the skin like a second layer. "My mother was a healer," she continued, her gaze shifting to the window, where shadows danced as the sun dipped lower. "She had this incredible ability to connect with nature. It was as if she could hear its secrets." Her voice dropped, becoming almost conspiratorial, inviting me into her world of enchantment. "She knew every herb, every root. People would come from all over to seek her help, for everything from a common cold to heartache."

As she spoke, the room seemed to melt away, replaced by images of a quaint cottage nestled in the woods, where the sound of bubbling brooks mingled with the sweet scent of lavender. I could see her mother, a figure of grace and wisdom, guiding Sophie through the art of healing, her hands moving deftly through the garden as she plucked herbs with a reverence that bordered on worship. "It was beautiful," Sophie sighed, a wistful smile gracing her lips, "but it was also isolating. We were different, you know? People didn't understand us."

I leaned in closer, entranced by the emotion in her voice. "What happened?" I asked, the question hanging in the air like a dare. There was a shadow that crossed her face, a flicker of something darker. "As I grew older, the attention shifted from my mother to me," she admitted, her fingers tightening into fists. "They saw my potential, my gifts, but they didn't see me. They only saw what I could offer."

Her words wrapped around me, drawing me deeper into her story. I could almost feel the chill of betrayal that had settled in her heart, a shiver that echoed against the warmth of her memories. "There were whispers in the town," she continued, her brow furrowing. "People came with their requests, but behind their eyes was greed, a hunger for power. They wanted to harness what I could do, twisting it into something I never wanted to be part of."

I swallowed hard, anger simmering just beneath the surface. "That's terrible," I murmured, my heart aching for the girl she had once been. The betrayal she felt rippled through me, the sharp edges of her recollections cutting into my own sense of safety. "What did you do?"

"I ran," she said simply, the weight of those two syllables heavy in the air. "I left. I thought if I distanced myself from it all, I could escape the shadows that loomed over our lives." Her eyes met mine, and I could see the depth of her pain. "But those shadows have a way of following you, don't they?"

The atmosphere in the room shifted, thickening like fog rolling in from the ocean. I could sense the raw truth in her words, the realization that no matter how far one goes, the past has a relentless grip. "You're not alone anymore," I said, my voice stronger than I felt. "We're in this together. Whatever those shadows are, we'll face them."

Her smile was faint but genuine, a flicker of light in the gloom that threatened to engulf us. "You're too good to me," she replied, shaking her head as if to dismiss the weight of my promise. "I don't want to drag you into my mess. You deserve better."

"I'm already in it," I countered, leaning back slightly but holding her gaze steady. "You're stuck with me now." The warmth in her eyes shifted, softening the hard edges of her worry. There was something liberating in that moment, a connection forged not just by our current struggles but by the vulnerabilities we dared to share.

Sophie hesitated, as if weighing the gravity of my words. "I just—" she began, then faltered. "What if my past becomes a danger to you? What if those people come looking for me?"

The thought chilled me, but I pushed it aside, unwilling to let fear creep into our sanctuary. "Then we'll face them together. We'll figure it out as we go. You're not meant to bear this alone." I reached out, placing my hand over hers, feeling the warmth radiating from her skin.

For a moment, the world outside faded, and all that existed was the quiet promise in the air. In her gaze, I could see the glimmer of hope mingling with the uncertainty, and I knew that whatever lay ahead, we would navigate the treacherous waters together.

"I'll tell you more," she said finally, her voice softening. "I need you to understand where I come from."

As she began to weave the intricate tapestry of her life, I leaned in, listening intently. Each word painted vivid pictures of a life both beautiful and cruel, of the vibrant colors of nature intertwined with the dark threads of human desire. It was a story of resilience, and with every sentence, my resolve deepened. I would stand by her side, come what may, and together we would conquer the shadows that dared to rise against us.

Sophie's words flowed like a river, and with each moment, the barriers between us began to dissolve. The sunlight faded into a delicate twilight, casting a dreamy glow across the room as shadows deepened. The evening air grew cooler, whispering through the open window, carrying with it the faint scent of blooming jasmine from the garden below. I could feel the warmth of her hand beneath mine, a tether to her past that I was determined to understand.

"After I left, I thought I was free," she continued, her voice a blend of wistfulness and strength. "But freedom has a way of eluding you when the past clings like a vine around your throat." Her gaze dropped, her fingers fidgeting with a loose thread on the couch. "I tried to build a new life, to bury the memories, but they were relentless. The whispers of my childhood followed me, mocking my attempts to forget."

I leaned closer, intrigued. "What did you do then? Did you go back?" The question hung in the air, as delicate as the evening mist that rolled in from the coast, and I could see her shudder slightly at the thought.

"No, never back to that town. I relocated, hoping the distance would smother the echoes." Her smile was bittersweet, a fleeting reminder of the innocence that had slipped through her fingers. "I went to a city filled with noise and chaos. The kind of place where nobody cared who you were or what you could do. It felt liberating at first."

A glimmer of a memory danced behind her eyes, a reflection of streetlights against wet pavement, bustling cafes, and the intoxicating rhythm of urban life. "But then," she sighed, "the city was just a different kind of cage. I lost myself in the crowds, yet I could still feel their eyes—those who sensed I was different, who sought to reclaim what they believed belonged to them."

"Did you ever confront them?" I asked, my curiosity piqued. "You could've faced them down. Showed them that you weren't afraid."

She chuckled softly, the sound laced with a hint of disbelief. "You have quite the imagination, don't you? Confronting them wasn't an option. They were shadows in the night, slippery and elusive. It wasn't until I met Alex that I learned how to fight back."

"Alex?" The name hung in the air like a spell, and my heart tightened instinctively. "Who's Alex?"

Her expression shifted, a flicker of warmth blooming in her eyes. "He was... well, he was a storm wrapped in charm. I met him at a farmers' market. I was selling herbal tinctures, trying to make ends meet." She smiled, lost in the memory. "He approached me with this ridiculous smile and asked if I had anything for 'a broken heart.' The look on his face told me he was joking, but I knew he was serious. There was an ache in his voice."

The image of Sophie at a bustling market filled my mind, her hands stained with the colors of nature, laughter bubbling around her as she navigated through the crowd. "What did you say?" I asked, enraptured by her storytelling.

"I told him to avoid heartbreak altogether. That it was a dangerous herb to consume." She laughed lightly, her eyes sparkling. "But then, he insisted on buying a bottle. The chemistry was immediate, like mixing oil and water."

"Were you two...?" My heart raced, a tumult of emotions surging at the thought of another person occupying such a significant space in her life.

"Complicated," she replied, her tone softening. "He was drawn to the same magic that had ensnared others, yet he was different. He didn't want to exploit it. He wanted to understand. He helped me learn to harness my gifts, to embrace the parts of myself I had spent years trying to hide." Her smile faded momentarily. "But even he had his shadows. They took him, and in the end, I lost him to the very darkness I had sought to escape."

I felt a pang of sympathy surge within me. "I'm so sorry," I whispered, wishing to reach through her pain. "That must have been devastating."

"It was," she replied, a tremor in her voice. "But that's when I truly understood what it meant to fight. I learned that healing isn't just about what you can do for others; it's about confronting your demons, even if they're made of memories."

Her words resonated deeply within me, echoing in the crevices of my own heart. "And you're still fighting," I murmured, emboldened by the fire I saw igniting in her eyes. "You're not just a survivor, Sophie. You're a warrior."

A small smile played on her lips as she met my gaze, the vulnerability of her past transformed into a strength that radiated warmth. "Thanks, but even warriors need allies." She glanced toward the window, where the night had unfurled its inky cloak, the stars blinking awake one by one. "Sometimes, the greatest battles come from within. But when the shadows begin to creep in, it's nice to know someone is there to help you light a path."

I nodded, feeling the gravity of our shared moment. We were both navigating the treacherous waters of our histories, each carrying burdens that threatened to drag us under. Yet, amidst the uncertainty, there was a fragile hope growing between us, a flicker of light in the dark.

"What's next for you?" I asked, the curiosity bubbling up within me. "What are you going to do now that you've faced some of the shadows?"

She pondered my question, her brow furrowing in thought. "I suppose it's about reclaiming my narrative," she mused. "I've spent too long running away, too long letting the past define me. I want to rewrite the story—to channel my gifts, to find a way to protect myself and the ones I care about."

"Maybe we can figure it out together," I suggested, excitement coursing through me. "We could even make a plan, confront the people who threaten you. I'm no healer, but I can be a damn good distraction."

The corner of her mouth lifted, the tension easing just a bit. "You really think so?"

"Absolutely. I can create a diversion. It could be epic," I joked, mimicking an exaggerated flourish. "I could wear a superhero cape, run around screaming, 'Fear not, citizens! The healer is here!'"

She laughed, a sound that felt like music to my ears, and I couldn't help but join her. In that moment, the weight of the world shifted, the laughter acting as a balm against the shadows lingering just beyond our reach.

"Okay, but you have to promise me one thing," she said, her expression suddenly serious.

"Anything," I replied, heart racing at the intensity in her gaze.

"Promise you won't let me retreat into my fears again. That you'll pull me back when I start to slip."

"I promise," I vowed, feeling the warmth of our shared resolve wrap around us like a blanket. Whatever lay ahead, we would face it together, lighting the way through the darkness, hand in hand.

As night deepened, the room glowed softly in the light of the flickering candles I had lit earlier, casting playful shadows against the walls. Sophie's laughter still echoed in my mind, brightening the heaviness of the stories she had shared. The world outside had grown quiet, the stars peeking through the velvety darkness, and I felt the magnetic pull of her presence, the undeniable bond that tethered us together in this moment of shared vulnerability.

"Okay, so we have our game plan," I said, my voice steady as I leaned back against the couch, trying to project confidence. "But how do we actually confront your past? Where do we start?" I could feel the weight of my own questions pressing down on us, the gravity of what lay ahead tangible in the air.

Sophie tapped her finger against her chin thoughtfully, a playful smirk crossing her lips. "I suppose we could begin with a good old-fashioned stakeout. You know, watch the shadows from the safety of the bushes like true detectives."

"Are we channeling our inner spies now?" I chuckled, imagining us crouched behind hedges, clad in dark clothing, clutching binoculars as if we were in some cinematic thriller. "I'll bring the popcorn for our vigilante movie night."

"Popcorn and binoculars," she teased, the sparkle in her eyes lifting my spirits. "That's the spirit! But really, I think we need to go back to the town. I haven't faced it since I left, and I need to know what those whispers have become."

My heart sank slightly at the thought. The place she had described felt like a ghost town, populated with specters from her past. "Are you sure about this? It could be dangerous."

"Dangerous? Please. I've survived worse. Plus, I'll have you," she countered, her tone defiant. "And we'll go together. Strength in numbers and all that."

The determination in her voice made my heart race, not just with fear but with an electric thrill. I wanted to protect her, yet I felt equally compelled to face whatever shadows awaited us. "Alright," I conceded, "but we go in with a plan. We find information, we observe, and if we need to bolt, we bolt."

"Deal," she said, extending her hand, and I shook it with a firm grip, sealing our pact. The thrill of adventure coursed through my veins, mingling with an undercurrent of anxiety.

As we spoke, the atmosphere in the room shifted; the air thickened with unspoken fears, anticipation blending with uncertainty. Sophie shifted on the couch, leaning in closer, her voice dropping to a whisper. "But I need to warn you, there's something else. Something I haven't told you."

My breath hitched, curiosity mingling with apprehension. "What is it?"

"There's someone I fear may still be lurking in the shadows. Someone from my past who wasn't just after my abilities but wanted me for himself."

The tension in the room tightened, a taut string waiting to snap. "Who? What do you mean 'wanted you for himself'?"

She hesitated, the flickering candlelight casting soft shadows across her face. "His name is Jonah. He was obsessed with the idea of harnessing my power. When I refused to play along with his twisted plans, he turned dangerous."

"Obsessed?" I echoed, the word sending chills down my spine. "What did he do?"

"I don't want to go into details right now," she replied, her eyes darting toward the window as if sensing something lurking just outside. "But he was relentless. After I left Oregon, I thought I had escaped him. But now... I can't shake the feeling that he might be looking for me."

A chill ran through me at her words. "You think he'll come after you again?"

"I don't know," she admitted, her voice trembling slightly. "But I can't ignore the feeling that he knows I'm back in town, that he can smell the magic I carry. He might be waiting, lurking just beyond the edges of my memory, ready to strike."

The air grew heavier, tension crackling like static electricity. "We'll be prepared," I said, determination flowing through me. "We'll keep our eyes peeled, and if he shows up, we'll be ready."

Sophie nodded, but I could see the flicker of doubt in her eyes. "It's not just him, you know. The entire town is filled with memories that could come flooding back. People who were kind one minute and turned against me the next."

"Then we'll confront them together," I reassured her, though I could feel a knot forming in my stomach. "We'll shine a light on those shadows. They can't hold power over you if you face them head-on."

Sophie met my gaze, the fierce spark of hope mingling with apprehension. "Alright, then. Let's prepare for tomorrow."

The night grew deeper, the atmosphere charged with unspoken emotions, a heady mixture of fear and excitement. We began discussing logistics, scribbling plans and ideas on a notepad. As the candlelight flickered, I felt an unshakeable sense of unity between us, an unspoken promise that we would not falter in the face of adversity.

Suddenly, a loud crash shattered the stillness, the sound echoing through the open window. My heart jumped into my throat as I exchanged a startled glance with Sophie. "What was that?" she whispered, her voice barely audible above the pounding of my heart.

"I have no idea," I said, standing up and moving toward the window. The world outside was cloaked in darkness, the streetlights flickering ominously. "Stay here. I'll check it out."

"Wait!" she hissed, grabbing my arm. "What if it's him?"

"Then I'll be ready," I replied, shaking off her grip but keeping my voice steady. "Just stay back."

As I peered out into the night, a figure stood silhouetted against the distant glow of the streetlight, half-hidden in shadow. My breath caught as the silhouette turned, revealing a face that sent a jolt of recognition through me. It was a face I thought I'd never see again, and the realization gripped my heart with icy fingers.

"Who the hell are you?" I murmured, the question lingering in the air like a dark omen as I turned to Sophie.

But before I could voice my fear, the figure took a step closer, and I felt a shiver run down my spine, the air thickening with tension as the shadows deepened.

Chapter 12: Seeds of Doubt

The late afternoon sun cast a warm golden hue over the farm, painting the rows of corn with an ethereal glow. I stood on the porch of the old wooden house, its splintered railings telling stories of summers past, and stared out at the land we had fought so hard to protect. The breeze carried the sweet scent of freshly tilled earth mingling with the faint aroma of wildflowers that dared to bloom amidst the encroaching chaos. Yet, despite the picturesque scene, a gnawing anxiety clawed at my insides, threatening to unravel the very fabric of my resolve.

"Hey, are you going to stare at the sunset all day or do you plan to help me with this?" Sophie's voice cut through my reverie, laced with a playful challenge. She was kneeling in the garden, her hands buried in the rich soil, a stark contrast to the pristine image of nature I had painted in my mind. Her hair, a cascade of dark curls, shimmered in the sunlight, each tendril capturing glimmers of gold as she worked. The sight of her brought a fleeting smile to my lips, yet it felt fragile against the backdrop of the storm brewing just beyond our sanctuary.

"I thought you enjoyed my company," I teased, forcing lightness into my tone, even as my heart felt like it was dragging anchors. She looked up, her brow furrowing slightly as she wiped her hands on her denim overalls.

"I do, but I could use a little help here. Unless you're too busy planning your dramatic confrontation with AgriCorp?" she said, a smirk dancing on her lips, but her eyes held a depth that betrayed her worry.

I sighed, dropping the act. "I don't want to think about them right now. They're spreading rumors, Sophie. They're trying to turn the community against us."

Her expression shifted, the levity of the moment evaporating like dew under the harsh glare of reality. "What have they said?"

"Just the usual—claiming you're a fraud, that we're using the farm for some sort of scam. It's maddening." I paced back and forth on the porch, my boots thumping against the worn wood. "I can't believe they're stooping so low."

"People love a good scandal," she replied, her voice steady despite the turmoil in her eyes. "Especially if it means they can ignore the real issues, like the terrible practices AgriCorp uses."

"Exactly," I said, stopping to lean against the porch rail, my heart aching with the weight of uncertainty. "But what do we do? I can't lose you, Sophie. You're the heart of this place. Without you..."

"Without me, you'd still have the land. You'd still have your dreams." She offered a soft smile, but it didn't quite reach her eyes. "Besides, I'm not going anywhere. We're in this together, remember?"

I wanted to believe her. I truly did. But the insidious whisper of doubt curled around my thoughts like smoke. AgriCorp had a way of twisting narratives, and I was terrified that one day, someone might actually believe them. The tension of the last few weeks had eroded our once unshakeable bond, leaving cracks in the trust I had fought to cultivate. "I just need you to trust me, Sophie. I know this is hard, but we'll figure it out. Together."

"Trust?" she echoed, her voice barely above a whisper. "It's not trust I'm worried about, but how far they're willing to go." Her gaze drifted towards the fields, where the sun dipped lower, casting long shadows that danced ominously across the crops. "Have you seen their latest advertisements? They're practically villainous."

"Right? Like they're straight out of a cheap horror movie," I chuckled, but my laughter felt hollow. "They're trying to paint us as the bad guys while they keep poisoning the land. How can people not see through it?"

"Fear makes for a convincing narrative." Sophie's expression darkened, her brow creasing with concern. "We've got to stand firm. Maybe we need to hold a community meeting, get everyone together, and address these rumors head-on."

"That could backfire," I warned, the unease crawling back into my veins. "What if more people show up believing AgriCorp's lies?"

"Then we counter them with the truth." Her determination sparked a flicker of hope within me. "We need to remind them what we're fighting for. We can't let fear silence us."

As she spoke, I felt my resolve begin to strengthen. If we were going to combat the smear campaign, we had to do it with passion and clarity. I took a deep breath, letting the crisp evening air fill my lungs, grounding myself in the present. "You're right. It's time we took the narrative back. We can't let them define our story."

Sophie's smile returned, igniting a warmth that spread through me. "Then let's do it. Let's gather the community, remind them what we're all about."

"Together," I affirmed, but beneath that promise lay an unspoken fear. What if our efforts weren't enough? What if the seeds of doubt AgriCorp had sown took root and flourished, choking out everything we had fought for? I pushed the thought aside, willing myself to focus on the task ahead. We had to be brave, to stand together against the tide, even if the waves of uncertainty threatened to pull us under.

In the fading light, as the shadows lengthened and night approached, I felt a renewed sense of purpose take hold. With Sophie by my side, I was ready to face whatever darkness awaited us. The fight was far from over, but the flame of our resolve flickered brightly, lighting the path forward into the unknown.

The next morning dawned with a heavy mist, cloaking the farm in an ethereal veil that mirrored the uncertainty swirling in my mind. I stood at the kitchen window, cradling a steaming mug of coffee, the rich aroma a comforting balm against the weight of impending decisions. Sophie was already outside, her silhouette barely visible through the haze as she tended to the garden, lost in her rhythm of planting and nurturing. The sight of her, steadfast and determined, nudged me toward action, but the doubts lingered like shadows, refusing to dissipate.

"Coffee won't fix the world's problems, you know," Sophie called out, her voice teasing yet somehow piercing through the thick fog of my thoughts. I turned to see her approaching the porch, her hands still dusty from the soil. "But it does help with the existential dread."

"Ah, a philosopher in the morning light!" I replied, setting my mug down with a clatter. "What do you suggest we do then? Start an impromptu gardening club? Maybe hold a poetry slam about sustainable farming?"

Her laughter rang out, bright and infectious, cutting through my gloom. "Why not? We can lure the community in with promises of fresh vegetables and pretentious sonnets about kale."

"Pretentious? I can't believe you'd question the depth of my poetic prowess," I said, mock offense coloring my tone. "Kale deserves an ode, if not a full-on ballad."

"Only if you plan to recite it while planting it," she challenged, folding her arms and raising an eyebrow in that infuriatingly charming way that sent my heart racing. "But honestly, I'm more interested in a real plan. We need to organize that meeting."

The lightness of our banter faded as the reality of our situation settled back in. "Right. A community meeting." I leaned against the porch railing, the wood rough against my palms. "Do you really think it'll make a difference?"

"It has to," she said, her tone shifting to something more earnest. "If we don't stand up now, we risk letting AgriCorp control the narrative. We can't let fear win."

The determination in her eyes lit a fire within me. "Okay, let's do it. We'll gather everyone and tell them the truth—why we're doing this and how AgriCorp is lying to them."

"Great!" she replied, her enthusiasm palpable. "Let's start spreading the word. I'll make a few calls to get the word out. You can work your charm on our neighbors. Maybe bake some cookies?"

"Ah, the age-old tactic of bribing people with baked goods." I grinned, appreciating how the simple act of planning together brought a sense of unity. "Fine, but only if we can make them those new chocolate chip recipes I found."

"Deal. But let's get moving before the mist turns to rain. I need to wrangle those pesky weeds before they stage a coup."

As we set to work, the air buzzed with a shared purpose. We walked through the rows of crops, our conversation flowing as freely as the breeze rustling the leaves. We discussed our strategy, what to say, how to frame our fight, and how we could reassure the community that we were in this together. Each word felt like an anchor, grounding us in our mission, fortifying our resolve.

Sophie paused by a particularly unruly patch of weeds, her brow creased in concentration. "You know," she said, her voice laced with a playful seriousness, "there are some folks out there who might just need a reminder of who we are and why this matters."

"Like the time old Mrs. Bennett thought I was trying to steal her prize-winning zucchinis?" I quipped. "She nearly chased me off the property with her broom."

"Exactly! If we can get them to remember that this is about community, about keeping AgriCorp from choking the life out of our land, we'll have them on our side."

Our laughter drifted into the air, a brief moment of levity amid the storm clouds looming over us. As we worked side by side, the rhythm of our movements fell into sync, a dance of sorts, where every weed pulled felt like a small victory against the tide of negativity we were up against.

As the day wore on, we finalized the details of the meeting, deciding on the barn as our venue. Its weathered wooden beams and rustic charm would provide the perfect backdrop for our message of resilience. I could already picture our neighbors filtering in, some curious, some skeptical, but hopefully all willing to listen.

Just as we wrapped up our planning, a familiar car rumbled up the gravel driveway, pulling me from my thoughts. I recognized the deep blue sedan belonging to James, the local farmer and a longtime ally. He stepped out, his brow furrowed as he approached us, clearly burdened by something heavy.

"Hey, you two," he greeted, his voice low. "I heard about what's been happening. I wanted to see how you're holding up."

"Like a field in drought," I replied with a half-hearted smile, gesturing for him to join us on the porch. "What's going on in your neck of the woods?"

"Rumors are flying, and it seems AgriCorp is working overtime. I got a call from a couple of folks saying they heard you two were swindling everyone."

Sophie tensed beside me, and I felt the knot in my stomach tighten. "Do you think they'll buy it?"

James shook his head, his expression grim. "Some might. They've got a lot of money and a slick marketing team behind them. But I know you both. I trust you."

"Thank you," Sophie said softly, her voice brimming with gratitude. "We're planning a community meeting to set the record straight."

"Count me in," he replied without hesitation. "I'll spread the word. If we're going to take a stand, we'll need everyone on board. We can't let them isolate you."

"Exactly," I said, my heart swelling with a mixture of relief and renewed determination. "We're in this together, and we need to show them that we're not backing down."

As we stood together, united by a common goal, I felt a flicker of hope ignite within me. Perhaps we weren't as alone as I had feared. Perhaps the bonds of community were stronger than the poisonous seeds AgriCorp sought to sow. The fight was just beginning, and with allies like James and Sophie, I felt ready to face whatever challenges lay ahead.

As dusk began to settle, painting the sky in hues of lavender and burnt orange, I could feel the anticipation buzzing in the air. The barn, our makeshift battleground, had transformed from a mere storage space into a gathering place for our community. Straw bales formed a makeshift seating area, and strings of fairy lights, borrowed from Sophie's collection, hung overhead, casting a warm glow that belied the storm of tension brewing beneath the surface.

I paced back and forth, the wooden floor creaking beneath my boots as I ran through my notes one last time. This wasn't just about dispelling rumors; it was about reclaiming our narrative and reestablishing trust. "This is it," I muttered to myself, rehearsing the words that felt both empowering and daunting.

"Just don't trip over your own bravado," Sophie teased, entering the barn with a basket of cookies balanced on her hip, a cheeky grin plastered on her face. "I brought reinforcements."

"Are those secret weapon cookies?" I asked, eyeing the basket with a mixture of hope and hunger.

"Absolutely! The kind that makes people feel guilty for ever doubting us." She winked, setting the basket down as she scanned the barn. "How many do you think will actually show up?"

"I don't know, but I'm hoping for a good turnout. At least the folks who know we're not frauds."

Sophie chuckled, folding her arms. "As long as you don't wax poetic about kale, we should be fine."

Just then, the first few neighbors trickled in, curiosity lighting their faces. Old Mr. Reynolds, with his straw hat and weathered hands, shuffled in, followed closely by the Johnsons, whose laughter echoed like music. The barn gradually filled, and I could feel the weight of their collective gaze upon us, some expectant, others skeptical.

"Are we going to sit down and eat those cookies, or are we going to stand here all night?" Mr. Reynolds asked, eyeing the basket with a twinkle in his eye.

"Only if you promise not to critique my baking skills," Sophie quipped, her eyes sparkling with mischief.

The laughter that followed helped to ease the tension coiling in my stomach. As I glanced around at the familiar faces, I felt a surge of determination. It was now or never. I stepped forward, my heart pounding like a drum, the warmth of the barn wrapping around me like a blanket.

"Thank you all for coming tonight. I know there's been a lot of chatter lately," I began, my voice steady yet tinged with vulnerability. "And I want to address those rumors head-on. We're here because we care about this community, this land, and the future of sustainable farming."

I paused, scanning the faces before me, searching for a flicker of understanding. "Sophie and I have worked tirelessly to bring something new to this farm, something that honors our roots while also looking to the future. But AgriCorp has decided to make us their target."

Murmurs rippled through the crowd, some nodding, while others exchanged wary glances. I could feel the weight of skepticism in the air, thick enough to cut with a knife.

"Let's be honest. AgriCorp is scared," Sophie chimed in, her voice rising with passion. "Scared of what we represent. They're trying to paint us as frauds because they know we stand for something different."

"Why would we believe anything AgriCorp says?" someone shouted from the back, the voice rising with anger. "They've been ruining this land for years!"

"Exactly!" I said, seizing the momentum. "We're fighting for our land, our community, and our future. We can't let their lies drown us out."

As the room filled with murmurs of agreement, I felt the tide shifting. The energy began to pulse, building into something hopeful. Sophie passed out cookies as if she were distributing medals of valor, her smile infectious, making everyone feel a part of something larger than themselves.

Then, just as the atmosphere began to crackle with camaraderie, the barn doors swung open with a crash, and the cool evening air rushed in like an unwelcome guest. The tall figure of Sheriff Daniels stood in the entrance, his expression stern, casting a long shadow over our gathering.

"Evening," he said, his voice echoing in the sudden silence. "I hope I'm not interrupting."

An uncomfortable hush descended as he stepped inside, the warmth of the barn contrasting sharply with the chill of his presence. "I'm here about the complaints regarding this meeting," he continued, glancing around at the assembled neighbors.

"What complaints?" I managed, my heart racing as I exchanged worried glances with Sophie. "This is a community gathering. We have the right to meet."

"AgriCorp has raised concerns about your little get-together," he replied, his eyes scanning the crowd. "They're claiming you're inciting unrest, stirring trouble."

"Trouble?" I echoed incredulously, disbelief rippling through me. "We're simply sharing information. We're fighting for our rights!"

"Rights or not, you need to disperse. If they press charges, I can't protect you," he warned, his voice lowering ominously. "You all know AgriCorp doesn't play fair. You might be risking more than you realize."

Gasps erupted from the audience, tension crackling like static electricity. I could feel the fear settle over the crowd like a thick fog.

"Wait," Sophie interjected, stepping forward. "Are you really going to let them intimidate us into silence? This isn't just about us; it's about everyone who cares about this land!"

"Do you really want to go to war against a corporation with deep pockets?" Sheriff Daniels asked, his tone hardening.

"What's the alternative?" I shot back, my frustration boiling over. "To sit quietly while they destroy everything we love?"

The sheriff hesitated, and for a brief moment, uncertainty flickered in his eyes. But before he could respond, a voice from the back called out, "If we back down now, we'll never get a second chance!"

"Exactly!" Sophie shouted, her voice ringing with conviction. "We're all in this together. We either stand up for what we believe in, or we let AgriCorp win."

The barn erupted in a wave of murmurs and shouts, emotions flaring like a wild fire. Sheriff Daniels stood firm, but I could see the tension in his jaw, the way his shoulders squared.

Just then, a figure appeared behind him, stepping into the light. It was Ethan, a representative from AgriCorp, wearing that all-too-familiar smug grin. He leaned casually against the doorframe, arms crossed, and surveyed the scene with a predatory gleam in his eyes.

"Looks like you all have made quite a ruckus," he said, his tone dripping with condescension. "How charming to see you banding together in a futile attempt to resist progress."

A low murmur spread through the crowd, a mixture of anger and confusion, and I felt the air thicken with tension.

"Futile?" I echoed, stepping forward to confront him. "You think we'll let you destroy our community without a fight?"

"Oh, I'm counting on the fight," he replied, his smile widening. "Because the truth is, I thrive on it. It's the chaos that draws the best reactions."

Sophie shot me a look, her eyes filled with determination, but I could see the flicker of fear behind her resolve. The room vibrated with the palpable tension of unspoken fears, and I knew we stood at a precipice, teetering between hope and despair.

Ethan took a step closer, and I could feel the weight of his gaze on me, almost daring me to make a move. "You have no idea what you're getting into, do you?" he said, a chilling edge to his voice. "But trust me, you'll find out soon enough."

And with that, he turned on his heel, leaving the door wide open behind him, the night spilling in like a dark omen. My heart raced as I realized the gravity of what had just transpired. The stakes had just been raised, and we were standing on the brink of a confrontation that could change everything.

Chapter 13: The Confrontation

The meeting room felt more like a lion's den than a corporate office, all sleek surfaces and sharp edges designed to intimidate. I took a seat at the long, glossy table, the reflective surface mirroring my apprehension as I faced the trio from AgriCorp. They sat in a huddle, a well-rehearsed trio of poise and calculated disdain. To the casual observer, they projected an air of confidence, but I could see the flickers of amusement in their eyes as they leaned back, waiting for me to lay out my demands.

"Let's cut to the chase," I began, forcing my voice to remain steady despite the gnawing tension in my gut. "You need to stop your smear campaign against Sophie. It's not just reckless; it's cruel." The words felt foreign, as if I was reciting lines from a poorly written play rather than speaking from my heart.

One of the representatives, a tall woman with meticulously styled hair that was as rigid as her smile, arched an eyebrow. "You do understand, don't you? This is business." Her voice was smooth, like honey poured over broken glass. "What we're doing is standard protocol when dealing with someone of your... significant influence. We simply wish to ensure that we have all relevant information before proceeding."

"Relevant information?" I shot back, unable to mask the rising heat in my tone. "You mean digging into her past like it's some kind of entertainment for you?" The words hung heavy in the air, met with silence. They exchanged glances, and I could almost hear the gears turning in their calculating minds.

"You underestimate us," a burly man interjected, leaning forward, his fingers steepled in front of him like a villain in a noir film. "We have resources at our disposal that can unravel her life piece by piece. And trust me, there are pieces that will be far from flattering." His voice dripped with mockery, and I could feel the blood rush to my cheeks, a rush of both fury and fear.

I inhaled deeply, envisioning Sophie's smile, the warmth of her laughter—moments I had fought so hard to protect. "You don't know who you're dealing with," I said, my voice quieter but steady, a calm in the storm of their arrogance. "She's not some pawn you can toy with. You're risking more than just her reputation. You're risking everything."

At this, the woman leaned back, crossing her arms, her expression shifting from amusement to something more sinister. "Oh, but that's where you're mistaken. We aren't risking anything. You are. Every word you utter in defense of her only strengthens our resolve. It makes for a more compelling narrative."

I felt a cold sweat prickling my skin. They reveled in this twisted game, and I was the unwitting player. "You think you can manipulate me into silence? You think I'll back down?" I fought to keep my voice steady. "You underestimate my commitment to Sophie. I won't let you tear her apart."

With that declaration, I stood up, the chair scraping loudly against the polished floor as I made my way to the door, determination propelling me forward. The laughter that followed was as chilling as it was condescending, a sound that echoed in my mind long after I stepped out into the cold hallway.

The fluorescent lights buzzed above, casting a harsh glow on my skin as I navigated the maze of corridors, each step resonating with the weight of their threats. I pulled my phone from my pocket, my fingers trembling slightly as I dialed Sophie's number. The sound of her voice was a balm against the tension, but it was also a reminder of the danger that now loomed over her.

"Hey, it's me," I said as soon as she answered, trying to keep my tone light, though the tremor betrayed me. "Just wanted to check in. How's your day going?"

"Busy! But good, I think. I'm just finalizing the plans for the charity event next week. How's everything with your meeting?" Her cheerful tone contrasted sharply with the storm brewing inside me.

"Not great. They're not backing down. I think they're going to dig into your past. I don't want you to worry, but I need you to be careful."

There was a pause, a moment of silence that stretched like a taut string ready to snap. "What do you mean? What are they planning to do?" Her voice trembled slightly, and I could almost see her brow furrowing in concern.

"They want to use your history against you, Soph. It's a cheap shot, and it's not fair. But I won't let them succeed. I promise you that." The words tumbled out before I could fully think them through, but they felt right.

"Why do they care so much about me? I've done nothing wrong."

I sighed, my heart aching for her confusion. "Because you're a threat to their plans, and when people feel threatened, they lash out. Just keep your guard up, okay? I'll figure something out."

"Be careful," she urged, her voice softening. "You know how they are. They won't play fair."

"I'm counting on it," I replied, a fire igniting within me at the challenge. As the conversation ended, I felt a surge of adrenaline mixed with a sense of foreboding. The stakes had never been higher, and the weight of Sophie's world rested heavily on my shoulders.

As I stepped out of the building, the brisk autumn air hit me like a slap, invigorating yet terrifying. I could feel the weight of AgriCorp's threats swirling around me, a malevolent fog that threatened to envelop everything I cared about. I glanced up at the sky, dark clouds gathering, mirroring the turmoil within.

It was time to play a different game—one where I set the rules and dictated the terms. The fight had only just begun.

The streets outside buzzed with the vibrant energy of early evening, but I felt the weight of the world pressing down on my shoulders. As I walked, the cacophony of honking cars and chattering pedestrians faded into the background, leaving only the relentless thumping of my heart. Each beat was a reminder of the challenge I faced, a pulse of urgency fueling my steps as I headed to the one place that always felt like a refuge: the coffee shop on the corner, with its worn wooden tables and the intoxicating aroma of roasted beans.

Pushing through the door, I was greeted by the familiar warmth that enveloped me like a hug. The cozy ambiance was punctuated by the low hum of conversation and the occasional hiss of the espresso machine, creating a perfect backdrop to gather my thoughts. I slid into my favorite seat by the window, the seat that overlooked the bustling street outside, and let out a sigh of relief.

"Hey, is that the face of someone who just had a delightful chat with corporate villains?" The teasing voice belonged to Jamie, the barista, who had a knack for reading people as well as he could read coffee grounds. His messy hair and playful grin were constants in my chaotic world.

"More like the face of someone who just walked into a den of snakes. I swear, they were practically hissing at me," I replied, forcing a laugh, though it felt hollow.

Jamie's expression shifted, his humor replaced by genuine concern. "What did they want this time? You're not still dealing with those AgriCorp jerks, are you?"

"Yeah, unfortunately." I leaned back, running a hand through my hair, trying to shake off the remnants of the meeting. "They want to dig into Sophie's past. It's like they think they can take a wrecking ball to her life and just walk away."

His brow furrowed as he filled a cup with steaming coffee, the rich aroma wafting toward me. "That's ridiculous. Sophie's a great person. Why would they even care?"

"They're scared of her. She has this uncanny ability to connect with people, to inspire them. If they think exposing her past will diminish that, they're sorely mistaken." I took a deep breath, allowing the caffeine to seep into my system, warming me from the inside. "I just don't know how far they'll go to make their point."

"You'll figure it out. You always do." He gave me an encouraging smile, a reminder that I wasn't alone in this fight. "Just make sure to take care of yourself, too, okay?"

The sentiment settled in my chest, a small flicker of comfort amid the turmoil. I nodded, grateful for his support, but my mind raced with the confrontation that lay ahead. With my coffee in hand, I stepped outside, the cool air invigorating me, sharpening my focus.

As I made my way down the street, my phone buzzed in my pocket. It was a message from Sophie, and a wave of warmth washed over me as I read her words: How did it go? I'm worried about you. Let's meet up later?

I typed back quickly, I'm okay. Just need to think. Let's grab dinner at our place later? I knew the sanctuary of our home, filled with soft lighting and the aroma of spices simmering on the stove, would be a balm for both of our frayed nerves.

Just as I hit send, a shadow crossed my path, and I looked up to find a figure blocking the sunlight. It was a man, tall and broad-shouldered, with an air of authority that sent a shiver down my spine.

"Fancy meeting you here," he said, his voice low and smooth like melted chocolate. It was Mark, one of the more unscrupulous executives from AgriCorp, his presence a stark reminder of the threats lurking in the shadows.

"Mark," I said, forcing the word through clenched teeth. "What do you want?"

He chuckled, an infuriating sound that rolled off his tongue like an invitation to a game I didn't want to play. "I was just in the neighborhood. Thought I'd drop by and see how you're holding up. You seemed a bit... agitated in the meeting."

"Agitated? That's one way to put it. I prefer 'fighting for what's right.'" I crossed my arms, channeling every ounce of defiance I could muster.

He stepped closer, his eyes glinting with amusement. "You should know by now that fighting doesn't always yield the results you desire. Sometimes, it's wiser to play the game. I could offer you a way to make this easier for you, you know."

"By backing off Sophie? Not a chance," I snapped, my heart racing.

"Ah, but think of the possibilities. We both know your little crusade is a losing battle. What if I told you I could help? You wouldn't have to fight alone." His smile widened, and I felt a chill creep into the air between us.

"Help? You mean manipulate?" I retorted, my voice laced with disdain. "I don't need your kind of help. I'd rather fight with my own two hands than be your puppet."

"Such fire," he said, mockingly impressed. "But don't be naive. You can't save her alone, you know. There are things lurking in her past that will come to light, things that will threaten everything she's built."

I took a step back, every instinct screaming at me to get away from him. "You're sick, Mark. You think you can scare me into submission? I won't let you hurt her."

"Suit yourself," he said, shrugging nonchalantly, though the threat hung thick in the air. "But remember, the deeper you dig, the more dirt you'll find. And when it comes to secrets, you never know what might bite back."

With that ominous parting remark, he turned and walked away, leaving me standing there, heart pounding, a whirlwind of anger and fear coursing through my veins. His words echoed in my mind, a chilling reminder of the stakes involved.

Determined to fight back, I marched toward home, every step igniting a fierce resolve. The thought of Sophie and her laughter, her spirit unyielding, fueled my determination. She deserved better than the machinations of AgriCorp and the threats they wielded like weapons.

Arriving at our apartment, I was met with the familiar scent of garlic and onions sizzling in a pan, a comfort that wrapped around me like a warm blanket. Sophie stood at the stove, her hair tied up in a messy bun, an apron adorned with cartoon cats hanging loosely around her. The sight of her brought a smile to my lips, even amid the chaos swirling in my head.

"Hey! I'm making your favorite," she said, glancing over her shoulder, her face lighting up. "I thought we could use a little comfort food after your meeting."

I stepped closer, wrapping my arms around her waist, inhaling the delicious aroma wafting from the pot. "You always know how to make everything better."

"Tell me what happened," she urged, turning to face me, her expression shifting from playful to serious. "You look like you've just seen a ghost."

And in that moment, as I looked into her eyes, I felt the weight of my earlier confrontation melt away, replaced by the fierce desire to shield her from the storm on the horizon. "Let's eat first. Then I'll tell you everything."

As we settled into our cozy routine, laughter mingled with the clinking of dishes, creating a sanctuary amid the brewing storm. But deep down, I knew that the fight was far from over. With each passing moment, the stakes grew higher, and the game was just beginning.

The evening passed in a blur of laughter and warmth, a stark contrast to the frigid reality outside our apartment. Sophie's culinary creations filled the air with rich, savory scents, the kind that made the world outside seem distant and unimportant. Each bite of her homemade lasagna was like a delicious armor, fortifying my resolve against the looming threats from AgriCorp.

As we settled onto the couch, plates balanced precariously on our laps, I tried to maintain the easy banter we both loved. "So, did you add a secret ingredient to this? Because it's dangerously good," I teased, nudging her playfully.

"Maybe. Or maybe it's just my charm that makes everything taste better," she shot back, her eyes sparkling. I couldn't help but chuckle at her confidence. It was moments like these that made everything else fade into the background.

But as I watched her, that nagging weight returned, creeping into the corners of my mind. It was only a matter of time before the truth about AgriCorp's intentions came crashing down around us. "Sophie," I began hesitantly, my playful demeanor slipping. "I need to talk to you about something important."

She set her fork down, the playful glint in her eyes shifting to concern. "You're scaring me a little. What's wrong?"

With a deep breath, I laid it all out—the threats, the games, and the unsettling charm of Mark. As I spoke, Sophie's expression hardened, her brows knitting together in worry. "They can't just do that! They can't invade my privacy like that!"

"I know it sounds terrible, but they think they can unravel your past and use it against you. It's twisted, but that's how they operate," I explained, trying to mask my own growing anxiety with a veneer of calm.

Her eyes flashed with determination, a spark I had come to admire. "I won't let them win. My past is my own, and I won't be bullied into silence."

The fire in her voice ignited something in me. "That's the spirit! But we need to strategize. I've been thinking... what if we turn the tables?"

"What do you mean?" she asked, leaning closer, curiosity mixed with a hint of mischief dancing in her gaze.

"We could dig into AgriCorp's dealings, find something they're hiding," I proposed, excitement bubbling up alongside the fear. "There must be something in their history that we can use."

"Like a corporate skeleton in the closet?" Sophie mused, her lips curving into a smile that set my heart racing. "I like the sound of that. Let's become detectives."

The thought was exhilarating, the adrenaline coursing through me like a jolt of electricity. "Exactly! We can work together, keep each other safe, and hit them where it hurts."

As we brainstormed, ideas tumbling out like popcorn, the atmosphere shifted. The tension that had gripped my chest began to loosen, replaced by a sense of purpose. Our laughter filled the room, a melody of defiance echoing against the oppressive shadows of the day.

The night wore on, filled with plotting and playful banter, until the soft glow of the lamp cast a warm halo around us. Sophie's laughter danced in the air, but just as I began to believe that perhaps we could indeed fight back, my phone buzzed on the coffee table, shattering the moment.

The name flashing on the screen froze me in place. It was Jamie.

"Should I answer it?" I asked, a mix of curiosity and dread flooding through me.

"Of course! Maybe he has intel we can use," Sophie encouraged, leaning forward, her eyes sparkling with interest.

I picked up the phone, glancing at the message. *Urgent! We need to talk. Meet me at the old warehouse by the docks in twenty minutes. I found something about AgriCorp.*

"What is it?" Sophie asked, her voice tinged with concern.

"I don't know. But it sounds serious," I replied, adrenaline rushing back as I shot a look at the clock. "I'll need to go. I can't ignore this."

"Be careful," she warned, her expression turning grave. "You know what they're capable of. You shouldn't go alone."

"I'll be fine," I insisted, though the knot in my stomach tightened at the thought of facing Jamie without her. "I'll call you the moment I know anything."

Sophie stood up, her determination unyielding. "I'm coming with you. I won't sit back and wait for you to handle this. We're in this together, remember?"

I opened my mouth to protest, but the look in her eyes silenced me. She was right; we were a team, and there was no way I could protect her if she insisted on joining the fray. "Alright, but stick close to me."

With that, we grabbed our jackets and slipped out into the cool night air, the city alive around us, yet cloaked in an unsettling darkness. The streets hummed with life, but every sound felt amplified, every shadow a potential threat.

As we approached the warehouse, the towering structure loomed ahead, an ominous silhouette against the moonlit sky. The air was thick with tension, and I could feel my heart pounding in my ears.

We stepped cautiously into the shadow of the warehouse, the musty scent of damp wood and rusted metal invading my senses. "Jamie?" I called out, my voice echoing through the cavernous space.

Silence answered, and a cold shiver crept down my spine. Just then, the sound of footsteps echoed behind us, and I spun around, heart racing. Sophie's hand found mine, our fingers interlocking as we turned to face the darkness.

The figure that emerged from the shadows was not Jamie, but a tall man dressed in a tailored suit, his face obscured by the dim light. "I've been expecting you," he said, his voice smooth and dangerously calm.

My stomach dropped. I knew that voice. "Mark," I spat, stepping in front of Sophie protectively. "What are you doing here?"

He smiled, a predatory gleam in his eyes that sent a wave of unease washing over me. "Oh, I thought we could have a little chat. You've been digging into my business, and that's simply unacceptable."

Before I could react, he snapped his fingers, and two men stepped out from the shadows behind him, their intentions clear as they approached.

Panic surged through me as I tightened my grip on Sophie's hand. "Run!" I shouted, pushing her back even as I prepared to confront this unwelcome encounter.

But before we could escape, Mark's voice cut through the chaos, chilling my blood. "You see, it's too late for that. I've already got what I need."

A sly grin spread across his face, and just as I turned to pull Sophie with me, a sharp sound rang through the air—a gunshot, echoing ominously in the empty space.

Chapter 14: An Unexpected Ally

The sun dipped low on the horizon, casting long shadows that danced across the fields like whispered secrets. I stood at the edge of my family's farm, a place that had once been a sanctuary but had recently become a battleground. The air was thick with tension, the scent of damp earth mingling with the distant tang of iron from the old tractor that had seen better days. I could almost hear the heartbeat of the land beneath my feet, a steady thrum that resonated with my own. But today, it felt like a call to arms rather than a lullaby.

"Don't let them get to you, Lila," I muttered to myself, trying to ignore the gnawing worry that had taken up residence in my stomach. My resolve had been wavering lately, especially with AgriCorp tightening its grip on the local farming community, swallowing smaller farms whole like a hungry beast. Their ominous presence loomed over us, a reminder that the innocent charm of our little town was rapidly being consumed by the machinery of corporate greed.

I heard a rustle behind me, and as I turned, my heart skipped a beat. Emerging from the edge of the woods was Claire, her silhouette framed against the dying light. Her hair tumbled down her shoulders in wild waves, catching the golden rays and almost glowing. She had always been a force of nature—unapologetically herself, with an insatiable curiosity that had fueled our childhood adventures. Now, as an investigative journalist, that same spark lit her eyes with a fire that felt contagious.

"Lila! I thought I'd find you here," she said, her voice breezy but with an undertone that suggested she understood the weight of the world resting on my shoulders. She moved closer, and I could see the determination etched in her features.

"What are you doing here, Claire?" I asked, though deep down, I hoped she'd come with a plan. The weight of our shared history hung between us, a connection forged in laughter and tears. "Shouldn't you be chasing down another political scandal?"

She waved her hand dismissively, a grin breaking across her face. "I can do both, you know. The latest scandal in the town hall can wait. Right now, I'm more interested in what's happening on your farm." Her eyes gleamed with mischief, and I felt a flicker of hope ignite within me.

I gestured for her to join me, and together we walked toward the weathered wooden fence that bordered the fields. The fading sunlight painted everything in soft hues of orange and purple, a beauty that belied the storm brewing within the community. "I don't know how much longer we can hold out, Claire," I confessed, the words tumbling from my lips like the wind scattering autumn leaves. "Every day, it feels like AgriCorp inches closer to swallowing us whole."

Claire's expression shifted, her playful demeanor giving way to a serious resolve. "Then we fight back," she said, her voice steady. "You and I both know the truth about what they're doing. We just need to shine a light on it."

The determination in her voice resonated with my spirit, and I felt a surge of energy flow through me. "But how? They have connections everywhere—politicians who turn a blind eye, a community that's too afraid to stand up. It feels impossible."

"Nothing worth fighting for ever is," she replied, her gaze fierce and unwavering. "Remember when we used to explore the woods behind your house? We never knew what we'd find, but we always faced it together. It's the same now. We dig into their practices, expose their corruption, and rally the community to take a stand. You're not alone in this, Lila."

Her words were like a clarion call, and the weight on my shoulders began to lighten, replaced by a sense of purpose. With Claire by my side, I felt the gears of my mind begin to turn, plotting a course of action. "Okay, let's do this," I said, a smile breaking through my earlier gloom. "But we'll need evidence—something concrete to bring to the town."

"Leave that to me," Claire replied, her enthusiasm infectious. "I've been gathering whispers—rumors of land deals, shady transactions, and politicians with their hands in AgriCorp's pockets. If we can get just one of those documents, it could unravel everything."

I nodded, the knot in my stomach loosening as ideas began to swirl like the wind whipping through the fields. "And we'll need to talk to the other farmers—find out what they've experienced, what they know."

"Exactly," Claire said, her eyes bright with excitement. "You're not just a farmer, Lila; you're a community leader. If anyone can rally them, it's you."

With her encouragement, I felt a warmth spread through me, a rekindling of the fire I thought had been extinguished. "You really think we can make a difference?"

"I know we can," she replied confidently. "It's not just about the farm, it's about all of us. We need to remind the community what we're fighting for—our land, our families, our future."

As we talked, the night deepened around us, the stars twinkling into existence, igniting the sky with hope. There was an electricity in the air, a feeling of impending change that sent shivers down my spine. With Claire's passion fueling me, I knew we were about to embark on a journey that would not only challenge AgriCorp but might also unearth hidden truths buried beneath layers of deception.

We spent the next hours sketching out a plan, our laughter echoing off the darkening fields, the sound a lifeline in the oppressive quiet. With each idea we tossed back and forth, the storm clouds of despair began to part, revealing a glimmer of possibility. The fight wouldn't be easy, but for the first time in weeks, I felt a flicker of hope lighting my way. Together, we would dig deep, unearth the truth, and breathe new life into a community on the brink of surrender.

As the last hues of twilight faded into night, I found myself drawn deeper into the comforting familiarity of my childhood home. The kitchen was aglow with the soft light of a single bulb, illuminating the worn oak table that had hosted countless family meals and whispered secrets. I busied myself with the kettle, letting the rhythmic bubbling lull my thoughts, but Claire's presence invigorated the air, stirring a tempest of ideas that refused to settle.

"Do you still have that old newspaper clippings album?" Claire asked, her voice breaking through my reverie. She leaned back against the counter, arms crossed, exuding that signature confidence that had always made me feel a little more courageous.

I chuckled, recalling how we used to glue our prized finds into that album like we were preserving treasures. "You mean the one with the fuzzy edges from my attempts at scrapbooking? It's in the attic, somewhere between a stack of childhood toys and the ghosts of my fifth-grade art projects."

Claire's eyes sparkled with mischief. "Perfect! I'll bet it's a veritable goldmine of local history. Those articles could be the backbone of our argument against AgriCorp. If they've been up to no good, there's bound to be something in there."

She was right; my mother had a penchant for preserving anything that hinted at scandal, corruption, or local heroes. I set the kettle aside and gestured for Claire to follow me up the narrow staircase. The wood creaked under our weight, a nostalgic reminder of our younger selves who had raced up and down these stairs, chasing dreams as we chased each other.

Once in the attic, the faint smell of cedar and dust greeted us like an old friend. Boxes labeled in my mother's elegant script lined the walls, each one a time capsule waiting to be opened. As I rummaged through the clutter, I could feel Claire's energy pulsing beside me, her impatience palpable.

"Ah! Here it is!" I exclaimed, pulling out a tattered cardboard box that had seen better days. Its lid struggled to stay intact as I pried it open, revealing the album nestled inside, surrounded by loose clippings and faded photographs. "I hope the memories don't crumble to dust as we sift through them."

Claire leaned in, her eyes wide with excitement as I flipped through pages filled with yellowing newspaper articles. We found pieces on everything from local festivals to the occasional scandal—like the infamous chicken debacle where several town council members were accused of favoritism in awarding contracts to a local poultry farm. The mere thought of it made me smile.

"Look at this one," Claire pointed at an article dated over a decade ago. "It mentions how AgriCorp wanted to buy out that small organic farm down the road. They painted a pretty picture of growth and development, but the owner didn't sell. It looks like they've been at this for a long time."

"Yeah, and it only got worse," I muttered, the weight of the past settling heavily on my shoulders. "The community lost trust in those who promised to protect us. How do you convince them that they need to fight back when they're already battle-weary?"

Claire's brow furrowed in concentration as she studied the article. "We show them. We remind them that they have a voice, and we highlight the risks AgriCorp poses—not just to our farms, but to their families, their lives. This isn't just about agriculture; it's about our community's identity."

With renewed vigor, we dove deeper into the album, unearthing articles that chronicled AgriCorp's gradual encroachment on our town. We found documents outlining zoning changes, questionable land deals, and politicians who had pocketed promises in exchange for silence. Each revelation was like a piece of ammunition added to our arsenal, igniting our resolve.

"I can't believe how many times they've pulled this nonsense," I remarked, flipping to a particularly damning piece about AgriCorp's involvement in a local land rezoning scandal. "It's as if they operate in the shadows, and we've all just turned a blind eye."

"Not anymore," Claire declared, her voice a rallying cry. "We need to craft a story that's impossible to ignore. One that brings all these threads together. We'll hold a town meeting and invite everyone—farmers, families, anyone who has a stake in this community. Together, we'll shine a light on the truth."

The idea of organizing a town meeting was thrilling, yet daunting. "What if no one shows up? What if they're too afraid?" The doubts snuck in, like an uninvited guest.

Claire's laughter filled the attic, a rich, comforting sound. "Fear is a terrible motivator, but it's also an incredible unifier. If we can get even a handful of people to share their stories, it'll create a ripple effect. We have to inspire hope, not just fear."

I considered her words, the truth behind them resonating deep within me. "You're right. If we can get even a few farmers willing to step forward and tell their stories, it might embolden others. People need to see they're not alone."

With a plan forming, we spent the rest of the night sifting through the archives of our past, each article reinforcing our mission. We filled a small folder with the most incriminating evidence, a tangible reminder of why we had embarked on this path. The attic, once a space of nostalgia, transformed into our headquarters, a war room for the battles to come.

As dawn broke over the horizon, spilling light through the attic window, a sense of purpose settled over me like a warm blanket. The uncertainties still lingered, but with Claire by my side, I felt emboldened. Together, we would face the giants that threatened our home. As I looked over at her, hunched over the table, the glow of the morning sun catching the determined set of her jaw, I couldn't help but smile.

"Ready to change the world?" I asked, my voice filled with a blend of excitement and trepidation.

"With you? Absolutely," Claire replied, a spark of adventure in her eyes.

The world felt wide open, full of potential and possibilities, and for the first time in what felt like ages, I was ready to embrace it.

With the first light of dawn filtering through the kitchen window, I could hardly contain the excitement buzzing in my veins. Claire and I had spent the night poring over old newspaper clippings, unearthing the sordid history of AgriCorp, and my mind was a whirlwind of possibilities. The prospect of organizing a town meeting felt less like a daunting task and more like a call to arms. Our sleepy town, once lulled into complacency, was ready to wake up and stand against the tide of corporate greed threatening to drown it.

"I'll make the flyers," I declared, my fingers itching to dive into the task. "Let's put something together that makes people want to show up. We need them to feel this is personal."

Claire nodded, already tapping away on her phone. "We can also leverage social media. I know some folks in town who are active online. If we can create a buzz, we'll attract attention."

I couldn't help but grin at her enthusiasm. "I can already picture it: 'Fight for Our Farm! Together Against AgriCorp!' It sounds like a rallying cry from an old war movie."

"Just without the cheesy music," Claire added with a chuckle, her fingers dancing across her screen. "But let's give it some flair. Maybe even a hashtag? FarmersUnite!"

As I wrote out slogans, my heart raced with each word. We were crafting not just a meeting but a movement. The thought of fellow farmers and families coming together ignited a fire in me that had been smoldering for far too long. It felt like reclaiming something that had been taken from us—a sense of community, a voice.

After breakfast, I headed into town to distribute flyers while Claire worked on social media strategies. The morning air was crisp, carrying the earthy scent of freshly turned soil and the promise of a new day. The sun peeked over the horizon, illuminating the small businesses that lined the main street. Each storefront seemed to pulse with potential, and as I posted the flyers, I found myself approaching familiar faces—old friends, neighbors, and those who had once stood shoulder to shoulder in the fight for our land.

"Lila! What's this all about?" asked Ms. Thompson, the owner of the local bakery, her brow furrowed as she read the flyer.

"AgriCorp is trying to take over, Ms. Thompson. We're organizing a town meeting to discuss what they've been up to and how we can fight back. We need everyone's voices."

Her eyes widened, and a flicker of recognition passed over her face. "I've heard the whispers. My sister's farm was one of the first they targeted. She's barely hanging on."

"Then come to the meeting!" I urged. "We need to band together. If they can take her farm, they can take any of ours."

As I made my way down the street, I could feel a shift in the atmosphere. People were listening, and the urgency in my voice was igniting something in them. By the time I returned home, I was nearly breathless with excitement. Claire was sitting at the kitchen table, her phone buzzing with notifications like a swarm of bees.

"We're already getting traction online!" she exclaimed, her eyes sparkling. "People are sharing the flyer, commenting, asking questions. They're interested, Lila!"

I sank into a chair across from her, the weight of the day starting to settle in. "Do you think it'll be enough? Will they show up?"

"Absolutely," she replied, her confidence unwavering. "People are fed up, and they're looking for a reason to fight back. All we have to do is give them one."

Just as we began to strategize for the meeting, my phone buzzed with a text from my neighbor, Jake. His message was short and clipped: "We need to talk. Urgent." My stomach twisted into knots as I glanced at Claire.

"Something's going on," I said, my voice barely above a whisper. "I need to meet him."

"Go," she urged, her expression shifting from excitement to concern. "I'll keep an eye on the social media responses. You might need to rally the troops again."

I grabbed my jacket and hurried out the door, my heart racing with a mix of anticipation and dread. Jake lived just down the road, his farmhouse a modest one-story that had been in his family for generations. As I walked, I could feel the pulse of the community around me, a collective heartbeat that echoed the urgency of our cause.

When I reached his front porch, Jake was pacing, his expression taut as he ran a hand through his unruly hair. "Lila," he said, his voice low and strained, "it's bad. I just heard from the Smiths. They're selling out to AgriCorp."

"What? No! They can't be serious!" The words tumbled from my lips, disbelief washing over me. The Smiths were a cornerstone of our community, a family that had weathered storms together. "They were one of the strongest supporters against them!"

"I know," Jake replied, shaking his head. "But they're scared, Lila. They received an offer they couldn't refuse—money upfront, no questions asked. I don't think they understand what that means for all of us."

A chill ran down my spine, the gravity of his words settling in like a winter fog. "If they're selling out, others will follow. It'll create a domino effect, and AgriCorp will tighten its grip even more."

Jake's gaze met mine, urgency flashing in his eyes. "We have to act now. We need to convince them not to sell. If they see that the community is rallying, it might sway them."

"Then let's go!" I said, adrenaline surging through me. "We can gather everyone and show the Smiths that they're not alone. That we all have something worth fighting for."

As we raced back toward the center of town, my heart pounded in sync with the determination building within me. We reached the park, a central gathering place where families had picnicked and children had played for generations. It was here that our meeting would unfold, and it felt like the perfect battleground.

But as we began to set up for the meeting, a black SUV pulled up, sleek and menacing against the backdrop of the park. My stomach dropped as a well-dressed man stepped out, his demeanor sharp, his expression unreadable. I didn't need to see the logo on the side of the vehicle to know who he was representing.

"Lila," Jake muttered beside me, his body tense. "What do you think he wants?"

I squared my shoulders, feeling the weight of our mission heavy on my chest. "Only one way to find out," I replied, stepping forward with resolve.

As I approached the man, he flashed a smile that didn't quite reach his eyes. "I believe you've been causing quite a stir," he said, his tone smooth, like honey laced with poison. "I'm here to offer you a proposition."

A chill ran down my spine, and every instinct screamed at me to back away. "We're not interested," I shot back, my voice firmer than I felt. "You're not welcome here."

His smile widened, revealing teeth too white against the growing shadows of the day. "I think you'll want to hear what I have to say. The choice is yours, Lila. Join us, or watch everything you care about slip away."

In that moment, with my heart racing and the weight of my community behind me, I knew we were standing on the precipice of a fight far greater than I had anticipated. The stakes were high, and the air was thick with tension. I was about to reply when a commotion erupted behind me, and I turned to see a crowd of familiar faces, but their expressions were filled with confusion and fear, each whisper echoing the threat that loomed before us.

Chapter 15: The Unraveling Threads

The scent of damp earth mingled with the crisp autumn air as I stepped into the town square, a place where whispers floated like leaves caught in a breeze. In the center stood the old oak tree, its gnarled branches extending like arms yearning for the warmth of the sun. Underneath its sprawling canopy, a small crowd gathered, a tapestry of faces lined with concern and curiosity. They were my neighbors, my friends—people I'd grown up with, whose laughter echoed in the streets and whose stories intertwined with mine. Today, however, their expressions were taut with unease, each furrowed brow a reminder of the looming threat we all faced.

Sophie stood a little way off, her posture rigid but her eyes glimmering with a spark I recognized all too well. It was the fire of determination that blazed when she put her mind to something, like a candle flickering defiantly against the wind. I had seen it before, of course, but not often enough for my comfort. Each time she summoned it, I wondered what shadows loomed in the recesses of her mind, what past had left its indelible mark on her spirit. Today, as we faced the beast that was AgriCorp, I could sense her anxiety radiating like heat from sun-baked pavement.

"Are you ready for this?" I asked, my voice barely above a whisper as I sidled up beside her. I tried to sound casual, but the tremor in my tone betrayed me.

She shot me a sideways glance, her lips curving into a wry smile that didn't quite reach her eyes. "Oh, sure. Nothing like a little public spectacle to bring out the best in us, right?" Her sarcasm hung in the air, a thin veil over the tension coursing through her.

A gust of wind whipped around us, carrying with it a chorus of murmurs. The town hall meeting was about to begin, and the weight of expectation settled heavily on my shoulders. I looked out at the crowd, noting the familiar faces mixed with new ones, a patchwork of the town's heart and soul. The local newspaper editor, a plump woman with a penchant for floral dresses, waved at me from the front. I felt a flicker of warmth in my chest, her presence a reminder that I was not alone in this.

"Let's go," I urged, nudging Sophie gently as I led her through the throng. We maneuvered around clusters of townsfolk, their conversations buzzing with the kind of anxious energy that could only arise from uncertainty. A small boy darted past, his laughter ringing like a bell, a fleeting reminder that innocence still thrived amid the chaos we were about to unleash.

As we took our seats on the wooden benches, I could see the faint glimmer of the podium up front. It stood there, an unassuming piece of furniture, but I knew it would soon become a battleground. The room was charged with a palpable tension, as if the very walls were holding their breath in anticipation.

I turned to Sophie, who was now staring straight ahead, her jaw clenched as if bracing for impact. "Remember," I said, my voice low, "this is about more than just us. It's about the whole town. We're the voice they've silenced for too long."

She nodded slowly, her fingers tapping nervously against her thigh. I reached out and squeezed her hand, a small gesture meant to ground us both.

Moments later, the town's mayor, a balding man with an insipid smile, stepped up to the microphone, his voice booming across the hall. "Thank you all for coming. Today, we're here to discuss the recent issues surrounding AgriCorp."

As he spoke, I felt my heart race in sync with the rhythm of his words. We had unearthed evidence of AgriCorp's corruption, a tangled web of deceit and manipulation that snaked through the highest echelons of our local government. Sophie and I had spent sleepless nights piecing together the fragments, uncovering contracts that reeked of bribery and meetings that reeked of collusion. The plan was simple yet terrifying: expose them here, under the weight of community scrutiny.

Sophie's hand tightened around mine as the mayor's speech droned on, setting the stage for our moment. "I understand there are some concerns about AgriCorp's practices, but I assure you, they have always operated within the law..." His words dripped with complacency, each syllable a carefully constructed shield for the truth.

Before I could stop myself, the words spilled out. "But what about the emails?" My voice rang clear, slicing through the fog of his rhetoric like a knife. "What about the hidden deals? The collusion with officials?"

Gasps echoed through the room, rippling like waves across a pond. I felt Sophie's grip on my hand loosen, surprise and admiration mixing in her expression. The mayor faltered, blinking at me as if I had slapped him.

"You can't just throw around accusations without proof!" he sputtered, his carefully cultivated facade beginning to crack.

"Can't I?" I shot back, fueled by a surge of adrenaline. "I have proof. And I'm not the only one." I gestured to Sophie, who was now standing beside me, her eyes ablaze with the fire of justice.

"It's time for the truth to come out!" she declared, her voice strong and unwavering. "We're tired of living in fear while you play games with our lives!"

The crowd shifted, murmurs growing louder, and for the first time, I felt the swell of hope rising within me. Perhaps this was the moment we had all been waiting for—the moment when the townspeople would rally together to reclaim their power.

But just as the tide began to turn, a figure loomed in the doorway, a silhouette that froze the air around us. My heart sank as I recognized him: a tall man in a crisp suit, the unmistakable emblem of AgriCorp emblazoned on his lapel. The chill that radiated from him cut through the warmth of our gathering, a reminder of the danger that still lurked in the shadows.

As he stepped forward, the room fell silent, the collective breath of the crowd hitching in anticipation. I glanced at Sophie, who had gone pale, her resolve wavering like a candle in a storm. "We can't back down now," I whispered fiercely, desperate to reignite the fire in her.

Her eyes met mine, and in that moment, I understood. This wasn't just about AgriCorp or the town. It was about confronting the demons we both carried, the shadows that threatened to consume us. We would face them together, no matter the cost.

The man from AgriCorp strode into the room, exuding an air of practiced confidence, his shoes polished to a shine that rivaled the cold glint in his eyes. He was the kind of person who could command a room without raising his voice, and as he approached the podium, I could feel the tension coil tighter, a rubber band ready to snap. The mayor faltered, visibly shaken by the intrusion, and for a fleeting moment, the façade of authority he wore like armor crumbled.

"Gentlemen, ladies," the stranger began, his voice smooth like a well-aged whiskey, "I assure you, we have nothing to fear. AgriCorp operates on the highest ethical standards. Any claims of misconduct are mere fabrications, born from a desire for disruption." He smiled, but there was something predatory about it, as if he were sizing us up for dinner.

I caught Sophie's eye, and the flicker of apprehension there sent a jolt through me. This was the moment we had prepared for—the confrontation, the truth-telling. Yet the words felt heavy on my tongue. "And what of the reports?" I shot back, my own voice rising with fervor. "The documented collusion? The payments under the table?"

The man leaned in, the slight tilt of his head a mixture of condescension and amusement. "Ah, the documents. So easily manipulated, dear friend. A signature here, a date there—who's to say they're authentic?" His tone was almost playful, as if he were toying with the crowd, and I could feel the collective breath of the audience hitch in disbelief.

"Perhaps a little investigation would prove otherwise," Sophie interjected, her voice steadier than mine, a steel resolve threading through her words. "Or perhaps you'd like to share your version of events with the authorities?"

A ripple of approval surged through the crowd, and I could sense a shift—a moment where we collectively realized we were not just spectators in this drama but the leading cast. But the man merely chuckled, the sound like ice cracking on a frozen lake. "Authorities? My dear, I am the authority here. You think you're playing a game of chess, but I've already moved the pieces."

"Chess, huh?" I replied, my sarcasm spilling out. "Is that why you're looking at us like pawns? Because I've got news for you: this game is far from over."

With a dismissive wave, he turned back to the audience. "You're all being misled by these two. They're desperate for attention, hoping to ride the coattails of a scandal." He gestured broadly, his arms sweeping like a conductor orchestrating a symphony of disbelief. "Do you really want to put your trust in them? Think of the consequences. Think of your livelihoods."

"Think of our futures!" Sophie shot back, her voice rising like a beacon in the storm. The fire in her eyes blazed brighter than before, and I could see the townsfolk start to rally behind her words, their faces a collage of uncertainty slowly morphing into determination. "We deserve transparency! We deserve to know what's really happening!"

A few brave souls started to clap, tentative at first, as if they were unsure whether they were supposed to be on our side. Then the applause swelled, building momentum, echoing off the high ceiling. The man's confident smile faltered slightly, revealing the cracks in his façade, but he quickly recovered, adopting an expression of condescension that suggested we were mere children playing dress-up.

"Very well," he said, his tone dripping with mockery, "let's talk about transparency. Let's talk about the little secrets you've both been keeping." His gaze landed heavily on Sophie, and for a moment, a silence enveloped us. "How about the time you fled from... what was it, your hometown? Something about a family scandal? How does that fit into your quest for truth?"

The air crackled with shock, the crowd gasping collectively, as if I had just thrown a bucket of ice water over everyone. I felt the weight of his words, a hammer striking at the delicate glass of Sophie's past. I turned to her, and I could see the flush creeping into her cheeks, the tension tightening her jaw as she steeled herself against the onslaught.

"What does that have to do with anything?" I demanded, my heart racing. "We're here to talk about AgriCorp, not Sophie's past."

"Ah, but context is everything, isn't it?" he countered smoothly. "You're both so eager to expose the truth, yet you forget that the truth can be a double-edged sword. Everyone has skeletons, and some are more eager to bury them than others."

I felt Sophie's hand slip from mine, and my stomach twisted. This was no longer just an argument about corruption; it had morphed into a personal attack, and I could see the cracks in her armor. But before I could respond, Sophie stepped forward, reclaiming her space with a fierce defiance that surprised even me.

"Sure, I made mistakes," she said, her voice trembling slightly but carrying an undeniable strength. "But what does that matter when we're facing something far greater than our pasts? AgriCorp is taking advantage of all of us. Don't let them distract you from the real issue here!"

The audience began to murmur again, the tide slowly turning in our favor. I could see resolve in their eyes as they began to connect the dots, not just between our pasts but between their lives and the manipulation that had seeped into our community.

"Exactly!" I chimed in, riding the wave of momentum. "We all have histories we're not proud of, but that doesn't negate our right to fight for our present and our future! We're here because we care about our town, and we will not be silenced!"

The applause surged again, louder this time, a cacophony of voices rising in unity. The man from AgriCorp shifted uncomfortably, the predatory glint in his eye dimming as he recognized the growing defiance in the room. He had underestimated us, and now it felt like we were on the cusp of something monumental—a chance to break the chains of deceit that had held our community captive for too long.

"Very well," he said, the veneer of confidence slipping as he took a step back, retreating slightly into the shadows. "You want a fight? You'll get one. But remember, I always play to win."

And with that, he turned on his heel, striding out of the town hall like a dark storm cloud retreating from the sun, leaving behind an electric atmosphere of uncertainty and resolve. As the last echo of his footsteps faded, I could feel the power of the moment wash over us, the room charged with an energy that felt palpable.

Sophie stood beside me, her expression a mix of shock and determination. "Did we really just do that?" she asked, breathless and wide-eyed, as if she were waking from a dream.

"Yeah," I replied, a grin breaking across my face. "We did. And we're just getting started."

As the dust settled in the wake of the confrontation, the town hall erupted into a flurry of discussions, voices overlapping like a chaotic symphony. The shift in the atmosphere was electric; hope and fear danced in a tangled waltz, making every heart race in anticipation of what would come next. The townspeople, previously subdued by uncertainty, now buzzed with determination, their collective energy a palpable force that surged through the air.

Sophie stood beside me, her expression a mixture of disbelief and exhilaration. "I can't believe we just did that," she said, her voice barely above the clamor. "It felt... powerful."

"Powerful? Honey, that was downright electric," I replied, unable to suppress my grin. "We just called out a corporate giant in front of everyone. They might think twice before messing with us again."

But even as I said the words, a knot of anxiety twisted in my stomach. This was only the beginning, and I knew AgriCorp wouldn't take our defiance lightly. The sound of shoes scuffling and whispers bouncing off the walls was quickly overshadowed by the familiar rustling of papers as the mayor regained his composure and cleared his throat, trying to reassert control over the meeting.

"Let's focus on the facts," he implored, his voice shaky but determined. "We need to ensure that any actions taken are based on evidence, not just allegations." He shot a pointed glance at us, his attempt to steer the narrative palpable.

"Evidence?" I challenged, my tone sharp. "We have documents, recordings, emails! What more do you want?" The crowd shifted, murmurs of agreement swelling around us.

"Yeah, what's next, a character assassination?" Sophie interjected, her bravery igniting the fire in the room. "It's our lives at stake here!"

"Hold on!" a voice called from the back. It belonged to Mr. Thompson, the local baker, his flour-dusted apron a comical contrast to the serious nature of the discussion. "If what you say is true, why hasn't anyone done anything before? We've all been talking about this for years!"

His words struck a chord, a realization dawning on the faces around me. The fear of repercussions had kept many silent, and now that fear was beginning to unravel like a frayed thread, each revelation loosening the grip of complacency.

"Because they thought we'd never stand together!" I shouted, emboldened by the growing conviction in the room. "But look at us! We're stronger than they ever gave us credit for!" The applause erupted again, and for a moment, it felt like we could conquer the world.

Just as the tide seemed to turn in our favor, a shadow fell across the podium. The stranger from AgriCorp re-entered, flanked by two intimidating figures in dark suits. They were as out of place as sharks in a kiddie pool, their eyes scanning the crowd like predators sizing up their next meal.

"Really?" he said, his voice dripping with condescension. "This is the best you can do? A baker and a couple of meddling women?" His laugh echoed through the hall, cold and sharp. "You think you can fight a corporation with your quaint little gathering?"

"Oh, honey, this isn't a quaint gathering," Sophie shot back, her voice steady despite the tremor in the air. "This is the beginning of a revolution."

The tension shifted again, but the man merely smirked, unfazed. "Revolution, is it? I admire your spunk. But let's be real. I'm here to remind you that playing with fire can get you burned."

"What are you threatening us with?" I demanded, my heart racing as I felt the crowd tense, like a tightly wound spring ready to snap. "We're fighting for our town!"

"Ah, but are you?" he replied, stepping closer, his eyes narrowing. "Your little rebellion could cost you more than you realize. You may lose friends, family—maybe even your jobs. What will you have left to fight for when it's all gone?"

His words hung in the air, thick and suffocating, and I could see a flicker of doubt in the eyes of some townsfolk. But just as I thought he might have landed a hit, Sophie stood firm, her eyes blazing with defiance.

"Let me tell you something," she said, her voice cutting through the tension. "What we're fighting for is bigger than jobs or friendships. It's our integrity. It's our lives. You can try to scare us, but we won't back down."

The crowd erupted in cheers, and the man's confident demeanor faltered. But as quickly as it wavered, he regained his composure, turning to address the audience with a deceptive calmness.

"Fine. You want to play the hero? Very well. Let's see how far your bravery goes when faced with the real consequences of your actions." He leaned back slightly, gesturing to his companions, who moved to the sides of the hall as if preparing for an exit. "Just remember, the truth is often much darker than you think. You might want to watch your back."

As they turned to leave, a hush fell over the room, confusion and concern knitting the brows of my neighbors. "What does that mean?" someone whispered, and I felt my heart skip a beat, an ominous dread settling over me.

Sophie caught my eye, and in that moment, we both understood the unspoken fear that lingered between us. "We need to be ready," she murmured, her voice low and urgent. "Whatever he's implying, it's serious."

I nodded, my mind racing with the implications. This wasn't just about uncovering corruption anymore; this was about protecting our lives and our community from forces we barely understood. The weight of our fight had shifted, and the stakes had risen sharply.

As the crowd began to disperse, a sense of urgency propelled me forward. "Let's meet at my place," I called out to Sophie. "We need a plan, and we need it now."

She nodded, her expression a mix of determination and fear, and we quickly made our way out of the town hall, the cool evening air hitting us like a refreshing wave.

But as we reached the edge of the square, a sharp cry pierced the air, halting us in our tracks. A woman stumbled forward, her face pale, her eyes wide with terror. "It's... it's happening! They're here!"

The crowd turned, gasps echoing as headlights pierced the gathering dusk, illuminating the square with an unsettling glow. Dark SUVs rolled in, and I felt the blood drain from my face.

"What's going on?" I whispered, gripping Sophie's arm.

"Run!" she shouted, and before I could comprehend, chaos erupted. The townsfolk scattered, a cacophony of screams and shouts as the shadows descended upon us like an approaching storm.

With adrenaline pumping through my veins, I grabbed Sophie's hand, pulling her along as we sprinted toward the nearest alley, desperate to escape the encroaching darkness that threatened to engulf everything we had fought for. But just as we turned the corner, a figure emerged from the shadows, blocking our path, a smirk playing on their lips.

"Where do you think you're going?" they taunted, and my heart raced as the realization hit me—this was far from over.

Chapter 16: The Heart of the Matter

The hall echoed with the discontent of a community awakened, a symphony of anger and disbelief reverberating off the walls. Each voice was a thread in the tapestry of resistance we had woven over countless nights spent poring over documents, gathering testimonies, and digging into the murky underbelly of AgriCorp's operations. Sophie stood beside me, her posture unwavering, radiating a fierce strength that made me proud to call her my friend. The fluorescent lights above buzzed, casting a stark glow on the gathered faces, illuminated with urgency and determination.

I stepped up to the podium, my heart racing like a wild stallion. "Thank you all for being here tonight," I began, my voice steady despite the fluttering in my chest. "We're not just fighting for our homes; we're fighting for our future." The room fell silent, anticipation hanging in the air like the first drops of rain before a storm.

Sophie leaned in, her eyes blazing with conviction as she murmured, "We can do this. They can't silence us."

I nodded, taking a deep breath to calm the whirlpool of emotions swirling inside me. The night air had grown thick with humidity, the scent of impending rain mingling with the faint trace of sweat and anxiety. Our presentation unfolded like a well-rehearsed play. We unveiled the damning evidence: photographs of contaminated land, testimonies from farmers whose livelihoods had been ruined, and charts illustrating AgriCorp's disregard for environmental safety. With each slide, gasps erupted from the crowd, punctuated by murmurs of disbelief.

Then, just as the audience began to rally behind us, the air shifted. The door at the back of the room creaked open, and in walked Paul, the slick, polished CEO of AgriCorp. His tailored suit shimmered under the harsh lights, and his perfectly coiffed hair seemed to defy the laws of gravity. He exuded an air of calm confidence that sent shivers down my spine. A smug smile played on his lips as he surveyed the room, like a cat eyeing a cornered mouse.

"Ladies and gentlemen," he intoned, his voice smooth as silk, "I'm sure you've all heard quite the tale tonight." He stepped forward, drawing the crowd's attention with an unsettling ease. "However, I must remind you that the truth is often more complex than the narrative you've been led to believe."

I exchanged a glance with Sophie, who clenched her fists at her sides, her jaw set in determination. Paul was here to play a game, and I refused to let him dominate the board.

"Complex?" I shot back, my voice rising above the murmur. "What's complex is how a corporation can poison our land and expect us to bow down to their profits! Your so-called progress comes at a devastating cost to our community."

Laughter rippled through the crowd, igniting a sense of unity among us, and Paul's smile faltered. I seized the moment, my heart pounding with the thrill of confrontation. "You can't bury the truth with your fancy words, Paul. The people of Willow Creek deserve to know what's really happening!"

His eyes narrowed, the facade of geniality slipping ever so slightly. "Ah, but what you call 'truth' is merely a series of unfortunate coincidences." He waved a dismissive hand. "And believe me, Willow Creek has benefited tremendously from AgriCorp's investment."

"Investment?" Sophie interjected, her voice sharp as glass. "Is that what you call it? What about the farmers you've put out of business? The land you've destroyed? Those aren't just statistics; they're lives!"

"Don't be naïve, Sophie," Paul retorted, a glimmer of malice dancing in his eyes. "Change is inevitable. Some people just can't adapt."

The air thickened with tension, the weight of his words settling heavily over us. I could see the crowd shifting, uncertainty creeping in like a shadow. Were they questioning us? Doubting our resolve?

"Adapt?" I repeated, my voice steady but laced with defiance. "You expect us to adapt to a world where our homes are turned into toxic waste dumps? Where our children play in fields that should be fertile and lush?"

A murmur of agreement spread through the audience, but Paul, with his steel-cold composure, pressed on. "You're manipulating their emotions. That's all this is, a fear campaign to push your own agenda."

"Fear?" Sophie's voice cracked like a whip, cutting through his calculated calm. "This isn't fear. This is love—love for our home, our people, and the land that nourishes us. You wouldn't understand that, would you?"

The air crackled with energy, and I felt the tide shifting. Our community had finally found its voice, and it was beautiful. Just as I thought we'd gained the upper hand, Paul leaned into the microphone, his smile returning, though it no longer seemed genuine.

"Very well, let's talk about love, shall we?" He gestured to the crowd, his eyes sweeping over them like a predator assessing its prey. "You love this town, this quaint little place, but what about the future? What about innovation? If you wish to stay in the dark ages, that's your choice, but don't expect the world to wait for you."

The audience murmured uneasily, and I could feel my heart sink. He was trying to play on their fears, turning our resolve against us.

"Wait?" I echoed, desperation creeping into my voice. "You think we're going to wait for you to destroy everything we love? No. We're taking a stand tonight! We will fight for what's right, for our families, for our future!"

The intensity in the room reached a fever pitch, a collective heartbeat pulsing in unison. I could see it in the faces around me—determination, courage, and an unyielding spirit that couldn't be extinguished. Even as Paul attempted to wrest control of the narrative, he was fighting against the tide of our unity.

And as we prepared to dive deeper into the battle, I felt an unexpected thrill coursing through me. The stakes had never been higher, but neither had our resolve. This was our moment, and I would not let it slip away.

Paul's presence sliced through the atmosphere like a knife through butter. His smile had returned, but it was now tinged with something darker—a mix of arrogance and condescension that wrapped around him like an expensive cologne. "I understand your passion," he said, his tone dripping with feigned empathy, "but let's not forget the bigger picture. Progress sometimes requires a few sacrifices."

A few nervous chuckles broke out among the crowd, like leaves rustling in an uncertain wind. I could feel the unease, the wavering trust in the room, and it fueled my resolve. "Sacrifices?" I shot back, the fire in my belly igniting once more. "What you call sacrifice, Paul, we call destruction. You've already sacrificed enough lives, families, and dreams on the altar of profit."

Sophie nudged my arm, her eyes sparkling with approval, as though she could hear the war drums beating inside me. It was electrifying to stand shoulder to shoulder with someone who dared to challenge the norm. I could see the passion reflected in the eyes of our neighbors and friends, each of them riding the wave of defiance we'd created.

Paul shifted slightly, his calculated smile faltering for a split second. "I suggest you take a step back and consider your next move carefully. You might find that a more cooperative approach yields better results for everyone."

"Cooperation?" Sophie snorted, her disbelief palpable. "You mean to say we should cooperate while you destroy our land? That's quite the pitch."

He leaned in, hands clasped in front of him, like a predator sizing up its prey. "Think about it. You'd have access to resources, to innovation. Just imagine what we could accomplish together!"

"Together?" I echoed, letting the incredulity seep into my voice. "Is that what you tell the families who've lost their homes? What's left of their land after your company's been through it?"

A murmur of agreement rippled through the crowd, swelling like a tide against the shores of Paul's bravado. He couldn't afford to let that happen. "You're misunderstanding the situation," he insisted, but the confident edge in his voice was beginning to fray.

With a dramatic sweep of my hand, I pointed to the large screen behind us that displayed the evidence we had painstakingly gathered. "Let's talk about understanding. How about the time you promised farmers a fair price for their crops, only to turn around and undervalue their hard work?" The audience erupted in shouts of agreement, their anger fueling the flames of rebellion.

Paul's calm veneer began to crack, revealing a flicker of anger beneath. "You're stirring up emotions that could have serious consequences. I urge you to think twice before you proceed."

"Consequences?" Sophie shot back, her voice laced with sarcasm. "Is that your way of saying we should be afraid? Because I don't think you realize what you're up against."

I could feel the room tightening around us, like a noose, drawing the crowd into a collective heartbeat, synchronizing our hopes and fears. Paul seemed to realize he was losing ground; the steel in his gaze turned sharper. "You're playing a dangerous game, and I can assure you, I don't play to lose."

"Neither do we," I said, stepping closer, my voice low and unwavering. "We are not backing down. Not now, not ever."

As I glanced around the room, I saw more than just anger; I saw hope igniting in the eyes of the townspeople. They were tired—tired of being overlooked, tired of being pushed around. The energy was palpable, a thick current running through the air, and it wasn't just our words; it was the spirit of Willow Creek rising to defend itself.

But then, in a calculated maneuver that caught me off guard, Paul turned and addressed the crowd directly. "You're all being swept up in this emotional frenzy, but let's not forget that I can help you. I can bring jobs, investment, and prosperity. Are you willing to throw that away for a handful of empty promises?"

The room went silent. His words hung in the air like a fog, cloaking the fervor of our cause. I could see some faces turning toward one another, doubt flickering in their eyes. "Jobs?" I said, my voice rising again, straining against the weight of his manipulation. "What kind of jobs? The kind that destroy our heritage and pollute our water? Is that the future you want for your children?"

"Who are you to dictate what's best for us?" someone shouted from the back, and I whipped around to find Mrs. Langley, the town's unofficial matriarch, standing with her hands on her hips. Her brow was furrowed, and her sharp eyes glinted with the kind of steel that had weathered many a storm. "You think you can come in here and tell us how to run our lives? We know this land, and we're not afraid of you."

A cheer erupted from the audience, revitalizing the atmosphere. Paul's facade was beginning to crumble, the tension in his shoulders giving way to a flicker of vulnerability. I seized the moment, the air thick with anticipation. "We are not just residents of Willow Creek; we are its heartbeat. You may think you can play us against one another, but this community is stronger than you realize."

His eyes narrowed, calculating, as if he was plotting his next move. "This isn't over," he said, and I could hear the underlying threat in his voice, a warning that was both chilling and invigorating.

Sophie stepped forward, her voice steady and fierce. "No, it's not over. We're just getting started."

The energy shifted, a wave of camaraderie washing over us, as people began to stand together, reclaiming their voices and their power. I could feel the tide turning, an undeniable force pushing against Paul's cold certainty. He had underestimated us, and in that moment of collective resolve, I knew we had the upper hand.

The night wore on, charged with electric energy as we continued to share our stories, bolstered by the laughter and cheers of those who had gathered. Each testimony was a building block, reinforcing our case and solidifying our bond. In the midst of it all, I felt something shift within me—an awakening, a realization that our fight was about more than just saving our homes; it was about reclaiming our identity, our community.

And as I caught Sophie's eye once more, a silent understanding passed between us. This was our moment to shine, to break through the darkness, and no amount of polished words from Paul could extinguish the light we had ignited.

The charged atmosphere crackled like static, and I could feel the pulse of every heartbeat in the room aligning with my own. Paul's attempt at control was slipping, and I savored the sight of it—a man so used to wielding power suddenly stripped of his confidence. He squared his shoulders, his eyes glinting with a mix of annoyance and something darker, as if he were mentally recalibrating his strategy in real time.

"Listen, people," he said, raising a hand to quiet the room, but it only intensified the murmurs of dissent. "You're letting emotions cloud your judgment. I'm offering solutions, and you're choosing fear."

"Fear?" Sophie retorted, her voice sharp and clear. "You think we're afraid? We're standing up for our lives and our land. What are you afraid of, Paul? That we might actually fight back?"

The audience erupted into cheers, a chorus of voices rising in support. I felt the warmth of their collective spirit washing over me, infusing my own resolve with renewed vigor. Paul's face darkened, his carefully constructed persona threatening to unravel.

"Your so-called fight is misguided. You're all potential victims of your own ignorance," he replied, his voice losing its smooth veneer. "I'll remind you that AgriCorp is here to help, not hurt. You'd do well to remember that."

"Help?" I couldn't help but laugh, the sound ringing like a bell in the tense silence that followed. "You mean help yourselves to what little we have left? Your 'help' has already cost too much, Paul. We've lost trust, we've lost livelihoods, and we will not lose our community to your greed."

His lips curled in that all-too-familiar smirk, the one that made my skin crawl. "It's quite charming, really, this little display of solidarity. But I assure you, it won't stand against the kind of force I can unleash."

"What force?" I challenged, feeling the surge of adrenaline rush through me. "You may have the corporate muscle, but we have something far stronger: a community united in truth. You can't intimidate us into submission."

Paul stepped back, his expression shifting from frustration to amusement. "You really think your little band of neighbors can stand up against a corporation with the resources to bury you? I've seen it happen too many times. You'll be forgotten, just another statistic in the fight for progress."

A ripple of uncertainty crossed the crowd, and I quickly turned to face them. "But we're not just any statistic! We are Willow Creek! We are farmers, teachers, shop owners, and families. We have history here, and no amount of money can erase that."

As I spoke, I saw heads nodding in agreement, the flicker of courage igniting in their eyes. It was then that I caught sight of a familiar face in the back—a figure cloaked in shadows, leaning against the wall, watching intently. My heart raced, for I recognized her immediately: Emily, the local journalist whose articles often danced between sensationalism and truth. She had been a thorn in AgriCorp's side, unearthing stories that made them uncomfortable.

"Emily!" I called out, hoping to draw her into the spotlight. "We need your voice here! This is the time to shed light on what's really happening!"

Her gaze flickered to mine, uncertainty etched on her face. Paul's eyes darted toward her as well, and I could see the gears turning in his mind. He was calculating, and that made me wary.

"What's your plan, then?" Emily called back, stepping forward with a fierce resolve. "You want to take on AgriCorp? What's your strategy, and how do you expect to be heard above the noise?"

"By telling the truth," I said, lifting my chin defiantly. "We're going to gather our stories, our evidence, and we're going to present it to every outlet willing to listen. We'll show Willow Creek for what it truly is—a community worth fighting for."

Paul laughed, a hollow sound that echoed in the charged air. "And you think the press will help you? They thrive on sensationalism, on drama. You'll be just another headline to them."

"No," Emily replied, stepping into the fray, her confidence radiating like sunlight breaking through clouds. "We'll be a story about hope, resilience, and a community that refuses to back down. You underestimate the power of narrative, Paul."

The crowd erupted in applause, the energy in the room shifting like the winds before a storm. I glanced around, soaking in the palpable sense of unity that had taken root. But just as I felt we were gaining momentum, Paul's expression hardened.

"I'd be careful if I were you," he warned, his voice low, barely containing the threat. "I don't play fair, and I have resources you can't even begin to imagine."

I could feel the tension in the room spike, the air growing thick with apprehension. I stepped forward, closing the distance between us. "We're not afraid of you or your threats, Paul. If you think you can scare us into submission, you've miscalculated."

He leaned closer, a glint of menace flickering in his eyes. "It won't just be your livelihood at stake. You'll lose everything you love. Do you understand what I'm saying?"

And in that moment, as the tension reached its peak, a loud crash echoed from the back of the hall. The door burst open, and a group of men in dark suits stormed in, their expressions grim and determined. My heart sank as I recognized one of them—a familiar face from the AgriCorp legal team, a man who had taken a keen interest in shutting down our efforts.

"Paul," he said, glancing around the room, his eyes locking onto mine. "We need to talk. Now."

The crowd gasped, the air thick with confusion and fear as whispers rippled through the audience. Paul straightened, the cockiness fading from his face as he exchanged hurried words with the newcomer, his brow furrowed with worry.

"What's happening?" I whispered to Sophie, my voice barely audible above the mounting anxiety in the room.

"I don't know," she replied, her eyes wide as she tried to gauge the situation. "But it can't be good."

And just like that, the atmosphere shifted again, tension coiling tighter as I took a step back, my mind racing with possibilities. The fight wasn't over; it was just beginning. But what did Paul have to hide? The sense of dread settled in the pit of my stomach, cold and heavy.

"Ladies and gentlemen," Paul said, turning back to the crowd, a forced smile plastered on his face. "It appears we have some urgent business to attend to. But I assure you, this isn't over."

As he turned to leave with the men in suits, I felt an unsettling certainty wash over me. The battle lines had been drawn, but the war was just unfolding. A knot of apprehension twisted in my chest, and I couldn't shake the feeling that the worst was yet to come.

Chapter 17: The Reckoning

The room pulsated with tension, a charged atmosphere thick enough to slice through with a knife. I could feel it in the pit of my stomach, a relentless churn that matched the rising heat of the debate. Paul stood at the front, his dark eyes sharp as knives, spitting venomous words that dripped with disdain. He was a storm, and I was standing in the eye of it, surrounded by faces that mirrored my unease, but also my resolve.

"Look at this! Look at what they're doing!" he barked, gesturing wildly at Sophie and me, his fingers slicing through the air like swords. "They claim to speak for the community, but their actions speak louder. They're risking everything for some misguided notion of loyalty to a piece of land."

The murmurs among the crowd began to swell, rippling through like a wave breaking on a rocky shore. I watched as Sophie clenched her fists, her knuckles whitening in a silent vow. Her deep-rooted connection to this land—our land—was palpable, radiating from her like warmth from a hearth on a cold winter's night. I wanted to leap to my feet, to shout out my own truth, but fear gripped my throat, tightening like a noose.

Instead, I turned to Sophie. "You've got this," I whispered, my voice barely a breath. She met my gaze, her eyes glimmering with determination that ignited my own.

"Paul," she called out, her voice ringing clear and steady, cutting through the din like a lighthouse beam piercing a foggy night. "What you fail to understand is that this isn't just about land or homes; it's about our very essence. This community is woven into the soil, the trees, and the rivers that run through it. We are not just tenants; we are guardians of a legacy."

Her words settled into the room, settling like a blanket of snow that muted all else. People leaned forward, their interest piqued. I felt the collective heartbeat of the crowd synchronizing with her, each pulse a reminder of the bonds that tied us together. We were no longer just individuals worried about their homes; we were a tapestry of lives intertwined, each thread as vital as the next.

Paul, ever the bulldog, narrowed his gaze, trying to cut through the wave of unity that was rising. "Emotional rhetoric won't change the facts. You can't ignore the bottom line," he retorted, but his voice faltered slightly, revealing a crack in his armor.

"But the facts are not just numbers on a spreadsheet, are they?" Sophie pressed on, her voice gaining strength. "These aren't mere transactions. This is our life! Each of us has a story connected to this place. My grandmother planted those trees when she arrived here. My mother taught me to fish in that river." She pointed toward the window, as if it held the very essence of our dreams. "What do you have, Paul? A balance sheet?"

His face turned an ashen shade, a mixture of frustration and the dawning realization that his words were losing their potency. I could see him grappling with the intangible, a cold corporate demeanor clashing against the warm, messy reality of human connection. The murmurs around the room grew louder, a swell of voices gathering momentum like a chorus of birds rising at dawn.

And then, unexpectedly, I felt a surge of courage rise within me. "What are you willing to sacrifice, Paul?" I called out, my voice shaking slightly but fueled by the fire in my heart. "Is it worth losing a community? Is it worth tearing apart lives for the sake of profit? Because when you strip away the numbers, that's what you're doing—destroying us."

A ripple of agreement swept through the crowd, a wave of supportive murmurs that felt like a gentle tide lifting us all. I could sense the collective heartbeat of everyone in that room—resilience, determination, and an unwavering desire to protect what we loved.

For the first time, I felt the threads of fear start to unravel, replaced by something deeper—hope.

Paul opened his mouth, perhaps to rebut, but the words failed him. Instead, he stood there, fists clenched at his sides, jaw taut as if he were chewing on the very air. I could almost see the gears turning in his mind, the struggle of trying to maintain control over a narrative that was slipping from his grasp.

"Enough!" he finally shouted, his voice reverberating through the space, causing heads to snap back in surprise. "You think your little emotional appeals will hold up in the real world? This is business, not a community picnic!"

With that, he turned on his heel, storming to the side of the room, his frustration palpable. The tension hung in the air like static electricity, and for a moment, it felt as though the universe held its breath, waiting to see what would happen next.

Sophie looked at me, her expression a mixture of disbelief and exhilaration. "Did we just win that?" she whispered, and I couldn't help but smile, the corners of my mouth lifting in a way I hadn't expected. It felt like a crack in the storm clouds, a glimmer of sunlight breaking through.

But before I could respond, a voice piped up from the back—a woman named Clara, someone I had always admired for her fierce spirit. "We have a right to fight for our home! We will not be silenced by fear tactics or intimidation!" Her words were a spark, igniting the fire of rebellion within the crowd, as others joined in, their voices rising in a chorus of solidarity.

The room felt alive, electric with possibility. I knew that this was only the beginning, a small but significant step toward reclaiming our narrative. As the chants grew louder, I realized we weren't just a group of individuals fighting for our homes. We were a family, a community with shared hopes and dreams, and together, we would stand tall against whatever storm came our way.

A palpable energy coursed through the room, a vibrant current that electrified the air. Each chant, each cheer was a heartbeat echoing our resolve, a rhythm that resonated deep within me. It was intoxicating, this sense of community, like drinking in the first sweet breath of spring after a long winter. I glanced around at the faces, each one familiar yet imbued with newfound determination, and realized we were no longer just fighting for our homes; we were reclaiming our narrative.

As the crowd swelled with voices, I caught sight of Clara, her brown curls bouncing as she waved her arms like a conductor guiding an orchestra. "Let's show Paul what we're made of!" she shouted, igniting a fervor that swept through the room. It was one thing to speak of community; it was another to feel it vibrate in your bones, to know you were part of something bigger than yourself.

Paul, cornered now, shot us a glare that could wither a rose. "You think this is going to change anything?" His voice dripped with disdain, but I could see the uncertainty lurking beneath his bravado. He was losing ground, and desperation was a dangerous opponent. "You're wasting your breath."

"Tell that to the wind," Sophie replied, crossing her arms defiantly. "Because it seems to carry our voices farther than your hollow threats ever could." The crowd erupted in laughter, a ripple of joy cutting through the tension, and for a moment, it felt like we had transformed the atmosphere from dread to determination.

I couldn't help but admire Sophie; she was fierce and unyielding, a warrior in her own right. I wished I had her strength, her ability to stand tall in the face of adversity. But I also realized I had something to contribute—an emotional depth that connected us all. "We're not just asking for our homes," I said, stepping forward, feeling the weight of the room's gaze upon me. "We're fighting for our stories, our roots. This land nurtures us. It is not a commodity; it is a part of us."

The crowd nodded, murmurs of agreement building like a wave. My heart raced as I embraced this newfound courage. Each word felt like a seed, planted in fertile soil, ready to blossom into a vibrant fight for our future.

But Paul wasn't done yet. "Your emotional appeals won't matter when the court rules in favor of progress," he retorted, his tone icy, as if he thought he could freeze us in our tracks. "You can't stand in the way of progress, no matter how heartwarming your stories are."

"Progress?" Clara scoffed, stepping up beside me. "Is that what you call bulldozing our memories? You're talking about progress like it's a shiny new toy, but for us, it's our heritage. It's our children playing in the fields and our elders sharing stories on porches. Progress without respect is just destruction in a fancier package."

A collective murmur of agreement swept through the crowd again, and I felt the energy shift, a palpable charge surging through us. It was infectious, this unity. The more we spoke, the more we believed in our cause. I could see the fire in Clara's eyes, and it fueled my own. Together, we were a force to be reckoned with, a tempest that refused to be quelled.

Suddenly, a figure emerged from the shadows at the back of the room—a tall, elegant woman with silver hair cascading like a waterfall over her shoulders. I recognized her immediately: Grace, the matriarch of the community, whose presence commanded respect. She was the heart of our town, and when she spoke, everyone listened.

"Enough of this bickering," she said, her voice calm yet powerful, reverberating through the crowd like a bell. "We are not here to tear each other down. We are here to uplift our community. I have lived here longer than most of you, and I can tell you this—there is a strength in our connection to this land that no amount of money can buy."

Her words wrapped around us like a warm embrace, soothing the simmering tension. "This place has witnessed our joys, our sorrows, and our triumphs. It has held our laughter and our tears. We owe it to ourselves to protect it fiercely."

The room fell silent, the weight of her wisdom sinking in. Grace's gaze swept over us, her piercing blue eyes glimmering with conviction. "Let us remember why we fight. It's not for ourselves alone, but for future generations who will inherit our legacy."

A heavy pause lingered before the crowd erupted into applause, the sound rising like a symphony, filling the air with hope. I felt a swell of emotion well up inside me, an unshakeable sense of belonging and purpose. Together, we stood united, ready to face whatever storms lay ahead.

Paul stood at the edge of the room, visibly shaken. The steam had begun to dissipate from his earlier bravado, replaced by a simmering resentment that only seemed to bolster our resolve. I half-expected him to bolt, but instead, he took a deep breath, perhaps reassessing his strategy.

"You think you can just shout me down?" he shot back, his bravado faltering as he pointed a finger, but the anger was beginning to feel like a feeble echo. "You're mistaken if you think I'll let this go without a fight."

"Then bring it on," Sophie challenged, stepping forward, her chin held high. "We're not afraid of a little fight. Just remember—when you fight a community, you don't just fight individuals; you fight their dreams, their hopes, and their histories."

The weight of her words hung heavy in the air, and for a brief moment, I thought I saw a flicker of uncertainty in Paul's eyes. Perhaps the storm clouds of doubt were beginning to gather over him as well.

"Let's take this outside," he finally spat, a desperate attempt to reclaim control, but the crowd wouldn't have it. The cheers grew louder, a chorus of support drowning out his anger.

As the atmosphere charged with renewed energy, I could feel my heart racing, an electric pulse igniting my spirit. We were ready for whatever came next. This was not merely a battle for our homes; it was a celebration of our shared strength, a testimony of our resilience. The reckoning had transformed into a rallying cry, one that would echo far beyond the confines of this room and into the very fabric of our community.

The cheers reverberated through the hall, a euphoric swell that seemed to lift us off the ground. I stood, heart racing, savoring the taste of victory as the weight of our community's spirit wrapped around me like a comforting shawl. Each cheer was a heartbeat, and for the first time in what felt like forever, I could see a way forward. Paul was floundering, grappling with our collective resolve like a fish out of water, struggling to reclaim the narrative he thought he controlled.

"Your little community spirit might be inspiring, but it won't save your homes," he said, trying to regain some semblance of composure, though his voice wavered slightly. "You really think your emotions can outweigh contracts and legality?"

"Contracts can be renegotiated," Sophie shot back, her eyes flashing with fire. "What you can't replace is the heart and soul of this community. Those can't be bought or sold."

"Keep telling yourself that," he sneered, but the words held less power now, more a petulant cry than a confident retort. "You'll find that when push comes to shove, greed always wins."

But his confidence was eroding. The applause from the crowd surged again, louder this time, drowning out his attempts to sow doubt. My gaze shifted among our neighbors, their faces lit with determination and passion, each of us woven together in a tapestry of shared dreams and histories.

Grace stepped forward, her silver hair catching the dim light like a halo. "Let's not forget who we are," she said, her voice calm yet commanding. "We're not just fighting for our homes; we're fighting for our identity. Every tree, every stone tells our story. This is our history, and we won't let anyone erase it."

"History?" Paul scoffed, but there was a crack in his facade, a hint of vulnerability that hadn't been there before. "What about the future? You can't stop progress with nostalgia."

"Nostalgia isn't what drives us," Clara interjected, her voice steady as she stepped beside Grace. "It's about building a future that respects our past. We want to thrive—not just survive. A future without our roots is a future we don't want."

The crowd erupted again, a wave of affirmation washing over us, fortifying our resolve. I felt the ground solidify beneath my feet, an unwavering foundation of purpose that had been absent just moments before. We were no longer just individuals; we were an unstoppable force.

But just as our spirits soared, Paul drew in a breath, a new intensity sparking in his eyes. "Then let's take this outside," he said suddenly, the challenge hanging in the air like a heavy fog. "We'll see just how far your little crusade can take you."

A murmur rippled through the crowd, uncertainty creeping in. Was he bluffing? Would he really challenge us to a public confrontation? I could feel the tension shift again, like the wind before a storm. "What are you planning, Paul?" I asked, my voice steady even as adrenaline coursed through me.

"Let's put it to the test. A debate. We'll lay it all out there—facts against your stories," he declared, his voice taking on a new fervor. "We'll bring in the experts. You think you can sway public opinion? Let's see if you can sway the judges."

"Are you suggesting a public forum?" Sophie asked, a flicker of excitement igniting in her eyes. "Is that your grand strategy? Because I promise you, we won't back down."

"Oh, I'm counting on that," he sneered, a glint of something darker flashing across his features. "You'll have your moment to shine, and I hope you've got your facts straight, because I'll be bringing in the big guns."

His words hung ominously in the air, sending ripples of apprehension through the crowd. It was a bold move, and while the prospect of such a showdown thrilled me, it also filled me with trepidation. The stakes were rising, and we would need to prepare for whatever he had planned.

"What's it going to be, then?" Paul asked, arms crossed defiantly. "Are you all in, or are you going to cower behind your sentimental stories?"

I exchanged glances with Sophie and Clara. The fire in their eyes mirrored my own. "We're in," I declared, my voice unwavering. "We're not going anywhere."

The crowd erupted once more, but beneath the cheers lay an undercurrent of uncertainty. Could we truly hold our ground against the machinery of bureaucracy and profit? As the clamor subsided, I felt a knot of worry twist in my stomach. Paul was cunning, and I knew he wouldn't play fair.

In the days that followed, the community mobilized. We gathered in makeshift meetings at the local café, pouring over maps and historical documents like archaeologists unearthing the past. Sophie was a whirlwind of energy, her enthusiasm infectious. "We'll show them what this place means to us!" she exclaimed, her eyes alight with determination.

"Remember," I said, trying to rein in the fever pitch, "this is about more than facts and figures. It's about the heart of our community. Let's not lose sight of that."

But even as I spoke, doubt crept in, clawing at the edges of my resolve. What if our passion wasn't enough? What if Paul's 'big guns' were more formidable than we could imagine? The tension in the air was palpable, thick as fog, as the date for the debate drew nearer.

Finally, the day arrived, and the town hall buzzed with an electric anticipation. People flowed in, faces filled with excitement and fear, all gathered to witness this unprecedented showdown. The room was packed, a sea of eager faces reflecting our collective hopes.

Paul stood at one end, exuding confidence that felt almost tangible. He was flanked by a group of slick lawyers, their polished suits gleaming under the harsh fluorescent lights. They looked like sharks in a tank, all sharp edges and cold smiles.

As we took our seats, I felt the weight of a thousand eyes upon us. This was our moment to shine—or to crumble under the pressure. Sophie squeezed my hand, her warmth grounding me in the uncertainty swirling around us. "We've got this," she whispered, a smile breaking through her nerves.

But as the moderator called the meeting to order, a flicker of movement caught my eye near the back of the room. A figure slipped in, cloaked in shadow, their presence almost ethereal. I squinted, trying to make out who it was, my heart racing with a sudden sense of foreboding.

Then, as the crowd quieted, the stranger stepped into the light, revealing a face I hadn't seen in years—a face that brought a rush of memories tumbling back, a mixture of warmth and dread. My breath caught in my throat. This was not just any stranger; this was someone from my past, someone whose very existence could tip the scales in ways I had never anticipated.

With the weight of history hanging in the air, I knew one thing for certain: the debate was about to take an unexpected turn, and the reckoning was far from over.

Chapter 18: The Unexpected Twist

The sun dipped low on the horizon, casting an amber glow over the fields that had become a second home to me. Each blade of grass danced in the gentle breeze, whispering secrets of resilience and promise. I could smell the earth's warmth, the scent of ripening tomatoes mingling with the sharp tang of freshly cut hay. Yet, beneath the surface of this bucolic paradise, a storm was brewing, and it had a name—AgriCorp.

The community had rallied behind us, supporting our dream of cultivating the land without the heavy hand of corporate greed. Sophie, with her fiery auburn hair and laughter that could light the darkest corners of my soul, had become our beacon. But as much as I wanted to believe in our victory, the weight of the world was poised to descend upon us, and I could feel it in my bones.

As dusk painted the sky with strokes of violet and deep blue, I found myself on the porch, nervously twisting a strand of hair around my finger. Sophie was inside, her usual vibrancy muted, her laughter silenced by the looming threat of AgriCorp's machinations. We had faced challenges before, but this felt different—more insidious, more personal.

It was a day like any other when the first blow fell. We were gathered at the community center for an urgent meeting, the air thick with anticipation and anxiety. The town buzzed with chatter, voices rising and falling like the rhythm of an uncertain heartbeat. It was there, among the familiar faces, that AgriCorp unleashed their latest weapon—an insidious press release filled with rumors and half-truths about Sophie's past. They painted her as a deceitful outsider who had come to disrupt our idyllic way of life, planting seeds of doubt that flourished in the fertile soil of fear.

I watched the townsfolk's faces twist into masks of disbelief and concern, my heart racing as the words sunk deep into the crowd. "Is it true?" someone whispered, the question hanging in the air like a noose, threatening to choke the spirit from our cause. "What do we really know about her?" another voice cut through the murmur. I could see the flicker of uncertainty in their eyes, and it felt as though the ground beneath us was cracking, ready to swallow us whole.

Sophie had always been an enigma, a wildflower thriving in the cracks of convention. I had fallen for her not just for her beauty but for the fierce passion she poured into every seed sown and every dream whispered under the stars. But now, as I scanned the room, I could see the light dimming in her eyes, replaced by shadows of doubt that threatened to consume her.

I pushed through the crowd, feeling the weight of their stares on my back, each one a pinprick of betrayal. I reached her just as the press release finished its devastating round, and I grasped her hands, hoping to transfer a spark of my conviction into her trembling fingers. "Sophie," I said, my voice steady despite the tempest raging within, "this doesn't define you. You know that, right?"

But her gaze was unfocused, as if she were already retreating into a world where the colors were muted, and laughter was a distant memory. "They have the evidence, Clara," she murmured, her voice barely above a whisper. "They're right. I've been running away from who I am for so long, and now everyone knows."

The air thickened with tension, and the world around us faded. "You're not a mistake, Sophie. Whatever they've dug up, it's just a chapter in a story that's still being written. You are not defined by your past but by how you rise from it." I leaned closer, searching her eyes for the fiery spirit that had once captivated me. "You taught me that life isn't about avoiding the storms; it's about dancing in the rain."

A flicker of something—a spark, perhaps—passed over her face, but just as quickly, it was extinguished by a wave of despair. "You don't understand. The things they're saying... It's true. I've made choices, bad ones, and I can't hide from them anymore. I don't deserve your fight or anyone's loyalty."

Every word was like a knife, twisting deeper into my heart. How could she not see the strength in her vulnerability? I had seen her struggle, her victories, and her tenacity in facing a world that had often turned its back on her. This was the moment where I needed to bridge the chasm that doubt had opened between us. "I don't care about what they say, Sophie. I care about you. The real you. And I will fight for you, even if you can't fight for yourself right now."

But as I spoke, I felt the weight of the whispers swirl around us, wrapping tighter with each passing second. AgriCorp was sowing discord, and I could feel the community's trust slipping away like sand through fingers. Doubt was a powerful adversary, and we were losing ground.

Sophie pulled away, retreating into herself like a tortoise drawing back into its shell, and I felt a pang of helplessness wash over me. "I need time," she finally said, her voice barely a murmur.

And just like that, she turned, walking away into the house that had once felt like a sanctuary but now loomed like a fortress. The door clicked shut, leaving me on the porch, the chill of the evening air wrapping around me, empty and desolate. I was left standing in the twilight, my heart racing with an urgency to protect not just our farm but the woman I loved.

The battle lines had been drawn, and I could feel the pulse of a war beginning, one that would test not only our resolve but our very identities. I took a deep breath, steeling myself for what was to come. The sun might have set on our peace, but dawn was yet to break on our fight.

The following days settled over the farm like an unwelcome fog, shrouding everything in an oppressive silence. Morning light broke through the clouds, but even the sun seemed reluctant to shine, as if it too understood the weight of despair that hung in the air. The rhythm of our daily tasks continued, but there was a dissonance now—a lack of joy that permeated every corner of our once-vibrant sanctuary.

As I moved through the rows of crops, my hands worked on autopilot, planting and pruning, while my mind spiraled with thoughts of Sophie. Her retreat into herself felt like a personal betrayal, a denial of the fierce connection we had forged. She was my partner, my compass, and watching her shrink away was like losing a part of my own soul. Each time I glanced at the house, I half-expected to see her vibrant silhouette in the window, but the curtains remained drawn, casting shadows that echoed my growing sense of dread.

A week had passed since AgriCorp's malicious unveiling, and the community seemed to be split. Conversations were hushed, a mix of concern and curiosity echoing through town, as if we were all unwitting participants in some tragic theater. I'd hear snippets of gossip while shopping for groceries or at the post office, whispers darting around like sparrows. "Have you heard? She's not who she says she is." "Can we trust her after all this?" The words stabbed at me, bitter and biting, making my blood boil.

One crisp autumn morning, I found myself wandering the market square, the air brisk and invigorating. Vendors were setting up their stalls, the vibrant colors of fruits and vegetables clashing against the muted tones of the falling leaves. I exchanged pleasantries with a few familiar faces, but the conversations felt surface-level, a fragile mask over the brewing tensions.

It wasn't until I reached the end of the square that I spotted her: Sophie stood by a booth selling handmade soaps and lotions, her hair a cascade of copper that shimmered even in the soft morning light. She appeared lost in thought, her fingers idly tracing the edges of a jar labeled "Cinnamon Delight." My heart raced at the sight of her, the hope bubbling up like a summer brook after a long winter.

"Sophie!" I called out, my voice stronger than I felt. She turned slowly, her expression a blend of surprise and uncertainty. There was a flicker of recognition, but it quickly faded, swallowed by the shadows that had taken residence in her eyes.

"What do you want, Clara?" Her voice was steady, but the underlying tremor betrayed the emotions brewing just beneath the surface.

I stepped closer, the chill of the morning forgotten as I focused solely on her. "I want to talk. We need to confront this. Together."

"Together?" she echoed, an eyebrow arched in skepticism. "You mean confront the very real truth about my past? The truth that has everyone questioning me? Questioning us?"

"Exactly," I said, refusing to let her retreat into her fortress of isolation. "What do you think will happen if we hide from it? The rumors will grow, and they'll swallow you whole. We need to face this, Sophie. You deserve to tell your own story."

For a moment, I could see her weighing my words, the internal battle flickering across her face. The sun peeked through the clouds, illuminating her features, and for a heartbeat, I could see the woman I fell in love with. "What if I don't want to? What if I don't want to relive everything?"

"Then you have to trust me," I replied, my tone softer but insistent. "Trust that I won't let you face it alone. I know you're scared. But your past doesn't define who you are now. You are more than the mistakes you've made. You are more than what they say. Let's show them that."

She closed her eyes briefly, as if summoning a strength I knew was buried deep within her. "It's not that easy. There are things about my past that could tear us apart, Clara."

"Things that make you human," I countered, stepping even closer. "And I can't lose you to fear. Not when I know how incredible you are. Not when I see the good you've done here."

At that moment, I could feel the energy shift, the crackling tension between us almost tangible. I held my breath, waiting for her response, praying it wouldn't be another retreat.

Finally, Sophie opened her eyes, and I saw a glimmer of resolve peeking through the cracks of her facade. "Okay," she said, the word heavy with hesitation but also a flicker of hope. "But only if we do this together. I won't stand up there and make excuses for who I was. I want to be honest, no matter how ugly it may seem."

"Together," I promised, the warmth of her hand slipping into mine grounding me. "We'll stand together, and we'll face whatever they throw at us."

As we walked through the market, I could feel the eyes of the townsfolk on us, assessing, judging. The murmurs began to swell again, but this time they felt different, charged with curiosity rather than condemnation. Perhaps they sensed the shift in Sophie, the tentative strength that was slowly returning.

Then came the moment that sent a shockwave through the square. Just as we reached the edge of the market, a familiar figure emerged from the crowd. It was Lily, the town's sharp-tongued newspaper editor, known for her piercing insights and unyielding tenacity. Her notepad clutched tightly in one hand, she approached us, an expression of determination etched on her face.

"Sophie," she called, stopping just a few feet away. The crowd grew silent, a collective breath held in anticipation. "I'd like to hear your side of the story. The real story. If you're willing to share it."

Sophie stiffened, glancing at me as if seeking my reassurance. I nodded, squeezing her hand tighter. This was it—the moment she needed to seize control of her narrative, to reclaim her power from the whispers that had haunted her.

"Let's do this," she said, her voice steadier than I'd heard in days. "Let me tell you who I really am."

And just like that, the storm began to shift, the clouds parting ever so slightly as hope took root once more. As Sophie spoke, I could see her light beginning to rekindle, the fiery spirit I had fought for flickering back to life. The crowd leaned in, and for the first time in what felt like an eternity, I allowed myself to believe that we might just turn the tide in our favor.

The air was charged with a palpable tension as Sophie stood before the crowd, her hands trembling slightly at her sides. I could see the flicker of vulnerability in her eyes, but beneath that was a burgeoning strength that promised to break free. The townspeople watched, their faces a mosaic of curiosity and skepticism, as if waiting for a performance to unfold. It was time for her to tell her story, to reclaim her identity from the shackles of the past.

Lily, her notepad poised and ready, nodded for Sophie to begin. The weight of the moment settled over us like a warm blanket, wrapping us in the significance of what was about to happen. "I know that many of you have heard things about me," Sophie began, her voice steady despite the quiver of uncertainty threading through it. "Things that paint me as an outsider, as someone unworthy of your trust. But I'm here to tell you that those stories only tell part of the truth. They're the shadows cast by my past, not the full picture."

A few people shifted uncomfortably, and I could see the flicker of doubt in their eyes. "What does that mean?" someone called out, breaking the spell of silence. It was a voice I recognized—Ruth, the town's unofficial gossip queen, always eager for the next scandal.

Sophie took a deep breath, the air rushing into her lungs like a gust of wind through the trees. "When I moved here, I thought I could start fresh, leave behind the mistakes I made. But those mistakes follow you like a ghost. I spent years trying to outrun who I used to be. I made choices that hurt people—people I loved. I was young and reckless, thinking I could handle it all."

There was a collective intake of breath from the crowd, an electric buzz of engagement as they began to lean in, hungry for the details. "I've had my share of struggles—fights with addiction, relationships that were toxic, and a lot of pain I brought upon myself. But I'm not that person anymore. I'm standing here because I've fought hard to be better. I'm committed to making a life that reflects who I truly am. I want to be part of this community, to contribute, to grow."

"Is that really who you are, though?" a voice piped up from the back, cutting through the vulnerability like a knife. It was Stan, the local farmer who had always been skeptical of newcomers. "How can we trust you won't just run when the going gets tough?"

"Trust is earned," Sophie replied, her gaze fierce and unwavering. "But I'm here to stay, and I'm willing to do whatever it takes to prove that I'm not just a shadow of my past. I want to build something real here. With Clara, with all of you."

The murmurs among the crowd shifted. Some faces softened, while others remained skeptical, clinging tightly to their doubts. I could feel the weight of expectation hanging over us, the silent question lingering in the air—would they accept her?

"Building trust takes time," I added, stepping beside her, grounding her with my presence. "But we've all seen what Sophie can do. She's poured her heart into this farm, into this community. Isn't that what we should focus on? The actions she's taking now, not just the mistakes of the past?"

There was a slight shift in the crowd; a few heads nodded in agreement, while others still appeared torn, wrestling with their preconceived notions.

"Actions speak louder than words, Clara," Stan retorted, crossing his arms defiantly. "What happens when the pressure mounts? You think she'll just stand there smiling while everything falls apart?"

Sophie's resolve faltered for a split second, but she quickly straightened. "If I run away, it will only prove your point, won't it? But I promise you, I'm committed to this. To our farm. To you all."

"Then prove it," Stan challenged, his gaze penetrating, unwavering. "Prove that you're willing to fight for us, not just for yourself."

A challenge lay thick in the air, and I could sense the shift in momentum as the crowd began to buzz with excitement, suspicion, and anticipation. "What do you have in mind?" someone shouted from the back, voice laced with skepticism but also curiosity.

Sophie glanced at me, her eyes searching for guidance. "I'll do anything," she stated, her voice gathering strength. "What if I help organize a community event? Something to bring everyone together—to celebrate what we've built and create a dialogue? I want to show you that I'm invested, that I'm not just a passing shadow in your lives."

"An event?" Lily's pen was scratching furiously against her notepad. "What kind of event?"

"A harvest festival," Sophie replied, her excitement bubbling over. "We can showcase local produce, invite local artisans to sell their crafts, maybe have a small competition for the best dish using farm-fresh ingredients. It could be a way to not just support local businesses but also rebuild trust. A chance to show that we are all part of this community, no matter our pasts."

The crowd stirred, and I felt a surge of hope rise within me. This was it—this could be the turning point. "Yes! We could do a pie-eating contest," I chimed in, my enthusiasm bubbling over. "And let's not forget a dance-off!"

The murmurs turned into laughter, and for the first time in days, I saw genuine smiles breaking across faces. The weight of the world didn't lift entirely, but it felt lighter, infused with the possibility of something new, something unifying.

Yet just as I felt the warmth of optimism wrapping around us, a shadow loomed from the edge of the square. A figure approached, moving with an unsettling purpose. I recognized him instantly—Mark, AgriCorp's local representative, his tailored suit stark against the rural backdrop. His presence sliced through the joyous atmosphere, a reminder of the battle we were still fighting.

"Interesting turn of events," he drawled, an insidious smile spreading across his face. "I must say, I didn't expect such a... spirited defense of our little 'project' here. But don't think this changes anything. You're still outnumbered, and we're not backing down."

A chill swept through the crowd, my heart pounding in my chest. "What do you mean?" I managed to ask, my voice steady despite the dread pooling in my stomach.

Mark leaned in, eyes glinting with malice. "You think this festival will erase the doubts? The questions? You're all being played like pawns in a game you don't even understand."

And then, with a flourish, he produced a thick folder from inside his coat, brandishing it like a trophy. "I have everything I need to ensure AgriCorp will not only remain but thrive. And I'm more than happy to share it with the community if it means securing my position."

The laughter died instantly, replaced by an eerie silence as the weight of his threat settled over us. Sophie's hand tightened around mine, her body tense with uncertainty. I could see the flicker of fear behind her determination, and I knew in that moment that everything hung in the balance.

"Come see me if you want to know the truth," he sneered, turning on his heel and disappearing into the crowd, leaving nothing but a lingering sense of dread and confusion.

The air felt thick, as if time had frozen, and I could see the worried expressions morphing around me. This wasn't just about Sophie anymore; it was about all of us, the very heart of our community. And as we stood there, the shadows lengthening with the setting sun, I realized we were standing on the precipice of a greater battle than I had ever imagined.

The sound of laughter faded, replaced by the weight of looming uncertainty, leaving us to wonder just what Mark had planned—and what it might mean for all of us.

Chapter 19: The Turning Point

The sun hung low in the sky, casting a warm golden glow over the fields, the kind that makes everything appear just a shade more magical, as if the universe itself was in on some cosmic joke. I stood at the edge of our farm, the familiar scent of tilled earth and fresh hay swirling around me, comforting yet fraught with the tension that had begun to seep into our lives. Just weeks ago, the days were filled with laughter, sun-soaked afternoons spent dreaming over iced tea, and evenings wrapped in the sweet aroma of roasted vegetables. But now, a heavy silence loomed, punctuated only by the occasional rustle of the wind through the corn stalks, whispering secrets I was too afraid to hear.

I turned and walked towards the farmhouse, the soft crunch of gravel underfoot a rhythmic reminder of the upheaval. Claire was already waiting for me on the porch, her fingers tapping anxiously against the arm of her chair. There was an unmistakable fire in her eyes, a fierce determination that had only grown since AgriCorp's accusations started to claw at our credibility.

"Did you hear what they said?" Claire's voice was a low hiss, brimming with indignation. "They're trying to paint us as the villains in this story. Us! Like we're some sort of eco-terrorists just because we want to grow food sustainably."

I settled into the chair opposite her, the wood cool against my skin, the familiar comfort of home mingling with the anxiety that had become our constant companion. "I know, but we have to stay calm. If we lose our cool, they'll win. We need to plan our next move carefully."

She crossed her arms, her vibrant curls bouncing defiantly. "A plan? Or a fight? Because I'm more in the mood for a good old-fashioned brawl."

Despite the gravity of the situation, I couldn't help but chuckle. "You know the last time you suggested that, you almost took out a garden gnome. We can't afford to start throwing punches—not just yet."

Her lips curled into a half-smile, but the seriousness settled back into her eyes. "So, what do we do?"

Just then, Sophie bounded out of the house, her little feet barely making a sound on the porch. The brightness of her spirit was infectious, her wild imagination still untouched by the cruel realities of the adult world. "Mom! Are we having a meeting? Can I sit in? I promise to be good!"

I knelt to her level, brushing a lock of hair behind her ear, looking into her curious eyes that sparkled like the very stars we'd stargazed at just last week. "Yes, sweetheart, but this is going to be serious. You might hear some words that aren't so nice."

Her face scrunched in thought, and I could see her weighing the prospect of adult conversations against her own imaginative escapades. "Will there be snacks?"

"Of course," Claire interjected, standing up and tossing her hair back. "I'll bring out the good stuff."

With a flourish, she disappeared into the house, leaving Sophie and me in a bubble of anticipation. I ruffled her hair and stood, feeling a surge of determination. "We're doing this for you, Soph. We need to show everyone that we can stand up for what's right."

The firelight flickered in the gathering dusk as we reconvened in the living room, Claire returning with a platter of assorted snacks—cheese, crackers, and an oversized bowl of popcorn that Sophie immediately dove into, creating an impressive mess around her.

Once our allies had arrived—three loyal neighbors with a shared disdain for AgriCorp's tactics—we settled into the comfortable chaos of our small meeting. The air was thick with urgency and the scent of the fresh snacks, mingling with the faint aroma of wildflowers drifting through the open windows.

"Alright, team," I began, gathering my thoughts as the room fell silent. "We need to tackle this head-on. They're trying to sabotage our reputation, and we can't let them succeed. We know they've been cutting corners and ignoring environmental regulations. That's our angle."

"Can't we just yell at them until they go away?" Sophie piped up between mouthfuls of popcorn, her eyes wide with enthusiasm.

"We could," I said, suppressing a smile at her earnestness. "But I think we need a more strategic approach. We'll gather evidence of their wrongdoings, go public, and remind everyone why small farms matter."

Claire nodded, her brow furrowed in concentration. "We'll use social media, maybe even reach out to some local news outlets. If we can get enough momentum, we can turn this around."

As the plan took shape, I felt the weight on my shoulders lighten just a little. The camaraderie in the room—a mix of shared experiences and mutual frustrations—created a ripple of hope. We were a small but determined band, united against a giant that believed it could trample over us.

By the time we adjourned the meeting, the stars had punctured the sky, twinkling like tiny promises. The darkness felt less oppressive now, the weight of our mission translating into a tangible strength that surged within me. As I tucked Sophie into bed later that night, her little face lit by the soft glow of her bedside lamp, I promised myself that no matter what, we would fight for her future, one popcorn-filled giggle at a time.

In that moment, as she drifted into dreams, I felt the stirring of something fierce within—a determination not just to defend our farm but to reclaim the narrative that AgriCorp sought to distort. We were the guardians of this land, and with each passing day, I was more convinced that we would rise to the occasion, wielding our truth like a sword against the encroaching shadows.

As dawn broke over the horizon, spilling its golden light across the fields like a warm embrace, I felt a renewed sense of purpose. The air was crisp, laced with the earthy scent of dew-kissed grass, a perfect backdrop for the day ahead. Today, we would act—not as the cornered mice AgriCorp painted us to be, but as the fierce lions of our little kingdom. I brewed a pot of coffee, the rich aroma filling the farmhouse as I mentally rehearsed our strategy.

Sophie, bleary-eyed and barely able to navigate her way to the kitchen, stumbled in, her hair a glorious mess of curls, resembling a frizzy halo. "Is it morning already? Why is it so bright?" she mumbled, her voice a mixture of sleep and confusion, reminiscent of a young bear emerging from hibernation.

"Because, my darling, the sun has an appointment with us, and it never misses a meeting," I replied, handing her a cup of hot chocolate, the marshmallows floating like little clouds in the rich liquid. "And today, we're going to show the world what we're made of."

Sophie's eyes lit up, the promise of adventure washing over her sleepy demeanor. "Are we going to be heroes? Like in the books?"

I chuckled softly, running a hand through my hair, my thoughts swirling with the weight of the day ahead. "We'll be the kind of heroes who stand up for what's right. Sometimes, it's a lot more complicated than swinging a sword or wearing a cape."

Before I could elaborate, Claire burst through the back door, her face flushed with excitement. "I've been on the phone all morning with local farmers' markets and community groups. They want to help us! They've been watching what's happening and are ready to rally."

Her enthusiasm was infectious, and I felt a flicker of hope ignite within me. "That's fantastic, Claire! We need to harness that momentum. If we can get a coalition together, it might just tip the scales in our favor."

Claire nodded, already pulling her hair back into a no-nonsense ponytail. "I've set up a meeting for tonight. The more, the merrier. It's time we turn the tables."

"Can I come?" Sophie piped up, bouncing on her toes, her enthusiasm spilling over like the hot chocolate she nearly spilled on herself moments earlier.

"Absolutely, but you'll need to be on your best behavior," Claire said, raising an eyebrow playfully. "This isn't a storytime session."

Sophie pouted for a moment, but then she grinned, her little face alight with mischief. "I can be serious! I'll even wear my 'I'm here to save the world' T-shirt."

With a plan in place, we set out into the day, the sun now high in the sky, casting long shadows across the farm. Our first stop was the local community center, a quaint brick building adorned with a mural depicting the seasons of farming life—spring blooms, summer harvests, autumn colors, and winter quietude. Inside, the air buzzed with the familiar sounds of chatter and laughter, a comforting chaos that reminded me of the heartbeat of our small town.

As we entered, a group of familiar faces turned toward us, their expressions a mix of concern and determination. Janet, a sprightly woman with a penchant for outrageous hats and a heart that matched her colorful style, waved us over. "There you are! We've been waiting! We heard the news, and we want to support you."

"Thanks, Janet. Your timing is impeccable as always," I said, settling into a seat beside her. "We need all the help we can get. AgriCorp thinks they can run us out of business, but they don't know who they're dealing with."

"Exactly! They're messing with the wrong people," chimed in Mark, a burly farmer known for his unwavering loyalty and his impressive pumpkin-growing skills. "You've got us behind you. Let's show them that we're not just a bunch of small-time growers."

The room filled with nods and murmurs of agreement, the atmosphere shifting from somber to spirited. As Claire outlined our strategy, laying out the plan for a public demonstration, the energy crackled with possibility. We would stage a rally, inviting not only our loyal supporters but also the public to stand against AgriCorp's manipulations.

"What if we turn the farm into a showcase?" Janet suggested, her eyes sparkling with ideas. "We can have booths with samples of our produce, cooking demonstrations, maybe even a mini carnival for the kids!"

"That's brilliant!" Claire exclaimed, the enthusiasm infectious. "It'll draw people in and remind them of the joys of local farming, the real food they deserve."

"And we can share our story," I added, feeling the weight of the moment settle upon me. "It's not just about us; it's about everyone who believes in what we do and stands against the corporate machine."

The conversation flowed seamlessly, ideas bouncing back and forth like a lively game of tennis, everyone eager to contribute. Sophie, seated cross-legged on the floor with her notebook, scribbled furiously, already drafting a plan for her own booth—"Sophie's Fun Corner: The Future of Farming."

"Will there be a petting zoo?" she called out, her wide-eyed innocence cutting through the fervor of the meeting.

"Only if you're in charge of the animals," Claire shot back, winking at her. "But you might have to limit the petting to actual farm animals, not your stuffed ones."

Sophie placed a hand on her hip, feigning outrage. "But they have so much to teach the world! I could host a seminar on hugging cows!"

We erupted into laughter, the tension easing further with each chuckle. It was moments like these that reminded me of why we fought so hard for this life, why the farm meant everything—not just to us, but to our community. The resilience in this room felt palpable, a shared heartbeat of hope pulsing stronger with every passing moment.

As the meeting drew to a close, we agreed to meet again to finalize the details. I lingered behind, chatting with a few neighbors while Sophie helped clean up. Watching her, I felt a swell of pride. She was not just a bystander in this journey; she was becoming an integral part of the fight.

Later that evening, as we returned home, the sun dipped below the horizon, painting the sky in hues of pink and orange. I couldn't shake the feeling that we were on the cusp of something monumental. AgriCorp had stirred a fire in us, and together we would rise, armed with the truth and our unwavering determination.

The rally was set for Saturday, just two days away, and as the clock ticked closer to the event, a mix of excitement and nerves crackled in the air like a live wire. Each morning unfolded with purpose, my mind racing with ideas, plans, and the daunting weight of our mission. We transformed our farm into a vibrant stage, with colorful banners flapping against the blue sky, declaring our commitment to local agriculture and community resilience.

Sophie was a whirlwind of energy, flitting from booth to booth, her enthusiasm infectious as she rallied volunteers like a tiny general leading her troops into battle. "Okay, everyone! We need more balloons! And glitter! What's a party without glitter?" she exclaimed, her hands gesturing wildly. Claire and I exchanged bemused glances, suppressing laughter as we watched her bounce around, her boundless optimism a stark contrast to the serious undertones of our fight.

By Thursday, the word had spread throughout the community like wildfire. People were ready to stand with us. I could hardly believe the response—more than a hundred RSVPs flooded in from neighbors, fellow farmers, and even families from nearby towns. In the days leading up to the rally, Claire and I worked tirelessly to organize everything, from food stalls to workshops. We would demonstrate that small farms were not just quaint backdrops for Instagram posts but vital lifelines for health, sustainability, and community spirit.

As the sun dipped low on Friday evening, I found a quiet moment alone on the porch, the light fading to a soft twilight. I sipped a glass of homemade lemonade, the tartness invigorating against the warm breeze. My thoughts drifted to what lay ahead, the weight of the impending confrontation looming large. Would it be enough? Could we truly take on a giant like AgriCorp?

Just then, Claire plopped down beside me, a look of deep contemplation etched on her face. "You know," she began, her voice low, "I've been thinking. What if they retaliate? They have resources we can't even fathom."

I sighed, the thought twisting like a knife in my gut. "I know. But if we show strength, if we show unity, we might just scare them off. They thrive on intimidation, Claire. We can't let fear dictate our actions."

She nodded slowly, but I could see the concern etched in her features. "I just hope we're prepared for whatever comes next. The media might latch onto this. If we go viral, it could either be our saving grace or our downfall."

"Then we'll have to ensure it's the former," I said, trying to mask my own apprehension with optimism. "The rally will be a celebration of everything we stand for, and we'll let our voices drown out any negativity."

The night wore on, filled with laughter and a sense of camaraderie as our friends joined us for a final pep talk. Sophie, ever the enthusiastic cheerleader, took it upon herself to lead a makeshift warm-up session. "Everyone, stand up! We need to get our voices ready to yell at the bad guys!" she shouted, her tiny fists pumping in the air.

Laughter erupted as Claire and I clapped along, the tension of the previous days momentarily forgotten. "You're a natural-born leader, kiddo," I said, ruffling her hair affectionately.

"Of course! I have to keep you two in line," she quipped back, grinning widely, blissfully unaware of the storm brewing on the horizon.

Saturday arrived with a vibrancy that felt almost surreal. The farm was alive with color and laughter, the air filled with the tantalizing scent of fresh produce and baked goods wafting from the stalls. As the crowd gathered, I stood back for a moment, soaking it all in. The community had come together, united in a purpose that transcended the struggles we faced.

"Here we go!" Claire said, her eyes sparkling with excitement. We positioned ourselves at the front of the crowd, microphones in hand, ready to speak to the throngs of people that had gathered in solidarity.

As the sun beamed down on us, I could feel the adrenaline pulsing through my veins, the fear of what might happen today mingling with the hope that today could change everything. I opened my mouth to address the crowd, but just then, a black SUV rolled up the dirt path, dust swirling in its wake.

My heart raced. The vehicle had an ominous air about it, and my stomach twisted in knots as it came to a halt. The door swung open, and out stepped a man in a sharp suit, his face hidden behind dark sunglasses. He strode toward us with an air of authority, a stark contrast to the joy that filled the atmosphere.

"Who is that?" Sophie whispered beside me, her tiny fingers clutching my hand tightly.

I had no time to answer. The crowd shifted uneasily as the man approached, a smug smile playing on his lips. "Well, well, well," he drawled, his voice dripping with condescension. "Looks like the little farm that could has gathered quite the crowd. But I'm afraid you're all wasting your time."

Gasps rippled through the audience, the atmosphere shifting from festive to charged in an instant. My heart thudded loudly in my chest as I squared my shoulders, stepping forward. "And who exactly are you to dictate our actions?"

He chuckled, leaning against a nearby fence as if he were merely a spectator in this drama. "Just a concerned citizen, wanting to ensure that you understand the consequences of your actions. AgriCorp doesn't take kindly to defiance, and believe me, they have their ways of making things... uncomfortable."

The tension hung thick in the air, every eye on him, every breath held in anticipation. This was the moment we had been preparing for, yet the unease crept back in, shadowing our resolve. I took a deep breath, meeting his gaze, refusing to let fear consume me.

"We're not afraid of you or your threats," I said firmly, rallying my voice for the crowd to hear. "This is about standing up for what is right, and we won't be intimidated."

"Is that so?" he replied, his smile widening into something almost predatory. "Well, let's see how brave you are when the reality of your little rally sets in. Enjoy your day, folks."

With that, he turned and walked back to the SUV, leaving an unsettling silence in his wake. My heart raced, a cold chill snaking down my spine as I realized the depth of the threat that hung over us. Just then, Claire nudged me, her expression alarmed. "What do we do now?"

The crowd murmured, anxiety creeping in like an unwelcome guest. I could feel their eyes on me, waiting for a response, and I knew I had to act decisively. Just as I prepared to speak again, a loud crash echoed from the other side of the farm, followed by panicked screams.

"Is that...?" Claire began, her voice trailing off in horror.

Before I could finish processing what was happening, chaos erupted, and I knew then that the battle was only just beginning.

Chapter 20: The Final Showdown

The sun dipped below the horizon, painting the sky in shades of tangerine and lavender, a breathtaking backdrop for the tumultuous storm brewing in my heart. The fields stretched endlessly around me, their golden waves whispering secrets only the earth could understand. Sophie, her auburn hair catching the last light of the day, stood beside me, her presence a soothing balm against the chaotic thoughts swirling in my mind. I took a deep breath, inhaling the rich scent of soil mingled with wildflowers, grounding myself in the moment as the chill of impending confrontation settled into my bones.

"Do you think they'll listen?" Sophie's voice broke through my reverie, a mixture of hope and uncertainty tinged with the weariness of countless battles fought and lost. She was my anchor, the embodiment of the spirit we were fighting to protect—the spirit of our community, of family farms threatened by the relentless march of AgriCorp.

"I have to believe they will," I replied, my voice steadier than I felt. "We have the truth on our side, and with the stories of the farmers, we're not just fighting for ourselves anymore. We're fighting for everyone who's ever felt voiceless." As I spoke, the words swelled with conviction, igniting a flicker of courage within me. I wanted her to feel it, too, to share in the flickering flame of hope that refused to be extinguished.

The shadows grew longer, wrapping around us as if trying to hold us back, but we stepped forward, leaving our worries behind. Together, we ventured deeper into the fields, where the stars above twinkled like the eyes of long-lost friends, reminding me that we were not alone in this fight. A soft breeze rustled the corn stalks, and I could almost hear their encouragement.

"Remember when we used to sneak out here as kids?" Sophie mused, a nostalgic smile spreading across her face. "We thought we could build a fort and protect the world from monsters."

"Yeah, and we ended up building a pile of sticks that collapsed the moment we put our weight on it," I laughed, the sound light and free, momentarily distracting me from the impending showdown. "But we had a blast trying."

"Maybe that's all we need to do now," she said, her eyes sparkling with mischief. "Just make a lot of noise and hope it all works out."

"Make noise? Oh, I can do that," I quipped, grinning at her. "I'm practically a human megaphone when I'm passionate about something."

Our laughter echoed in the twilight, a fragile thread of joy in a web of uncertainty. Yet, beneath the surface of light-hearted banter, a current of tension ran deep. The stakes were high; AgriCorp had been like a shadow over our community for too long, their corporate machinations looming ominously. I could practically feel Paul's smirk, that arrogant tilt of his mouth, ready to dismiss our efforts with the wave of a well-manicured hand.

"I just wish we could somehow catch them off guard," Sophie mused, her tone shifting from playful to contemplative. "Expose their lies in a way they can't wiggle out of. They've been so careful, so calculated."

"Careful doesn't always mean clever," I replied, the seed of an idea germinating in my mind. "We need to strike at their weakest point—their arrogance. They think they own this town, but they don't know us. We're resilient, Sophie. We're stubborn."

"Like weeds in a garden," she added, her eyes bright with mischief.

"Exactly! And weeds have a way of choking out even the strongest flowers," I said, feeling a surge of determination. "What if we gather more stories? Reach out to those who've been silenced and give them a platform?"

Her face lit up with excitement, a cascade of possibilities dancing in her gaze. "Yes! We can invite everyone to share their experiences on the town square—create a living tapestry of our community. When they see the faces and hear the voices, it will be harder for AgriCorp to dismiss us."

A swell of hope washed over me, invigorating my spirit. We could rally together, a united front armed not just with facts, but with the heart and soul of our community. "Let's do it," I urged, already envisioning the flurry of activity that would ensue. "We'll collect stories tonight, make it our mission. Tomorrow, we'll flood the square with their truth."

The night air thickened with purpose, and as we walked back, a new resolve settled between us, igniting a fire that would carry us into the dawn of our final confrontation. Tomorrow would not be just another day; it would be a turning point, a declaration of our resistance against the corporate goliath threatening to consume everything we held dear.

As I turned to Sophie, ready to set our plan into motion, a rustle in the distance caught my attention. My heart raced, the thrill of adventure coursing through my veins. "Did you hear that?" I whispered, instinctively lowering my voice.

"What?" Sophie asked, her brow furrowing in concern.

"Something... or someone is out there."

The moment hung in the air, electrified with potential. We exchanged a glance, a shared understanding of the unknown that lay ahead. Whatever it was, we would face it together. I could feel the weight of the world on my shoulders, but with Sophie by my side, I knew we would find a way to confront the challenges looming before us.

The rustling intensified, a symphony of whispers riding the night breeze, as shadows played tricks on my mind. My heart drummed a frantic beat, each thud echoing in my ears as I strained to catch a glimpse of whatever lurked beyond the cornfield's edge. Sophie stood beside me, her confidence faltering for a moment, yet a glimmer of determination flickered in her eyes. "Should we check it out? Or call for backup? Maybe bring a snack as bait?"

"Because nothing says 'don't eat me' like a plate of cookies?" I replied, suppressing a smile even as my heart raced. The thought of an ambush involving baked goods was absurd enough to cut through the tension. But the gravity of our situation pressed down on us, and we couldn't let our fears drive our actions.

With a shared nod, we moved cautiously toward the source of the noise, each step heavy with anticipation. The moonlight cast ghostly silhouettes across the field, and the familiar scents of damp earth and wildflowers filled the air, but tonight they felt charged with something electric, something primal.

Suddenly, from behind a particularly dense cluster of corn, a figure stepped into view. "Whoa there! You two planning an escape from a horror movie or just out for a stroll?"

The voice was both familiar and disarming, cutting through the suspense like a warm knife through butter. I exhaled sharply, relief washing over me as I recognized Tyler, our neighbor and fellow activist. He had the kind of presence that could diffuse even the most intense of situations, his tousled hair and easy smile a comforting contrast to the tension we had been bracing against.

"Tyler! You scared the daylights out of us," I exclaimed, shaking off the remnants of fear that had clung to me like a second skin.

"Good, that's my secret weapon. Now, what's the plan?" He stepped closer, his expression shifting to one of keen interest. "I saw your light and thought I'd check in. Heard a little birdie say you're organizing some kind of rally tomorrow. Care to fill me in?"

Sophie and I exchanged glances, a silent agreement passing between us. We filled Tyler in on our plans, the urgency of sharing the stories of the farmers affected by AgriCorp's grip on our community. With each word, I felt the momentum building, fueled not just by our conviction but also by the unexpected solidarity blooming around us.

"Stories are the heart of it," Tyler said, his voice earnest. "People don't just need facts—they need to connect emotionally. When they see the faces behind the statistics, it changes everything. Count me in."

A wave of gratitude washed over me. Tyler's enthusiasm was contagious, and with him in the mix, it felt like we were gaining a small army to fight back against the looming giant. "We'll meet at the square at dawn. Bring anyone who's willing to share their story. The more voices we have, the harder it will be for AgriCorp to sweep us under the rug," I declared, feeling more empowered by the minute.

The moon hung high, casting a silvery glow over the fields, and for a brief moment, it felt as if the universe conspired to light our path forward. But as I turned to leave, the urgency of tomorrow gnawed at my insides. I couldn't shake the feeling that we were running out of time, that AgriCorp would retaliate in some way we weren't prepared for.

"Let's gather at my place afterward," Sophie suggested, her voice steady. "We can brainstorm and gather our thoughts over coffee. I make a killer cup."

"Just as long as you don't accidentally brew it with AgriCorp's logo on it," Tyler quipped, earning a playful shove from Sophie.

"Hey! My coffee is pure, unlike their practices. You'll see," she shot back, her laughter infectious as we made our way back, the thrill of collaboration lighting our footsteps.

The night slipped away, surrendering to the cool embrace of dawn. I woke up with a sense of purpose thrumming through me, but the weight of anxiety clung like a second skin. I dressed quickly, pulling on a sturdy pair of jeans and a flannel shirt that smelled faintly of lavender—an aroma that always reminded me of home, of summer evenings spent helping my grandmother in her garden.

As I stepped outside, the morning air greeted me with a refreshing chill, and the world came alive with the sounds of chirping birds and rustling leaves. I made my way to the town square, the anticipation bubbling beneath my skin. A few early risers were already setting up tables and chairs, their voices weaving together like a vibrant tapestry.

Sophie arrived soon after, her eyes alight with determination. "I've got flyers! And coffee, the kind that'll wake the dead," she said, a lopsided grin breaking across her face.

"Perfect! Let's hang these up everywhere. We need everyone to know this is happening," I replied, my excitement bubbling over.

As we worked, people began to gather, drawn by the whispers of our mission. Faces I recognized and some I didn't appeared, each person bringing their own story, their own stake in the fight against AgriCorp. The atmosphere buzzed with an electric energy that fueled my spirit, transforming my nervousness into a palpable sense of solidarity.

As the sun climbed higher, the crowd thickened, and my heart swelled with hope. Each voice that joined us was a reminder that we weren't alone; we were part of something bigger, a collective force standing against the tide of corporate greed. The stories began to flow, pouring out like sweet summer rain. Each tale shared, from lost crops to shattered dreams, built a narrative stronger than any one individual could muster.

But just as I felt we were gaining traction, a figure loomed at the edge of the square, a dark silhouette against the brightening sky. Paul stood there, flanked by a few suits that dripped with corporate arrogance. I could feel the collective intake of breath from the crowd, a hush falling over us like a shroud.

"Ladies and gentlemen," Paul's voice sliced through the air, smooth as silk but laced with venom. "What a charming little gathering you have here. However, I must remind you, this is not the way to achieve what you want."

The tension coiled tightly, like a spring ready to snap. My heart raced as I prepared to respond, knowing this was the moment everything could shift. The crowd held its breath, waiting for the first spark to ignite the fire of confrontation.

The crowd simmered with anticipation, eyes locked on Paul as if he were an unruly guest at a family gathering, and we were all waiting for him to make a fool of himself. He stepped closer, his tailored suit stark against the rustic backdrop of our town square, the polished surfaces of his expensive watch and shoes catching the morning light in a way that felt distinctly out of place among us. I could almost hear the collective heartbeat of our community, the rhythm of resistance pulsing through the air like a drum.

"Charm?" he scoffed, his lips twisting into a mockery of a smile. "What you're engaging in is pure sentimentality. Farmers don't need the illusion of community; they need cold, hard cash." His voice dripped with condescension, a calculated venom that made my skin crawl. "And that's exactly what AgriCorp offers. Not these—" he gestured dismissively at the crowd, "—emotional tales of hardship."

Sophie stepped forward, her voice steady yet fierce. "What you call 'sentimentality' is our reality, Paul. You can't drown out the truth with dollar signs." Her words sparked a ripple of agreement among those gathered, and I felt my resolve hardening like steel.

"Oh, please," he retorted, his condescending smirk only widening. "What is your 'truth' worth? A few sob stories? I'll tell you what it's worth: nothing. You'll find that out soon enough." He leaned in, as if sharing a secret, his voice lowering to a conspiratorial tone. "Your little gathering here? It's cute. But you're stepping into a world that doesn't play by your rules."

Just then, a voice from the back called out, "We're tired of being bullied, Paul!" It was James, a local farmer whose land had been seized under the guise of "expansion." The crowd erupted in a chorus of agreement, their voices weaving together in a tapestry of defiance.

Paul turned his piercing gaze toward James, eyebrows arched in disbelief. "Ah, the victim. Such a tragic story, but tell me—what is it you plan to do about it? Nothing but complain, I assume." He was toying with us, like a cat with a cornered mouse, and my gut churned at the sight.

"Enough!" I found my voice rising above the noise, shaking off the cold dread that threatened to overwhelm me. "This isn't just about complaints; this is about action. This is about people standing together, refusing to let you and your corporation run roughshod over our lives!"

Paul's smile faltered for a split second before he regained his composure, a flicker of irritation sparking in his eyes. "Is that so? Let me remind you, you're playing a dangerous game, my dear. AgriCorp has deep pockets and even deeper connections. You think this charming little protest will change anything? You'll just end up hurting yourselves."

"Like that's ever stopped us before," I shot back, my heart racing. My words hung in the air, daring him to respond. "If you think we'll cower in fear because of some financial threat, you clearly don't know who you're dealing with. We have something you can't buy."

"What's that? Your precious ideals?" His voice dripped with scorn. "Let me tell you, ideals don't pay bills or put food on the table. They won't save your farms from the reality of economic survival. You'll need to wake up, little girl."

The anger bubbling in my chest threatened to spill over. "I'm awake, Paul. And I see you for what you are—a bully hiding behind your wealth." My voice rose, the crowd leaning in, drawn by the palpable energy crackling between us.

"Careful now," he warned, his tone sharp. "You're out of your depth." He shifted slightly, the glint in his eye promising retribution, a storm brewing just beneath the surface.

But before I could respond, Sophie stepped up beside me, her presence a reassuring anchor. "You know what? Let's make this interesting. Why don't we invite you to share your side of the story? We're all ears." Her tone was deceptively casual, but I could sense the challenge beneath her words.

The crowd murmured in surprise, and I shot Sophie a look, half bewildered and half impressed. "You sure about that?"

"Absolutely," she replied, her eyes sparkling with mischief. "Let's give him a platform. The truth always finds a way to rise, doesn't it?"

Paul's expression twisted, clearly caught off guard. "You think I would lower myself to this? I don't need to explain myself to you or anyone here. My actions speak for themselves. And, frankly, they are far more powerful than your—" he waved a dismissive hand, "—whimsical tales of woe."

The crowd simmered with a mix of excitement and apprehension. "He's afraid," I whispered to Sophie, the realization hitting me like a gust of wind. "That's why he won't engage. He knows we have the power of the truth behind us."

"Then we push him," she said, determination lighting her face. "Let's invite him to join the stories, to stand here and face us. Show us who he really is. Besides, wouldn't it be fun to watch him squirm?"

"Fun isn't quite the word I'd use, but I get your point." I smiled at her, bolstered by her unwavering spirit.

"Let's do this!" Sophie shouted, turning back to the crowd. "If Paul wants to talk, let him! We have nothing to hide!"

The collective energy shifted, the crowd echoing her sentiments, voices rising in a tidal wave of support.

"Fine," Paul said, straightening his jacket, trying to regain control. "If that's how you want to play, I'll humor you. But don't expect any sympathy from me."

"Sympathy isn't what we're after," I countered, my heart pounding in my chest. "What we want is accountability."

As he stepped forward, the tension in the air thickened. I could feel the eyes of the townsfolk on us, each one a testament to the stakes involved. This was more than a debate; it was a reckoning.

Just then, a sudden commotion erupted at the edge of the crowd. A figure burst through the throng, breathless and wild-eyed. "You need to hear this! It's urgent!"

The crowd turned, confusion rippling through us like a shockwave. I glanced at Sophie, who mirrored my concern. The air crackled with an unspoken fear, a premonition that something monumental was about to unfold.

"Who are you?" Paul snapped, annoyance cutting through the tension.

"Please! Just listen!" The newcomer, a young man with disheveled hair and dirt-smeared clothes, struggled to catch his breath. "It's about AgriCorp. They've got plans—plans that will change everything for this town!"

A hush fell over the square, the collective breath held as the realization hit. Whatever news he carried had the potential to shift the tides in our favor or shatter our fragile hopes.

"What kind of plans?" I demanded, stepping forward. My heart raced, a mix of dread and anticipation weaving together.

He met my gaze, urgency blazing in his eyes. "Plans to... to take more than just the farms. They're going after the land itself. And there's something even worse..."

The words hung in the air, laden with impending doom, each syllable crackling with the promise of revelations yet to come. The crowd leaned in closer, the murmur of anxious voices swirling around us like autumn leaves caught in a tempest, waiting for the storm to break.

Chapter 21: Unraveling the Lies

The fluorescent lights flickered overhead, a staccato rhythm that matched the quickening beats of my heart. Claire stood at the front of the room, her eyes alight with fervor as she meticulously pieced together the evidence we had unearthed, each slide a nail driven deeper into AgriCorp's coffin. I had known from the start that this moment would be pivotal, but witnessing the shift in the audience—initially skeptical, now leaning forward with a hunger for truth—was electrifying. Each gasp that escaped their lips reverberated through me, a shared recognition that we were not just individuals presenting data; we were the harbingers of justice.

"Look at the manipulation!" Claire exclaimed, her voice slicing through the charged atmosphere. "These figures are not just numbers—they represent families, livelihoods! AgriCorp has played us like puppets, pulling strings behind the scenes while we remained blissfully unaware."

I stole a glance at Sophie, who stood beside me, her fingers entwined with mine. Her grip was firm, a grounding presence amidst the storm of emotions swirling around us. I could see her determination, a fierce resolve battling against the tide of vulnerability that flickered in her eyes. The air felt heavy, laden with the weight of our mission, yet it was also filled with the unmistakable scent of revolution—like rain on dry earth, promising renewal.

As Claire clicked to the next slide, an image flashed across the screen: a collage of headlines, each one revealing a different aspect of AgriCorp's misdeeds. From environmental degradation to labor exploitation, the sins of the corporation were laid bare for all to see. Murmurs rippled through the crowd, a collective consciousness awakening to the truth we had fought so hard to reveal.

"Do you see?" I murmured to Sophie, my voice barely above a whisper, yet thick with emotion. "They can't hide anymore."

She met my gaze, her expression a blend of hope and trepidation. "This could change everything, couldn't it?" she asked, her voice steady but her eyes betraying a flicker of fear.

"Everything," I affirmed, squeezing her hand gently, willing her to absorb the gravity of what lay ahead. "But it's just the beginning."

Suddenly, a voice pierced the tension—a deep, authoritative tone cutting through the rising tide of our momentum. "What proof do you have? You can't simply make claims without solid evidence." It was Richard, the well-coiffed PR executive from AgriCorp, his posture rigid, a human barricade between us and the truth.

Claire squared her shoulders, her confidence unwavering. "Our evidence is irrefutable, Richard. You've underestimated the power of your complacency. We've dug deeper than you ever imagined. This isn't just a battle of words; it's a war of truth."

A ripple of applause broke out, igniting a fire within the room. The tension was palpable, electric, and I could feel the shift as the audience began to rally behind us. Their energy surged like a wave, crashing against the shore of corporate greed. They chanted our names, a chorus of defiance that pushed back against the suffocating presence of AgriCorp.

With each chant, I felt the doubts that had once plagued me dissipate into the air like smoke. We were not alone. This was a movement, a collective uprising against the tyranny of profit over people. Claire continued her presentation, her words weaving a tapestry of truth that enveloped the audience, pulling them into our narrative.

But then, amidst the rising cheers, I caught a glimpse of Sophie, her face pale as if the very blood had drained from it. The vibrant energy that had surrounded us began to wane, replaced by a subtle shift—a shadow creeping in where there had once been light.

"Hey," I said softly, leaning closer, my voice just for her. "What's wrong?"

She took a deep breath, her eyes darting to the back of the room where shadows seemed to coalesce. "It's just... something doesn't feel right," she whispered, her brow furrowing. "I thought this would be the turning point, but it feels like they're just waiting for us to slip up."

Before I could respond, a commotion erupted at the entrance. The double doors swung open with a force that sent a hush cascading through the crowd. In strode a group of sharply dressed executives, their expressions a storm cloud of anger and indignation. Richard's face paled as he recognized the urgency in their stride, the way they seemed to draw power from their collective presence.

"Ladies and gentlemen," one of them spoke, a tall man with a hawkish gaze. "We have evidence of an orchestrated smear campaign against AgriCorp. These claims are unfounded and will not be tolerated."

His words fell like a stone into the pool of fervor that had just begun to swell, and I felt a wave of fear wash over me. The air shifted again, this time with a weight that pressed down on my chest, threatening to suffocate the hope we had ignited.

"What do you mean by 'smear campaign'?" Claire challenged, her voice sharp and clear. "We're here to share the truth!"

"Truth?" the man scoffed, a patronizing grin spreading across his face. "Let's see how well the truth holds up in a court of law."

I exchanged a look with Sophie, a shared realization dawning in our eyes. This was no longer just about us revealing the truth; it was a battle for survival. AgriCorp wasn't going to roll over. They were ready for war, and the stakes were higher than we had ever anticipated.

As the tension in the room thickened, I could feel the atmosphere shift palpably, like the air before a summer storm. The tension between the two factions—us, armed with undeniable truths, and them, an imposing wall of corporate authority—seemed to thrum in the silence. Richard stood awkwardly beside the group of executives, looking a little lost, like a sheep caught in a pack of wolves.

"Evidence of a smear campaign?" Claire's voice sliced through the uneasy quiet. "You mean the facts we've gathered? That's not a smear; that's a spotlight on your failures. If you've got something to say, now's your chance to back it up."

Her challenge hung in the air, daring them to retaliate, but the hawkish man merely laughed, a sound devoid of mirth. "Ah, the young and naïve. You think this is a game of honesty? We will crush you with the very laws you think protect you." He leaned in closer, a predator sizing up his prey. "Don't think we haven't prepared for this. We've been waiting for you to make your move."

Sophie's grip tightened around my hand, her knuckles whitening as the room seemed to darken with looming threats. I could see the uncertainty in her eyes, battling against the embers of hope we had kindled. "This isn't just about us anymore," she whispered, her voice barely carrying over the hum of anxious murmurs. "This could get ugly."

"Let it get ugly," I replied, my voice steadier than I felt. "We have the truth on our side." But deep down, the gnawing worry began to settle in. What if the truth wasn't enough? What if they had the power to spin the narrative, to twist it in a way that made us look like the villains?

Claire stepped forward, undeterred, her eyes blazing with defiance. "We are not afraid of you. We will expose what you've done, and we will fight this until the very end."

At that moment, I felt the crowd rallying behind us once again, a swell of support that threatened to drown out the looming threats. The energy shifted back, the electricity of the room crackling with renewed determination. "We are the community!" one voice called out, and soon a chorus followed, echoing through the venue, shaking the very foundation of AgriCorp's façade.

But the hawkish man held up a hand, silencing the growing tide. "You're playing with fire, and we know how to extinguish it." He gestured behind him, and I caught sight of a tall woman stepping forward. Her presence was commanding, with sharp features and a gaze that seemed to pierce through the growing haze of resolve.

"Let's not forget who has the money and the resources," she said coolly, her voice smooth but laced with an edge. "A legal battle can go on for years. We will bury you in paperwork and legal fees. You'll wish you'd never dared to take us on."

Claire squared her shoulders, unyielding. "You think we'll back down? We've fought too hard for this. You can't silence us. You can't intimidate us into submission."

"Ah, the ever-idealistic crusader," the woman retorted, tilting her head, amusement flickering in her eyes. "But idealism doesn't pay the bills or put food on the table."

"Actually, it does," Sophie chimed in, her voice firm as she stepped forward beside Claire. "Because idealism—when paired with action—creates movements. We are not alone in this. You might have money, but we have the hearts of the people, and they are worth more than your corporate interests."

The crowd erupted again, a wave of cheers rising like a tide, the moment emboldening me. It felt as if we were on the cusp of something monumental, a point of no return. I could sense the heartbeat of rebellion pulsating around us, and it was intoxicating.

But the hawkish woman merely smirked, folding her arms. "We'll see how long that lasts when the news breaks that you've been misleading the public. How long do you think this rebellion will last when your credibility is in question?"

The tension snapped in an instant, like a taut string severed. I glanced at Sophie, who met my gaze with a fierce glimmer of resolve.

"They're trying to intimidate us," she murmured, and I could see the fire in her eyes igniting further. "We can't let them get away with this. We need to be smart, play our cards right."

Just as I was about to respond, a commotion broke out at the back of the room. An older man in a faded baseball cap and a weathered denim jacket pushed his way through the crowd, his face a mask of indignation. "You all listen here!" he called out, his voice rich and booming. "These people are fighting for us! They're digging up the dirt that needs to be brought into the light!"

Sophie and I exchanged glances, surprise mixed with a flicker of hope. The man continued, rallying others around him. "We've had enough of AgriCorp lying and stealing from our community! It's time we stand together and demand accountability!"

The crowd erupted into cheers, a swell of emotion washing over us as the man's passion ignited something deep within each of us. Suddenly, more people began to speak out, a cascade of voices rising in solidarity. "Down with corporate greed!" "We deserve better!"

Claire beamed, clearly invigorated by the outpouring of support. "This is our moment!" she shouted, her energy infectious. "We are the truth! We are the change!"

But as we basked in the glow of collective fervor, I couldn't shake the nagging feeling that we were still in dangerous waters. The executives from AgriCorp stood unflinching, calculating. They weren't done yet. This was merely their opening act.

As the crowd continued to roar, I felt a pang of uncertainty. We had sparked a fire, but fires could be extinguished just as easily. I glanced at Sophie again, her eyes bright with determination, and I resolved to push aside my fears. We had come too far to falter now.

"Let's make sure our voices are heard loud and clear," I said, my tone firm. "Together, we'll gather our evidence, and we'll show them that their intimidation tactics won't work."

Sophie nodded, and as the crowd continued to chant, I allowed the warmth of camaraderie to envelop me, reminding me that we were not alone. Together, we were an unstoppable force. But in the back of my mind, the question loomed: Would it be enough?

The room reverberated with the pulse of collective outrage, a living, breathing entity determined to challenge the corporate Goliath before us. Sophie and I stood at the epicenter, our hearts thundering in sync with the chants echoing off the sterile walls. The executives, still poised and seemingly unshakeable, appeared to sense the rising tide of defiance; their expressions shifted, the smug confidence cracking, revealing glimpses of concern.

"Let's take this outside," one of the hawkish man's companions suggested, his voice low but tinged with irritation. "We can't allow this circus to continue in here."

But the crowd wasn't having it. "No!" a voice shouted from the back, igniting a ripple of agreement. "This is our space! We'll speak our truth right here!"

I felt Sophie's grip tighten around my hand as she leaned closer. "We can't back down now. This is our chance to show them we're serious."

"I'm with you," I whispered back, my own resolve hardening like steel. The energy was palpable, a force of nature that coursed through our veins, urging us to press on.

As Claire raised her voice above the clamor, I caught sight of a familiar face slipping through the throng. It was Jake, my old college buddy, and a rather talented journalist known for his hard-hitting exposés. His presence cut through the noise, and I felt a swell of hope. Maybe he could lend us some of his media magic.

"Hey!" I shouted, trying to catch his attention amidst the cacophony. "We need your help!"

Jake's brows furrowed as he approached, his expression shifting from surprise to determination as he absorbed the atmosphere. "What's going on? This looks intense."

"AgriCorp is trying to bury the truth, and we're not letting them," I explained, quickly filling him in on the events. "They're here trying to intimidate us into silence, but we have the community on our side."

"Good," he replied, a spark igniting in his eyes. "You know I live for this kind of story. Just tell me what you need."

Claire interjected, her voice cutting through the chatter. "We need to get our findings out there, and fast. We can't let AgriCorp spin this narrative before we do."

Jake nodded, his fingers already flying over his phone as he began drafting a post. "I'll get this live. A rallying cry for the community. They need to see what's at stake."

The energy in the room shifted again, a collective breath held in anticipation. People were turning to their phones, sharing the news and rallying friends. The atmosphere crackled with the electricity of unity, and for the first time, it felt like we were harnessing the kind of power that could bring a corporation to its knees.

Yet, even as I reveled in the moment, a dark cloud loomed on the horizon. I could sense the eyes of the AgriCorp executives drilling into us, their palpable frustration mingling with a simmering fury. The hawkish man stepped forward again, voice dripping with disdain. "You really think this will change anything? You're merely a gnat buzzing around a giant. The truth is, we have the resources to bury you."

"Why don't you try?" Claire shot back, her composure unyielding. "We're not here to roll over; we're here to fight."

A moment of silence hung between us, tension vibrating like a plucked string. Then, the woman in charge, her gaze steely, replied,

"Fighting is one thing. Surviving the aftermath is another. We will make your lives a living hell."

The crowd began to murmur, uncertainty creeping back in. I could see the flickers of doubt on some faces, and I knew we had to reinforce our message, to fan the flames of rebellion that were beginning to flicker.

"Listen!" I called out, raising my voice to cut through the murmurs. "This isn't just about us anymore. This is about every person who has suffered under corporate greed! Every worker who has been mistreated! Every family affected by their negligence! We have the power to change this narrative, to stand tall against intimidation. Are you with us?"

The crowd erupted once more, a cacophony of voices shouting their solidarity. But amidst the cheer, a nagging thought clawed at me. What if we weren't prepared for the kind of fight that lay ahead?

Just then, a sharp sound echoed through the room, silencing the crowd. A loud bang followed by the unmistakable sound of glass shattering reverberated off the walls, a chilling reminder of the stakes at play.

"What the—?" I turned, eyes wide, just in time to see a figure slipping through the shattered window, a masked face obscured beneath a black cap. Panic surged through the crowd as the intruder vaulted over the broken glass and charged toward us.

"Get down!" someone yelled, and chaos erupted. The energy that had previously felt so empowering now twisted into a frenzy of fear as people scrambled to escape.

Sophie pulled me down behind a nearby table, her eyes wide with terror. "What the hell is happening?"

"I don't know!" I shouted back, my heart racing. "But we need to get everyone out of here!"

The figure, now fully visible, reached for something at their side. My mind raced, thoughts spiraling as I tried to make sense of the situation. Were they here to silence us, to take our voices before we could truly fight back?

"Stay close!" I urged Sophie, just as the figure pointed something shiny toward Claire, who was still standing defiantly, fists clenched.

"Stop! You have no idea what you're getting into!" Claire yelled, her bravery shining through the chaos. But her words barely reached me as adrenaline coursed through my veins.

In that heart-stopping moment, time seemed to freeze. The crowd pressed against the walls, watching in horror as the masked intruder's finger tightened on the trigger. A sharp crack echoed, a deafening sound that left us all breathless.

And just like that, the world tipped on its axis, hanging in the balance between defiance and fear, as I held my breath, not knowing if we would emerge from this chaos intact.

Chapter 22: A Heart Divided

The sun hung low in the sky, casting a warm golden hue over the kitchen, where the scent of freshly baked bread mingled with the earthy aroma of rosemary and garlic. I leaned against the counter, watching Sophie as she rolled out the dough with a grace that always left me in awe. Flour dust danced in the air, creating a whimsical, almost ethereal quality to the moment. Her hair, a cascade of chestnut waves, bounced lightly as she hummed an unfamiliar tune, the soft cadence of her voice weaving through the afternoon like a comforting blanket.

But that tranquility shattered the moment her phone rang. The sharp trill cut through the warm atmosphere, jolting me from my reverie. I observed her expression shift in an instant, the joyful lines of her face erasing themselves as if someone had turned off the lights in a theater. The call seemed to reach into the very core of her being, twisting her features into a mask of dread.

"Who is it?" I asked, my voice a low murmur, filled with concern.

Her fingers tightened around the phone, and for a moment, I feared she might shatter it. "It's... it's him," she whispered, barely audible above the sudden roaring silence that enveloped us. The man who had haunted her past—his name hung heavy in the air, a malevolent specter that twisted in the shadows behind her eyes.

I stepped closer, closing the distance between us, my heart pounding as the weight of her fear washed over me. "Sophie, you don't have to answer it. We can just—"

But before I could finish, she lifted the phone to her ear, a blend of determination and trepidation flooding her expression. "Hello?"

Her voice trembled slightly, betraying the steely facade she fought to maintain. I watched, helpless, as she listened, the shadows creeping back into her features, painting her with a vulnerability that made my chest ache. I wanted to reach out, to pull her into my arms and shield her from whatever threat lurked on the other end of that line, but I knew she needed to confront this.

"I don't want anything to do with you," she said, her voice suddenly fierce, a spark igniting in her hazel eyes. "Leave me alone." The finality in her tone echoed in the room, a resounding declaration that met with an unsettling silence on the other end.

As she hung up, I stepped forward, enveloping her in my arms. The warmth of her body felt like a sanctuary against the chilling dread that had seeped into the room. "What did he say?" I asked softly, feeling her heartbeat racing beneath my palm, a wild drum echoing the chaos in my mind.

She shook her head, biting her lip, as if trying to swallow the words that threatened to spill out like shattered glass. "He knows where we are," she finally said, her voice cracking under the strain of the revelation. "He's coming for us."

A sense of fury ignited within me, hot and insistent. "He won't touch you," I growled, gripping her shoulders with a fierce tenderness, my own fear igniting a protective instinct that had lain dormant for far too long. "I promise you that."

Her gaze met mine, a flicker of gratitude tempered with uncertainty. "I can't let you put yourself in danger because of me. This is my fight."

"Together, then," I countered, unwilling to relinquish the strength we found in each other. "You don't have to face this alone. We'll figure this out. Just tell me what you need."

In the quiet that followed, I felt a connection pulse between us, raw and electric, as if the air itself crackled with unspoken words. She nodded slowly, the weight of our shared resolve hanging heavy in the air.

We moved to the living room, the sunlight now casting long shadows across the floor as evening began to settle in. I couldn't shake the unease gnawing at my gut. I settled on the couch, pulling out my laptop and searching for any information I could find about her past—anything that could give me a clue as to what we were dealing with.

Sophie sank into the armchair opposite me, a fragile silhouette in the dimming light. Her usual vibrancy seemed dimmed, replaced by an unsettling stillness as she stared into the depths of her own thoughts. I wanted to reach out, to bridge the chasm of worry that stretched between us, but the fear of shattering the moment held me back.

As I scrolled through endless articles and snippets of data, I felt a twinge of guilt for dragging her into my world of research. "I wish I could do more than just sit here," I said, glancing up to meet her gaze.

"You being here is enough," she replied softly, a tender smile breaking through her worry, reminding me of the woman I had fallen for—the one who radiated strength and resilience, even in the face of uncertainty.

Suddenly, the air thickened with tension as her phone buzzed again, its intrusive vibration slicing through the fragile moment. We exchanged a look, both of us knowing it was him again.

"Do you want me to get it?" I asked, my instincts screaming for me to protect her, to shield her from any further hurt.

Sophie shook her head, her resolve firming. "No, I can do this."

She reached for the phone, hesitating only briefly before answering. "What do you want?" The calm in her voice was a stark contrast to the tumultuous chaos surrounding us, yet beneath it lurked an undercurrent of defiance that I found utterly captivating.

The conversation hung in the air, charged with danger and unyielding tension, as I watched her navigate the conversation with a strength I admired. I clenched my fists, ready to pounce if necessary, but she held her ground, a warrior in her own right.

"You won't intimidate me," she asserted, her voice rising with each word. "I'm not afraid of you."

The fierceness in her tone sent a rush of adrenaline coursing through my veins. I would protect her, I vowed silently, even if it meant facing the ghosts of her past head-on.

As she hung up once more, a sense of calm washed over her. "We'll figure this out, together," she said, her voice steady, filled with determination.

"Together," I echoed, feeling the certainty of that promise settle between us like an anchor amidst the storm.

As dusk fell, the sky transformed into a canvas of vibrant oranges and deep purples, yet inside, a heavy stillness blanketed the room. The warmth of the day faded, leaving only the faint glow of our living room lamp to battle the encroaching shadows. I could feel the atmosphere shift; it was as if the walls themselves had absorbed the weight of our fears and were now pressing in on us.

Sophie's breath came in shallow bursts, the tension palpable in the air. I wanted to ease her mind, to sweep her away from the looming threat that hung over us like a storm cloud. But the truth was, we were trapped—not just in this room, but in the very past that had come clawing back into her life. I watched her, a tempest of emotions flitting across her features. The resolve she'd shown moments ago began to fray, and I knew I needed to do something to pull her back from the edge of despair.

"Let's take a walk," I suggested, standing and extending my hand toward her. "It'll help clear our heads."

Her eyes flickered with uncertainty, but after a brief moment of contemplation, she took my hand. The warmth of her palm against mine sent a jolt of reassurance through me, as if she could feel the strength in my resolve.

We stepped outside, the cool evening air wrapping around us like a gentle embrace. The world outside felt alive, pulsating with the sounds of crickets serenading the twilight. The stars began to peek through the deepening sky, shimmering like tiny beacons of hope. I led her down the familiar path by the lake, where the surface reflected the first glimmers of moonlight, creating a silver ribbon that wound through the dark.

"I used to come here to think," I confessed, glancing sideways at her as we walked. "There's something about the water that makes it easier to sort through the chaos in my head."

She nodded, her expression softening slightly. "It's beautiful," she murmured, and I could see the tension in her shoulders ease just a fraction.

We reached the weathered wooden dock, the planks creaking beneath our weight as we stepped onto it. Sophie leaned against the railing, gazing out at the water as if it held the answers we were both searching for. I stood beside her, the night air thick with unsaid words.

"What did he say?" I asked gently, breaking the silence that had settled like a shroud around us.

She sighed, her gaze fixed on the moon's reflection rippling in the water. "He knows about you," she admitted, her voice barely above a whisper. "He made it clear that he wouldn't hesitate to come after you if I didn't play along."

My heart clenched at the thought of that man, lurking like a shadow, threatening the life we were building. "Sophie," I began, a fire igniting within me, "I won't let him hurt you. I won't let him come between us."

A small smile flickered on her lips, but it didn't reach her eyes. "I appreciate that, but this is my fight. I need to deal with him on my own."

"Like hell you will," I shot back, frustration bubbling to the surface. "You've already faced him alone once. I won't sit by and let you do it again."

Her laughter was soft, tinged with disbelief. "And how do you plan to stop him? We don't even know where he is."

"Then we find out." The determination in my voice surprised even me. "We dig up whatever we can. If he wants a fight, he'll get one. But I'll be damned if I let you face this without me."

Sophie turned to me, her hazel eyes glimmering with something between admiration and irritation. "You really think we can take him on?"

"I believe we can do anything if we're together," I replied, meeting her gaze with unwavering certainty.

The tension between us shifted, becoming something electric, something fierce. The lake mirrored our passion, the ripples creating a symphony of chaos that echoed our hearts. For a moment, the looming threat felt far away, just two souls standing against the night, united in our resolve.

But just as quickly as it came, that moment was interrupted by the sudden vibration of her phone, which she had left on the bench by the dock. We exchanged wary glances, both of us knowing who was likely on the other end. "You should get that," I said, even though the words felt heavy in my mouth.

She hesitated, a battle of emotions playing out on her face. "What if it's him again?"

"Then we'll face it together."

With a nod, she turned and walked back to the bench, the weight of our fears hanging thick in the air. I followed closely, my heart racing. Sophie picked up her phone, and I could see her hand tremble slightly as she glanced at the screen. The caller ID flashed a name that made my stomach drop—James.

"Who's James?" I asked, trying to keep my tone neutral, though jealousy pricked at me like a thousand needles.

She took a deep breath, her voice steadier than before. "An old friend. He was my confidant during... well, during the time I was running."

My heart sank. "Running from him?"

Sophie nodded, her expression shifting into something vulnerable. "He helped me navigate through a lot of things. I haven't spoken to him in years, and now..." She paused, glancing at the phone with uncertainty. "I don't know why he's calling me now."

"Maybe he knows something," I suggested, hoping to pierce through the veil of unease that surrounded her. "Could he help?"

"I can't drag him into this. I won't put him at risk."

But there was a glimmer in her eyes, a spark of hope mingled with fear. "What if he could help?" I pressed gently. "What if he has information that could turn the tide?"

She stared at the phone, the tension in her body palpable. "I don't know," she whispered, wrestling with her instincts.

"Then why not find out? You can always hang up if it gets too uncomfortable."

Sophie chewed on her bottom lip, and in that moment, I could see her weighing the risks against the potential rewards. Finally, with a deep breath, she pressed the green button and raised the phone to her ear.

"James?" Her voice quivered slightly, the uncertainty evident. "It's been a long time."

As she spoke, I could sense the shift in her demeanor, the familiar ease creeping back in as she conversed with someone from her past. I stood back, watching as she reconnected with an old ally, all the while feeling the shadows creeping back in. It was strange how something so simple could feel both comforting and threatening.

I caught snippets of the conversation, her laughter laced with tension, the playful banter a stark contrast to the reality we faced. She leaned against the bench, her body relaxing as the weight of her fears began to lift, if only slightly.

Then, suddenly, her laughter faded, replaced by a serious tone. "What do you mean you've seen him?"

My heart raced as I leaned closer, trying to hear every word. The moon cast an ethereal glow around us, illuminating the intensity of the moment. Whatever James had to say, it felt pivotal—a turning point in our battle against the darkness that threatened to engulf us.

"I need to know where," Sophie continued, her voice now steady and resolute. "If you have any information, please share it. I can't let him hurt anyone else."

I held my breath, every instinct tuned to her response. The shadows shifted, the air thick with anticipation as Sophie listened intently, her face a mask of determination. I felt the ground beneath us shift, a reminder that even in the darkest moments, there was always a flicker of light, always a chance to reclaim what was lost.

Sophie's expression shifted dramatically as she hung up the phone, the playful banter evaporating like mist in the morning sun. "He knows where I am," she said, her voice tight, every word laced with urgency. I felt a shiver run through me, but I wouldn't let fear take root; I refused to let it poison the moment we had fought so hard to reclaim.

"Did he say how he found you?" I asked, my tone steady despite the tumult raging in my chest. The vulnerability in her eyes made it clear that this was no ordinary situation. It was as if we had been thrust into a thriller novel, the pages turning faster than we could read.

"No, but he has his ways," she replied, a bitter smile gracing her lips. "He always did."

I paced the dock, hands stuffed into my pockets, staring at the water rippling beneath me. "What do we do now? Can we go to the police?"

Sophie shook her head vehemently. "And tell them what? That I'm being stalked by a ghost from my past? They won't take me seriously."

The realization hung between us, a palpable tension threading through the air like static. "What if we just leave?" I suggested, the idea tumbling out before I could consider the implications. "We could go somewhere far away, anywhere he won't think to look."

"And live in hiding?" she retorted, incredulous. "I won't let him dictate my life any longer. I want to fight back, not run."

The fire in her eyes sparked something in me—a reckless resolve. "Then let's fight. Together."

Her smile, tentative yet bright, made my heart skip. "You really mean that?"

"Absolutely," I replied, stepping closer. "This isn't just your fight anymore. We're in this together."

Sophie took a breath, the tension in her shoulders easing slightly. "Okay. But if we're doing this, we need a plan. We can't just charge in without knowing what we're up against."

The warmth of her determination washed over me, igniting a flicker of hope. "Let's start with James. If he knows something, we need to find out what it is. The more intel we have, the better prepared we'll be."

"Agreed," she said, her confidence returning like the tide. "He mentioned he's been doing some digging on his end. Let's see if he can shed any light on what we're dealing with."

As we turned back toward the house, a flicker of movement caught my eye across the lake. A dark figure emerged from the trees, hidden just beyond the reach of the fading light. My heart raced as I squinted into the growing shadows, instincts on high alert. "Sophie," I hissed, grabbing her arm.

"What is it?" she asked, her voice dropping to a whisper, her gaze darting to where I was pointing.

The figure stepped closer, and my pulse quickened. "I don't know," I admitted, suddenly feeling exposed and vulnerable, standing there like a deer caught in headlights. "But we should get inside."

We bolted back toward the house, adrenaline coursing through our veins. My mind raced with possibilities, each one darker than the last. What if it was him? What if he had come to finish what he started?

As we burst through the front door, I locked it behind us, the sound echoing in the stillness. I could feel Sophie's eyes on me, gauging my reaction, but I was too busy scanning the room for potential threats. "Should we call James?" she asked, her voice taut with urgency.

"Let's wait," I said, trying to keep the tremor from my voice. "I don't want to risk alerting anyone else."

We moved to the living room, and I settled against the wall, attempting to catch my breath. "I should check the windows," I said, moving toward the nearest one.

Sophie remained still, her expression a mix of worry and determination. "What if it was just someone out for a walk?"

"Or someone looking for you," I countered, the words spilling out before I could bite them back. I pulled the curtain aside and peered out. The shadows danced just beyond the porch light, but the figure had disappeared, leaving only the quiet rustle of leaves in its wake.

"Nothing," I said, stepping back. "But I don't like it. We need to stay alert."

"Agreed," Sophie said, her jaw set, determination etched into her features. "We can't let fear take over. It's time to take back control."

We spent the next hour piecing together a plan, bouncing ideas off each other like tennis balls, the energy in the room morphing from anxious to hopeful. With every word exchanged, it felt as though we were constructing a fortress against the darkness that threatened to invade our lives.

"Let's meet James tomorrow," she proposed. "He can help us strategize. Maybe he knows how to flush him out."

"Good idea," I replied, feeling a sense of camaraderie grow between us. "And I'll do some research on my end. There has to be something we can use to our advantage."

As the clock ticked on, an unexpected sense of calm washed over me, wrapping me in the comforting notion that we were finally taking charge. I glanced out the window again, peering into the darkness, half-expecting to see the figure lurking. The night was still, but my mind remained alert, racing with possibilities.

Just as we settled into a semblance of peace, Sophie's phone buzzed violently on the coffee table, the sound slicing through the silence like a knife. We exchanged a glance, and I felt a surge of adrenaline spike through me. She hesitated, glancing at me before reaching for it, the weight of anticipation thickening the air.

"Could it be James?" she wondered, but her voice held an edge of uncertainty.

"Only one way to find out," I urged, tension coiling in my gut.

With a deep breath, she picked up the phone and glanced at the screen. Her eyes widened, and in an instant, the color drained from her face. "It's him," she whispered, her voice trembling with fear.

"Answer it," I said, my heart pounding. "We need to know what he wants."

Sophie hesitated, her fingers hovering over the screen, but just as she prepared to swipe to answer, the lights flickered ominously. The sudden darkness felt like a harbinger, a sinister warning that sent chills down my spine.

"Did you pay the electric bill?" she asked, a hint of humor surfacing as her nervousness crept into her voice.

"No, but I was planning on getting around to it," I replied, forcing a smile despite the gravity of the moment.

Before she could respond, a loud crash echoed from outside, reverberating through the walls like a thunderclap. Our hearts raced in unison as we exchanged horrified glances. "What was that?"

"I don't know," I said, voice barely above a whisper. "But we need to check."

As I moved toward the door, Sophie grabbed my wrist, her grip fierce. "Wait! What if it's him?"

"Then we'll face him together," I replied, steeling my resolve.

With a deep breath, I turned the handle, every muscle in my body tensed for whatever awaited us. The door swung open to reveal the inky darkness, swallowing the light behind us. A foreboding silence enveloped us, broken only by the distant sound of something shifting in the shadows.

"Sophie..." I began, but the words hung in the air, thick with dread.

Then, as if the universe were mocking our bravery, we heard a voice cut through the night. "You thought you could hide from me?"

The icy dread pooled in my stomach, freezing me in place. Sophie's face paled as the figure stepped into the light, a familiar silhouette emerging from the depths of the night. My breath hitched in my throat, and I felt the ground shift beneath me as everything spiraled into uncertainty.

Chapter 23: The Reckoning of Truths

The night wrapped around us like a thick velvet cloak, heavy and electric with anticipation. Stars twinkled above, seeming to whisper secrets only the cosmos understood. Sophie stood beside me, her profile illuminated by the soft glow of lanterns flickering to life in the village square. Each light became a tiny beacon, a promise of hope against the encroaching darkness. I could feel the weight of our community's gaze upon us, a mix of admiration and apprehension swirling in the cool air, as if they held their breaths, waiting for the first note of the symphony we were about to conduct.

With her hands trembling at her sides, Sophie's eyes danced between the faces of our friends. I knew she was searching for courage amidst the swirling uncertainty. I turned to her, the corners of my mouth pulling into a reassuring smile. "You're not alone in this, you know. Your truth is our truth now," I said, my voice a steady current in the storm of emotions. It was both a promise and a challenge, and I saw her chest rise as she inhaled deeply, steeling herself against the onslaught of memories.

Her voice was a delicate tremor when she finally spoke, but it carried the weight of her past. "You all deserve to know," she began, glancing at the gathered crowd—friends who had become family, united by more than just proximity. "I didn't grow up here, not in the way you think. I came from somewhere else, a world wrapped in shadows where survival meant bending the truth to fit the lies told to me." Each word was a fragile thread, weaving together the tapestry of her existence. "I ran from it, hoping to find a place where the echoes of that life wouldn't chase me down."

Her revelation hung in the air, thick and palpable, as we all leaned closer, straining to catch every nuance. The wind picked up slightly, rustling the leaves overhead, almost like nature itself was holding its breath, urging her to continue. She straightened her shoulders, finding her rhythm as she recounted the threads of her history—the betrayal of those she had trusted, the scars that crisscrossed her heart like a topographical map of pain.

"I thought I could escape it all by coming here," she said, her voice gaining strength. "But the past isn't so easily discarded, is it? It waits for moments like this, lurking in the shadows, ready to spring forth." There was an intensity in her gaze, a flicker of defiance that shone through her vulnerability. I could see it then, the very essence of what made Sophie extraordinary—a fierce spirit battling against the currents of fate.

A shiver coursed through me as I remembered the shadows that threatened her, the whispers of danger that had set our world on edge. I clenched my fists, my nails digging into my palms as I willed away the anger bubbling just beneath the surface. "We'll face him together, Sophie. Whoever he is, whatever he wants, we're not backing down," I declared, the conviction in my voice drawing a collective murmur of agreement from our friends. The embers of solidarity glowed brighter, fueling our resolve.

Sophie nodded, and for a moment, the flickering lanterns around us seemed to pulse in time with her heartbeat. "I need to tell you about the pact I made," she continued, her voice steady now. "The reason I thought I could outrun the past." She paused, her expression growing serious. "In that other life, I swore an oath to protect something greater than myself—a land that holds magic, life, and untold secrets. I believed if I severed ties with my past, I could protect it from falling into the wrong hands."

A soft gasp floated through the crowd, and I felt my heart quicken. Magic? It was something we had always thought existed only in stories, bedtime tales spun from the imaginations of hopeful dreamers. And yet, here we stood, at the brink of something we couldn't entirely comprehend. The air thickened with an electric charge, anticipation swirling around us as the truth began to unfurl.

"The magic is bound to the land, and it chose me as its guardian," she explained, her eyes brightening with the weight of revelation. "But the moment I left, I abandoned my duty, and it unleashed chaos—chaos that has followed me here." Her gaze turned distant, lost in memories that shimmered just beyond the veil of time. "And now it's returned, knocking at our door."

Our friends exchanged uneasy glances, the gravity of her words sinking in like a stone dropped into still water, sending ripples through our gathering. I could almost hear the unspoken questions, the fears that pulsed beneath the surface. "And this pursuer?" I asked, my voice breaking the tense silence. "What does he want?"

"He wants to harness that magic for himself," Sophie replied, her voice steady, though a flicker of fear danced in her eyes. "He believes he can control it, bend it to his will. But he doesn't understand the land—or the consequences of such a choice." Her hands clenched into fists, determination weaving itself into her words. "He's come for me, but I won't let him take it."

In that moment, the fire within her ignited something in me. I felt it rise, a surge of fierce loyalty, of readiness to stand alongside her against the storm that threatened to tear us apart. "We'll fight for you, Sophie. We'll fight for our home," I declared, my voice ringing out clear, cutting through the weight of uncertainty that had settled upon us. I glanced around, meeting the eyes of our friends, each one of them nodding in solemn agreement.

As the stars twinkled down, casting a glow upon us, the bond we shared transformed into a palpable force, wrapping around us like a shield. Sophie was no longer just a girl with a haunted past; she was a beacon of hope, a thread that tied us together, and together we would confront whatever darkness awaited us. The truth had unraveled, revealing not just her struggle but the strength of our community—a tapestry woven from love, resilience, and an unwavering determination to protect the very essence of who we were.

The night deepened around us, a tapestry of shadow and starlight weaving an intricate dance of uncertainty and resolve. As the air crackled with the weight of Sophie's revelations, an unmistakable energy pulsed through our group—a wild, chaotic symphony of fear and determination. I could see it reflected in the eyes of our friends, each one grappling with the new reality we were faced with. What had once been a quiet village, nestled among the hills, was now at the precipice of a battle far beyond our comprehension.

Sophie, still reeling from the gravity of her own truth, turned to me, her voice barely above a whisper. "What if he comes for them too? What if this ends up hurting everyone I care about?" Her vulnerability hung in the air like mist, wrapping around us and forcing the others to lean closer, caught between sympathy and anxiety.

I reached for her hand, feeling the warmth of her skin against mine. "We'll protect them, Sophie. We've always looked out for each other, and now we'll stand as one." The words felt inadequate, but they were all I had, a fragile lifeline thrown into turbulent waters. Her eyes flickered with gratitude, yet a shadow of doubt still lingered, threading its way through the fabric of our gathering.

Just then, a loud crash echoed through the square, causing everyone to jump. The sound reverberated like a gunshot, sharp and jarring. A wooden crate tipped over in the corner, its contents spilling out—a jumble of apples, their sweet scent mixing with the damp earth beneath us. "Is that how we're announcing our impending doom? With a fruity explosion?" I quipped, trying to inject a moment of levity into the chaos. Laughter erupted, breaking the tension and drawing smiles from familiar faces. But the laughter faded quickly as reality pulled us back to the task at hand.

"Let's not wait for him to come to us," I said, glancing around at the determined faces of our friends. "We can't let fear dictate our actions. If he's hunting Sophie, we need to draw him out and face him on our terms. This is our home, after all." The murmurs of agreement swelled, a chorus of voices rising in a battle cry against the darkness that threatened to envelop us.

As we brainstormed, ideas spiraled around us, each one more outlandish than the last. "What if we set a trap?" suggested Mark, his brow furrowed in concentration. "We could lure him here with a false sense of security. Make him think we're vulnerable."

"That's all well and good until he realizes it's a trap," Sophie countered, her eyes narrowing as she considered the implications. "He's not just some brute; he's cunning. He knows how to manipulate situations to his advantage."

"And you know him personally, right?" I added, trying to keep the mood light despite the seriousness of the topic. "Is he one of those 'truly misunderstood' villains with a tragic backstory?" The playful sarcasm hung in the air, but there was a flicker of genuine concern behind my words. I knew Sophie had been running from something—someone—for a long time, and now that she had brought it to light, we all shared the burden of her past.

Sophie met my gaze, the fire within her reigniting. "He's worse than that. He's calculated, and he knows how to exploit weaknesses. I've seen it firsthand." Her voice shook slightly, but there was a steeliness beneath the tremor that made my heart race. "He won't hesitate to hurt anyone who stands in his way, including you all."

"And that's why we need to be smarter than him," I replied, my tone more serious now. "We'll build a plan. If he's coming for you, then we'll make sure he finds an entire village ready to stand against him." A shared resolve pulsed through the group as we began piecing together a strategy, laying our fears bare and honing our strengths into weapons against the encroaching darkness.

The hours slipped away, transformed into a tapestry of whispered strategies and hopeful laughter that rang through the night air. We gathered supplies—old nets, ropes, and an assortment of odd tools from the village—while rallying together a network of watchers to keep an eye out for any signs of movement beyond the hills. It felt like preparing for a harvest festival rather than a confrontation with an unseen enemy, and yet the undercurrent of tension was palpable, crackling like static in the air.

As the night wore on, I found a moment to pull Sophie aside. "Are you okay?" I asked, sensing the whirlwind of emotions swirling beneath her exterior. She looked at me, her eyes reflecting the moonlight, a mix of fear and gratitude etched on her face. "I didn't want to drag you all into this," she confessed, her voice barely above a whisper. "I thought I could handle it alone."

I couldn't help but chuckle softly. "Handle it alone? That's so last season. Haven't you figured out yet that we're a team? You don't have to face this alone anymore." I squeezed her hand, feeling her warmth spread through me, an anchor in the churning sea of our circumstances.

"Thank you," she said, her voice trembling with unshed tears. "You don't know how much that means to me." There was a weight in her words, a sincerity that caught me off guard. I nodded, determined to banish any lingering doubts.

"Just promise me one thing," I replied, my tone shifting to something more serious. "Promise me you'll let us fight for you, even if it gets tough. You deserve to have people at your side, fighting alongside you."

She met my gaze, her resolve solidifying like the roots of an ancient tree digging deep into the earth. "I promise," she whispered, her voice steadying as she returned my grip, squeezing my hand in affirmation.

And in that moment, a bond formed—a pact forged not just of words, but of understanding and shared strength. We turned back toward our friends, their laughter echoing across the square, a reminder that even in the face of adversity, there was room for hope. As we stood together, united against the shadows that threatened our lives, I felt an unwavering sense of purpose settle within me. This was our home, and we would fight tooth and nail to protect it, weaving our stories into a tapestry of resilience and love.

The moon hung low, a guardian in the night sky, casting silver light upon the square where our plans were coming together, each detail intertwining with our hopes and fears. As Sophie and I stood side by side, I could feel the thrill of adrenaline humming in my veins, a potent mix of anxiety and determination swirling like a tempest within me. The village had transformed into a hive of activity, a cacophony of whispers and laughter punctuated by the occasional clank of tools as our friends prepared for the unexpected battle ahead.

"Alright, who's taking the first watch?" I called out, scanning the group gathered beneath the lanterns. There was an air of camaraderie among us, laughter mingling with the seriousness of our situation. It was a fragile balance, but we were holding it together. Mark stepped forward, puffing out his chest like a rooster ready to crow at dawn.

"I'll take it! I'll shout like a banshee if anyone even looks sideways at this place."

"Oh, please," I laughed, "as if anyone could take you seriously with that hairstyle." His wild curls bounced in defiance, and the laughter erupted around us, momentarily lifting the weight pressing down on our shoulders.

"Don't worry, I'll take good care of the village," he said, mock seriousness etched across his face. "Besides, I'm pretty sure the ghosts in the woods would prefer me to scare them off rather than have them sneak up on us."

Sophie rolled her eyes playfully, but I could see a flicker of warmth light her expression, a spark of hope that had dimmed in the wake of her past. It was infectious, and I felt my spirits lift as our banter echoed against the backdrop of the looming threat. "Ghosts, huh? Maybe I should start writing ghost stories, then. You could be my muse," I teased, shooting him a conspiratorial wink.

With the tension slightly eased, we turned back to our preparations. The strategy session morphed into a rallying cry, with plans being crafted, improvised defenses erected, and roles assigned. Each person brought something unique, a skill or a talent that we'd never fully appreciated before this moment. It was remarkable to witness—a mosaic of our strengths emerging from the shadows, each piece vital to the whole.

As the hours slipped away, I noticed Sophie retreating into herself again. Her laughter had quieted, her smile dimming as she contemplated the enormity of what lay ahead. I approached her, feeling the gravity of the situation tugging at my heart. "Hey," I said softly, "what's going on in that head of yours?"

She met my gaze, a flicker of vulnerability breaking through her brave façade. "What if I've put all of you in danger? What if he comes for you, and I can't protect you?" Her voice trembled, each word heavy with the weight of her fears.

"Then we'll face it together," I assured her, refusing to let her pull away. "You have to believe that. This isn't just your fight. We're in this as one. Remember?"

Her eyes searched mine, and after a heartbeat, she nodded, a fragile resolve settling back into place. "You're right. I can't let him win by isolating myself." There was a flicker of fire rekindled in her spirit, a glimpse of the warrior I knew she could be.

With a newfound determination, she threw herself into our preparations. "Let's finish this. I refuse to hide any longer." We worked late into the night, our hands and minds united in purpose.

It felt good, this momentum, a heady rush that drowned out the fears lurking at the edges of our minds.

But as the first light of dawn began to creep over the horizon, painting the sky in strokes of pink and gold, a tension settled in the air, heavier than before. The village square transformed into a battleground, the remnants of laughter giving way to silence, a hush that felt almost reverent.

"Are we ready?" I asked, my voice low but steady. The weight of what was to come hung like a shroud around us. Each face turned toward me, resolve written in the lines of their expressions. We were all scared, but there was something more powerful at play—an unyielding desire to protect what was ours.

As we took our positions, a sudden rustle in the underbrush broke the silence, the sound sharp and jarring. My heart raced as I turned to face the direction of the noise, every instinct screaming that we were being watched. Sophie stepped closer to me, her hand slipping into mine, a small but potent gesture of unity.

"Did you hear that?" she whispered, her voice taut with tension.

"I did," I replied, my heart pounding like a war drum. The air thickened, every breath a reminder of what we were fighting against.

From the trees, a figure emerged, cloaked in shadows that clung to him like a second skin. He moved with a confidence that sent a chill racing down my spine. I squinted, trying to make out his features, but the light of dawn did little to illuminate his presence. Instead, it felt as if the shadows were wrapping around him, shielding him from our gaze.

"Ah, Sophie," his voice rolled through the air, smooth and taunting. "I was wondering when you'd come out to play."

Every instinct within me flared, ready to leap into action, but I forced myself to remain still, to gauge the situation. The laughter of the night before felt like a distant memory, replaced by an eerie silence as we collectively held our breath.

"Why are you here?" Sophie's voice was a mix of defiance and fear, her grip tightening around my hand.

He stepped forward, a sly smile curving his lips. "I've come to collect what's mine."

Before I could react, he raised a hand, and an otherworldly light flickered to life, casting strange shadows around us. It shimmered like a mirage, bending the air, and a low hum began to vibrate through the ground, shaking the very foundations of our resolve.

Panic surged through the crowd, but I stood rooted, heart racing as the ominous glow pulsed in time with the threat looming before us. The world seemed to shrink around us, closing in as dread coiled tight in my chest. Sophie's eyes widened in terror, and I sensed the stakes had just risen dramatically.

"Let the games begin," he said, laughter dripping with malice as the light expanded, swallowing the dawn in a maelstrom of chaos. In that instant, everything shifted, and I knew we were teetering on the edge of an abyss, a battle that would decide our fate.

I turned to Sophie, ready to confront this darkness together, but the ground beneath us trembled, and before I could utter a word, the earth split open, a chasm of shadow and light erupting between us. The world spiraled as I reached for her, but the darkness consumed everything, and as the ground fell away, the last thing I heard was her scream.

Chapter 24: Shadows and Light

The scent of burnt coffee lingered in the air, mingling with the sweet, cloying notes of the floral arrangements that adorned the community center. I tucked a loose strand of hair behind my ear, feeling the soft hum of the crowd around me. Conversations buzzed like the static of an old radio, filled with murmurs of concern and the occasional laugh that seemed to ripple through the tension, a reminder of the warmth that resided in our small town. The painted walls, adorned with memories of potlucks and holiday celebrations, felt alive, as if they too held their breath in anticipation of the confrontation that loomed ahead.

Sophie stood beside me, her fingers laced through mine, a steady anchor in the swell of uncertainty. I could see the nervous flicker in her eyes, a reflection of the storm brewing beneath her calm exterior. Today, she was ready to face the shadows of her past, and as much as I wished to shield her from it all, I knew that this was a necessary step for her to reclaim her truth. Her courage had always fascinated me, a quiet strength that emerged like the first light of dawn breaking through the thickest clouds. And yet, beneath that fortitude lay a vulnerability that tugged at my heart.

As the clock struck three, the doors swung open with a creak that seemed to echo through the hall. In stepped a figure that sent a shiver down my spine. He was cloaked in shadows, his presence more felt than seen, as if he were a dark fog creeping through the room. My heart raced as his eyes met mine—sharp, cold, and piercing, glinting like shards of glass that promised pain and fear. I squeezed Sophie's hand tighter, feeling her pulse quicken beside me.

The room fell silent, an electrifying hush that engulfed the vibrant chatter like a predator stalking its prey. It was then that I realized just how deeply the townsfolk were intertwined; every gaze was a thread woven into the fabric of our shared history, their collective heartbeat thrumming in the air, vibrant and palpable. This was not merely a confrontation between Sophie and her past; it was a battle for our community's soul, for the resilience that defined us.

"Well, well, look who decided to show up," he said, his voice smooth as silk, yet laced with malice. The way he pronounced Sophie's name twisted my insides, a chilling reminder of the hold he had on her, the grip that once threatened to pull her under.

"You don't belong here," I shot back, my voice louder than I intended, a mix of protective instinct and the adrenaline surging through me. The eyes of the townspeople bore down on him, curiosity mingling with indignation.

He laughed, a low, mocking sound that reverberated through the silence. "Isn't it quaint? You think you can protect her?" His gaze shifted to Sophie, and I could almost see the tendrils of his influence wrapping around her, memories of fear and confusion resurfacing. "Tell me, Sophie, do you really believe that they can save you from the truth?"

"Truth? Or your twisted version of it?" I countered, my heart racing as I stepped forward, fueled by a sense of duty. It was one thing to be afraid of the darkness, but it was an entirely different beast to stand against it.

Sophie's breath hitched, but she found her voice, quiet yet steady. "I've lived in your shadow long enough. It's time I stepped into the light." The words hung in the air, a beacon of strength that cut through the suffocating tension. I watched as her shoulders straightened, a transformation igniting within her.

"Ah, how poetic," he sneered, his features twisting into a mask of mockery. "But you forget—light only exists because there's darkness to define it. And you, my dear, are nothing without me."

A murmur swept through the crowd, a mixture of disbelief and anger, but Sophie remained steadfast, her eyes fierce, igniting a fire in my heart. This was no longer just about confronting her past; it was about our future, a promise forged in the flames of adversity.

"You are wrong," she stated, the steadiness in her voice a testament to her resolve. "I am not defined by what you did to me. I am not a victim; I am a survivor."

The atmosphere shifted, a ripple of strength flowing through the room as her words settled like a storm breaking after a long, oppressive heat. The crowd seemed to inhale, absorbing her declaration as a collective promise of support, an affirmation that we were all in this together.

The man faltered, the edges of his confidence blurring as he surveyed the sea of faces, some hardened with resolve, others softened by empathy. In that moment, I saw not just Sophie but the entire community standing tall, unified in the face of a common adversary.

"You think you can just walk away from me?" he spat, venom dripping from his words.

Sophie's chin lifted, defiance radiating from her like sunlight breaking through the clouds. "No, I'm walking towards my own future, one that you don't control. You'll never have that power over me again."

It was a defining moment, a turning point where shadows began to retreat under the brilliance of her bravery. I felt an overwhelming surge of love for her, admiration washing over me in waves. Together, we would unravel the chains of her past, stitch the wounds with threads of hope, and transform the pain into a tapestry of resilience.

In the silence that followed, I knew the confrontation was only beginning, and though the shadows loomed large, the light within us flickered with the promise of new beginnings.

The air felt charged, vibrating with the collective energy of our community as Sophie stood her ground, embodying the very spirit of defiance. I watched her, captivated by the transformation unfurling before me like petals of a blooming flower. Gone was the timid girl shackled by doubt; in her place stood a woman radiant with purpose, her voice echoing through the hushed room, cutting through the remnants of his shadow like a beam of sunlight breaking the dawn.

"Control?" he scoffed, the bravado slipping from his words like water through a sieve. "You really think you can step away from everything I've built around you? I made you who you are!" His laughter, low and sinister, wrapped around the room like smoke, trying to suffocate the light.

Sophie shook her head, her expression resolute. "You made me afraid, not whole. That ends today." She stepped forward, drawing strength from the murmurs of support swelling from the crowd behind her. Every hand clasped together was a testament to the unyielding bond we shared, a web of loyalty and love woven intricately through our lives. It fueled her, and I felt it wrapping around my own heart, igniting a fire that pushed back against the darkness he represented.

"You think you're strong because you've rallied these people?" He sneered, motioning dismissively toward the gathering. "They're just pawns in your little game. You're still just a girl hiding behind a facade of bravery."

My jaw clenched. "And you're just a bully trying to reclaim what you lost," I shot back, unable to hold my tongue any longer. "Sophie's strength doesn't come from this place; it comes from within. You can't snuff out that light, no matter how hard you try."

A ripple of surprise flickered through the audience, a mix of shock and admiration as they witnessed the battle unfold. I could feel the weight of their gazes, the silent encouragement propelling Sophie to rise higher. She was no longer alone; she was part of something far greater, a tapestry woven from resilience and hope.

"Is that what you tell yourself? That your love can save her?" he spat, his demeanor shifting from bravado to a kind of desperation I hadn't expected. "Love is a weakness, and she's going to see that when the world turns its back on her."

I could almost feel Sophie's heartbeat quickening beside me, her determination shimmering in the air. "You've had your turn at wielding fear," she declared, her voice steady and unyielding. "But it's time to let go of the past. I'm not who I was when you left. I'm more than the girl you thought you could manipulate."

With each word, the light in her eyes grew brighter, illuminating the shadowy corners of the room. I could see the flickers of recognition among the townsfolk, the realization that Sophie was no longer a victim of his machinations. She had become a force to be reckoned with, a beacon of courage.

He stepped back, uncertainty creeping into his posture, but I could see the gears turning behind his glassy eyes, calculating and desperate. "You think you can stand against me? You're just one woman in a room full of memories I can twist against you," he taunted, trying to regain control of the narrative. "What will they think when they hear the truth? That you're just a scared little girl pretending to be strong?"

A murmur rippled through the crowd, but I sensed the tide had shifted. They were no longer just spectators; they were warriors, standing shoulder to shoulder with Sophie. "Let them hear it," she replied, her voice steady. "Let them hear how you tried to break me. Let them know the lengths I went to reclaim my life."

There was a moment of charged silence, as if the entire room held its breath, waiting for the inevitable storm to break. And when it did, it was with a sudden rush, like a dam bursting, the voices rising together in a chorus of support. "We stand with you, Sophie!" they called out, the unity palpable, echoing off the walls like a battle cry.

"You think you can manipulate this?" he shouted, but the bravado was fading, his confidence waning under the sheer force of our unity. "You're a fool, and this will all come crashing down around you."

"No," Sophie countered, and I could see her standing taller, her stance becoming a fortress of strength. "You've underestimated me for the last time. You're the one whose walls are crumbling, not mine."

With each exchange, the tension twisted tighter, a vine choking the life out of him. I could see the façade cracking, the man who once loomed over her beginning to shrink under the collective weight of her truth. The room swirled with energy, and I could feel the pulse of resolve beating in time with the shared hope that filled every corner.

"Maybe I should just walk away," he sneered, but his words were tinged with uncertainty. "Let you all have your little moment. But we both know the truth will come back to haunt you."

"No truth is stronger than the one I hold now," Sophie declared, her voice a clarion call that silenced his bluster. "And if you dare to haunt me, I'll face you again and again. I'm no longer afraid."

In that moment, I realized something vital: fear was a ghost, and Sophie had exorcised it. She stood firm, illuminated by the glow of newfound strength, while he faltered, the darkness that once enveloped her now chasing shadows in retreat. The crowd erupted into applause, their support washing over us like a wave, lifting our spirits higher.

But just as the tide of triumph surged forward, he stepped back, a glint of something dangerous crossing his face. "You think this is over?" His voice dropped to a low hiss, like a serpent coiling in the grass. "You've made a powerful enemy today, Sophie. I won't just fade into the background."

I felt the hairs on my neck stand up. "What do you mean?" I asked, the urgency rising in my voice.

He smirked, a chilling expression that sent a shudder through me. "Oh, you'll see. Shadows don't just disappear. They linger, waiting for the right moment to strike."

As he turned to leave, I caught a glimpse of something darker in his eyes, a promise of chaos lurking just beyond the horizon. The energy in the room shifted once more, an undercurrent of apprehension as we processed the weight of his words. But as I looked at Sophie, determination radiated from her; she was ready for the fight. Together, we would meet whatever darkness lay ahead with unwavering resolve, our bond stronger than any shadow that dared to cross our path.

The applause that had erupted in the wake of Sophie's declaration faded into an unsettling stillness, a thick silence that seemed to stretch and curl around us like smoke. The man, the shadow that had haunted her for far too long, retreated with an unsettling grin, his presence lingering like a bad dream that refused to dissipate with the morning light. I could feel the heat of his words echoing in the room, the threat of his ominous promise looming just outside the fragile cocoon we had created.

Sophie's eyes were locked on the door, where he had vanished, a mixture of triumph and concern swirling within her. I squeezed her hand tighter, grounding her, as I whispered, "We'll deal with whatever he throws our way. Together."

"Together," she echoed, though the uncertainty clung to her words. I understood that even as we faced down the past, the scars left by it could take a long time to heal. The gathered crowd began to murmur amongst themselves, a blend of disbelief and resolve knitting them closer as they processed what had just transpired. It was a testament to the bonds we had forged, a unity forged in the fires of adversity. But as they stood there, supportive yet uneasy, I couldn't shake the nagging feeling that this was only the beginning.

The crowd began to disperse, voices rising and falling like a tide washing over the shore, but Sophie remained rooted in place. "I didn't expect him to show up," she admitted, her voice barely above a whisper. "I thought... I thought I was done with that part of my life."

"Clearly, he had other ideas," I said, forcing a lightness into my tone even as my heart pounded. "But you were incredible up there. You took control, and that's what matters."

She looked at me, her brow furrowed with a mixture of gratitude and lingering doubt. "But what if he decides to come back? What if he tries to hurt the people I care about?"

The shadows of her fears cast a pall over our moment, and I brushed my thumb across her knuckles. "We won't let that happen. We have each other, and we have everyone here. You've shown them you're stronger than he ever realized. And besides," I added with a smirk, "you're not a girl who hides anymore. You're a woman who fights."

That seemed to spark a flicker of hope in her eyes, but it was quickly overshadowed by the dark clouds gathering in my own thoughts. I had seen that smirk on his face before he left; it wasn't just a threat—it was a promise. And it left a bitter taste in my mouth, one that lingered long after the applause had faded.

As the community center emptied, I glanced around at the remnants of the day's energy—the scattered chairs, the fading bouquets, and the lingering echoes of voices. Each detail was like a ghost haunting the space, reminding us of the battle we had just fought. But I felt something else too, a sense of urgency creeping in. We needed to take action, to solidify the unity Sophie had inspired among us.

"Let's gather everyone tomorrow," I suggested. "We can have a meeting to discuss what happened and how to prepare for anything he might do next. We need to be ready."

Sophie nodded, her determination resurfacing as she glanced at the door through which he had departed. "That sounds like a plan. I won't let him intimidate me or anyone else again. We'll show him we're not afraid."

The drive home felt heavier than usual, the weight of unspoken fears settling between us like an unwelcome guest. The sunlight filtering through the trees cast dappled shadows across the road, a stark contrast to the darkness that still clung to my thoughts. I could feel Sophie's unease, the way it radiated off her in waves, and I wished I could take it all away with a simple embrace.

When we reached her house, the familiar sight of her garden—flowers bursting with color—felt strangely out of place against the ominous cloud that hung over us. I helped her inside, but the warmth of the sun seemed to vanish as we closed the door, leaving us in the dim glow of the living room.

Sophie turned to me, her expression a mix of gratitude and uncertainty. "I'm glad you were there today. I don't know how I would have done it without you."

"You're stronger than you give yourself credit for," I replied, my voice soft. "But I'll always be here to remind you of that. You're not alone in this."

As she smiled, a flicker of her old spirit returned, but it was quickly overshadowed by a shadow darting across the window—a movement that sent a chill racing up my spine. My heart thundered in my chest, a primal instinct urging me to protect her, to shield her from whatever darkness loomed on the horizon.

"Sophie," I murmured, stepping closer to the window. "Did you see that?"

"What?" she asked, her brow furrowing as she joined me.

I strained my eyes against the dusk settling outside, trying to discern the shifting shapes in the growing shadows. "I thought I saw someone," I replied, my voice barely above a whisper. "Someone lurking just beyond the edge of the light."

Just then, a loud bang echoed from the back of the house—a sound that rattled the very frame of our resolve. It came from the kitchen, a thunderous noise that shattered the fragile calm, and we both jumped, instinctively stepping closer to one another.

"What was that?" Sophie's voice was a mix of fear and determination, and I could feel her pulse quickening beneath my fingers as I held her close.

"I don't know," I breathed, the adrenaline surging through me. "Stay here."

"Like hell," she shot back, her eyes sparking with defiance. "I'm not letting you face anything alone."

I couldn't help but admire her bravery even in the face of danger. "Fine, but stay behind me." We moved toward the kitchen, every creak of the floorboards beneath us amplifying the tension in the air. I reached for the handle of the kitchen door, feeling the cool metal beneath my palm, and I glanced back at her.

"On three?" I asked, my voice steady despite the unease coiling in my stomach.

"On three," she confirmed, her eyes locked onto mine.

"One... two..."

Before I could say "three," the door swung open with a violent crash, revealing the darkness that lay beyond, the kitchen flickering ominously under the failing light.

And there, in the doorway, stood a figure cloaked in shadows, a familiar silhouette that sent chills racing down my spine. It was him—the darkness returned, grinning with a malevolence that felt like ice clawing at my insides.

"Did you really think I'd let you go?" he sneered, and I felt Sophie stiffen beside me, the air thick with danger as we both braced for whatever chaos lay ahead.

Chapter 25: The Breaking Point

The air in Willow Creek felt different after that day, almost electric, charged with a tension that clung to my skin like an unwelcome layer of humidity. The sun hung low in the sky, casting long shadows that danced across the quaint streets, and while the townsfolk returned to their daily routines, the echoes of our confrontation lingered, a soft hum beneath the surface of normalcy. Sophie walked beside me, her gaze focused on the cobblestones as if they held secrets only she could decipher. I longed to reach out, to draw her back into the warmth of companionship, but a chasm had formed between us—a divide that felt insurmountable.

"Do you remember the old oak tree by the creek?" I ventured, attempting to ignite a spark of nostalgia. "We used to sit there for hours, dreaming up wild adventures."

Her response was a faint smile that flickered briefly, like a candle struggling against a gust of wind. "I remember," she replied, her voice a soft murmur, weighted with something unnameable. The light in her eyes, usually so vibrant, seemed dimmed, as if a storm cloud had settled just above her head.

I tried to focus on the world around us: the vibrant flower boxes that adorned the windows of every cottage, the gentle burble of the creek that wove through the town like a silver thread. But my heart was heavy with concern for Sophie. The town felt almost like a character in our story, a backdrop to her silent struggles. Each familiar face we passed wore a veneer of joy, blissfully unaware of the turmoil brewing beneath the surface.

As we approached the café, the scent of freshly brewed coffee mingled with the sweet aroma of pastries, a seductive invitation I found hard to resist. "Let's grab a coffee," I suggested, hoping to coax her out of her silence. "It's on me. They have that new mocha that everyone's raving about."

She hesitated, her fingers twitching against her side as if contemplating a decision of monumental importance. Finally, she nodded, and together we stepped inside, the bell above the door jingling cheerfully. The café was bustling with the familiar clatter of mugs and chatter, a comforting cacophony that felt at odds with the tension hanging between us.

As we settled into a cozy corner booth, I watched Sophie as she absently traced the rim of her cup. Her usual exuberance seemed muted, replaced by a distant expression that gnawed at my insides. "Sophie," I said softly, "what's going on in that head of yours? You know you can talk to me."

She met my gaze, and for a moment, I saw the walls she had built around herself begin to waver. "It's just... everything feels different now," she confessed, her voice barely rising above the ambient noise. "I thought I was prepared for the truth, but now... now I feel lost."

"Lost?" I echoed, my heart aching at the vulnerability in her tone. "You're not lost, you're right here. We're right here."

But her eyes, usually so full of fire, flickered with doubt. "But am I? Or am I just pretending to be? I don't even know what I want anymore."

"Neither do I," I admitted, the honesty spilling out like the coffee from the pot. "But maybe that's okay. We can figure it out together."

She looked away, her expression turning contemplative, and I felt an overwhelming urge to shake her out of her reverie, to pull her back from whatever abyss she was teetering on the edge of. The silence stretched between us, a taut line that threatened to snap, and I could almost hear the gears of her mind turning.

"I keep thinking about what happened," she said finally, her voice steadier now. "About everything we uncovered. It feels like a weight I can't shake off."

"Do you want to talk about it?" I asked gently, not wanting to push too hard. "I mean, really talk about it?"

She sighed, the sound heavy and loaded, as if it carried the burdens of her past. "I don't know if talking will help. What if it just makes it worse?"

"Sometimes talking makes it better," I replied, wishing I could be the balm to her wounds. "It can clear the air."

"Or stir up a storm," she countered, her brow furrowing in that endearing way I had come to adore.

I reached across the table, taking her hand in mine, feeling the coolness of her skin. "Whatever the storm looks like, we can weather it together. I promise."

She stared at our hands, her fingers curling slightly around mine as if testing the warmth of my reassurance. "I wish I could believe you," she whispered, a tremor of vulnerability threading through her words.

In that moment, I realized that the battle we fought outside, against the tangible enemies of our past, was nothing compared to the emotional struggle she faced within. It was a fight for her heart, her mind, and her very soul, and I felt like a mere spectator in a game where the rules had shifted dramatically.

"Just give me a chance," I urged, not entirely sure what I was asking of her. "Let's be real with each other. No more secrets."

She nodded slowly, the shadows in her eyes deepening momentarily before flickering back to the surface. "Okay," she said, her voice softer now. "Let's try."

As we talked, the walls began to crumble—one confession at a time. Each word was a brick removed from the fortress she had built, revealing the tender heart beneath. She spoke of dreams deferred, of past hurts that had shaped her, and I listened, my heart aching and swelling all at once. It was as if I were peeling back layers of an intricate painting, uncovering the vibrant strokes hidden beneath the muted tones of her past.

But as she spoke, I couldn't shake the feeling that while I was making progress, the specter of her past loomed large, an ever-present reminder that some battles were not easily won.

Sophie leaned back in her chair, a thoughtful frown etched across her forehead as she absently swirled the remnants of her coffee. I watched her, captivated by the way the light caught the golden strands of her hair, illuminating the chaos of her thoughts. Each flicker of her gaze told a story, one I longed to unravel. The café hummed with life around us, laughter and clinking cutlery blending into a symphony of normalcy, yet here we sat, suspended in a bubble of unresolved tension.

"I used to think bravery was about big gestures, you know?" she finally said, breaking the comfortable silence that had settled like a heavy blanket between us. "Like saving the day with a grand act."

"Like jumping in front of a train?" I joked, trying to lighten the mood, but the shadow that flickered in her eyes told me I had missed the mark.

She chuckled softly, the sound brittle, then continued, "But now I see it's the small things, too. Like admitting when you're scared or letting someone see the parts of you that feel broken. That's what real bravery is."

I felt a pang of admiration for her vulnerability, the way she navigated her feelings with a raw honesty that felt both terrifying and beautiful. "And you, Sophie, are braver than most," I replied, squeezing her hand gently. "Just look at everything you've faced."

Her smile faded, replaced by a distant look, as if she were peering into a fog that obscured her view of the present. "What if I'm not brave enough to face what's coming?"

"What's coming?" I asked, suddenly on alert. "What do you mean?"

She sighed, a sound laden with resignation. "I've spent so long burying my past, pretending it doesn't exist. But it does. It's like a ghost, haunting me."

"What do you mean?" I pressed, leaning forward. "What happened?"

Her lips parted, and for a heartbeat, I thought she might finally share the truth she had guarded so fiercely. Instead, she shook her head, the vulnerability giving way to defiance. "Not now. I can't. I'm not ready."

That familiar knot tightened in my stomach. "Sophie, we can't keep dancing around this. You're carrying a load that's too heavy for one person."

"Maybe that's how it has to be for now." Her voice was firm, but I could hear the wavering underneath. "Maybe I need time to figure it out."

Time. A concept that had always eluded me, and one that felt particularly slippery now. "You know you don't have to do this alone," I said, my tone softer. "You've got me, right? I'm not going anywhere."

"Promise?" she asked, her eyes searching mine for any sign of insincerity.

"Absolutely. Cross my heart." I made the motion exaggeratedly, a grin breaking through the heavy atmosphere.

A small smile tugged at her lips, but it faded almost instantly, and the weight returned, thicker than before. We spent the rest of the afternoon in companionable silence, sipping our drinks as the café buzzed around us, the world seemingly unaware of the storm brewing in the heart of Willow Creek.

As the sun dipped lower in the sky, casting a warm golden hue across the town, I felt an urgency welling inside me, an instinct that warned me we were running out of time. I wanted to protect her, to shelter her from the past that loomed over us like a gathering storm.

But how could I help her when she was so determined to shoulder it all alone?

Eventually, we left the café, stepping into the embrace of the evening. The cool air felt refreshing, yet I could sense the tension swirling around us, a thick fog that refused to lift. We strolled along the main street, the glow of shopfronts illuminating our path, but the normalcy felt like a mask, concealing the deeper currents of emotion that swirled beneath the surface.

"Do you want to go to the park?" I suggested, pointing toward the small expanse of green where we'd spent so many afternoons. "We could walk, maybe clear our heads."

"Sure, why not?" she replied, though the enthusiasm was lacking.

As we reached the park, the faint sound of children's laughter echoed in the distance, mixing with the chirping of crickets as twilight settled in. The familiar swing set swayed gently in the breeze, a reminder of our carefree days. I settled onto one of the swings, nudging it into motion, and looked at Sophie, who stood a few paces away, her arms crossed tightly over her chest.

"Come join me," I called out, trying to coax her back to that carefree spirit. "You know you want to."

She hesitated, then slowly made her way over, sitting beside me. The chains creaked softly as we swung, a rhythmic motion that felt oddly soothing.

"I remember when we used to come here after school," she said, her eyes brightening momentarily as memories flickered in her mind. "You'd always try to see how high you could go."

"Always," I replied, laughing. "And I think I succeeded every time—at least in my mind."

We shared a moment of laughter, but it was short-lived. As the laughter faded, an uncomfortable silence settled, heavy and foreboding.

"Do you think we'll ever go back to how it was?" Sophie asked, her voice low, almost hesitant.

"Back?" I pondered, feeling a pang of nostalgia for the simplicity of our past. "I think we can create something new. Something better."

"Easier said than done."

"True," I admitted, the sincerity of her words sinking in. "But we can't go backward. We can only move forward."

She nodded, her gaze fixed on the ground, where shadows played tricks in the fading light. "What if forward is scary?"

"It probably will be," I said, my heart racing as I met her gaze. "But we'll face it together. I won't let you face it alone."

"Even if I push you away?" she challenged, a spark of defiance breaking through her melancholy.

"Especially then," I replied, my voice firm but gentle. "That's when you'll need me the most."

Her silence hung between us, and I could see the internal battle waging within her, a war against the fears that threatened to consume her. I longed to reach out, to pull her into the warmth of my arms and shield her from everything that haunted her, but I knew that sometimes, the best way to help someone was to let them fight their own battles.

"Okay," she said finally, her voice barely a whisper, yet laced with determination. "I'll try."

"Good," I smiled, feeling the weight shift ever so slightly. "That's all I ask."

As we swung back and forth, the stars began to sprinkle the sky, each one a reminder of the countless possibilities that lay ahead. It was a fragile peace, but it was ours, and in that moment, it felt like just enough.

The twilight deepened around us, wrapping the park in a soft cocoon as the stars began to twinkle overhead. Sophie's laughter lingered in the air, a fleeting reminder of who she was when the shadows didn't loom quite so large. I felt a shift within myself, an urgency urging me to keep her close, to bridge the gap that threatened to swallow us whole.

"Do you ever wonder what would happen if we just... packed up and left?" I asked, breaking the spell of silence that had settled over us. "Like, right now. Just drove away and didn't look back?"

Her brow arched in curiosity, a glimmer of mischief igniting in her eyes. "Oh? And where would we go? Paris? Bali? Or maybe just to the next town over for some overpriced coffee?"

I grinned, imagining us in a sun-drenched café overlooking the Seine or lounging on a beach where the waves lapped at our feet. "Why not all three? We could be wanderers, adventurers, the embodiment of 'carpe diem.'"

"Carpe diem?" she teased, shaking her head as if my suggestion were absurd. "You sound like a cliché from a bad romance novel."

"Maybe so," I countered, pushing off the swing and standing up. "But every good story needs a bit of whimsy, don't you think?"

"I suppose," she replied, rising to her feet as well. "But let's not romanticize running away. It's not like our problems will disappear just because we drive a few hundred miles."

"True," I admitted, my smile faltering for a moment. "But it would be nice to pretend for a bit, wouldn't it?"

As her gaze drifted toward the darkening horizon, I caught the slightest hint of wistfulness in her expression. The wind tousled her hair, and for a heartbeat, I imagined she was seeing the world beyond Willow Creek—a world without burdens, without ghosts haunting her every step.

The sound of laughter from the playground snapped her back to reality, and she turned toward the noise, a hint of longing shadowing her features. "You know, I used to think I could escape by going to college in the city," she mused, her tone almost wistful. "I thought the busy streets would drown out the whispers of my past."

"Did they?" I asked, intrigued by the depths she was willing to reveal.

"Not really," she replied, a wry smile playing on her lips. "Turns out, the past has a way of sticking around, no matter how fast you run."

I stepped closer, sensing her vulnerability hovering just beneath the surface. "You don't have to run anymore, Sophie. You can face it. I'll help you."

She turned to me, her expression suddenly serious, the flicker of laughter snuffed out. "What if I can't face it? What if I'm not strong enough?"

"Strength isn't always about facing everything alone," I said softly. "Sometimes it's about allowing someone else to carry the weight with you."

The air thickened between us, a charged silence that felt almost electric. I could see the turmoil in her eyes, the struggle between wanting to confide in me and the instinct to retreat into the safety of her own walls. I held my breath, waiting for her to break the stillness, to let me in just a little more.

"Do you really want to know?" she finally asked, her voice barely above a whisper, laced with trepidation.

"Yes," I replied, every fiber of my being attuned to her honesty. "I'm here. Always."

She inhaled sharply, her chest rising and falling with a rapid cadence that mirrored the conflict in her heart. "It's about my family. I thought I could outrun the shadows, but they followed me. Every time I thought I was free, they dragged me back down."

"What do you mean?" I pressed, desperate for her to share the secrets that threatened to engulf her.

"My father... he was involved in things that are better left buried," she said, her voice trembling. "When I finally thought I was free from him, I realized he still had a hold on me."

"Your father? How?" I asked, the pieces starting to connect in my mind.

"The decisions he made, the enemies he made... they don't just disappear," she continued, her voice breaking. "I've spent my life trying to distance myself from that world, but it's always been there, lurking just out of sight."

Suddenly, the shadows around us felt denser, as if the trees themselves leaned in closer to listen. My heart raced at the implications of her words, a mix of fear and anger swirling within me. "What do you mean? Are they... are they still after you?"

"I don't know," she admitted, her voice barely above a whisper. "But I've started getting these messages. Cryptic, threatening. Like someone knows about my past and wants to drag me back."

My stomach twisted at the thought, anger bubbling just below the surface. "Why didn't you tell me sooner? You shouldn't have to go through this alone."

"Because I didn't want to involve you," she shot back, her eyes blazing. "I thought I could handle it. But now..."

I stepped closer, closing the distance between us. "Now you need me, and that's okay. We'll figure this out together, I promise."

The tension was palpable, each word hanging in the air like a promise, but just as I thought we were breaking through, the sudden shriek of a siren pierced the night, shattering the fragile moment. My heart leaped into my throat, and I turned instinctively toward the sound, dread settling heavily in my stomach.

"What was that?" Sophie asked, her eyes wide, fear threading through her voice.

I scanned the park, the shadows stretching ominously as the siren grew louder, echoing through the streets of Willow Creek. "I don't know, but it doesn't sound good."

Before I could say another word, a dark figure emerged from the trees at the edge of the park, moving swiftly toward us. My instincts kicked in, adrenaline surging through my veins as I turned back to Sophie. "We need to get out of here."

"Why?" she asked, confusion etched on her face.

"Just trust me," I urged, grabbing her hand and pulling her toward the exit. But as we turned, the figure stepped into the light, revealing a familiar face—one I had never expected to see again.

"Hello, Sophie," he said, a smirk twisting his lips. "Miss me?"

In that moment, time froze, the world narrowing to the two of them, and the weight of everything shifted once more, teetering on the edge of chaos.

Chapter 26: A New Path Forward

The tires hummed against the asphalt, a rhythmic serenade that punctuated the quiet moments between us. As Sophie leaned against the window, the wind tousled her hair, sending strands fluttering like flags in the breeze. The Midwest unfolded before us, a patchwork quilt of golden fields and rolling hills, a testament to both the resilience of nature and the people who cherished it. We had set out with a purpose—one that felt as vast and open as the landscapes we were traversing—and slowly, the edges of her sadness began to soften.

"Do you remember that summer we spent at the lake?" she asked suddenly, her voice breaking through the drone of the tires. Her eyes sparkled with a mix of nostalgia and mischief, igniting a warmth in my chest. I glanced over, taking in the way her lips curled up at the corners, a ghost of the smile that had once illuminated her face so brightly.

"How could I forget? You thought you could teach me to catch fish, but all I caught was a sunburn," I replied, a laugh escaping me. "And you spent most of the time chasing dragonflies instead of actually fishing."

She laughed, a sound like music, pulling the tension that had lingered between us into the rearview mirror. "Well, I wasn't going to let a silly fish steal my summer fun."

In that moment, the car was a sanctuary—a small, contained world where laughter echoed, and memories danced between us like fireflies on a warm evening. The diner we stopped at later had character, the kind you couldn't find in glossy travel brochures. It was the kind of place where the walls told stories, adorned with photos of patrons long gone and neon signs flickering in cheerful defiance of age. The scent of fresh coffee mingled with the unmistakable aroma of fried food, a comforting embrace that wrapped around us as we slid into a booth by the window.

I ordered a slice of pie, the waitress insisting it was homemade, and as I took my first bite, the sweetness enveloped me like a childhood memory. "You've got to try this," I urged, pushing the plate toward Sophie. She hesitated, eyeing the slice with a mix of desire and caution, a testament to her newfound resolve to prioritize her health. But then she caved, a gleam in her eye that suggested she was ready to indulge, if only just this once.

"This better be worth the calories," she said, taking a tentative forkful and lifting it to her lips. As the taste hit her, her eyes widened, delight bursting forth. "Okay, you win. This is divine!"

Our conversation flowed as freely as the coffee refills, and I felt the weight of unspoken words begin to lift. We shared stories of our childhood adventures, the mischief we caused, and the dreams that had once felt so vivid. I couldn't help but notice how the small acts of joy—the diner's jukebox playing classic tunes, the way the sunlight caught the dust motes dancing in the air—pulled her closer to the surface of herself. It was as if each laugh and shared memory cracked open a door, allowing the light to flood in and illuminate the corners of her heart that had grown dim.

Later, as we resumed our journey, the horizon painted itself with the deep purples and burnt oranges of a fading sunset. I glanced at Sophie, who was staring out the window, her expression contemplative. I knew she was still grappling with the shadows of her past, but tonight felt different. There was a newfound determination in her gaze, as if she was ready to confront the ghosts that had haunted her.

"Sophie," I ventured, testing the waters. "What if we stopped at the old campsite tomorrow? You know, the one by the river?"

Her gaze flicked to me, surprise etched on her features. "You mean the one where we camped out that one summer and nearly got eaten alive by mosquitoes?"

"Exactly!" I laughed. "But remember the stars? They were so bright, you could almost reach out and touch them."

She paused, her smile softening. "I remember. That night felt like magic. I hadn't seen a sky like that in years." There was a flicker of something in her eyes—recognition, maybe, or a hint of the adventurous spirit I had known.

With the night wrapping around us like a velvet cloak, I couldn't help but feel that we were on the cusp of something transformative. The road stretched ahead, a tangible promise of adventure, and the warmth of our laughter felt like a fire against the coolness of the evening. I knew that Sophie had a journey of her own to navigate, one laden with heartache and hesitation, but I was determined to walk alongside her, to help her carve out a new path.

As we drove on, I made a silent promise to her and to myself: that no matter how tangled the roads ahead might become, we would face them together. The world outside the window blurred into streaks of color, a reminder that life, in all its chaotic beauty, was worth every moment of uncertainty. And just like that, as the stars began to blink into existence above us, I felt a sense of hope unfurl within me, a delicate flower pushing through the cracks of the pavement, vibrant and alive.

As dawn broke, the soft light spilled into our tiny motel room like a whisper, coaxing me from sleep. I turned to find Sophie still nestled under her covers, the peace of slumber hugging her tightly. She looked so serene, a quiet contrast to the storm of emotions swirling beneath the surface. I wondered what dreams danced behind those closed eyelids. Were they filled with laughter and adventure, or did shadows of doubt still linger?

I tiptoed to the window, drawing back the curtain to reveal the world waking up outside. The Midwest stretched endlessly, a canvas painted in soft greens and golds, and as I inhaled the crisp morning air, I felt an exhilarating sense of possibility wash over me. Today was the day we'd revisit our past—a site filled with laughter, youth, and perhaps a few more mosquito bites than either of us would like to remember.

After a quick breakfast—just coffee and granola bars that crunched like brittle leaves—we piled back into the car, my excitement bubbling over. "So, ready to face the great outdoors?" I asked, trying to inject a note of bravado into my voice as I glanced sideways at Sophie, who was meticulously tying her hair into a tight bun, her brow furrowed in concentration.

"Only if you promise to bring bug spray this time. I still have nightmares about those mosquitoes," she replied, her lips quirking into a teasing smile.

"Bug spray is my middle name!" I declared, though I realized my name was technically "Taylor." Regardless, I shot her a mock-serious look. "But if the mosquitoes want to tussle, I'm game for that too."

We both laughed, and for a moment, the weight of the past seemed lighter, even whimsical. As the miles rolled by, the countryside began to shift subtly, morphing into a landscape dotted with old barns, their wooden sides weathered but proud, and fields bustling with harvests ready for gathering. Each sight felt like a postcard from the heart of America, the kind of backdrop that could ignite nostalgia in anyone who dared to dream.

As we approached the campsite, a flutter of anticipation stirred within me. Memories flickered like fireflies in the fading twilight of my mind—the crackling campfire, marshmallows roasted to a perfect golden brown, and Sophie's infectious laughter echoing against the quiet of the night. This was where we had spun tales under the stars, hearts open, spirits unburdened.

The entrance loomed before us, the sign almost hidden by overgrown foliage, as if the woods had conspired to reclaim its territory. "Here we go," I said, my voice a blend of eagerness and nostalgia.

We parked the car and stepped out, the earthy scent of damp pine and rich soil enveloping us like an old, familiar cloak. The sound of leaves rustling in the gentle breeze echoed around us, a soothing symphony that welcomed us back to this cherished sanctuary.

Sophie breathed in deeply, her eyes sparkling as they swept across the familiar terrain. "It's even more beautiful than I remembered," she murmured, and I could sense a shift in her energy—a thawing of the frost that had clung to her for so long.

We walked down the familiar path leading to the riverbank, the gentle gurgle of the water harmonizing with our footsteps. Sophie paused, her gaze fixed on the shimmering surface of the river, as if she could see echoes of the past mirrored there. "I was so carefree here," she said, her voice barely above a whisper. "I wish I could feel that way again."

"Then let's make that happen," I declared, a sudden surge of determination fueling my words. "We'll create new memories, ones that make you laugh so hard you snort. It'll be epic."

Sophie looked at me, surprise flickering across her features before she broke into a grin. "You always did have a way with words. I just hope I can keep up with your level of epicness."

We settled on a grassy patch near the water, surrounded by the scent of wildflowers that danced in the breeze. I reached into the cooler I had packed, pulling out a couple of sandwiches and a thermos of lemonade. As we ate, I began to recount stories of our past camping trips, embellishing them with wildly exaggerated details.

"Remember when you tried to start that campfire and ended up burning the marshmallows into little blackened nuggets?" I teased, mimicking her dramatic attempt to salvage the charred remains.

Sophie giggled, shaking her head. "You mean the 'flambé marshmallow incident'? It was a culinary adventure gone awry! I was just trying to impress you."

"I was definitely impressed," I replied, "but not in the way you intended."

Her laughter was like music, vibrant and infectious, lifting both our spirits higher. It was the sound I had missed—the symphony of her joy that resonated through the air, weaving between the leaves and the flowing river.

As the afternoon sun dipped lower in the sky, casting golden glimmers across the water, we ventured to the riverbank. Sophie, ever the adventurer, dared me to wade in. "Just a quick dip," she challenged, her eyes sparkling with mischief.

I hesitated, remembering the icy chill of the water, but the playful glint in her gaze urged me on. "Alright, but you're coming with me!"

Before I could second-guess myself, I grabbed her hand, and together we splashed into the river. The cold water sent shivers through us, but laughter erupted like a burst of fireworks, bright and effervescent.

"You are crazy!" she squealed, retreating a few steps, only to be caught in a wave of water I splashed in her direction. The scene was chaotic, filled with shrieks of surprise and bursts of laughter that echoed off the water.

Suddenly, a mischievous spark flickered in her eyes. "You know what? I'm tired of being careful," she declared. "Let's really make a mess of it."

With that, she lunged toward me, and before I could react, she pulled me under the water. The world above transformed into a swirling blur, the sunlight fracturing around us like a shattered glass window. When I broke the surface, gasping for air, Sophie was doubled over, laughter bubbling from her like a brook overflowing after a rainstorm.

"You are so on my list!" I spluttered, half-laughing, half-reprimanding her, though the truth was, I wouldn't have had it any other way.

As the sun began its descent, painting the sky in hues of pink and lavender, I knew we were forging new bonds—one where laughter intertwined with vulnerability, weaving a fabric of memories rich enough to overshadow the shadows that lingered in Sophie's heart. In that moment, I realized we were not just revisiting the past; we were creating a new narrative, one where joy could coexist with healing, and where friendship could light the darkest paths.

The sun dipped below the horizon, casting a shimmering glow on the river as we finally pulled ourselves from the cool water. My heart raced not just from the thrill of the splash but from the deepening bond I felt with Sophie, the laughter shared a lifeline we both desperately needed. We stood there, water dripping off our hair and clothes, breathless and exhilarated. In that moment, I could see the walls she had built around herself beginning to crack.

"Okay, Miss Adventure," I said, playfully pushing my wet hair out of my face, "what's next on our agenda? A thrilling hike or a quiet contemplation by the fire?"

She considered for a moment, eyes sparkling with a hint of mischief. "How about a fire? I'm ready to roast some marshmallows and reignite our culinary mishaps."

"Now you're speaking my language," I replied, the warmth of our playful banter creating a sense of ease that had been missing for so long. I led the way back to the campsite, our footsteps squelching in the mud as we left behind the river's embrace.

By the time we reached our tent, twilight had settled in, wrapping the world in a soft, velvety embrace. I set to work gathering firewood while Sophie rummaged through our supplies, her determination visible as she prepared for our next culinary endeavor. The campfire soon crackled to life, its warmth radiating against the cooling night air, inviting us to gather around its flickering glow.

As we sat cross-legged on the ground, I took in the scene before me: Sophie, her laughter spilling out like a waterfall as she recounted tales of our childhood, her spirit noticeably lighter. The fire danced, casting playful shadows on her face, making her look almost ethereal against the night.

"So, tell me," I prompted, leaning forward, "what is the most embarrassing thing you've ever done at a campfire?"

Her laughter slowed, and she bit her lip, a sign that she was deep in thought. "Hmm, let me see... Ah! The time I got so excited about roasting marshmallows that I forgot to pay attention and nearly set my hair on fire. You thought it was hilarious," she said, shaking her head.

"I still think it's hilarious! But seriously, if you're willing to let your hair sizzle for the sake of a golden marshmallow, that's commitment," I teased, unable to contain my grin.

"Hey, at least I know how to make a good comeback," she shot back, a spark of her old self shining through the cracks of uncertainty.

As the night deepened, we reached for the skewers and set our marshmallows to roast. I held mine too close to the flames, and it quickly caught fire. "Whoops!" I exclaimed, waving it about like a little torch. "Just trying to add some drama to the evening."

Sophie burst into laughter, her joy mingling with the smoke rising from the fire. "If we're going for drama, I think we need a little more flair. How about a s'more-off? Winner gets to choose our next destination!"

"Challenge accepted!" I grinned, rallying my inner competitor. We hurriedly constructed our s'mores, slathering chocolate and graham crackers with exaggerated seriousness. As we tasted our creations, it felt like a simple joy—one of those moments that seemed to stretch out, infinitely precious.

"This is definitely the best s'more I've ever had," Sophie declared, her eyes bright in the firelight. "And you know what? This might just be the best day ever."

Before I could respond, her expression shifted, the smile fading slightly as if she had remembered something unspoken. "But, you know, it's so easy to pretend everything is okay here, isn't it?" she said quietly.

The air between us thickened, tension curling around the flames like smoke. "Sophie," I began, wanting to reach for her, to assure her that we were indeed on a better path, "it's okay to not be okay."

She shook her head, a flicker of frustration passing over her features. "But I don't want to be that person anymore—the one who can't shake off the past, who always finds a way to ruin moments that should be good. I hate feeling like a burden."

"You're not a burden," I insisted, my voice steady. "You're human. You're allowed to feel everything, the good and the bad. Just because today has been light doesn't mean tomorrow will be. It's all part of the journey."

She looked down, her fingers tracing patterns in the dirt. The fire crackled between us, the silence stretching out, charged with unspoken truths. I could see her battling with her thoughts, the past warring with the present, and I wished I could sweep away the remnants of her pain, as if it were merely smoke dissipating into the night sky.

But just as I opened my mouth to continue, the sound of rustling nearby drew our attention. We both froze, eyes darting toward the darkness that loomed beyond our firelight. The woods seemed to hold their breath, the nighttime sounds momentarily silenced.

"What was that?" Sophie whispered, her earlier bravado fading into uncertainty.

"I don't know," I replied, my heart racing. "Could just be a raccoon, or maybe a deer." But even as I spoke, the rustling grew louder, more insistent.

"Raccoons don't usually sound like they're staging a rebellion," she muttered, her voice laced with trepidation.

The rustling crescendoed into what sounded like shuffling footsteps, deliberate and heavy. I shot up, straining my ears to catch any further sounds. "Stay here," I said, trying to sound braver than I felt.

"No way am I staying here!" Sophie shot back, her eyes wide. "If there's a creature out there, I'm not letting you face it alone. It's about teamwork, right?"

I couldn't help but smile despite the adrenaline coursing through my veins. "Teamwork it is, then. Let's grab the flashlight."

As we fumbled for our gear, the rustling stopped, replaced by an unsettling silence that felt pregnant with tension. Heartbeats quickened, and as I switched on the flashlight, the beam pierced the darkness, illuminating the path ahead.

"What do you think it could be?" Sophie asked, her voice a whisper.

Before I could answer, the beam of light landed on something moving in the shadows. My breath caught in my throat. Standing just beyond the treeline was a figure—a silhouette etched against the dim glow of the moon. It was too large to be any woodland creature, and my stomach dropped.

"Is that...?" Sophie started, her eyes wide with disbelief.

The figure stepped forward, and in the beam of light, I caught a glimpse of something that made my heart race for entirely different reasons. A face, familiar yet distorted by the shadows—someone I had never expected to see again.

"Surprise!" the figure called, a grin stretching across their face, sharp and disarming, the kind that could slice through the darkness and into the very heart of our fragile moment.

Everything shifted in that instant, the night holding its breath, as the air grew thick with a tension I couldn't place. I felt Sophie's hand grip mine tightly, and in that silence, I understood we were standing on the precipice of something new—something that could either bind us closer together or tear the carefully woven fabric of our journey apart.

Chapter 27: The Blossoming Garden

A soft breeze whispered through the vibrant blossoms as we stepped into the community garden, an oasis that felt worlds apart from the bustling streets we had left behind. The air was thick with the sweet, intoxicating scent of honeysuckle and the earthy undertones of freshly turned soil. A riot of colors splashed against the backdrop of emerald green leaves, as flowers unfurled their petals like open arms inviting us into their world. Marigolds stood guard at the entrance, their golden crowns nodding approvingly at the visitors they had welcomed.

Sophie, her auburn curls bouncing in the breeze, knelt beside a patch of vibrant zinnias, her fingers trailing gently over the soft petals. "Look at these," she said, her voice laced with awe, "they're like confetti in the wind." I couldn't help but smile at her childlike enthusiasm. In her eyes, I saw a spark of hope flicker to life, a contrast to the weight that had so often pressed down on us during our journey. Here, amidst the blossoms, we were two wayward souls, seeking refuge from the chaos that the world often thrust upon us.

As we wandered deeper into the garden, I marveled at the intricate tapestry woven by the hands of the community. Raised beds brimmed with kale, tomatoes, and peppers, their leaves dancing merrily under the warm sun. Nearby, a small wooden sign read "Take What You Need" above a flourishing herb garden. It was a simple invitation, a testament to the spirit of sharing and generosity that enveloped the space. "Can you imagine if we could do something like this?" Sophie mused, her voice low and contemplative. "A place where people can come together, grow food, and heal."

I watched her, captivated not just by her words, but by the transformation occurring within her. The shadows that had clung to her since the start of our journey seemed to dissipate, replaced by a lightness that danced in her green eyes. "You want to create a sanctuary?" I asked, my heart racing with excitement. "A retreat?"

She turned to me, her expression a mixture of determination and vulnerability. "Yes. A place where people can escape, even if just for a few hours, and connect with nature and each other."

The vision blossomed like the garden itself, rich with possibilities. We could establish workshops on gardening, cooking classes featuring the very produce we'd grow, and meditation spaces among the trees. I could already imagine children laughing and playing, their laughter mingling with the buzz of bees and the gentle rustle of leaves. I felt the weight of the world lift off my shoulders as I pictured families coming together, forging bonds that transcended their everyday lives.

"But how?" I asked, reality creeping in like a shadow. "We're just... us."

Sophie chuckled, the sound light and airy, like the petals of a dandelion floating on a summer breeze. "Maybe 'just us' is enough. We could start small. Organize weekend workshops, gather volunteers. If we build it, they will come, right?"

"Are you quoting 'Field of Dreams' at me?" I teased, nudging her playfully with my shoulder.

"Hey, it's a classic for a reason!" she shot back, laughter brightening her face, making her look radiant. "You know what they say, a little bit of madness goes a long way."

The atmosphere thrummed with an energy that was almost palpable. We set to work, our hands sinking into the cool earth, the sun warming our backs. We planted seeds for herbs and vegetables, imagining the flavors that would spring forth. Each scoop of soil felt like a promise, each seed a dream that we hoped would take root and flourish.

"Let's make a plan," I said, wiping the sweat from my brow. "We can outline our ideas, gather supplies, and even start a social media page to reach out to the community."

Sophie nodded eagerly, her enthusiasm infectious. "We could share gardening tips, recipes, and maybe even stories of people who have found solace in nature."

The notion ignited something deep within me, an ember of purpose that I hadn't realized I'd been missing. It wasn't just about gardening or building a retreat; it was about weaving together a community, creating a tapestry of shared experiences and collective healing.

As we worked, the sun began to dip low in the sky, casting a warm golden hue over the garden. It felt as if the universe conspired to bless our venture. Sophie paused, her hands resting on her hips as she surveyed our small section of the garden. "You know, this could be the start of something beautiful," she said, her voice barely above a whisper, yet filled with conviction.

"Beautiful and a little chaotic," I replied, unable to suppress a grin. "But that's part of the charm, isn't it? Life is messy, and so are gardens."

She laughed, a sound that rang out like a bell, clear and bright. "Then let's embrace the chaos. After all, who needs perfection when you have passion?"

Just as I opened my mouth to respond, a sudden rustling in the nearby bushes caught my attention. I turned, expecting to see a squirrel or perhaps a wayward bird, but instead, I was met with the curious gaze of a young girl. Her big brown eyes shimmered with intrigue, a tiny flower crown perched atop her head like a badge of honor.

"Are you planting a garden?" she asked, her voice soft yet bold, full of the innocent confidence that only a child could possess.

"Yes, we are!" Sophie exclaimed, kneeling to meet the girl at eye level. "Would you like to help us?"

The girl's eyes widened with delight, and she nodded vigorously. "Can I plant some seeds?"

"Absolutely," I said, my heart swelling at the sight of her excitement. "What kind would you like to plant?"

As we welcomed her into our small circle, I felt an overwhelming sense of hope wash over me. This little girl, this innocent and curious soul, was a reminder of the impact we could have—how one small seed of an idea could grow into something magnificent, nurtured by laughter, community, and love.

Together, we planted our seeds, laughter ringing out under the warm glow of the evening sun, each moment a step closer to the sanctuary we dreamed of creating—a place where we could all find healing among the blossoms.

The sun dipped lower, casting a golden light across the garden as Sophie and I worked side by side, our hands dirty but our spirits buoyant. The little girl, whose name turned out to be Lila, dug her fingers into the soil with an enthusiasm that was contagious. "Look!" she squealed, pulling up a clump of dirt to reveal a wriggling earthworm. "Is this a snake?"

"Nope, just a worm," I said, chuckling as I gently retrieved the slimy creature from her grip. "But a very important one. They help the soil breathe and make it rich for our plants."

Lila's eyes widened in awe. "So, it's like a superhero for the garden?"

"Exactly!" Sophie exclaimed, clapping her hands together. "You're a garden superhero now, too. The more you help, the stronger it becomes."

The girl beamed, clearly delighted with her newfound identity. I watched as she continued to dig with fervor, transforming our small patch into a treasure trove of possibilities. It was inspiring to witness her innocent joy; it ignited a flicker of childlike wonder within me that I hadn't realized I had lost amid adult responsibilities and the weight of expectations.

"I can't believe how quickly she's picking this up," I said to Sophie as we shared a quiet moment, observing Lila's antics. "It's like she's never met a weed she didn't want to wrestle into submission."

Sophie snorted, the sound bubbling up like champagne, effervescent and delightful. "A true warrior of the garden! We should probably give her a cape."

"Or a shovel with a glitter handle," I added, playfully rolling my eyes.

Just then, the tranquility was pierced by a voice that was rich and booming. "Well, well, what do we have here?"

I turned to see a tall figure approaching, a man whose wide-brimmed hat shadowed his face. He moved with a gait that suggested he owned the very earth we stood upon. As he drew closer, I noticed the sun catching glints of gray in his beard and an inviting warmth in his blue eyes.

"Hi, I'm Sam," he introduced himself, extending a calloused hand toward Sophie and me. "I run the community garden here. And who might these two be?"

"Sophie and... well, I'm kind of just along for the ride," I admitted, shaking his hand.

"Just along for the ride, huh?" Sam mused, a knowing smile creeping onto his lips. "Usually, those who wander in here end up planting roots, you know."

"Are you suggesting we might become permanent residents?" I joked, raising an eyebrow.

"Only if you want to." He winked, making me feel like he saw right through my casual facade. "This garden is open to all who seek it. And it seems you've already made a good start."

Lila jumped in, her small hands on her hips. "We're making it super amazing! I'm a superhero, and we're planting seeds!"

Sam laughed heartily, the sound rumbling like distant thunder. "That's the spirit! The more, the merrier. This place thrives on community, after all."

Sophie and I exchanged glances, a shared understanding passing between us. Sam's arrival felt like a sign, a confirmation that our budding dream could indeed sprout into something real and meaningful. "We're hoping to create a retreat here," Sophie shared, her eyes sparkling with enthusiasm. "A place for learning and connection."

"Ah, I see," Sam nodded, the corners of his mouth lifting. "Well, you've come to the right place. We could use some fresh energy around here. We've had some challenges lately."

"Challenges?" I asked, curiosity piqued.

"Nothing too terrible," he replied, scratching his beard thoughtfully. "Just a few folks who forgot that gardening requires more than just a green thumb. There's been some vandalism, and weeds have taken over in places. A little community spirit has been missing."

Sophie's brow furrowed, the realization hitting her. "That's terrible. But it sounds like a perfect opportunity for us to rally the community back together."

"Exactly!" Sam said, his eyes lighting up with excitement. "If you're willing, I could use your help to organize a clean-up day. Get folks out here to pull weeds and plant some new seeds, both in the ground and in the hearts of our community."

I glanced at Sophie, the thrill of the idea electrifying the air between us. "Count us in," I said before she could respond, my voice brimming with newfound confidence. "We'd love to help."

"Great!" Sam clapped his hands together, the sound echoing through the garden. "We can set up a planning meeting next week. I know a few people who'd be eager to join."

As we continued to chat, I felt an unfamiliar excitement bubbling within me. This was more than just a garden; it was a chance to cultivate relationships, to bring people together in a shared mission of growth and renewal. I envisioned our little retreat transforming into a vibrant hub of activity, where stories would be exchanged, laughter would echo, and friendships would blossom like the flowers around us.

Lila interjected, her voice chirping like a bird. "Can we have a picnic when we're done? I love picnics!"

"Absolutely," Sam said, nodding. "Picnics are a must. Food and friends go together like sunshine and rain."

"We'll bring homemade cookies," I added, imagining the sweet scent wafting through the air.

"Only if you're making the chocolate chip ones," Sophie teased, her eyes dancing with mischief. "We wouldn't want anything inferior to spoil the picnic."

"Don't worry," I said, my hands raised in mock surrender. "I'll whip up a batch worthy of your discerning palate."

The laughter that followed wrapped around us like a warm blanket, a promise of the camaraderie that lay ahead. With each passing moment, the garden transformed from a mere collection of plants into a canvas of dreams and connections. We were no longer just two wanderers; we were part of something larger, a tapestry woven from the threads of hope, healing, and shared purpose.

As dusk settled over the Appalachian foothills, casting a gentle twilight glow, I felt a sense of belonging bloom within me. The community garden wasn't just a sanctuary for flora; it was becoming a sanctuary for us all, a place where we could find solace in the chaos of life, united by the simple act of planting seeds—both in the earth and in each other's hearts.

With the twilight casting a soft hue across the garden, we began to map out our plans. Sophie and I huddled with Sam, sketching ideas for the upcoming clean-up day on a scrap of cardboard we found near the shed. Lila sat cross-legged on the ground, her flower crown slightly askew, as she colored the cardboard with bright, erratic scribbles, adding her own touch of whimsy to our brainstorming session.

"Let's call it 'Roots and Shoots Day,'" I suggested, inspired by the mingling of laughter and dirt that seemed to bind us together in this makeshift team.

Sophie grinned, "And we can promote it as a day of growth! For the garden and the people."

Sam nodded appreciatively. "I like it! We can put up posters around town and spread the word online. Who knows, we might even draw in some new volunteers."

Just as we were getting into the groove of planning, the garden's tranquil atmosphere was punctuated by a commotion near the entrance. A group of teenagers burst in, laughter trailing behind them like confetti. Their boisterous energy contrasted sharply with the calm we had cultivated. They were equipped with spray paint, backpacks slung low, clearly more interested in mischief than mayhem.

"Hey, what are you doing?" Sam's voice boomed, effectively halting their antics.

The teens froze, wide-eyed, like deer caught in headlights. One of them, a lanky boy with a shock of bright red hair, stepped forward, feigning innocence. "Just checking out the garden, man. No harm meant."

I could almost feel the tension crackle in the air. Sam took a step closer, crossing his arms over his chest, a formidable figure against their youthful recklessness. "This isn't a playground for vandalism. We're trying to build something good here."

Sophie and I exchanged worried glances, the atmosphere shifting like the weather before a storm. Just as I opened my mouth to diffuse the tension, Lila piped up, "We're making a garden sanctuary! Do you want to help?"

The teenagers blinked, taken aback by the little girl's earnestness. Their laughter faded, and I could see them weighing their options. It was a moment of hesitation that felt fraught with potential.

"Are you serious?" the girl with bright blue hair asked, crossing her arms. "A sanctuary? Sounds boring."

"Boring? No way! We're planting flowers and making it super fun!" Lila exclaimed, her eyes shining with the conviction of a child who had never yet learned the art of cynicism.

The girl hesitated, her brow furrowing as she looked from Lila to Sam and back again. "Okay, but can we have a bonfire later?"

Sophie jumped in, her excitement spilling over. "A bonfire sounds like a perfect idea! We could roast marshmallows, tell stories—"

"And sing!" Lila interjected, twirling in a circle as if she were already dancing around a flickering fire.

I couldn't help but chuckle at the sight. There was something so delightful about her unfiltered enthusiasm that began to chip away at the hardened exteriors of the teens.

The lanky boy scratched his head, glancing at his friends, who exchanged unsure glances. "Maybe we could help out a little," he said slowly, as if testing the waters. "But only if there's a bonfire."

"Deal!" Sam said, his voice radiating warmth, and I could see the immediate shift in the energy surrounding us.

As they joined our circle, I felt a strange sense of unity forming, one that pulled together the loose threads of our disparate lives. Perhaps the garden wasn't just a retreat for those seeking solace but also a place of unexpected connections—a melting pot for people from all walks of life.

With a new group of helpers on board, the planning kicked into high gear. Lila took the lead, her small hands demonstrating how to plant seeds while the teenagers watched, bemused but engaged. I found myself captivated by the way she effortlessly brought everyone into the fold, her innocence bridging the gap between generations and lifestyles.

"Do you think we can plant a giant sunflower?" she asked, her voice brimming with ambition.

"Why not?" I replied, grinning at her enthusiasm. "Let's make it the tallest one in the whole garden!"

As we began to dig deeper, laughter mingled with the chatter about bonfire songs and marshmallow roasting techniques. I caught a glimpse of Sam standing off to the side, a small smile gracing his rugged features. He seemed to embody the spirit of the garden itself—solid, nurturing, and filled with quiet strength.

But just as the atmosphere lightened, I noticed a shadow pass overhead, cutting through the sunset glow. A group of older men had appeared at the edge of the garden, their expressions stern and their postures rigid. They stood in stark contrast to our joyful chaos, a storm brewing just out of sight.

"What are you doing here?" one of them barked, his voice like gravel, as he pointed a finger at Sam. "This land belongs to the community, not some hippie project."

"Hey! We're just trying to make a positive change," Sam shot back, stepping forward with a protective stance.

I could feel the tension snapping like a taut string. Lila, oblivious to the growing discord, continued to chatter about flowers. The teens exchanged uneasy glances, and the warmth we had cultivated in the garden seemed to dim as quickly as the light fading from the sky.

"Positive change? This is a waste of space. We need to be using this land for something productive, not some... retreat," the man sneered, his disdain palpable.

"Who decides what's productive?" I found myself interjecting, my voice steady despite the quickening beat of my heart. "This is a space for growth in all forms. Can't you see how important it is to the community?"

He turned his piercing gaze on me, the intensity of it making my stomach flip. "This community has its priorities, and you don't seem to fit into them."

An uneasy silence descended, the air thick with confrontation. My heart raced as I looked at Sophie, her brow furrowed in concern. The tension in the air felt like a tightrope, and I could sense the precarious balance teetering on the edge of something explosive.

"We're all trying to do something good here," Sam said, his voice low but firm. "This garden is for everyone, and it's about time we come together instead of tearing each other apart."

But as the man continued to glare, a disquieting thought gnawed at the back of my mind—this was not just a conflict over a garden. It was a clash of ideals, a fight for the very soul of the community we had hoped to nurture.

And just as I opened my mouth to respond, a loud crash echoed through the garden, shaking the leaves and sending a flock of birds soaring into the sky. We turned, startled, to see a large sign that had been affixed to a nearby tree had fallen, splintering upon impact.

Emblazoned on the shattered wood were words that sent a chill coursing through my veins: "This Garden is Under Threat. Beware."

The unease spiraled into full-blown tension, and I could feel the fabric of our little sanctuary fraying before my eyes.

Chapter 28: The Seeds of Tomorrow

I sank my fingers deep into the warm, rich soil, feeling its coolness against my skin. The earth breathed beneath me, a living tapestry of life bursting with potential. Around me, the garden thrived in riotous color—zinnias danced in the breeze, their petals vibrant against the backdrop of leafy greens, while tomatoes, heavy with promise, clung to their vines like precious jewels waiting to be plucked. Each plant told a story, each bloom whispered secrets of growth, patience, and the quiet determination it took to flourish.

Sophie was nearby, a blur of energy, her laughter ringing out like wind chimes on a breezy afternoon. She knelt beside me, hands streaked with dirt, her hair a wild halo catching the sunlight. "Do you think we'll be ready for the festival?" she asked, her eyes sparkling with enthusiasm as she flicked a stray petal off her cheek. "I mean, we still have so many herbs to harvest, and I'm pretty sure the carrots are planning an underground revolt."

I chuckled, brushing my palms on my jeans as I straightened up. "If the carrots have anything to say about it, they'll probably throw a party and forget to show up. But yes, I think we're on track. We just need a bit of luck and a sprinkle of determination."

"Luck? Is that all it takes?" she teased, feigning disbelief. "I thought it was all about your gardening magic."

"Oh, you know I sprinkle fairy dust on every seed I plant," I replied, rolling my eyes playfully. "That's the real secret."

As we continued our work, more hands joined us—neighbors, friends, even curious strangers who had wandered in, drawn by the vibrant blooms and the scents wafting through the air. The garden had become a refuge for everyone, a place where worries could be left at the gate, and laughter could flourish like the sunflowers towering above us. Each workshop felt like a celebration, a gathering of kindred spirits sharing tips, stories, and the occasional gardening mishap that turned into a shared giggle.

I loved watching Sophie transform in this nurturing environment. Gone was the shy girl who had hesitated at the edge of the garden, afraid of her own abilities. In her place stood a confident woman, vibrant and alive, a spirit intertwined with the community we were building. She had taken to teaching like a fish to water, guiding newcomers with infectious enthusiasm, as though she had been doing it all her life. It was remarkable to witness; she was blooming just like our flowers, finding her voice and strength among the petals and soil.

One sunny afternoon, as the golden hour bathed the garden in a warm, honeyed glow, I caught her in a moment of quiet reflection. She stood by the rows of sunflowers, their heads turned toward the fading light, a smile tugging at her lips. "You know," she began, her voice barely above a whisper, "I never thought I could be this happy, planting flowers and making friends. It feels... magical."

"It is magical," I replied, stepping closer. "You're not just planting flowers; you're planting hope. You're giving people a reason to smile, to gather, to believe that things can change."

Her eyes glimmered with a mixture of joy and vulnerability. "But what if it all falls apart? What if the storm comes and washes everything away?"

I hesitated for a moment, choosing my words carefully. "Then we rebuild. Together. Just like we've done before. This garden isn't just about the flowers; it's about the community we're creating. And communities—like gardens—are resilient."

That night, as we wrapped up our work and watched the sunset bleed into the horizon, I felt an unsettling shift in the air. A rumble of thunder rolled in the distance, a dark cloud looming over our vibrant world. I glanced at Sophie, who seemed to sense it too, her smile faltering as the wind whipped through the leaves, carrying whispers of change.

"Do you think it'll rain?" she asked, her voice tinged with concern.

"I hope so," I said, though doubt crept into my heart. "The plants could use a drink. But it's also a warning sign, isn't it?"

"Yeah," she murmured, her gaze distant. "Everything feels a bit too perfect right now."

The next day brought more than just rain. A storm swept through, its ferocity shaking the very foundations of our garden. Winds howled like wild animals, uprooting seedlings that had barely taken hold. I watched helplessly as branches snapped, petals flew, and the vibrant colors we had nurtured faded beneath a shroud of gray. Sophie stood beside me, her expression a mix of horror and determination.

"We can't let it go like this," she shouted over the roar of the storm. "We have to do something!"

With that, we sprang into action, rallying our neighbors, our friends, our newfound family. We raced against the elements, securing stakes, covering the vulnerable with anything we could find—tarps, blankets, our own bodies when necessary. It was chaos, a dance of frantic energy, but amidst the turmoil, I felt a surge of connection that anchored me.

As the rain poured down, I caught glimpses of resolve in the faces around me—determination, hope, and fierce loyalty binding us together. We were not merely a collection of individuals; we were a community, and we would face this storm as one.

With every gust of wind that threatened to steal our dreams, I felt the seeds of tomorrow taking root, stronger than before. No storm could wash away what we had built, and as we fought for our garden, we were also fighting for each other, proving that even in the face of adversity, love and resilience would always thrive.

As the days stretched into weeks, the garden transformed into a vibrant tapestry of color and life, a riot of reds, yellows, and greens, each plant reaching for the sky as if competing for attention. The air hummed with the sound of buzzing bees and the distant laughter of children, their innocence and joy weaving seamlessly into the fabric of our community. Each morning brought a renewed sense of purpose; I relished the predictability of watering the plants, trimming the edges, and chatting with Sophie about our upcoming harvest festival.

The idea for the festival had blossomed organically, a collaborative effort borne from our workshops. It was more than just a celebration of our fruits and vegetables; it was an invitation for everyone to participate in the joy of growth and togetherness. As the date approached, I found myself caught up in the frenzy of preparations. Banners were painted, recipes tested, and a playlist of upbeat tunes curated to fill the air with good vibes.

Sophie flitted about the garden like a hummingbird, her enthusiasm infectious. "We need more signs! Bright colors! Something that screams 'This is going to be the best day ever!'" She paused, tapping her chin thoughtfully. "How about we make a giant sunflower banner? I mean, who doesn't love sunflowers?"

"Only people who are really, really sad," I joked, shaking my head. "But I'm not sure we have time to craft a masterpiece when we still need to finish the canning. And let's not forget about the flower crowns."

"The flower crowns! How could I forget?" she gasped, placing her hands over her heart in mock horror. "What would a harvest festival be without a bunch of slightly lopsided floral headgear?"

"Exactly! And the best part? They're the perfect way to distract from the fact that my hair is a disaster every single day." I gestured at my messy bun, which had become a daily norm, a sign of my dedication to the garden rather than personal grooming.

As the festival approached, our garden took on a life of its own. The sun poured down generously, nurturing our crops while also pushing us into a delightful frenzy of activity. We chopped vegetables, baked pies, and practiced our speeches, though it was mostly Sophie who flourished in front of an audience. She had a knack for storytelling that captivated anyone who dared to listen.

On the eve of the festival, our excitement was palpable. The sun dipped low in the sky, casting a warm glow over our preparations. Sophie and I stood together, surveying our work. "Do you think we've done enough?" she asked, biting her lip in a moment of vulnerability.

"Enough? We've done more than enough! This place looks incredible," I assured her, wrapping an arm around her shoulder. "You've put your heart into this. Everyone will feel it."

Her smile widened, but just as quickly, a shadow flickered across her face. "I just hope no one remembers the time I accidentally threw a tomato at Mr. Jenkins. I still can't look him in the eye."

"Don't worry, he's still in therapy over that," I teased, trying to lighten the mood. "Besides, it could have been worse. You could have hit him with a zucchini."

As the evening settled in, I found myself enveloped in a swirl of emotions—excitement mingled with trepidation. What if it rained? What if no one showed up? The doubts crept in, whispering their insidious thoughts.

"Do you want to talk about it?" Sophie asked, catching the flicker of worry on my face. "You seem a little distant."

"It's just... what if we fail?" I admitted, looking out over the rows of flourishing plants. "What if this beautiful space doesn't bring people together the way we hoped?"

Sophie shook her head, determination dancing in her eyes. "We won't fail. We've already succeeded just by creating this garden. If the festival flops, at least we know we tried. And we'll have the most beautiful garden in town, even if it's just for us."

Her optimism was like sunlight cutting through a cloud, illuminating my doubts and making them feel smaller. We retreated to her small cottage nearby, where she had been experimenting with some recipes for the festival. The scent of fresh herbs mingled with the warmth of baked goods, wrapping around us like a cozy blanket.

"Here, try this!" She thrust a spoonful of her latest concoction into my hands.

I hesitated, eyeing the vibrant green mixture suspiciously. "Is that pesto or an alien life form?"

"Just taste it!" she insisted, laughing.

I took a cautious bite, and the flavors burst across my palate, bright and refreshing. "Okay, wow. This is actually really good. You're a genius!"

"I know," she replied, flipping her hair dramatically. "And don't you forget it."

As we sampled our way through her creations, the laughter and chatter blended with the warm light spilling from the kitchen window. The world outside faded away, leaving only the moment, our friendship, and the promise of tomorrow.

But as the night deepened, I received a text that made my heart sink. It was from a friend who had promised to bring her family to the festival. "Sorry! We can't make it. Something came up." Just like that, a ripple of disappointment washed over me. I could only imagine how many others would follow suit.

"Bad news?" Sophie asked, catching my expression.

"It's nothing," I said quickly, trying to hide the frustration bubbling up inside me. "Just a friend who bailed on the festival."

"Just a friend?" She raised an eyebrow, refusing to let me brush it off. "How many people do you think will show up? We can't count them before they arrive!"

"Fine, you're right. It's just... I thought this would bring people together. I want it to be special."

"It will be special. But only if we focus on what we've created, not on who hasn't shown up. I mean, look at this pesto. I didn't spend hours making it for a small crowd, right?"

Her lightheartedness was a balm to my worries. As the clock ticked closer to midnight, we gathered our energy, fortified by the laughter and a newfound resolve. Tomorrow, we would open the gates to our garden sanctuary, and even if it wasn't perfect, it would be ours.

The morning sun rose slowly, casting a golden hue over our little corner of the world. The air buzzed with anticipation as I flung open the garden gate, my heart racing at the thought of the festival unfolding before me. Colorful banners danced in the gentle breeze, and the scent of fresh herbs wafted through the air, mingling with the lingering aroma of baked goods. I could hear laughter and music filtering through the trees, a sweet serenade of joy that filled me with warmth.

Sophie was already at the center of the festivities, directing the chaos with her usual flair. "Come one, come all! Step right up! We have the finest tomatoes in town, and the tastiest carrot cake you've ever had!" She twirled around, her flower crown tilting jauntily to one side, and I couldn't help but smile. This was the Sophie I had come to adore—vibrant, full of life, and utterly fearless.

"Your sales pitch needs some work," I teased as I joined her, slipping my arm through hers. "A little less carnival barker, a little more charming gardener."

"Fine! I'll work on my delivery. But I refuse to tone down my enthusiasm. It's not my fault if you're too busy being a wallflower!"

"Hey! I'm not a wallflower; I'm just a—"

"A vibrant perennial?" she interrupted, stifling a laugh.

"Exactly!" I said, laughing despite myself. "In any case, we need more people to stop by if we want this festival to be a success."

As if summoned by our conversation, a few neighbors wandered over, drawn by the scents and sounds. They greeted us warmly, their arms laden with homemade dishes and fresh produce. The garden quickly transformed into a lively marketplace where laughter and chatter mingled like the colors of our flowers.

"Look at this place!" one neighbor exclaimed, her eyes shining. "I can't believe how much it's grown since last year. It's beautiful!"

Sophie glowed with pride, her cheeks flushed with happiness. "Thank you! We've poured our hearts into this garden. It's not just a space; it's a community. Come, taste this!" She eagerly handed them samples of her pesto and homemade breads, beaming as they savored each bite.

As the festival buzzed around us, I found myself wandering through the rows of sunflowers and zinnias, inhaling the sweet fragrance of blooming flowers. Children dashed past, giggling and racing each other, while couples strolled hand in hand, sharing the day with relaxed smiles. But amid the joyous chaos, I felt a tug of uncertainty gnawing at the edges of my mind.

"I thought more people would show up," I said quietly to Sophie later as we restocked our tables. "I know we invited a lot of folks."

"Patience, my anxious perennial! It's still early. People are probably sleeping in after a long week. Besides, we're having fun, right?" She smiled, her enthusiasm unwavering, and for a moment, I felt my worries ease.

But as the sun climbed higher, the steady stream of people began to slow. I glanced around, hoping to see more familiar faces among the crowd. My stomach tightened as I watched Sophie entertain the guests, her laughter infectious, but the crowd seemed thin, and the vibrant energy began to wane.

"What do you think we should do?" I asked, concern creeping into my voice.

"More games! A little competition always gets people riled up," she suggested, her eyes sparkling with mischief. "How about a tomato toss? Winner gets to take home a basket of our freshest produce!"

"A tomato toss? What are we, a farm-themed carnival?" I laughed, but deep down, I admired her determination.

"Exactly! And who doesn't love the idea of hurling tomatoes at a target?" she grinned, and before I could respond, she bounded away to rally the guests.

The tomato toss quickly became the highlight of the day, drawing laughter and cheers from onlookers. It was a scene right out of a whimsical storybook—adults giggling like children, cheeks stained with juice and laughter echoing through the garden. I watched Sophie gleefully demonstrate her own technique, her laughter a sweet melody that wrapped around me.

In the midst of the chaos, an unexpected figure appeared. I squinted, recognizing a familiar face emerging from the crowd—Mr. Jenkins. He strode forward, his brow furrowed in concentration as he surveyed our festivities. My heart raced. The last time I had seen him, he had been the unwitting target of Sophie's tomato mishap.

"Is this a festival or a demolition derby?" he quipped, crossing his arms over his chest, his lips twitching with barely contained amusement. "I hope you have some insurance, just in case."

"Oh, we're fully covered for flying produce," I retorted, unable to hide my grin. "But I can't promise we have a warranty on messy hair and bad fashion choices."

He chuckled, shaking his head as he approached the tomato toss setup. "I'd like to sign up. I could use a little amusement today."

"Really?" Sophie's eyes sparkled with mischief as she turned to him, her excitement palpable. "Just keep in mind; I've trained in the ancient art of tomato throwing!"

"Then prepare to be schooled, my dear," he shot back, an unexpected glimmer of playfulness shining in his eyes.

As they prepared for their duel, I noticed a sudden shift in the atmosphere. The air thickened, an unfamiliar tension creeping into the joyous vibe. Glancing over my shoulder, I spotted a figure lurking at the edge of the garden—a woman with dark hair pulled back in a tight bun, dressed in crisp business attire that felt out of place among the colorful chaos. Her expression was unreadable, eyes scanning the scene with a mix of curiosity and something else I couldn't quite place.

"Do you know her?" I asked Sophie, gesturing discreetly.

She shook her head, her brow furrowing. "No idea. But she looks like she's on a mission. Should we invite her in?"

Before I could respond, the woman strode forward, cutting through the laughter and chaos like a knife. "Excuse me," she said, her voice low and measured, "is this where the harvest festival is taking place?"

Sophie nodded, trying to mask her surprise. "Yes! Would you like to join us?"

"I'm afraid I'm not here for festivities," she replied, glancing around as if assessing the garden's worth. "I represent a developer interested in this property."

A knot tightened in my stomach. "What do you mean?"

She continued, her voice unwavering. "This garden, while charming, is not in alignment with our plans for revitalizing this area. I need to discuss your intentions here."

Sophie and I exchanged a worried glance, the festive air suddenly heavy with uncertainty. The laughter faded into the background as the reality of her words settled in like a storm cloud gathering overhead. The garden we had poured our hearts into, our little sanctuary, was suddenly under threat.

"Revitalizing?" Sophie echoed, her tone defensive. "We're revitalizing this community, not tearing it down. This garden means something to us."

"It means something to many," I added, feeling my voice grow steadier. "This is not just property; it's a lifeline for our community."

"Lovely sentiments," she replied coolly, "but you'll need to make way for progress. I'd like to discuss options with you both."

I felt a shiver race down my spine. What did progress mean if it came at the cost of what we had built? The laughter faded, leaving an uneasy silence where the joy had once flourished. Behind us, the tomato toss continued, but I couldn't shake the feeling that our celebration was teetering on the edge of a precipice.

With a deep breath, I steeled myself, ready to fight for our garden. The stakes had suddenly risen higher than I ever imagined, and as the laughter of the festival danced on the wind, I realized that we were not just nurturing plants; we were fighting for our future.

Chapter 29: The Harvest of Love

The sun poured through the windows of the barn, igniting a mosaic of colors on the rustic wooden floor. My fingers lingered over the surface of a perfectly ripe pumpkin, its skin a vibrant orange, a reminder of the bounty we'd cultivated over the season. I could hear the distant laughter of children chasing each other among the rows of sunflowers, their bright faces reflecting the joy of the harvest festival. Today was not just about reaping what we had sown; it was a celebration of resilience, community, and newfound hope.

Sophie leaned against the barn door, her golden hair catching the light like spun sugar. I couldn't help but smile at the sight of her, her laughter ringing out like music as she tossed a sunflower into the air, catching it with effortless grace. There was something almost magical about the way she had blossomed over the past few months. She was no longer the woman burdened by her past; she had transformed into a force of nature, as vibrant and unyielding as the fields that surrounded us.

"Is that a pumpkin I see, or just a big orange conspiracy?" she quipped, her eyes twinkling with mischief. I chuckled, shaking my head at her antics, knowing she would have a dozen more puns ready for the day ahead. Her humor was one of the many facets that drew me to her, the way she found joy in the simplest moments, effortlessly lighting up even the cloudiest days.

"I think it's both," I replied, playfully rolling the pumpkin back and forth between my palms. "But if we're going to pull off this festival without a hitch, we should probably start by not losing half the pumpkins in a 'conspiracy.'"

She feigned a gasp, placing a hand over her heart in mock indignation. "You wound me! I am simply trying to add a touch of flair to our festivities. What is a harvest festival without a little fun?"

I couldn't argue with her logic, especially when it came to adding a sense of whimsy to our hard work. As the morning wore on, the barn filled with the rich aromas of spiced cider and fresh-baked bread. The townspeople bustled about, laughter mingling with the sound of chopping and the occasional thud of someone dropping a basket. Each familiar face brought a wave of warmth, an affirmation that our efforts had not gone unnoticed.

As Sophie and I moved through the crowd, handing out samples of our produce, I felt a swell of pride. Not just for the farm, but for the community we had helped nurture. Each smile, each compliment, reminded me that we were all in this together, bound by our shared stories and struggles. It was a tapestry woven from the threads of joy and hardship, laughter and tears, and it was beautiful.

Suddenly, a voice broke through my reverie, a familiar one laced with urgency. "Emily! We need you over by the hayride!" It was Mark, one of the local farmers, waving his arms frantically, his face flushed with concern.

"What's happened?" I asked, my heart quickening as I glanced at Sophie, who looked equally puzzled.

"There's a problem with the wagon! It tipped over when we tried to load the kids," he explained, breathless from the exertion. "Can you help? We need to get it sorted before more children get hurt."

Sophie's eyes widened, her playful demeanor shifting to one of determination. "Let's go," she said, and without hesitation, we both followed Mark through the throngs of festival-goers. The scene unfolded before us like a mini drama, with parents looking on anxiously as a small group of kids gathered around the fallen wagon.

When we arrived, the sight was more chaotic than I had anticipated. The wagon, an old wooden cart laden with hay, had tipped onto its side, spilling its contents everywhere. The laughter of the children had turned to nervous chatter as some of them poked at the hay, while others stood frozen in confusion.

I knelt beside the wagon, my mind racing through the options. "Okay, everyone! Let's make this a fun game," I announced, my voice rising above the noise. "If we all work together, we can turn this into a hay maze. What do you say?"

The children's eyes lit up at the idea, and the nervous energy transformed into excitement. "A maze! Yes!" they chorused, some jumping up and down.

Sophie took charge, her natural leadership shining through as she rallied the older kids to start moving the hay into a new pile. "If you guys stack it up high, we can make tunnels and everything!" she encouraged, her enthusiasm contagious.

As I joined in, the sense of community tightened around us like a warm blanket. We worked in sync, children laughing and shouting directions, the air thick with the sweet scent of hay and the thrill of shared effort. The wagon was soon forgotten, and the joy of creation took over.

Minutes slipped by in a flurry of laughter and teamwork, and before long, we had built a makeshift maze that would entertain the children for hours. It wasn't just a triumph of resourcefulness; it was a testament to our bond, our ability to adapt, and our knack for turning chaos into joy.

Amidst the hustle and bustle, I caught Sophie's gaze. In that fleeting moment, we exchanged a knowing smile, a silent acknowledgment that we were more than partners in farming; we were partners in life, navigating whatever twists awaited us. The festival had transformed from a simple celebration of harvest to an emblem of our resilience, and with each shared laugh, each cheer from the children, I felt a sense of belonging deep within me, the kind that roots itself in your very soul and grows stronger with every passing season.

As the sun arched higher in the sky, bathing the festival in a golden glow, the joyful chaos of the hay maze began to settle into a delightful rhythm. Children darted in and out of the makeshift tunnels, their laughter like a symphony of summer, while parents snapped photos, their faces glowing with pride and amusement. I stood at the edge, my heart swelling at the sight of Sophie guiding a gaggle of giggling kids, her own laughter mingling effortlessly with theirs.

"Emily! Come on! Help me scare them!" she called, her eyes dancing with mischief. I raised an eyebrow, intrigued.

"Scare them? What do you have in mind?" I stepped closer, curiosity piqued.

She grinned wickedly, an idea sparking behind those brilliant green eyes. "I'm thinking...ghost stories! But we'll tell them in the maze, make it a spooky adventure."

"Oh, you devious mastermind!" I laughed, shaking my head in mock exasperation. "And I suppose you want me to wear a sheet?"

"Only if you promise to moan dramatically!" she shot back, her laughter infectious.

Just then, a group of children burst through the maze, eyes wide with excitement. "Can we have a ghost story, please?" one of them pleaded, her freckled face glowing with anticipation.

I exchanged a look with Sophie, her enthusiasm fueling my own. "Alright, gather around!" I called, and soon a circle of eager faces surrounded us. As I wove together a tale of friendly spirits and enchanted pumpkins, Sophie joined in with exaggerated gestures and gasps, drawing the children deeper into our whimsical narrative.

As I spun the story, I caught glimpses of adults nearby, their smiles genuine and relaxed. For many, the festival was a much-needed escape from their daily grind—a moment to connect, unwind, and share laughter with neighbors. I realized how easily we had woven our lives into the fabric of this community, and how, despite the trials we had faced, joy had managed to flourish.

"Then the ghostly pumpkin rolled toward the farmer, glowing with magic!" I exclaimed, my voice rising for dramatic effect. "And what did the farmer do? He... danced!"

At this, the children erupted into giggles, and I felt a rush of exhilaration, the warmth of their joy wrapping around me like a favorite blanket. Just then, a whistle cut through the laughter, a sound sharp enough to pull my focus.

"Alright, folks! Time for the pie-eating contest!" Mark's voice boomed across the grounds, a playful challenge that stirred the crowd. "Who's ready to see who can devour a pie the fastest?"

A chorus of cheers erupted, and Sophie looked at me, her eyes gleaming with mischief. "We have to join! It's a rite of passage at this festival."

"Is that so?" I arched an eyebrow, feigning reluctance. "And what if I'm not a pie-eating champion? I'm more of a 'savor every bite' kind of girl."

"Oh, come on! It's all in good fun! Plus, think of the glory if we win!" She clasped her hands together, her expression a mix of determination and delight.

Before I could argue further, she had already dragged me toward the makeshift stage, where tables were set up for the contest. The smell of cinnamon and baked crust filled the air, sending my senses into a delightful spiral of temptation. I couldn't help but grin as the announcer called out our names, my competitive spirit rising.

We lined up alongside a motley crew of contestants, a mix of seasoned festival veterans and bright-eyed newcomers. I exchanged a glance with Sophie, a silent pact forming between us—whatever happened, we were in it together.

"On your marks, get set, go!" The whistle pierced the air, and chaos erupted as we dove face-first into the plates of pie before us. The crowd roared with laughter and encouragement, and in that moment, nothing else mattered.

Sophie was a whirlwind beside me, her laughter a melodic counterpoint to the messy endeavor. Crust flew, filling splattered, and we were two unstoppable forces of nature, caught in the frenzy of fun. Between bites, I managed to crack jokes about the pies being "mysteriously haunted" from the earlier story, causing even more laughter to erupt from the onlookers.

Halfway through, I glanced at Sophie, and we both burst into laughter, her face smeared with whipped cream and my own dripping with pie filling. "If we don't win, at least we're the most entertaining!" she shouted through bites, her determination unwavering.

In a moment of sheer inspiration—or perhaps sheer madness—I turned to the audience, raising my arms in mock defiance. "Ladies and gentlemen! Prepare yourselves! We will conquer these pies in the name of deliciousness!"

The crowd erupted in cheers, urging us on, and as the contest reached its climax, the friendly rivalry intensified. The announcer's voice became a blur in the background as I focused solely on the pie before me, its sweet, spicy aroma intoxicating.

As we neared the end, Sophie and I were neck-and-neck, our eyes locked in playful challenge. In a final surge of energy, we both shoved the last bites into our mouths, the crowd counting down as if we were crossing the finish line of a race.

"Three, two, one... time!" The announcer's voice rang out, and we both sat back, breathless and triumphant. The crowd erupted into applause, laughter and cheers swirling around us like confetti.

The results were announced, and while we didn't take home the pie-eating crown, we were declared the "Best Duo" for our unabashed enthusiasm and comedic flair. Sophie leaned in, her breath still labored from the contest, and whispered, "We were amazing. Who needs a crown when we have a title like that?"

I laughed, the sound rich and full, and for a moment, everything else faded away—the doubts, the fears, the shadows of our past. Here, in this joyful chaos, we had found something precious: not just a community but a family, stitched together through laughter, love, and the unyielding spirit of togetherness.

The laughter of the crowd reverberated in my ears, mingling with the sweet aroma of baked goods and the earthy scent of freshly turned soil. Sophie and I stood side by side, the remnants of pie still clinging to our cheeks, a testament to our spirited contest. I glanced at her, her eyes glinting with mischief as she wiped a smudge of cream from her lips, and I couldn't help but chuckle.

"Did we just become local legends?" she asked, her voice teasing, yet warm with genuine excitement.

"Only if local legends wear pie-stained clothes," I quipped, gesturing to the splotches of filling on her shirt. "But I think that adds to our charm."

She feigned offense, placing a hand dramatically over her heart. "Charm? I'd say we're downright fabulous!"

Just then, a commotion erupted nearby, pulling my attention from our banter. A group of children clustered around a towering scarecrow, its tattered clothes flapping in the breeze, while their parents stood at a distance, some appearing concerned. As I moved closer, I overheard snippets of conversation that piqued my curiosity.

"Did it move?" one little girl whispered, her wide eyes filled with awe and fear.

"Of course not! It's just a scarecrow!" her older brother replied, though even he sounded a bit unsure.

Sophie followed me, her interest piqued. "What do you think happened?"

I shrugged, but the unease in the air tugged at me. "Let's check it out."

As we approached, I could see that the scarecrow had somehow lost its balance, tilting precariously as if it were about to topple over. "It's just a little tipsy," I reassured the children, trying to dispel their fears. "Let's help it stand tall again!"

With a chorus of cheers, the kids rushed forward, eager to lend a hand. Sophie and I joined in, carefully maneuvering the straw-filled figure upright. "There we go! No scarecrow left behind!" I joked, and the children giggled, their earlier worries forgotten.

But as I stepped back to admire our handiwork, something caught my eye—a glint of metal peeking out from beneath the straw. I knelt down, brushing aside the hay, and my heart dropped. It was an old pocket watch, tarnished and slightly rusted, but unmistakably a relic from another time.

"Sophie, come look at this!" I called, holding it up. The kids gathered around, their curious faces leaning in closer.

"Whoa! Is it magic?" one boy asked, eyes wide.

I chuckled nervously. "I'm not sure, but it definitely has a story to tell."

As Sophie examined the watch, a flicker of recognition crossed her face. "This looks like the one that belonged to...." Her voice trailed off, and I watched as her expression shifted from curiosity to something more serious, more contemplative.

"What? Who did it belong to?" I pressed gently, sensing a deeper connection beneath her words.

She hesitated, as if weighing her next words. "My grandfather. He lost it years ago during the last harvest festival. He always said it was lucky, that it kept time in ways we could never understand."

I felt a chill creep down my spine, an unexplainable connection forming in the air around us. "Lucky, huh? Maybe we've stumbled upon something special."

The children, oblivious to the weight of the moment, began making wild guesses about the watch's powers. "Maybe it can slow time down!" one shouted, his imagination running wild.

Sophie smiled at their innocence, but her gaze lingered on the watch. "Maybe it's more than that," she murmured, more to herself than to me.

Just then, the announcer's voice rang out again, cutting through the lighthearted chatter. "Ladies and gentlemen! The next event is the unveiling of the harvest mural! Gather around the main stage to witness the magic!"

Sophie's eyes sparkled with enthusiasm once more, and she nudged my shoulder. "Let's go! This is going to be epic!"

I tucked the watch safely into my pocket, the cool metal pressing against me as we joined the throng of festival-goers heading toward the stage. The energy in the air was palpable, a wave of excitement and anticipation washing over the crowd as they took their places.

As we settled in, I couldn't shake the feeling that the watch was more than just an object. It was a key, somehow intertwined with the stories of our community. I glanced at Sophie, her face illuminated by the fading sunlight, and wondered what revelations the day might still hold.

The unveiling began, and the artist, an elderly woman with a warm smile and paint-streaked hands, stepped forward, her voice carrying the weight of countless harvests. "This mural represents the spirit of our community," she began, gesturing toward the vibrant colors that danced across the canvas. "It tells the story of our triumphs, our struggles, and our unbreakable bonds."

As the curtain was pulled away, gasps of awe filled the air. The mural depicted scenes of harvests past, families working together, children playing, and the rich tapestry of life that intertwined us all. But then, something strange caught my eye.

In one corner, amidst the bustling images, was a figure that looked strikingly familiar—a woman with long, flowing hair and a fierce gaze. My heart raced as I leaned closer, squinting at the details.

"Emily, look!" Sophie exclaimed beside me, her voice almost a whisper. "That's... that looks like my grandmother."

The realization crashed over us like a wave. Sophie's grandmother had passed away long ago, and yet here she was, immortalized in this mural, as vibrant as the day she had lived. But what truly sent shivers down my spine was the figure next to her—a man with the same pocket watch I had found.

My breath caught in my throat. "Sophie, do you see that?" I gestured toward the mural, the implications swirling in my mind.

But before she could respond, a sharp gasp came from the crowd, and I turned just in time to see the elderly artist clutch her chest, her eyes wide with fear. "No, no, it can't be!" she cried, stumbling back.

Gasps spread like wildfire as the energy in the crowd shifted from joy to confusion, the lively festival morphing into a scene of concern.

"What is happening?" Sophie whispered, her hand tightening around mine.

I didn't have an answer, but I could feel the tension thickening in the air, a storm brewing beneath the surface of this beautiful day. Just as the murmur of worried voices began to swell, a flash of movement caught my eye.

Someone, cloaked in shadow, slipped away from the stage, disappearing into the throng of onlookers. I felt a strange pull in my gut, a sense that this figure held the key to unraveling the mystery that had just unfolded.

"Stay here," I said to Sophie, my heart pounding with urgency as I moved to follow. I had to know more, had to uncover the truth behind the watch, the mural, and the figure that seemed to haunt both Sophie's past and our present.

As I pushed through the crowd, the laughter and music faded into a distant echo, replaced by the frantic beat of my heart. I was close, so close to uncovering something monumental, something that could change everything.

But just as I caught sight of the shadowy figure, it turned to face me, and I froze, recognition dawning like a chilling breeze. The familiar face was someone I had never expected to see again.

"Emily," the figure said, their voice low and filled with a strange mix of warning and urgency. "We need to talk."

Milton Keynes UK
Ingram Content Group UK Ltd.
UKHW042004281024
450365UK00003B/154